MAGIC'S DAUGHTER

THE BROKEN REALMS CHRONICLE
BOOK ONE

T.J. FISHER

Published 2025 Broken Realms Publications
Copyright © 2025 T.J. Fisher
Paperback ISBN-13: 978-1-7329150-7-7

Dedicated to my friend Rebekah.
You're dearly missed.
Kiira's love of horses is for you.

CONTENTS

The Klaroni Cordillia
Ebony Spires
Volpean River
The Fores
V
The Kingdom of Klynotia
Aria Bells
Lael Lake
Meldari River
Lisean River
Chalcena River
Aradyll
The Kingdom of Lorea
Loreston Lake
Tayrus River
Relgrak Peninsula
Map of the Broken Realms
The S

Temple
os
Torchid
Lezza Mera
Tarnished Plains
Ristern Mera
Byloraan
Night Crystal Quarries
The Shadow Desert
Jearut Oasis
Slate Cliffs
Storm Gulf
Falls
Magician's Cloister
The Tears of Apelgo
Corsair Cay
Tilkt Point
Reana

BEATEN

Today, in particular, tended towards savory in lieu of the typical sweetness of harvest. The brine of the sea hung heavy on the cool breath of morning, clinging to the air and in Kiira's lungs; the first signs of a typical humid and wet winter to come. Dreamy pastels of cornflower and poppy watered the dawn, promising a balmy day.

I can't wait for The Yielding Festival.

She smiled. The annual week-long celebration had all of Lorea reveling with towering bonfires, spiced meats, and flavored wines. This year had been deemed especially promising. It was to be the biggest harvest in seven years and had been the main topic of conversations for a month.

Kiira disturbed the earth with her toes simply for the sensation of feeling the coolness between them. The usually dense, smooth dirt of the training ring was cool and damp, numbing her bare feet.

"Stop daydreaming, Kiira," her brother Liem chided. "I have things to do."

"And I have new recruits to torture," Liem's best friend Folen added.

Leaning against the rough, sturdy wooden rails, she rolled her eyes before cuffing the sleeves of her tunic. "Relax, gentlemen. As usual, you will both be late for your appointments," she said, smoothing her braid and pushing an errant frizzy curl behind her ear. Her mocking tone produced a snort from her brother and a wry, unbelieving grin from Folen.

From her lower back, Kiira unsheathed dual twelve-inch bone-handled knives from the pliable leather corset cinched around her waist. Running her thumb and pointer finger along the flat of the blade, she focused her magic and the faintest sparkle of green added a layer of protection to the honed edge; the casting preventing injury but paralyzing the person whose skin it touched. It was an effective method for training. Any of them could attack ruthlessly and injuries were minimized to ugly purple and yellow bruises. She couldn't, however, vouch for the injury it would do to Liem's and Folen's pride today when she won.

She released her control of the magic and felt the slightest parching at the back of her throat. Water would be her first stop after winning this duel.

Licking her lips, Kiira crouched into a carefully balanced stance, her muscles loose but tense and poised for action. She focused her attention on the two men opposite her, looking for weaknesses to exploit. They were both wearing darker clothing, making them more difficult to see in the early morning darkness. Clever. Kiira flipped her two blades with a practiced ease and smirked, teasing her opponents.

This is going to be too easy.

Liem and Folen didn't stand a chance. As much as they liked to think they had the advantage—two against one—she was the best knife fighter in the military. Both men were skilled, but neither had the drive for perfection she did.

Liem and Folen circled like vultures, and Kiira matched their movements, her strides long and easy. Unless she goaded them into attacking first, they would wait for the ideal opportunity. She had made the mistake only once of letting Liem and Folen surround her. The result left her paralyzed for a few hours and it was an experience she never wanted to repeat.

A hint of a smile crossed her lips as an idea came to mind and, easing her stance, Kiira dropped her guard, giving her opponents the sense of an easy mark.

Folen was the first to take the bait with a feint to her right. Liem moved from her left for what he likely thought would be an effortless takedown. Sandwiched, Kiira tucked her shoulder, rolling under Liem's guard and slicing his forearm with a quick, efficient stroke. The blade would have cut deep if not for her casting. He dropped, thudding against the compacted dirt in an ungainly position. If she didn't still have Folen to deal with, the shock on her twin's face would have been immensely satisfying. She would gloat later during the evening meal.

Kiira tumbled again, distancing herself from Folen.

Crouched and ready to face him—she waited. With Folen, patience was her advantage, since his strength couldn't match her lissome fighting style.

"Well played, my pearl, but you will not best me," he taunted.

"Ah, but you forget, Folen, I am the best"—her tone was light with confidence—"and stop using your awful endearments on me. There is *nothing* between us."

"You wound me, Petal," Folen said, placing a fisted hand over his sternum in mock distress.

Kiira just managed to stop herself from rolling her eyes—again. Folen used the momentary distraction to jump forward, bringing down a pair of whistling blades toward her exposed arm. She whirled to his left, forcing him into a few unsteady forward steps, but he quickly corrected. His left hand swiping at her ribs, she blocking with her right, his strength testing the fortitude of her muscle. Magic crackled from the connected blades. She stabbed at his ribs, but he stepped and parried easily. They danced across the training ring—sometimes jumping over Liem—steel ringing against the silent morning and neither gaining the advantage. Flashes of green and amber sparked in the dull light each time their knives connected.

Kiira crouched into a spinning kick. Folen easily jumped, but she used the momentum to gain space. Her breaths—full and quick—added a light fog to the air in front of her. She narrowed her focus.

What is your weakness today?

The corner of her mouth ticked up.

The same as every other day.

Kiira again relaxed her stance slightly and he stepped, taking the bait. She could sense Liem trying mightily to warn his friend, but the paralyzing magic flooding his veins prevented him from doing anything other than breathing, blinking, and maintaining the casting on Folen's knives.

Folen took another wary step, the soldier in him cautious, yet pride making him unwilling to lose the advantage of a clear opening. Just before he was in striking range, Kiira softened her features and gave him an affectionate smile.

It had the desired effect.

Folen, solely focused on her demeanor, didn't react quickly enough when she stepped into his guard and sliced one knife down his forearm and the other across his neck. He landed in an ungainly heap at her feet.

Stooping, she clucked her tongue at him. "Folen, you are a hopeless flirt. You should not allow the charms of a woman to affect you so." She smiled and ruffled his hair. His eyes conveyed an amusing mixture of annoyance and pleasure at his defeat. "Worry not, the casting is subtle this time. The paralysis should wear off in an hour or so, just in time for the lads to see." Kiira winked and wandered over to her brother.

"My dear brother"—she grunted while straightening his body. She wanted to embarrass him, not leave him in pain from an awkward angle—"not one of your better days I'm afraid. You will have to tell me why when you can speak again. I'll see you at the evening meal!" Kissing her fingers, she gave him a light tap on the cheek and whistled a bright, happy melody as she jogged away.

THE RAYS of a new day warmed her as they skimmed atop the castle's outer defense wall, a loving caress to her chilled skin. The plush grass tickled her feet as she glided with long strides in the retreating shadow. Kiira loved the thrill of a run, and this was her favorite place to experience the pounding of her heart and the rhythmic pattern of her feet as they connected with the earth. It was freedom. It was beautiful. Simple. Out here she didn't have to listen to the thumping of boots or virile grunting of thousands of soldiers training. Out here, next to the tan-stoned sentinel protecting her home, was hers.

Starting on the second lap, Kiira glanced back at the sound of additional footfalls interrupting her trance. She spotted Leo Moredell, the Earl of Wirlen, and her second in command. He was one of the few that, like her, appreciated the comfortable silence the thick stones provided. His long strides slowed to match hers momentarily before he gave her a taunting grin and pulled away, his long legs affording him an advantage. She frowned at his back, debating whether to increase her pace to outdistance him. Kiira took a cleansing breath. No, today she would just enjoy the clear air.

As she finished, the burn in her legs begged for the release through the Warrior's Dance. A small shiver rushed down Kiira's spine from a momentary breeze as she stopped at a crest on the land. The sun was well in the sky and the small hill afforded her a view several leagues outside the protective walls of the castle grounds, the distant glittering waters of Lorestan Lake winking against the breaking sun. The simple beauty was a love letter to her soul as bright tendrils of light kissed verdant fields. This view was why she chose to stretch here each morning.

Closing her eyes to focus, Kiira let deep, even breaths guide her through somnolent movements, gliding from one stance to the next. She used the time to meditate on the teachings of Windrah. Today she focused on a verse from her favorite paean.

Your constant love reaches the heavens; your faithfulness extends to the skies. Your righteousness is towering like the mountains; your justice is like the depths of the sea. We are in your care.

"Good morning, Princess," Leo said, interrupting her thoughts as he trotted up beside her, an easy smile on his lips. His rich brown hair tufted into odd angles. "Did you enjoy your run this morning?"

"Good morning." Kiira finished her stretch and straightened. "Yes, I did. I thought to keep pace with you today, but decided your taunting was not worth the effort."

He laughed as he started his own routine of the Warrior's Dance. "I am glad to hear it."

A few moments of companionable silence followed before Kiira spoke again. "I will be working with the mounted archers today. They are still weak with reverse shots. This afternoon I would like to drill with unexpected targets, and also begin working the new recruits on close range combat. How many of the conscripts do you think will pass the testing?"

"Honestly," Leo said, "there is a good group this year. At least three quarters of them will do well, but they have only been here a week and much can change. We've certainly had surprises in the past."

Kiira couldn't argue. After a few moments of reflection, she returned her focus to Leo.

"For the close range practices, have the senior archers paired with the recruits; I want to be able to devise a training schedule based on skill."

When Leo finished his stretches, he and Kiira made for the private building belonging to the Archery Commander. Technically, it should be hers, but even a princess didn't need a castle suite and a two-room building, so she had passed it to Leo.

"We'll meet tonight after the evening meal in the library to discuss the training regimen. The last thing I want to do is drag myself down here again."

"Of course, Princess," Leo said with a smile. After a slight pause, he continued with less formality. "How did your sparring go this morning?"

"Wonderful!" she crowed, raising fists in victory as she spun to face him. Kiira gave him a triumphant grin before opening the door to Leo's comfortable study and living space. The smell of warm wood infused the air, inviting her to take a deep breath. Fisting either hip, a self-appreciating glint touched her eyes. "Liem was out in three moves. Folen gave me a fair fight, but he has a weakness for a pretty smile. I left them crumpled in a heap on the training ring."

"You're ruthless," Leo said, chuckling as he shut the door.

Once their privacy was assured, Kiira stepped into Leo's arms and gave him the most wide-eyed, innocent look she could muster, resting her hands on his muscled chest. "Only to those who think they are better than me," she said.

Leo chuckled and pulled her close. "My love, I would never dream of saying I was better than you; though I, too, am not immune to your pretty smile," he rumbled, hovering just above her lips.

"Then you have nothing to worry about," she teased, her eyes sparkling with playful affection.

An amused huff passed his lips before he kissed her soundly. Kiira leaned into him so as not to float away. This was her second favorite part of each morning.

The distant sound of conversation drifted through the cracked window. Kiira pulled away, wrinkling her nose at the disruption. Leaning back to absorb the desire in his earthen eyes, Kiira shamelessly soaked up every ounce of love she could see. These were eyes she wished to gaze upon for the rest of her life, and their secret needed to end. Stepping away, she played with the tip of her braid while she spoke. "Leo, you need to speak to my father soon. I have managed to keep recent inquiries at bay, but my influence will not last much longer. Father has been restless about my betrothal as of late, and it is not right to hide what is between us any longer."

"I was planning on speaking with him during the week of the Yielding Festival. The King always seems to be in an agreeable mood during that time," Leo said.

Kiira shook her head. "No, I have a gut feeling that time is running short. Please go to him tomorrow during Open Court."

Leo studied her for a moment before staring at the wall.

"What's wrong Leo? Why do you hesitate? Do you not—"

Leo stepped to her, cutting off her words. Running his fingers through the escaped curls of her hair, he cradled her tilted head. "Never doubt I love you, Kiira." He kissed her. "If you believe it is the right course of action, I will go tomorrow."

"Thank you Leo," Kiira said, before brushing his lips with a kiss.

"No, I should thank you," he replied, hugging her close. "You chose me."

CHAPTER 2
FORGIVEN

Deep night lingered as day teased the horizon. Sleep smothered out most sounds save for a restless sea and a few happy crickets. Soon, a chorus of roosters would crow across the castle grounds and beyond, beckoning the world to wake. A whisper of a breeze twirled through white clouds, bringing with it the first signs of cooler temperatures and the beginning of yet another meager harvest.

A solitary candle flickered dimly, creating a wispy silhouette of Terren as he sat cross-legged on the open-air balcony attached to his rooms.

One breath in.

You make a way where there is no way.

One breath out.

Fog swirled in response to his deep, steady breaths. Droplets clung to his bare torso like a second skin.

Breath in.

You are provider and shield.

Breath out.

Reciting the words from chants he learned in the temple focused his mind and brought peace to his soul. Something he desperately needed each day since returning home. He relished this solitary time in the mornings.

Terren took in one last deep breath of the cool fog and exhaled before blinking his eyes open. It was light enough now he could define the edges of the utilitarian balustrade in front of him. Beyond, the sun's weak rays pierced the fog, casting the land in an ethereal glow. He stood in a fluid motion, resting his forearms on the railing to cast an appreciating eye upon the fresh day.

Tendrils of light darted through the misted morning, highlighting portions of the barren landscape to his left and right, where the flat fields meandered toward the sea, the highest reaches of the castle still shadowing the space directly before him. Dune grass bent severely as the breeze from the coast cleared, the fog wrapping the land. The brief moment of tranquility tipped his lips into a rare smile before thoughts of the coming day twisted them back into a laden frown.

Klynotia was a beautiful kingdom, and he had missed its simple beauty during his travels, but it was broken, more so than when he'd forsaken it twelve years ago. Before long, all shadows would scatter and reveal the truth. Magnificence lay deep in the heart of his kingdom, and he vowed to see it restored. The people deserved more than the hard living they knew. For now, he had to turn a blind eye, though it pained him.

Sighing, Terren stretched the stiffness from his muscles as he passed the threshold to the warm, dry interior of his suite. The two guards posted inside his room gave him a cursory glance before returning to their permanent expression of boredom.

They must feel punished for being assigned to protect me. Worst lie I've ever heard … my protection.

Since Terren's return to the kingdom, the four-man guard had been his shadow, solely tasked to ensure he did not disappear again.

If only they knew how easily I could evade them.

The prospect was tempting, more often than he cared to admit. He longed for the freedom from princely burdens; yet this was the choice he made to dedicate himself to the well-being of his people.

I came back for them. My comfort is a small price to pay. I just pray I can ease their burden soon.

Sighing louder, he closed the door to his bath.

Eyes closed, Terren focused all of his energy on an imaginary opponent. Each envisioned stroke of the enemy sword was aimed to kill, giving him the incentive needed to respond appropriately. The wraith opponent in his mind's eye—broad and fierce—equaled his skill with a sword. A worthy challenge. Often, he pictured the face of the king as he played out these mock fights, preparing for the day when his imaginary battles manifested. The king would have no qualms about killing him, and Terren refused to let futile loyalty stay his hand from doing the same.

He held a shoulder parry before swinging into a chest attack and slicing upward in a perfect arc to protect his head. Fluid and sure steps moved him through the small clearing as he danced with the invisible enemy. Stepping to the side to avoid an imagined thrust, his boot crunched an errant pinecone. His eyes snapped open.

'*You should return soon,*' Kamaria said within the confines of his mind, interrupting his swordplay. '*Your watchmen already think you take dreadfully long baths.*' Her distaste at the four-man guard simmered in the undercurrent of her emotions and echoed across their link.

Terren did not blame her for the sentiment. He briefly glanced at the sky to confirm her statement. Time had gotten away from him while he was here in the Shade Realm; the sun already brushing the points of the towering pine. At least in the Sun Realm, time moved slower. There it would still be early, but he had probably missed the morning meal.

Sheathing his sword, he walked over to where Kamaria, his massive Shade Bear, blended into the shadows of the forest. She was so still that only their intimate connection allowed him to know where she lay, otherwise he would have walked past her without a second glance. This camouflage was a Shade Beast's greatest asset.

He stood in front of her giant nose. Warm, moist breath washed over his entire body and flattened his hair. Craning to look into one of her large, opaque, black-and-grey-ringed eyes, he said, '*It is only for a season that you have to endure restrictions on our times together. If I could visit the Shade Realm every day, you know I would.*'

She chuffed. '*I know, but that doesn't mean I have to like the fact that you don't.*'

Terren gave a sad smile. He rested against her snout, burying his face into the prickly, grey-flecked fur. He sympathized with Kamaria's feelings, but Klynotia was where he needed to be, and she knew his heart. His Bear would stick by him, despite her attitude.

Kamaria tilted her head. Smiling, Terren scratched the underside of her enormous snout. It didn't take long for a low, pleasant rumble to sound from the back of her throat. Her bitterness eased like the snow melts of spring. '*I at least have a few more minutes that I can relax with you,*' he reminded her.

Terren reclined on her giant paw, using one of her claws to prop his feet, and took deep breaths of pine as he sunk further into Kamaria's warm fur. He enjoyed the still moment. It was always like this with his Bear. Neither of them needed to talk or share emotions to be happy. They just were, and it was enough.

As the sun rose, light flooded the intimate clearing, only to be cut short by the broad trees dominating one another for space. His mother would have said the massive size of the forest was Gimetii's way of competing with his brother Liioh's enormous Beasts.

Terren preferred the Shade Realm. He liked the dark green prickly boughs and the rich brown of the flakey trunks. Birds chittered gaily and the distant sound of the sea filtered through the forest. It was similar to the Sun Realm, but here the land was raw and unspoiled by the selfishness of people. Here, the Shade Beasts, both wild and tame, ruled with undisputed power. Terren couldn't truly put into words his impressions of the Shade Realm, but whole seemed the best explanation. Centuries had barely changed its original design.

'*Are you going to try again today?*' Kamaria asked.

'*Yes, just like I do every day,*' he replied.

'*Why do you persist with such a stubborn girl?*'

'*She is my sister.*'

'*That is not a reason,*' Kamaria scoffed. A thin white cloud escaped her snout to punctuate her words.

Terren considered giving his reasons—again—but she would never grasp the bond he used to have with his sister and what he desired to have again. Kamaria understood brothers and sisters in the sense of camaraderie. It was what she felt for her fellow Beast, but she would never understand his devotion. Instead, he replied, '*it is every reason.*'

There was a comfortable silence between them for a moment.

'*When will I see you again?*' She asked.

'*In a few days.*'

She huffed. An ache built in his chest as turmoil seeped across their link. He wished desperately to ease her heartache.

After a short hesitation, she asked, '*Yepenzi?*'

Terren smiled. It was an affectionate term that Kamaria used often. '*Yes, partner of my mind?*'

Jumbled feelings passed through their mental link as she attempted to explain her turmoil in the human tongue. Finally, she simply said, '*I love you.*'

'I love you too, Kamaria.'

TERREN RAPPED on the door to Sairah's suite, ignoring the uncomfortable shifting of his guards. They were likely tired of the same routine each morning, but where he went, they went. How many more times would they have to witness his failure?

Ny, please let her answer today. I really want to make things right between us.

This was not the first time he had prayed the simple request. The looming, thick oak separated them. Errantly, he remembered something Naanel, his mentor at the temple, used to say. "Everyone who asks will receive, and anyone who seeks will find, and the door will be opened to those who knock."

If only.

Other than his first attempt, in which Sairah viciously shouted at him to stay away before slamming the door in his face, his sister had completely ignored his presence for the past three months. The icy disregard hurt, but wasn't unexpected.

Twelve years was a long time to be gone, and his sudden departure, with little more than a letter promising a return, did not inspire confidence. Rather than shielding a fragile ten-year-old from harm, he subjected her to the unpredictable demands of a tyrant, using his own brokenness and self-centered longing for freedom as a flimsy justification. Looking at it now, the price of his freedom had been far too much. It ruined a relationship he treasured. Terren couldn't blame Sairah for holding a grudge.

He knocked again after his customary few minutes passed. A stir of footsteps sent a flicker of hope through his chest, even though the door would likely remain shut. Sairah was proud and strong, and would never approach him first, but she still loved him. He believed it in his soul. They were family. He just needed to coax it out of her.

He sighed. One day she will open the door, one day. The heel of his boot scraped against stone as the black barrier of thick wood ripped open to flood light into the hallway. A shadow—framed by the door—stood before him.

Sairah.

Terren let his vision adjust, and once he could see her lovely face, he smiled. Today she wore a pale lavender long-sleeved silk gown that hugged her willowy frame with understated grace. Accented with a silver circlet artfully braided into her long, thick black hair, she looked breathtaking as it fell in polished waves from a night's loosened braid. The back light of morning sun highlighted a few strands of red to complement the color of her tan skin and dress.

The firm set of her mouth and angered eyes could not diminish what a beauty his sister had become over the years. Sairah's expression should have been a clear message of her current frame of mind, except for the subtle curiosity. This is good, he thought, a step forward.

"What do you want, Terren?" Sairah asked, through hissing teeth.

"The same thing I wanted when I knocked on your door nearly three months ago. I want to talk," he said.

"Will you ever leave me alone?"

"No. Not until you let me speak my piece. Then you can tell me to permanently go away … but even then I will still pursue you," he replied.

She scrutinized his face, looking for justification to keep him at arm's length. Finally, Sairah growled her disgust, but said, "I might as well talk to you, maybe then you will actually take the hint since the slamming door was not enough"—she turned into the room—"this better be worth my time."

Terren stepped through the door and stopped the two guards, attempting to follow. "No, you will stay out here."

The captain shook his head. "I'm sorry, Your Highness, but King Grayten's or—"

"I said no. You have my word I will not leave this room via any other means than this door, but you will not be present for this conversation." The captain startled, yet a spark of respect in his expression shone through.

Good. Let them see I am not the timid prince they think.

It was a gamble letting the men see this side of him. Terren didn't want to reveal too much too soon, but he hoped they would keep this amongst themselves. The captain nodded and stepped back.

He shut the door and gave all of his attention to his sister.

Sairah sat next to a small oval table with the remnants of her morning meal. She was poised save for the steady tap of a perfect nail against wood. Her flushed cheeks diminished some of the ire settled on her face. Terren took a moment just to memorize her.

He had seen her in dim light during a few scattered evening meals when Grayten required they dine with him, and in hurried passing in the hallway, but this was the first time Terren had a chance to see her in the full light of day.

She has grown so much.

Sairah favored their father with her square jaw and lighter skin, but the hair and eyes were directly from the Isokanii bloodline. Her edged curves were softened by femininity as if she had been carved from stone then polished smooth.

"Well? Say what you came to say and then get out."

Terren cleared his throat. "Sairah, I shouldn't have left you when I ran and for that I am sorry."

She scoffed. "Save it, Terren, there is nothing you can say that will earn my forgiveness."

He shook his head, eyes downcast. "I wish for your forgiveness, but do not expect it. I am only apologizing for my actions and my failure."

Sairah eyed him warily.

"I was selfish and failed at the one thing I promised mother; to protect you." He lowered his voice. "It is no excuse, but I was not in a good place emotionally when I left, I made a very poor decision because of it, and I know it caused you pain." Terren slowly raised his eyes to meet her gaze, silently willing her to understand the regret he carried. After several heartbeats of silence, he turned for the door.

Just as he touched the handle, Sairah hoarsely said, "Do you even know what happened to me? What your actions allowed for?"

"I could guess, but no, I don't actually know," Terren said quietly, facing her again.

"Let me enlighten you." She grimaced. "He had me tortured. Beaten till my bones broke and I was painted black and blue, all to coax you out of hiding. Did you even notice I wear long-sleeves in the heat of summer?"

Terren had.

A tear slipped down her cheek as she whispered, "My father." Swiping a hand across her face, she once again turned her cold wrath towards him. "Your excuses, Terren, are pathetic."

Every word burrowed into his skin, despite Sairah's tempered delivery. Terren pressed his lips into a thin frown. He hid his whitening knuckles beneath crossed arms and glared at nonexistent specks of dust.

I subjected her to that torture. My selfish actions. May the gods forgive me.

Snakes writhed in his gut. He fought against ideas of retribution toward the men who afflicted such evil upon Sairah, even if it was at Grayten's command.

But I am not my father and Ny expects better of me.

Terren would deal with the men responsible, but not with violence.

He took a deep breath to carefully compose his next words. "I was not naïve enough to believe Grayten would let you go unnoticed after my departure, and I'm not surprised he stooped as low as he did." Terren fidgeted his jaw a moment to harness the guilt constricting his chest. "What you endured I cannot change. It devastates me more than words will express. Leaving Klynotia changed my life, and once I was in my right mind I deeply regretted abandoning you every day I was gone."

"Then why did you never come back for me?" Sairah asked, her voice sticky.

Terren softened. He was ashamed to admit the truth, but she deserved to know. It was the least he could offer after discarding her to a madman. Quietly, he said, "I was afraid, Sairah. I wish something more dramatic to be the truth. Yet, even something impressive would never be able to paint me in a positive light. I plotted hundreds of ways to come back for you and what stopped me each time was fear."

She sneered. "Then why come back now? Did the stars finally align enough for you to stop being a coward?"

The malice in her words was a slap to the face, but he wouldn't let her see it.

Terren took a deep breath and, straightening his posture, he said, "For many reasons, but mostly I finally realized Grayten cannot hurt me"—she scrunched her face—"which you probably do not believe, given your experiences, but it is the true."

Sairah cast a critical eye over him. "If you are not afraid of him, then why allow him to keep you under lock and key, hounded by guards even while you sleep? Why do you not confront him?"

"I want Grayten to think I am still afraid of him."

"Why?"

"I will tell you someday, but not today." Having spoken his piece, he wanted to give her time to digest all he said. Still facing her, but with one hand on the door, he added, "I hope you can find the grace to forgive me someday. I love you, Sairah, and I do not want a future without you in it." The words were unceremonious, but honest. He turned to exit.

"Terren, wait," Sairah whispered. He let go of the door and turned. Tears discolored her cheeks. She slumped in her chair, not looking him in the eyes. "I want"—she swallowed, flicking her eyes to him for a second—"I too want my brother ... promise"—she sniffled—"promise me you will never abandon me again, and I can work at forgiving you."

Terren took three long strides and gathered Sairah into his arms. He held her entire weight from the floor, cradling her head against his chest as she began to cry in earnest. "You have my solemn promise that I will never intentionally leave you again. I will do whatever it takes to protect you and shield you, even if it means my death."

Muffled into his chest, she said, "Thank you."

MEMORIES

Using the tip of his finger, he lifted the small white bud of the snowdrop away from the unmelted spring ice still covering the ground.

Loralyn would be thrilled to see them so early.

He'd taken extra care to make sure the hundreds of blossoms would thrive this time. After years of careful propagation, the perennial flowers finally surrounded the entire shack and grew down the hillside.

Every spring, the tiny white petals surfaced above the snow after a long mountain winter and filled him with both sorrow and happiness. Symbols of hope for warmer weather also reminded him of his loss. He'd planted them while mourning the death of his wife and unborn daughter. Choosing a different flower might have been better, but at the time of planting, all color had been washed from his world—it seemed appropriate. He could still recall the morning before he'd lost her.

"Zerrec," she said with a hard thump between his shoulder blades. "Wake up you lazy man! The baby is moving."

He lifted from the pillow, forcing his body into an uncomfortable arch. "What?" The sleepy question accompanying a smile. "Did the baby wake you? Is everything okay?" He asked, an arid throat making his words soft in the early morning. He twisted into a more comfortable position.

"Everything is fine. Here," she said as she grabbed his hand to rest on her showing stomach.

The soft movement under his palm brought awareness to his sleepy mind. Zerrec smiled. Their child was moving! How wonderful to feel the promise of more under his fingers. He pulled a small portion of magic and used it to examine the child. The baby was perfect. Ten tiny perfect fingers, ten tiny perfect toes, and he could "see" she had a button nose —just like her mother. Zerrec hoped their baby had her mother's emerald eyes too, but he wouldn't mind his stormy gray, either. Truly, it didn't matter. After a few losses, they were going to have the most beautiful and perfect little girl. Zerrec offered a pleased grin to his wife.

Loralyn smacked him playfully. "You cheat. You know the gender! We were supposed to keep it a surprise!"

"How could I not know? I have to make sure everything is perfect."

Loralyn's eyes sparkled with tenderness.

They sat in silence for a time until the baby stopped moving. Zerrec groaned, flopping onto his back. "I might as well get an early start on the garden, but I would much rather stay here with you."

"Ha! You would rather not tend the plants at all!"

Plants were her passion. Thick heavy vines crowded every corner of their one room home in the mountains; keeping the normally thin air so thick he could almost quench his thirst. The plants flourished because of Loralyn's core gift of Nature. Zerrec clasped his wife's left wrist and brushed soft strokes across the faint magician's mark below her palm.

"True, but my duties are only temporary." Being forced to take it easy— his orders—was driving her mad, but he wouldn't endanger her or the baby, not when he could do something about it. Her bed rest would be worth every second when they could hold their little girl for the first time.

"You could let me—"

"No, Lora. We've already talked about this. Rest is the only thing keeping you from losing this child," Zerrec said with firm, sure words. "I'll not see us lose another." Even his Blood magic couldn't save their last child and it had broken both of them.

She sighed. "You're right. At least give me something to do. If I cannot move around to tend the plants, give me something I can do here."

His wife's pleading melted his stubbornness. "The garden looked a bit sad yesterday. How about you make a tonic to liven the plants?"

Loralyn beamed. She knew he was pacifying her, but at least she had a project to take most of the day. "I'll need a leaf from each of the plants, my jars, and water."

Zerrec placed a savoring kiss on her knuckles. "I shall return, my lady, with the bounty of our garden and the other requested items post haste!"

She snorted. Pulling her hand from his, she said, "be gone you love-sick fool, or I shall punish you for taking so long."

He wobbled, pulling on a boot. "Oh! My lady, you wound me. You know I am a most loyal and faithful servant"—he pulled at the other boot—"what punishment is there for such a person?"

Loralyn gave him a mischievous smirk. "I shall force you talk to the plants!"

Zerrec fisted a hand to his heart and stumbled toward the door. "My lady, such a wound I could not recover from."

His wife's soft laugh touched his ears as he closed the door. He smiled, knowing he'd lightened the heaviness weighing on her.

ZERREC'S KNEES crackled as he stood from his crouched position. That memory was lifetimes ago and plants were the only thing left in this world connecting him to his two loves. Soon the snow would melt to reveal Privet, Holly, and Dogwood shrubs he planted in his Loralyn's honor. They would hide the worn wood planks forming the walls of his home. Loralyn would be proud of his garden. A man without a natural green thumb or Nature Magic to assist his efforts.

He'd lost everything when she and their child died in the breaking, but at least his hope wasn't wholly gone. Zerrec wandered over to the large patch of tilled soil where he'd planted orange peonies to remind him of what he had—Kiira. Closing his now sapphire eyes, he almost felt Kiira next to him, with her emerald eyes and wide smile, a copy of his Loralyn. He missed his new love each day, and he hoped to see her again. At least when the Peonies blossomed, they would be a bright reminder of the princess' vitality, enthusiasm, boundless creativity.

When he'd planted the orange flowers, a wish took residence in his heart for his core magic to be Nature so he could make the blossom grow large and as fragrant as she. The desire promptly left him. If he'd been gifted with another magic, his life could never have been sustained this long and he never would have met Kiira. Instead, he would have wasted his life pining for what was lost and broken, only to die miserable and alone.

Kiira gave him hope.

Though, with ten years of distance since I last laid eyes on her, my hope dwindles a little more each spring.

Zerrec considered unearthing his scrying crystal from beneath the floorboards to glimpse his former pupil and love. Anything to feel closer to her—to feel as if she was near. He shook his head, releasing the foolish idea. It would only increase his longing.

A spring wind sent him inside for warm tea. Crunching through the snow, Zerrec knew one day he would have Kiira. One day he would hold a child with emerald eyes and he could restore a life lost. He just needed to be patient.

One day.

CHAPTER 4
ANNOUNCEMENT

Soft light of early evening cast a warm glow, muting the variegated greens decorating her room. The fading sunlight did the exact opposite to the vases of flowers and plants scattered about. Jemma kept the curtains open just for this reason. Stepping over to a large gathering of Starfire Lilies, Kiira inhaled their heady fragrance. Pulling a bit of magic, she coaxed the large blooms to deepen their perfume. Her father and brother would hate the additional floral scent infusing the space; but nature, especially flowers, had a way of revitalizing her spirit, and she needed any energy she could get after a rigorous day of training.

Stretching, Kiira turned to find Skehtra curled in her favorite reading chair, situated close to the smoldering fire. It looked wondrously inviting. She inspected her appearance and patted the sleeve of her once white tunic. Wispy clouds of dirt and horse hair puffed into the air. Kiira coughed.

That's what I get for riding and having close quarters combat practice in one day.

Jemma would have a fit if any part of her dirt and sweat layered body touched a single item in the pristine room. Except, the longer she eyed the plush chair, Jemma's good-natured ire and Skehtra's displeasure at being disturbed seemed worth the chance for comfort.

Kiira's stomach growled—loudly—startling her from her daze.

"It seems that it was a good thing I grabbed a few tidbits to tide you over, my lady," Jemma said, with a warm and loving smile as she entered the room with a steaming pail of water.

The soft-spoken, gentle manner of the lady's maid was illuminated by the equally soft creases enhancing her happy eyes and framed by tendrils of crisp Magnolia white hair that had come loose from her maroon cap throughout the day. Kiira appreciated that about Jemma, and it was why the woman was her closest confidant. Hardly anything phased her. She was completely loyal, and the mother-figure Kiira needed after the tragic death of her own mother.

"So it seems," Kiira said with a laugh. She rubbed her hands together with undisguised glee. "Though, I doubt any food will compare to this hot bath."

"Then it is right perfect this is the last pail of water. It's just the temperature you like, my lady."

"Thank you, Jemma."

Kiira peeled out of her dirt and sweat encrusted clothing and gratefully sank into the hot water, groaning in relief. She had not been kind to her body today, pushing herself as hard as any of the trainees. Dirt loosened easily, floating to the surface. The hot liquid eased her tired muscles and bubbles foamed and popped along the surface of the water. She smiled, easing up to her neck into the soapy liquid. There was little that couldn't be solved with a hot bath.

After a couple of dips below the surface to soak her hair, Kiira rested against the edge to let Jemma wash the matted strands. It never failed. Even within the confines of a braid, her honey curls still managed to tangle. A soft hum and the relaxing scent of lavender filled the room as soap tingled her scalp. Kiira relished having her hair washed by Jemma. Her strong fingers eased all the tightness away. Once Jemma was finished, Kiira grabbed her favorite clove-scented soap to scour her skin clean. The combined smell of lavender and clove reminded her of the morning pastries served every year on the anniversary of her birth. Once clean, she stepped behind the dressing screen. "Jemma," Kiira whined. "Do I have to wear this?"

"Yes, my lady. The King made the request to me earlier today."

"Why?"

"I have not a clue. I do know that their Highnesses' Prince Marko and Lady Liane will be in attendance," Jemma replied.

Kiira poked her head out from behind the screen. "What? They have traveled from the duchy?"

"Tis true, my lady."

A sinking thought wormed through her mind.

Father must have something really special planned for Uncle Marko and Aunt Liane to be here. Gods above, I hope it isn't a marriage announcement.

Kiira grudgingly stepped into a pale pink silk gown, allowing Jemma to lace the corset. An emerald green sash fitted her waist before draping down the back and she stepped into matching silk slippers. If she arrived in her preferred attire of a tunic, trousers, and riding boots, her aunt Liane would be scandalized. The mere fact she trooped around in such clothing normally was already a frequently visited topic and its level of atrocity.

Perhaps uncle and aunt are just visiting. Marko and father are close.

Unfortunately, her thoughts did little to soothe the worry clinging to her like the uncomfortable silk of her gown. Instead, Kiira busied her mind by selecting which nuts and dried fruit to eat while she closed her eyes to enjoy the gentle touch of Jemma styling her hair. She looked in the mirror as Jemma stepped away, and was surprised to see that the completed style was rather elaborate. Wispy curls framed her face with thin silk ribbons matching her sash braided throughout, accenting the glossy ringlets as it cascaded down her shoulder and back.

Kiira frowned at the image reflecting back at her.

Maybe he finally found an acceptable match.

The distaste of her father finding a man made her mouth go dry, and she found it difficult to swallow. She loved her father, and his past candidates were always acceptable men, but she wanted Leo. Kiira shook her head and took a deep breath, refusing to let her thoughts travel down such a terrible road. If he did announce a marriage alliance, she would just have to fight it like the others, relying on her close relationship with her father to sway decisions in her favor.

The temple bells chimed. She was going to be a few minutes late. She sighed, yet another topic for her aunt to comment upon. Clearing her throat, she said, "Well, I suppose I should be on my way."

Kiira, on the verge of a run, navigated to the room her father used for council meetings and private dinners. Guards opened the door as she approached. The room was as expected.

Okay, so maybe he doesn't have something special planned and I … am only over-reacting?

The utilitarian meeting hall suited its function, and the simplicity of the space didn't diminish the beauty of the room. It was like her mother told her, 'sometimes less is more'. The only adornments were a few iron candelabras and a hand-carved large rectangular table. The dark stained oak, worn in odd places, distinctly contrasted the light sandy walls. The matching sturdy chairs boasted an array of scratches, tarnished markings from years of consistent use, adding softness to the otherwise plain room.

Liem, Uncle Marko, Aunt Liane, and her father shared space near a low fire on the opposite wall, sipping whatever drink had been chosen for the evening. Dressed in stark white cotton tunics, black trousers, oiled black leather boots, and sleeveless doublets, the men could not have looked more splendid. Her aunt, dressed in the finest clothes, dripping with jewels, of course.

"I apologize for my tardiness, Father, I found the bath to be far too enticing this evening." She stepped into her father's welcoming embrace, and he placed a light kiss on the top of her head. A servant handed her a goblet as she stepped back.

"It's a wonder you even know what a bath is, child," Lady Liane commented before taking a sip of wine.

"A surprise to many I'm sure," Kiira replied, giving her aunt a pleasant smile.

"You look splendid this evening, and actually came at the perfect time," Herretus said, intervening before the conversation spiraled. "We were just discussing the progress on the new training regimen your brother has introduced. You should fill us in on the details of how the archers fair while we eat."

Liem escorted her to the table before taking his own place by her side, while their aunt and uncle sat opposite, and their father at the end. It had not escaped her notice that her brother was dressed in a doublet the same shade as her gown accented with emerald thread embroidery. Kiira gave him a pointed stare, and he shrugged, unconcerned by the obvious attempts of color matching. Jemma and Clay thought it the greatest jest to dress them in matching colors because they were twins. If it did not bother him, then she would shrug it off as well—for now.

"I caught a glimpse of the archery training today," Marko said. "The mounted archers have improved since my last visit."

Kiira took a bite of the cubed rosemary potatoes before replying. "Thank you, Uncle. I have been working diligently with them to improve their skill. The trainees are also coming along nicely in such a short time. They work hard, and I appreciate their efforts."

Herretus nodded. "The archery division has flourished under your care. I'm so proud of you. Please keep me informed with weekly updates."

"Of course, Father," Kiira said. A droplet of relief eased the tightness in her shoulders. Surely he wouldn't ask for weekly updates if he meant to see her married and sent away.

Herretus nodded. The conversation veered to topics regarding her uncle's duchy and other dealings in the kingdom. As the meal concluded, her father cleared his throat and when she looked up at him, something about his expression made her stomach twist into a hundred knots. His goblet hand raised, he said, "I have some wonderful news to share."

Kiira barely swallowed around the lump in her throat.

"As you know, Prince Terren of Klynotia has returned from his long absence and I have been in communication with King Grayten for a proposal of marriage between Kiira and his son."

"Please tell me you turned down that overzealous magic-hating tyrant," Liem scoffed.

Herretus looked pointedly at Liem before turning his gaze back to the group. "No. In fact, I have accepted his terms. The ending celebrations of the Yielding Festival this year will include your marriage, Kiira, to the prince of Klynotia. I will make the official announcement to court in the morning."

Kiira stiffened, fork clattering to the table, splattering a bit of food on her sleeve.

No! No, no, no, no! This can't be happening; goddess please let this not be true!

Her frantic thoughts outpaced her tongue. All eyes were on her, waiting for a response.

"I have to agree with Liem on this, Herretus," Marko said, clearing his throat and turning to his brother.

"I think it's a wonderful idea. Kiira is far too old as it is and should have been married years ago. Maybe marriage will temper some of her inappropriate behaviors," Liane said.

"Liane, I do not appreciate you speaking about my daughter so negatively. Kiira knows how to act appropriately when necessary."

"Really, Herretus. You let the girl run around playing soldier."

"Liane, you know she is afforded the same opportunity as any of the women in this kingdom."

"She should be cultivating the relationships of the court in her mother's absence. That is her duty," Liane replied.

"She does, Aunt Liane, when necessary," Liem chimed in defending Kirra. "Just because she does not send you correspondences does not mean she neglects them."

"Liem," Herretus rumbled.

Marko waved a hand. "All of that is beside the point. Brother, do you truly think this a good match? Klynotia is known for the persecution of magicians, you know as well as I how many we have taken in as refugees. The children do well at keeping their abilities unnoticed, but it does not mean Kiira should deliberately be put into a situation that could get her killed. Does King Grayten know? And the prince?"

"Neither have been made aware of her gift. I will leave it to Kiira to decide if and when she chooses to reveal her magic," Herretus replied.

"So, you are knowingly placing my sister into a dangerous situation? Why?" Liem asked.

"Because I am trying to cultivate a better relationship between the two kingdoms. There has been tension between our lands for generations. We can thank the gods a war has not yet occurred," Herretus answered.

"Or it is opening a door for Grayten we don't want him to have," Marko countered.

"I am amazed to see that none of you have noticed how my normally outspoken niece has turned three shades paler since the announcement," Liane remarked, taking a sip of her wine.

Kiira felt a strong hand on her shoulder. "Kiira, are you alright?"

She dazedly turned to her brother for several drawn out seconds. Liem squeezed, trying to elicit some sort of life from her. Kiira blinked and clasped her hands beneath the table with enough strength to whiten the knuckles. Starved for air, she managed, "Father, please, I beg you. Please do not send me away like this. You know how much I love this kingdom, please."

"I know, child, I know, but this is not about sending you away. I am certainly sad to have you leave, but you are well past the age you should have been married, and you could hardly do any worse. All the men that have asked me in the past were dismissed by me or you. There are no others wanting to come forth. It is time," Herretus said.

I could hardly do any worse?

Kiira frowned.

I could hardly do any worse!

Her lungs pinched.

Liem leaned forward. "Father, I understand your reasoning, however, this really—"

"What if I said there was someone willing to marry me within the kingdom?" Kiira blurted. "What if this man had every intention of speaking to you on the morrow, during your weekly Open Court? Would you repudiate the agreement?"

All eyes turned to her.

"What?" Herretus asked. His brows rose briefly before he narrowed his eyes in suspicion.

"Promise me you will not go through with this marriage contract, give me your word I can marry the man of whom I speak without punishment and I will tell you," Kiira tumbled through the words, trying desperately to control her world being uprooted.

Aunt Liane wore a shocked expression as she flattened a palm to her chest. "Have you been courting a man in secret?" So much accusation dripped in every word of the sentence that Kiira's poor standing with her aunt just dropped several more steps.

"I will make no such promise, now tell me who it is," Herretus replied, his voice deep and dangerous.

Kiira pinched her lips and shook her head. "I will not betray him." She pushed unfelt confidence into her shoulders. Her father could be a formidable man to encounter when he was unhappy. She could count on her hand the number of times she had evoked her father's ire. It was unnerving to have all of his brewing energy directed at her. Not to mention the addition of her aunt's judgmental frown.

Anger born of displeasure simmered in her father's eyes. "You have been courting a man unchaperoned?"

Kiira almost flinched at the clipped tone, but she had assumed this would be his reaction when she dared to mention the courtship. Herretus was doing a surprisingly marvelous job of keeping his rightful anger muted. She kept her tone respectful as she said, "Nothing has happened that would change my value as a bride." Kiira snapped and a faint green glow came from her left wrist under the silk of her sleeve. "Trinesteo, I bind myself to my word and upon my honor as the princess, Father. I would never."

Some of the storminess in Herretus' gaze dissipated. Her casting indicating she spoke only the truth.

"I need a moment," her father said.

The heavy scrape of his chair was jarring, and his coiled pacing did nothing for her own nerves. She kept her eyes trained on her father near the fireplace. Uncle Marko joined him and they spoke in hushed tones. She could use her magic to listen, and the thought was tempting, but that would be disrespectful. Kiira didn't think it was worth boiling the hot water she already seemed to be sitting in.

'Kiira, what were you thinking!' Liem exclaimed through a mental link, gripping her hand to gain her attention.

'I love this man, Liem. We hid our courtship because we did not know if father would approve,' she replied. *'I am not a fool. I realize my age and knew father was looking for a suitable marriage. It is why this man was going to speak with father on the morrow at my insistence. We have only been courting for half a year, it's not like this has gone on for a long time.'*

'Half a year!'—he glanced at their father—*'Kiira, you should have expressed your interest in this man. Even I would not court a lady without father's knowledge,'* Liem said.

'Do not chastise me, Liem,' she replied, and pulled her hand from his grasp. *'I had my reasons for keeping it quiet.'*

'Is he a commoner?' he asked.

Kiira shook her head in decline.

Herretus cleared his throat as he approached the table. He gave them both a pointed look, knowing they had been communicating. Uncle Marko stood behind his brother with a heavy frown. Obviously, the conversation had not gone the way he anticipated. Her father leaned heavily against the chair back and focused on Kiira. All hope she held ebbed away, fear flowing into its place. His voice was controlled despite the situation. "I am deeply disappointed in you, Kiira. I expect better from my children. Therefore, you will honor my agreement with King Grayten and marry Prince Terren at the conclusion of the Yielding Festival."

Kiira paled. Tears gathered in the corners of her eyes. Desperately, she whispered, "Father, please—"

"No!" Herretus barked, making her Aunt Liane jump. "I have heard enough. My decision in this matter is final."

Tears clouded her vision, threatening to spill. Kiira silently pleaded with him to be understanding and to forgive her, yet the longer she held his gaze, the glassier his eyes became. Any pleas from her lips would be fruitless. As much as her heart was breaking in this moment, this situation was of her own creation, and she should have pushed Leo to speak with her father sooner. Her lips trembled. Kiira looked at Liem and saw the one thing she didn't want to see—pity. The emotion would do nothing for her. A single hiccuped sob escaped her lips before she snapped her fingers and disappeared in a leaf green cloud of smoke.

CHAPTER 5
DINNER CONVERSATION

The refreshing scent of sandalwood touched his senses as he pulled a clean black linen tunic over his head. It had become a favorite scent of his while living in the Shadow Desert, and since his return, Lucen, his servant, took to folding packets of the strong spice into his clothes. It was a rare spice in the Sun Realm, and an appreciative smile crossed his lips. Lucen did many small, unexpected gestures like that to serve him.

Terren's smile faded.

I still do not understand how he can be so loyal after what he suffered because of me.

It was not the first time the thought crossed his mind, especially after Lucen divulged what he endured at the hands of Grayten. If the scars on his servant's hands were any indication, he suffered as much as Sairah, possibly worse.

Terren studied the valet, who worked efficiently about the room. Lucen had been his servant and confidant for years before he fled the kingdom. Now, he was the only person next to his sister and Kamaria he could deem a friend.

The valet paused in a patch of light, shifting objects from one place to the next, keeping the room tidy. The late sun turned Lucen's pale blonde hair nearly white, aging him far more than a few summers over thirty. Pale lines marred his tanned skin and his tall, thin frame stooped, burdened with a sadness he should have never known. Still, this did not diminish his warm hazel eyes, proud angular features, and humming the notes to a jaunty Klynotian dance. Clearing his throat, Terren said, "Lucen, why do you remain loyal to me? You have every right to hate me, and I would not hold it against you in the slightest."

Lucen froze before turning to face Terren. His prematurely aged eyes turned kind, and he gave a small smile. "I am loyal because you are my friend and I yours, my prince."

"I was no friend to you, Lucen, leaving you the way I did." He scowled at the stone floor with crossed arms. "I wish you would hate me, like Sairah does. At least then I could work to gain your trust and friendship again."

"Why do you feel it necessary to gain forgiveness?"

"I failed, Lucen. I need the people closest to me to know I am not the same man who abandoned them," Terren said, hating the hint of desperation clinging to the conviction in his voice.

Lucen walked over to place a strong hand on his shoulder. "Terren." It was rare indeed for the valet to use his given name. Terren looked him in the eyes. "I will admit I was angry and bitter when you left. It was especially difficult during the king's administrations, and I held on to every ounce of dislike I had; until the very moment I saw your face again."

Terren gave him a skeptical frown.

Lucen nodded. "Yes. The moment I met your eyes upon your return, all of it, my anger and bitterness, melted." He smirked. "I tried to hold on to it, I really did, but I couldn't."

I don't deserve his friendship.

Terren shook his head, refusing to look at his friend. "Why?"

"You are a good man, Terren. And do not shake your head. You are, whether you believe it about yourself or not. I witnessed the struggle captivating you every hour when you were a younger man. I may have been hurt by your action, but your leaving was certainly not unexpected. What really matters is you came back. That speaks volumes about your character. The moment I looked into your eyes I saw the man I knew to be there all along. You just needed to find him."

Pained, Terren said, "I thought about you and Sairah every day I was gone, and still I left you to suffer. I do not deserve your loyalty. How will I ever show anyone I am worthy to be their leader?" He scrubbed his hands through his hair and over his face, thoughts of failure pestering him.

"Terren, my friend, stop." Lucen made sure he had his attention before continuing in a quiet tone. "If you let the guilt at what the people suffered and still suffer because of your father affect you, then you will never accomplish what you came back to accomplish."

His head snapped up to look at Lucen, and Terren glanced worriedly over at the assigned guards. They shouldn't be able to hear the conversation, but it was still a concern.

Have I been negligent at hiding my intentions?

He turned an insistent gaze toward the valet. "What do you know?"

All he received in a response was a knowing smile. An itch of fear crawled down his neck to his fingers. Then he saw something else in Lucen's smile. Respect. No secret would be uttered by him. Terren would remember this in the days to come.

"Forgive yourself, my prince, and those that have it in their hearts to forgive you, will," Lucen replied.

"Thank you."

"Anytime," he said. "Now, you better leave, the evening bells will chime soon and Ny only knows you shouldn't be late to a summons."

Terren grimaced before acknowledging the reminder. "What do you think he has to say?"

"Only the gods know," Lucen replied, shrugging. "In the twenty years I have served in this castle, I have yet to understand the mind of the king"—he glanced over his shoulder at the guards—"and I do not wish to attempt such a thing."

The manservant went back to his cleaning, and Terren gave a curl of a knowing smile to his back. Facing the door, he took a fortifying breath, pressing his shoulders to his ears and stretching his neck as he strode toward the exit. The suffocating four-man guard encircled him. He wanted to shake them loose as much as he wanted to escape the depressing grey walls of the castle. Every corner of the stone building clawed at his peace. It didn't fit; none of it. The heavy tread of footsteps and the crackle of torches, those were indications of life. Yet here life was dimmed by anxiety clothing every servant and distress decorating every room. There was no talking, singing, or laughing, not a hope of a smile or even so much as a quiet hum. Life was nonexistent within the confines of this castle or the borders of the kingdom. A dimness he felt the moment he crossed into Klynotian lands, like a boulder on his chest. Grayten thrived on the oppression. It sickened him.

Terren stepped into the dining hall just as the evening bells tolled. Perfect timing. That would earn him a favor with Grayten. A bright spot glowed in the middle of the windowless room where the table was placed.

Darkness lurked in corners, patiently waiting for the halo of the few candelabras arranged down the middle of a long gnarled oak table to be snuffed so it could once again consume the space.

It matches the rest of the atmosphere clinging to this forsaken castle.

The guards detached from Terren, allowing him to approach the king. Grayten dined alone this evening, as he regularly did, but what of the summons? What made this night special enough for Terren to be in the king's presence? Terren expected and waited for the worst possible news as he eased into the circle of light encompassing the table to give a stiff bow.

The king, already feasting greedily, grunted at the sign of respect before continuing to devour his plate of boiled potatoes and roasted venison, the same fare eaten every night when Terren was a child. So many wonderful spices and flavors could be added to the food, but the king preferred plain, unseasoned dishes. It matched the rest of the unsavory aspects of the castle, Terren thought, as the screech of silverware on metal plates and loud slurps of ale from Grayten filled the room.

Terren took care, making sure no emotion could be detected in his features as he waited for the king to indicate the reason for his summons. He glanced around the room, spotting the statuesque servants along the wall as they waited for instructions from Grayten, ghostly presences praying just to keep the king pleased—to survive another meal. Terren shifted his stance—he was hoping for the same. Grayten was calculating, but also unpredictable, as evidenced by Terren's sudden invitation to what tended to be a solitary meal. Terren should be grateful. He preferred this awkward silence to the canting discussions about the quality of Klynotia's people.

The king remained engrossed in his food, and to pass the time, Terren let his thoughts wander to one of the many places he visited in his travels. These were pleasant memories easily pictured and full of splendid meals with exceptional friends. If only he could once again be amongst his mother's family. They knew how to feast!

The burbling of liquid into an empty chalice ruptured his idyllic visions. The king cleared his throat before using the dark-brown ale to wet it. Terren took the opportunity to unobtrusively study Grayten. It was foolish of him not to notice before, but something about tonight had the king in an uncommonly pleasant mood, and he'd downed more ale than usual. Dare he believe there was even a hint of a smile? Years ago, this behavior would have sent shivers down Terren's spine. Now it gravely concerned him. Thanks to the strong drink, his eyes were brightly burnished instead of dim, cold, and calculating. Definitely concerning.

A loud burp signaled the end of his fifth mug of ale. Grayten waved his empty vessel merrily a few times before shouting, "More!" He slammed the tankard to the table in waiting for the refill before taking another long drink. Some of the sticky liquid trickled down his chin and neck. Terren clenched his jaw attempting to hide his disgust. Grayten leaned forward clumsily, his head swaying, the glassy shine of his eyes making his normally chilling features idiotic. It took a second for the king to focus his eyes on Terren. "I have good news for you, Son!"

Terren tensed. Anything Grayten considered good news could not bode well for him.

"Well, don't be insolent, boy, ask me what it is!"

"What is the good news, Sire?" Terren asked, his voice carefully lifeless.

"We're taking a trip," Grayten said, louder than necessary. The slightly slurred words stumbled out and echoed around the stone room, punctuated by a belch.

"To where are we traveling, Sire?"

Another belched flapped the king's lips. "I've found you a bride! Her dowry's not bad either." Grayten looked longingly at the half-empty mug in his hand.

"What?!" Terren jolted forward, a hard ball forming in his stomach as though he had been punched.

"Are you deaf?" Grayten rumbled in annoyance. "I have arranged a marriage for you."

Terren gritted his teeth. "I did not mishear, Sire, I am simply surprised."

Grayten slammed his fist on the table, making the nearby servant jump. "Do not speak to me in such a manner, boy! I'll tell you this now, nothing will change my mind. This marriage is going to happen whether you like it or not, in case you had any ideas to do things your own way." The king glared at him.

"No, Sire, I am entirely at your service," Terren said, forcing as much reverence in his voice as he could muster, despite his growing horror. He glanced helplessly at anything, fighting to keep a deep frown from his features and ignoring the knotting sensation pooling in his gut. "Who is the bride, my lord, and when do we leave?"

"You are to wed the princess from Lorea, Kiira, she's a right beauty that one," Grayten said, pride radiating from him. "King Herretus and I arranged the ceremony to take place three weeks from now in their kingdom at the end of the Yielding Festival." His words were even more slurred as he finished a sixth mug. "We leave within the week!"

Terren paled—a rarity for him. Marriage was not a calculation in his plans. For the first time since his return, he could not think of a way to work around or secretly defy the king's order. Despair pulled at his heart, sending a deep ache through his chest, and he fought the urge to rub the black hole forming there.

"Well?" Grayten asked, interrupting his thoughts. "What do you have to say? Show a little enthusiasm, Son!"

He couldn't. Enthusiasm was lost to him, even a false one to satisfy the king. "May I be excused, Sire? I would like some time alone to absorb this," Terren said.

Grayten waved a dismissive hand, already focused on the piece of venison pinched in his fingers and lips. Terren gave a stiff bow, nearly stumbling out of the light and away from the table, the sound of his boots muffled by the pounding of blood in his ears. In the hall, the four guards moved to take up their position around him. Dazed and unsure of what else to do, Terren let the men lead him back to his quarters.

Lucen looked up from the arrangement of Terren's evening meal as the door swung open. Terren glanced at the food and then at his manservant briefly, hoping he was casual enough to hide the shock still reverberating in his mind. But Lucen, attuned to his needs, still noticed and concern etched his features. He tried to follow Terren into the baths, but Terren stopped him with a shake of his head. He would tell the manservant what had happened later. Right now, Terren wanted to be away from this place and with his bond partner. Lucen was a good friend, but his Bear understood him like no one else.

Shutting the door, he mentally shouted, *'Kamaria, I need you!'*

Immediately, he felt her presence and concern. Finding the deepest shadowed corner, Terren opened a doorway to the Shade Realm and stepped through.

CHAPTER 6
BAD TIDINGS

A dull ache pulsed for a moment between Zerrec's shoulder blades, the signal from his magic that a permitted visitor just crossed the edge of his property. It would be Taam or Sael, the only two people who tolerated his existence. Somewhat outcasts themselves, the hunters had been easy to bribe. Only fools turned away three golds a week.

The villagers, though, despised and feared him, and didn't consider Zerrec the rightful owner. Centuries may have passed, but this was his land before the realms broke, certainly long before a village rooted itself at the base of the mountain. The villagers would never know since he kept to himself, but this little rotting shack set squarely in the middle of parceled land high in the Aria Bells was always his. A few brave individuals tried their hand at retribution because Zerrec forcibly acquired the previous residents' possessions. They shouted murder, but technically, murder was too strong of a word for the shriveled excuse of a living being. With the help of his magic, he simply assisted ending the man's misery by accelerating an already advanced pneumonia, which would have killed him, anyway. He did the old coot a favor.

The villagers to this day still sometimes attempted to band together to overpower him, but thanks to the magic guarding the boundary of his land, any vandals became disoriented as they crossed. It was a simple and effective casting. Why the villagers never learned from their past attempts and continued to pursue a useless endeavor for a piece of land that didn't belong to them was beyond him.

"You are coming along nicely," he said to the sprouted plants near his knees. "Kiira would be pleased at your progress so early in the season and in such unfavorable conditions."

He bent to examine the delicate beginnings of his winter harvest. He would need to build a shelter soon to protect the rich green leaves from the cold temperatures of the mountain. Kiira would have scolded him for being so careless with the plants, but he liked the way the steep angle of the morning sun gave the tiny leaves shadows of contrast.

He smiled at the image of Kiira's frustrated brow, always following pursed lips when she was upset or confused by someone's actions. A sharp pang in his chest had him wishing she was here now just so he could see it. Kiira's passion for healthy plants infected him in the same way his beautiful Loralyn once had. It's what sustained him in his isolation these past ten years. Tending greenery was both a comforting and arduous task. Zerrec enjoyed how the work reminded him of his two loves, but tending the garden always stirred a deep hurt that would never leave. His Loralyn was gone and Kiira, the balm to a centuries-deep wound, was far away. A quick, icy breeze froze the thoughts in place, and he returned his attention to the churned soil before him.

Zerrec gently held the baby leaves with his fingertips. "I am pleased the fertilizer has been good for your roots. I'll have to see if I can find the recipe for the tonic to help keep you from being so fragile. It will not be as strong as Kiira's or Loralyn's but it will still help." He touched the ground. It was time to place the prepared hot stones to keep the roots warm. Spaced evenly, the slowly cooling rocks would protect the plants until the sun became more pronounced on his little patch of mountainside. Zerrec could use magic to heat the ground, but the casting would exhaust him for no reason, and it was no match for time-honored methods. Kiira would approve of his traditional care.

The sound of pebbles skipping down the heavy slope caused him to turn. The uneven tread of Taam's steps greeted him before he saw a head bob into view. An old injury prevented the seasoned hunter from being as lithe as his partner. Zerrec met Taam's weathered eyes, well hidden beneath careless facial hair. The hunter squinted in return, and his permanent frown deepened. A well-used knit cap protected his thick, dirt-crusted mane from the slight chill of the mountain. Zerrec, on multiple occasions, attempted to picture Taam clean, and it just didn't fit. The gruff exterior seemed to manifest from his personality.

Taam tossed his pack on the ground and pulled out items wrapped in oilcloth. "Got what you requested, and an extra portion of meat from this week's kills," he said, his voice muted behind the nest around his mouth.

"Excellent," Zerrec replied. He pulled the agreed payment from his pocket and flew the pieces across the space between them, dangling them before Taam's nose.

Taam snatched the payment from the air with an annoyed grunt, but he never complained. The hunter disliked dealing with a magician, but distrust could always be outweighed by the right amount of gold. They stared at each other for a few long moments and, just as blandly as before, Taam continued. "News flew in two days ago."

Zerrec raised a brow at the mention of the winged birds trained to fly all over Lorea from the capital. His land was in Klynotia, but the closest village squatted on the Lorean border. It's why he came here after banishment.

"Princess Kiira is set to marry Prince Terren from Klynotia. Someone last night in the tavern mentioned something about the Yielding Festival. He heard it from the Bird Master. It's all he said." He shrugged. "Thought you'd want to know since you're always asking about the kingdom." Without waiting for an answer or even saying goodbye, Taam left.

Zerrec stood frowning at the spot where the hunter had been. It was too outrageous to believe.

Kiira? My Kiira? Marriage?

"This is unacceptable," he said, though no one heard.

Rage roiled in his limbs, thrummed in his ears, and made his hands twitch. Unspeakable feelings settled in his chest. His breath skittered from him like the mountain salamander did from a shadow. She would be taken from him. Herretus knew he wanted Kiira. The king knew he claimed her as his own many years ago, despite a refusal to let her marry him. A tingling sensation crept over his face as his fevered brow cooled again to match the mountain air. His eyes flashed in sync with flared nostrils.

Kiira—my Kiira—no one is as good for her as me. Only I can treat her as she truly deserves.

Zerrec strode briskly into his lean-to dwelling. A few blinks adjusted his vision to the filtered light of shuttered windows. The simple shelter was not an ideal home, but it suited his needs. Now, in light of the information just given, the musty bouquet of damp earth and lean-to walls was not enough.

If he was to rescue and care for Kiira, and he would, he needed something sturdier and more refined.

He leaned heavily against an open-shelved dividing wall, escaped strands of his ice-blonde hair wavered as he tried to capture his breath. All of his feelings for the princess came to him with perfect clarity. He needed her. He gathered a thinning woolen quilt from his bed. Zerrec pressed the worn fabric to his face and inhaled deeply. Sadly, the fragrance he desired had long since faded, but his memory filled in the missing scent as easily as if he just received the gift. He knew every inch of the six hundred precise squares, the pieces meticulously sewn together by Kiira's hand. This quilt was precious.

"I need to see her," he said, "If I can see her, it will put my mind at ease." Draping the quilt across his shoulders, Zerrec pulled at several loose floorboards to reveal a generous hole and gingerly lifted a misshapen oval. Carefully, he removed the protective cloth to reveal a polished claw-like crystal. The black opaque square and spired points marked his hand as he balanced the precious crystalline in the center of a small table.

Satisfied the crystal would not topple, Zerrec caged his long fingers around the seeing stone. With a pulse of power, the smooth surfaces wavered and settled on his love. Looking upon her now, he berated himself for not scrying her more often. She was as lovely as he remembered, perhaps more so. At the moment, Kiira was shouting orders, acting as commander. Her accomplishment at multiplying and strengthening the archery division made him proud, but the position was far beneath her full capabilities. Perhaps if he still held a place of honor in Lorea, she would be the woman he imagined. His rash act ten years past still guilted him, and Zerrec regretted not being around to push Kiira to study her powers as a magician more diligently.

Though it seemed his desires hardly mattered anymore. Soon she would be thrust into the arms of another and he would lose her completely. He sneered at the thought. That would not do.

Zerrec rotated the image, obsessively scanning her features, searching for signs of distress. An outside observer would say she was fine, but not him. Pain lurked in the depths of her emerald eyes. His nostrils flared.

Herretus will pay for this! Kiira must be saved.

"She doesn't deserve anyone else!" Zerrec growled. "She doesn't deserve anyone but me."

Fire simmered in his sapphire eyes. A vicious snarl tore from his lips. With barely controlled rage, a stream of fire blasted from his hands. Yellow and blue flames licked at his meager possessions, zealously consuming the dry posts of his bed and leaning bookshelf.

He leaned on his knees, a little worse for casting strong magic outside of his school. He narrowed his eyes at the soon-to-be blighted interior, not really seeing the space.

I will destroy this other man, he resolved, *and free my love from bondage.*

Kiira was the only woman who could replace the love he lost centuries ago and he would not lose his love a second time.

DISCONSOLATE

"Kiira!" Leo jumped as she appeared in the room in a swirl of smoke. She connected eyes with Leo, tears brimming on her lower lids before trickling down her cheeks. She had no will to remain standing. Melting to the floor, she dropped the thin control she had over her emotions. Rushing to her side, Leo gathered her in his arms, settling them both into a cushioned armchair. "Kiira, what's wrong? Talk to me."

Thick sobs choked away words. Leo responded by tightening his grip on her waist. Kiira savored his touch as his work-roughened hands stroked her hair and traced her jaw and breathed in his warm breath as he placed gentle kisses on her head, all the while whispering words of encouragement. Sadly, they only added to her misery. She would never have any of this. Her hopes, her plans, had dissolved into mere dreams.

Leo remained silent, holding her until she calmed, and her tears were reduced to just a few quiet, sharp breaths. Once she was still, Leo hesitantly asked, "Is there anything I can do to fix it?"

Kiira buried her face deeper into his muscled chest. He squeezed her closer in response.

"Will you tell me what's wrong or do you need more time?" The hesitation in his voice suggested he might have clued into the reason for her sorrow.

She turned to look absently around the room, contemplating how to share what troubled her. Various candles in different states of use were scattered around the room, making it inviting and warm. Scrolls and other stacked papers indicated Leo had been in the middle of something when she came. Such a normal activity. This simple wooden cabin, always a safe-haven, was now an aching reminder of what she was losing. Kiira rolled the words around on her tongue, grimacing at the awful taste they left.

Is there such a thing as a kind way to break his heart?

She sat up slowly, determined to look him in the eyes. As painful as it would be to see his reaction, she owed him that much. Her voice was thick and despair made her words sour. "You have lost me, Leo."

The hand that was gently rubbing her back stilled. His face twisted in pain and there was a waver in his response. "The king has made an arrangement."

Kiira nodded.

He frowned, concentrating on a knot in the wooden floor. "Do I have a chance if I still go to the Open Court?" His tone bordered on hopeful, but even she could hear the muddling of doubt.

Kiira shook her head and swallowed—hard. "In my attempt to back out of the arrangement I revealed our relationship." Hurriedly, she added, "I did not give him your name, but if you go to the Open Court father will put the pieces together and you would be punished. He is the angriest I have seen him in a while. I could not bear to see you punished because of me. So, no, you have no chance."

"You are only allowed to share half the blame, Kiira. I, too, kept the relationship secret when I should have gone to the king months ago. I don't understand," Leo said, "you were able to push away others in the past. What made this one different?"

A tear rolled down her cheek. "This *one* is the prince of Klynotia," she replied, not caring to disguise her disgust. "And as my father so generously pointed out, 'I could hardly do any worse'."

Leo sat bolt upright, nearly toppling her off his lap. "What? Kreshkt!" His arms tightened around her waist. A hiccupped laugh escaped Kiira's lips. He gave her a rueful smirk before settling back into a relaxed position against the cushions and shifting her closer.

She twisted to look at him and saw that his wry expression had melted into a simmering resentment. "You have every advantage over him, Leo. If I had a choice"—her chin trembled—"I love *you*."

The pad of a calloused thumb caressed her lower lip. He lingered on her face longer than necessary. Leo pulled her close and kissed her softly. "There really is nothing to be done?"

Defeated, Kiira buried her face in his shoulder. She had already made her father angry and if Leo tried anything, he could be killed. "I can think of nothing," she mumbled. Raising her eyes to his, she said, "My *punishment* for courting you unchaperoned and without his knowledge is that I must marry the prince." More tears clouded her vision. Her voice was barely a whisper. "If you are to be protected I have to go through with this."

"Kiira, I would die for you."

"Noble, but what would your death accomplish? You would be gone, I still forced to marry, and doubly miserable because of it."

Leo nodded and pressed his lips into a thin line, wanting to believe there was another way, but he would soon come to her conclusions. He would do anything for her, and *if* he entertained the idea of going before the king, she would stop him. Leo's death would be devastating. "Kiira I..." After a range of emotions crossed his face he said, "You did at least tell him that we never—"

"Of course, but he was still livid," Kiira replied. "Please don't be angry with me too," she pleaded. After a few heartbeats, she said, "He will make a court announcement tomorrow."

Leo tensed. As an earl, he would be expected to attend the king's proclamation. When he finally spoke, his words were slow and deliberate. "Kiira ... I. Love. You. This is not your fault, I could never be angry with you for this." He took in a scattered breath. "Really this is my fault. I am losing you because I did not act soon enough. I knew not long after we became more than friends that I wanted to marry you and I did nothing. I am the worst kind of fool."

Kiira pressed her lips together. Finally, she said the only thing that really mattered. "I love you too, Leo. I will never love anyone as I have loved you."

He tightened his grip on her, pulling her as close as their sitting position allowed. Leo tilted her chin and pressed a deep, longing, heartbreaking kiss onto her mouth. She briefly considered stopping him, to make their loss a clean cut, but she could not find the space in her heart to utter the words. What she really wanted was more. To know the depths of his love and devotion. A stirring in her chest made the decision. Kiira grazed his lips as she whispered, "Love me, Leo."

He pulled back and looked down into her eyes.

"I want to be yours," she said softly when he did not respond, running a hand down his chest toward the hem of his untucked tunic.

Leo gently grabbed her wrist. Wrapping her hand between his large ones, he placed a soft kiss on her knuckles with an agonized expression. "Kiira, every fiber in me wants to feel every inch of you, but I will not."

"I'm giving you permission." She hated how desperate she sounded, but with his words she could feel the connection between them thinning and she did not want to lose the man she loved.

"I know, but I will not do it," he said with a mixture of deep regret and conviction.

"Why?" She furrowed her brow.

Leo studied their clasped hands. Though he did look at her, his rich brown eyes were filled with sorrow seeded by pain. "As much as I already despise the prince for having the privilege of loving you in that way, it will be a privilege for him and him alone as your husband. Believe me, I am testing the limits of my restraint, but I will not treat you like a common lady of pleasure."

Kiira frowned. Hurt laced her voice as she asked, "You think I asked because of another reason besides loving you?"

"I think you want it because you love me, but I question your motivation," Leo said. He looked away.

"I would never regret us," Kiira said, fisting his shirt. Her eyes blazed with fierce conviction.

"You are hurting and angry with the king for making you do this, but I know you, Kiira. You value the gods' commandments and you still respect your father, even if you are not feeling it. Being with me would create a blistering lie in your life so vast it would corrode at your dignity because you perjured yourself to your father and deliberately disobeyed the gods. I love you too much to let you do that."

Kiira could feel the fury rising. The man she loved was a coward! But she suspended her emotions momentarily, letting her mind move in place of her body. She looked at the grip Leo had on her. His thumb rubbed over her calloused hands harder than necessary. It was his one last grasp of her belonging to him. The tension pulling at his shoulders, radiating through his neck, crashed into her like a strong current. This was one of the few times she had ever seen Leo truly scared. The mild pain he was causing along her fingers seemed minimal with that knowledge. Kiira deflated. As much as she welcomed anger, the truth of his words hit their mark and buried deep. All the furious energy sapped from her and she felt broken and restless, like a wave shattered on the beach.

What I need is time alone.

Gently removing her hands, Kiira stood and smoothed her wrinkled dress. Leo was on his feet in an instant.

"Kiira, I—" he paused when she placed a hand on his chest.

She gave him a reassuring smile. "Thank you for your honesty. I need you to handle everything with the archers for a few days, please. I will be taking a leave of absence."

Tears threatened to spill over his eyes. It was the second time she had ever seen him in such a state. For the first time since she had appeared in his room, he showed complete heartbreak. Leo hoarsely said, "Kiira…"

Placing a hand on his cheek, she stood there for a moment, savoring the warmth of his skin. Leo's jaw flexed, stopping every word he wanted to say as his erratic heartbeat thudded under her palm. She studied his eyes for a moment, his amazing brown eyes. This would be the end. Kiira would see him again, of course, but this was a final marker for their relationship. They would go back to as it was before, princess and subject. Finally, she said, "I love you, Leo. Nothing will ever change that. Nothing. But you are correct, the comfort I seek cannot be found with you." She stepped back. "We will speak again."

He frowned in desperation. "When will that be?"

"I know not, but you have a piece of my heart. To stay away from you, even with my impending marriage, is impossible," Kiira said.

She gave him one last sad smile.

I will never regret us.

With a snap of her fingers, Kiira disappeared.

CHAPTER 8
NO CONTESTATION

'*T*erren!' Kamaria shouted, terrified. Her frantic heart beat in time with his own as she ran toward him. A spray of dirt pelted him as she slid to a stop between two massive trees. *'Are you hurt? What foe has rent you?.'* The force of her mental communication almost toppled him.

'I have no mortal wound, only I am to be married!' he spat between their connection, sinking to the ground and covering his face with his hands, as if this would shield him from this new circumstance. *'All of my plans, ruined!'* He let his despair and anger flow unchecked between them as he mentally relayed to his Bear the entire conversation with Grayten in a matter of seconds.

Kamaria was silent, but he could feel the shock of his revelation travel to her core. It was not what she planned, either. Terren came to her out of desperation, grasping for any solution to free him of this obligation. He hated to admit it, but she would soon reach the same conclusion as he. She snuffled his back, wetting him thoroughly. Reluctantly, she admitted, *'There is no desirable option.'*

Hearing the acknowledgement anchored the reality of his position. Terren foolishly hoped everything was a horrible dream, though he should have known better. The authenticity of his situation settled somewhere in his stomach, making him sick again. *'No, there is not,'* he agreed.

He gritted his teeth in anger. His honor bound him to treat the princess of Lorea with kindness and not hold this development against her. She was sure to be a victim as much as he. If the rumors about her were true, she was not like any traditional woman of court, that still didn't change his opinion of the situation.

Terren lay on his back and stared at the sky. Millions of stars twinkled back at him as the tips of trees created voids of space in his vision. How this marriage changed his plans. He would be responsible for another. Were the hundreds of men and women in the kingdom not enough of a burden that the gods thought he needed one more? A wife, no less? He would have to be especially careful with his actions moving forward. Having the princess around would make it more difficult to conceal his subtle movements to take the crown. He had to wonder, would she support him, or try to undermine him?

Marriage wasn't even the most disparaging aspect. Terren didn't care to be responsible for a wife, but could make do with the circumstance. No, the worst part would be the Lundemai. He had just returned to Klynotia and now soon he'd be gone for another year. How was he supposed to gain the favor of the people with absence? His father would be sure to honor the marriage tradition in an act of good faith toward the agreement, and Terren, from what little he knew, didn't picture King Herretus as one to stray far from tradition.

He chewed at the corner of his lip. This marriage was such a detriment. Maybe he could move his plans forward? He was strong enough. Fighting Grayten would be nothing, especially after the old man was in his cups.

'Terren, you know as well as I that attempting a coup now would do nothing. You have no support and the kingdom would only look upon your act as unlawful violence,' Kamaria said, interrupting his trail of thought. *'Remember the heart of your plans.'*

He sighed, hating the reminder. Hating she was correct.

'Maybe it will not be as bad as you think?' She was trying to encourage optimism.

It only stirred the bitterness simmering in his heart.

'What is that even supposed to mean? Are you not upset?' Terren snapped and pinned his gaze at one large eye. He scrubbed his face with his hands again. His life threads were a disheveled mess.

I will not lose control. I will be better than him.

Terren obsessively repeated the phrases, willing them to be true. He needed to be calm, not irrational. He was not impulsive; not anymore.

'Do not be so short sighted, Yepenzi, of course I am angry. Already I have considered what this means for our relationship. I am only trying to be the eye in your storm,'

Kamaria said. A small measure of guilt melted through him. She nudged him, attempting to push his hands from his face to lighten his mood, but ended up slicking his entire front with her wet snout. It was comical and Kamaria huffed a warm breath of irritation when her actions did not rouse him.

Terren shifted to lean against her muzzle, resting his head to stare at the treetops, the steady in and out of warm air washing around him. Her breath smelled of dusk berries. The familiar scent eased some of his tension. The hand-sized berries grew all over the forest and were a favorite for Kamaria. His bitterness ebbed like water pulling from the shore. He could not be happy, nothing could bring him joy at a forced marriage, but at least he could face this new circumstance with a friend and a sound mind.

'When do you leave for Lorea?' she asked.

He squeezed his eyes and let out a long sigh. *'A few days. You will follow?'*

'Of course. I would not leave you to weather this alone, even if I do not like the idea of sharing you. If I had known it would be this soon, I would never have bonded,' she said.

A rock settled in his heart, forcing it to trip over the new obstacle. *'How...how could you say that?'* For the first time in years, Terren could feel tears begin to blur his vision. *'You regret choosing me?'* Terren asked, the betrayal sinking slowly through him. How could she?

'Oh, Yepenzi!' Kamaria was silent. She tried to hide it, but he could feel her turbulent emotions as she considered how to best formulate her words. *'That was unforgivable. I should not have been so careless. I do not regret bonding with you. I just ... I just don't want to share you.'* Her words were tender. She let her emotions fill in the gaps her words could not express. She had expected a marriage, of course, knowing of his obligations as the crown prince, but that didn't mean she had to like it.

'You're jealous,' Terren said, piecing together what his Bear was feeling.

'No,' she said a little too quickly. *'Maybe,'* Kamaria admitted in a mumble.

'You worry for nothing. I will have no love for this woman, not like I love you,' Terren said.

Kamaria did not feel relief at his statement, as Terren expected. Instead, she distanced herself from the idea entirely.

'You should protect the traveling party,' Kamaria said.

Terren had to lean back to make sure he was hearing her correctly. She was deflecting, and this especially was an odd thing for her to say. Terren wouldn't let Kamaria wallow in her feelings. He would confront her about this, but they were both too emotional for a reasonable conversation. He would wait until after the wedding to discuss what she felt. For now, he took what she said at face value. *'I shall have my sword and knives as usual. Do you feel as if I need more?'*

'Yes, always, you are such a fragile thing,' she said.

As unclear as her statement was, Terren trusted her instincts. As a Shade Beast, his Bear was connected to the transcendental in a way he never could. It was one of the first things he learned during his training to become a Shadow Walker. *'Okay, Kamaria, I will take extra precautions in protecting the retinue.'*

CHAPTER 9

MERCENARIES

The rancid, sickly sweet smell of ale-tarnished wood kept Zerrec from leaning comfortably against the back of his seat. It didn't do any good. No matter how straight he sat, he could feel grime soaking through the thick layers of his clothing. Smoked-imbued air clawed at his lungs, making him uncomfortable. The only thing exposed to the squalid surroundings was his face, and he was regretting the decision. Zerrec coughed as a fresh cloud of smoke blurred his vision.

I am going to burn my clothes and bathe three times when I am finished here.

Looking into the rough, wooden tankard, he twisted the vessel around on the table, contemplating the dark brown liquid supposedly passing for ale. He grimaced, refusing to let this drink touch his lips. He knew the tastes of finely crafted ales, and this viscous substance definitely could not be classified as such. The only reason he bought anything was because this tavern did not take genially to non-paying customers. If not for the drink in his hand, Zerrec would have a knife at his throat before someone tossed him through the door into the slurried road. That would have been infinitely worse than not paying for the questionable drink.

Truly, this blackwater skerry was his only option, even if he didn't want to be here. Corsair Cay should be wiped from the realms—in his opinion— but it was the best place to find the type of mercenaries he needed. In order to save Kiira from the forthcoming marriage, he required assistance; he needed someone to be his eyes and ears within the citadel.

48

It is the only reason that I am subjecting myself to this festering hole. For her.

A flood of laughter filled the room as a gaggle of inebriated pirates tumbled into the already crowded space, crew from the last of the ships making a port for the night. A few out-of-tune instruments struck up what should have resembled a song but sounded more like a chorus of squawking barn animals. To Zerrec's great displeasure it livened the mood of the disintegrate men. He sneered. The Knobby Seas Pub was the worst tavern in the realm, and, sadly, the best one on this crumbling rock.

Zerrec scanned the newest additions and spotted a man, maybe two, to suit his needs. Rubbing his finger across the base of his palm, a gold coin shimmered into existence. He trickled the weighted, shining piece of metal through his long fingers as he studied the room from beneath the cowl of his cloak. The flash of coin should bring him the type of man he wanted, and if it didn't, well, he could easily separate out the chaff.

A chair scraped in front of him and Zerrec looked up to see a stocky, bare-chested man heavily tattooed with snarling predators and other things too faded to tell one line from the next, taking a seat at the table. He was a floating head on a sea of ink. A puckered scar marred his face from his right ear to his lower left chin. A slipped knife, perhaps? Two other men sat with him.

"Fellows like you don't usually find themselves in places like this," said the large one, his voice guttural and threatening.

"We could have a lot of fun with this one, Ricker," said his companion. This one spoke in a deep baritone that did not match his sickly physique. It was a wonder the man had enough muscle to remain upright. Greasy hair hung in stringy clumps around a pock-marked face, and Zerrec saw nothing but stupidity in his ale-sotted grey eyes.

"How much do you think he would sell for, boys?" The last man asked as he took his seat, the chair raging in loud creaks and groans that it should be forced to hold so much weight. This man was the ugliest feculent of the three, with tiny eyes hidden above bulbous cheeks that, unfortunately, enhanced his multiple chins. Long, coin-thick dreads hung heavy at various lengths, which were probably cut when boredom struck during windless sails.

His hair must be what pulls his face into a wrinkled mass.

"We could get a couple golds in the trade, he looks strong and he—" Ricker gasped suddenly and reached for his throat, sputtering as his fingers clawed the table. Both of his companions drew back, eyes wide, only to find their own throats empty of air as well.

Zerrec held a fisted hand next to his tankard of ale, a dim, crimson glow peeking out from beneath his long sleeves. The three men in front of him gasped soundlessly, their eyes pleading him for oxygen. Each second their blood deprived lungs struggled for air, suffocating under the weight of his magic, gave him a thrill. The power of life in his hands. The men turned feeble and sluggish, and the corner of Zerrec's mouth ticked up in satisfaction. Now he had their attention. He released the casting. The stocky man, Ricker, and his companions took favorable breaths in recovery while scrambling to get away. Zerrec fisted again, forcing the men to remain seated. They all strained against the invisible bonds but may as well have been glued to the chairs. His core magic allowing him to control every fiber of their bodies. "Have a seat gentlemen; you wanted to do business, let's do business," he said.

"We don't do business with sods like you," said the sickly man, his voice strained as he struggled against the magical imprisonment.

"Truly? That is not the impression I had a moment ago," Zerrec replied, his tone dangerously sweet.

Ricker darted his eyes back and forth between Zerrec and his two companions. "W-well, I s'pose we could reconsider for a gentl'man like yourself." The other two nodded a hasty agreement, and Zerrec released the hold he had on their muscles. He studied the eyes of the men, leaning into the dim light of the oil lamp set between them. Aware of his power, Ricker and his two repulsive friends lacked the confidence to meet his eyes, but it did not disguise their ruthlessness.

"Gentlemen," Zerrec said, his voice smooth and inviting. "I have no time for pleasantry, so straight to business. How do you feel about killing people?"

The three thugs briefly looked at one another and simultaneously leaned in. He could smell the lanky man's rancid breath, and only sheer will kept him from leaning away to escape the toxic odor.

Ricker asked in a harsh whisper, "Who'dya need snuffed out, mate?"

"All in good time," Zerrec said, once again meeting each of their eyes in turn before continuing. "I can pay each of you three golds a week until my need of you is finished"—he wrinkled his nose—"all I ask is that you complete whatever task I assign without question or hesitation, which includes having excellent hygiene. I'll not work with mongrels."

Ricker looked at his two friends in silent conversation. With a nod from his pals, the leader looked back at him. "You 'ave a deal." He spit in his hand before offering it to seal the agreement. The thought of touching his hand, even gloved, repulsed Zerrec. In its place, he dropped a small leather pouch laden with twenty-one gold coins.

Standing, Zerrec said, "Meet me at the Felsian Tavern on the mainland two days hence. The pouch contains enough for your first week of pay, and to make yourselves presentable."

Zerrec stood to leave, but paused and eyed the trio warily. "Should you entertain ideas of running off with my gold, well, I think you already know what would happen."

Without further acknowledgement, Zerrec pushed his way through the sweaty, drunken men, cringing with each person he touched. He breathed a sigh of relief when he was out of the disgusting space, except the air outside seemed nearly as hostile as inside the tavern. What should have been a refreshing harvest air was tainted by the smell of rotting wood, stagnant seawater, and fermentation.

I'll have to ensure I am not diseased after leaving this island.

Zerrec turned down the lumpy, deeply rutted road and strode into the night.

CHAPTER 10
EMOTIONLESS

Golden light bloomed in her hand. Harsh contours from the sudden radiance shifted amongst the dusty shelves, straining with hundreds of books and scrolls as she took the last step into the library. Sleep had outpaced her thoughts, and with plenty of night left, she sought comfort in her favorite spot. Fondness brought Kiira here. Built at the heart of the castle, these shelves were crammed with poems, stories, and ballads of scorned, delighted, and jealous lovers. This papered sanctuary, overflowing with some of her favorite stories, now mocked her. A mirthless laugh escaped her lips.

Irony, at its finest. Mother would doubtless call me dramatic; but I do not care.

Kiira placed the fireless bloom on the newel post cap carved to resemble a mushroom. She coaxed tendrils of the light to curl around the baluster, highlighting the intricately carved design of vines and leaves. The thick handrail still held the richness of new stain, since few visitors wanted to climb to the zenith of the library tower. The time and energy required for such artistry always impressed her, and normally, the elaborate baluster would inspire her imagination, speaking to the heart of her magic. Today, she blinked, numb to anything that would normally bring her joy.

She bent into the small window seat, keeping her back to the sardonic scrolls and barbed books. Heavy fog bathed the land as it meandered south toward the Reana Sea in unflattering shades of grey and blue, the lifeless colors fitting her mood. She let out a deep, frustrated sigh. Usually, the library brought her joy; the scent and feeling of the room giving her a sense of peace. Not today. Today her future husband would arrive and she would be there in the Grand Hall, showing everyone a brave face.

A bright meow alerted her to Skehtra's presence just before the Wolfcat cub jumped onto the bench with her. She stumbled over the fluffy pillows and condensed into a silver ball of fluff between Kiira's stomach and the window. The cub's solidarity was a comfort; an anchor. Her lip tipped into the hint of a smile. "Of all the things to humor me, I'm not surprised it was you," she said and rubbed the top of her companion's head.

Just a few months ago, she'd come across the tiny Wolfcat cub dangling mid-air by one back paw and fiercely struggling to get free from the rabbit's snare. Kiira had been nervous to go near the cub since Wolfcat mothers were viciously protective of their offspring, but her heart ached to see the cub struggling so mightily, only to be left so miserable. After releasing the cub, Kiira had expected Skehtra to scamper after her mother, but the little ball of fluff stayed glued to her side.

Even when I tried to shoo you away, you still tottered after me. She smiled. *I guess the goddess knew I would need you as a companion.*

A tiny glimmer of peace sparked and comforted Kiira. She stroked the cub with a heavy hand, eliciting a purr that pushed back the silence of the empty library. It was amazing how something so small could produce that amount of noise. "What would I do without you, Skehtra?"

Hearing her name, the cub tipped her head just enough to peer at her with contented eyes. Kiira scratched under the cat's chin and a heavy purr vibrated up her spine to the base of her skull. Skehtra blinked a few times when the special attention ended. At first curiosity sparkled in her eyes, but then she seemed to pick up on Kiira's mood and the expression morphed into sympathy. Kiira gritted her teeth.

The last thing I want is sympathy. What a useless emotion!

No one could understand the deep loss she felt except Leo.

I love him so much.

A choked sob escaped her throat, and Kiira took several refreshing breaths. "I will not be angry at you though," she whispered and scratched behind the cub's large, pointed ears. Skehtra closed her eyes in pleased satisfaction.

The first rays of dawn pierced the horizon and Kiira turned her gaze to the outside again as night's blanket slowly rolled away to reveal the tempered pulse of life awaiting a new day. The brightening sky rippled as watery blue mixed with ruffles of pink, white, and orange. Spacious white clouds added depth by reflecting an overlay of brilliant hues. Explosions of color painted every corner of the kingdom with the approaching light. The Seas of Reana traded places with the night sky as fathomless black eased into a deep blue and glittered with reflecting light. The rich green land, sporadically broken by fields healthy with harvest, sparkled from morning dew. How she loved nature.

Why, though, did today have to be such a spirited morning? A morning befitting the arrival of her betrothed, her father would say. Prince Terren of Klynotia would see the best of the kingdom. For her, the blinding light of dawn was merely a reminder that time progressed despite her wishes.

Warmth penetrated the window, making her hiding spot less desirable. She was about to move from the perch when the soft creak of hinges echoed up the tower. Kiira briefly considered disappearing again, not in the mood to deal with people until necessary, but running would not change her fortune. The tortured groan of used stairs followed weighted steps. It was Liem. He was one of the few people privy to her favorite secluded spaces.

Kiira waited. Eventually, she could feel him hovering, accessing the situation. "I know, I know … I am supposed to be in the Grand Hall soon for the announcement. No need to lecture me, Liem."

"That is not what I was going to say," he huffed.

She twisted enough to meet his gaze. "Then what are you here to tell me?"

Liem raised his eyebrows as he crossed his massive arms. "Actually, I was going to ask how you were doing and where you've been the last week. I know you have attended to your duties as Commander, but otherwise you might as well have been a specter. I told father to give you space to process, but he's become increasingly worried about you, as have I. However, since you think all I am capable of is annoying you, then never mind."

"'Tis what twin brothers are for, to *be* annoying," she said with an affable shrug in an effort to hide her pain. Unfortunately, it was that effort that caused a floodgate to open, and unbidden tears formed in her eyes. Struggling to speak, she turned away. "How do you think I am, Liem? Terrible is the answer. I have cried myself to sleep each night since father's news, and I'm not much better this morning."

In two easy strides, Liem closed the distance between them and wrapped her in a tight embrace. Skehtra let out a yowl of protest at his sudden approach and retreated. Kiira sobbed into Liem's shoulder as his steady presence conveyed he would carry the weight of her burden if possible. He could be a thorn in her side, but he also never failed to be her best friend when she needed him most. He understood her on a level no one ever could. Kiira thought nights of crying would have spent her tears, but it seemed her emotions had other plans. Short, strangled gasps filled the room as her brother's tunic turned damp. "I've … lost … everything," she hiccuped out before another round of tears began.

"I know," Liem replied.

He knew. Kiira had already felt his sorrow multiple times this week, and she could feel it now. Their connection as twins allowed her to feel some of his pain. If she dropped the magical barrier protecting her mind, she would feel a torrent. Liem was losing a lot, too, with this marriage. It seemed selfish to continue to cry about her heartbreak, but cry she did until there was nothing left—again. She pressed a little more into Liem's shoulder, taking comfort in him, then let out a heavy sigh. He let go but kept a hand on her shoulders as if she might crumble if he completely broke contact. She might. Liem held her gaze for several long seconds, searching for what she couldn't guess. All Kiira could process was she probably resembled a water logged corpse, eyes red and swollen and a lifeless expression. Noticing the kindness and understanding filling his caramel eyes, she gave him a mirth-less smirk before concentrating on her laced fingers.

Liem pulled her from the illusioned safety of the window seat. "Come. You need to clean up and get to the Grand Hall. Being late would be bad form." He said, commanding, steady, and gentle.

She nodded and let him lead her down the steps to her suite.

CHAPTER II

THE POISE OF A PRINCESS

A deep silence settled on the Grand Hall in the dying echo of closed doors. Her father watched her contemplatively, but the feel of his gaze diminished beneath the sound of her hollow breaths. A physical pain pushed at her chest as she stared absently at the riot of colors produced by the sunlight pouring in through the stained glass windows. The overlapping jumble of tints and odd shapes matched the feeling in her stomach, and the stillness of the empty room did nothing for her fragile emotions. She wrapped her arms around her torso to keep from falling to pieces. Her father had just informed the court that their royal guest would be arriving this evening. It was more than official. It was real.

Herretus finally broke the heavy stillness with steady, even strides marked by the thud of his boots. The gleaming tips broke her view before he tipped her chin. His look was cautious and loving. "Kiira, my precious daughter, I asked you to stay so that we could talk. An arranged marriage is not the end."

"It is when you love someone else," she replied, pulling her chin away; her voice barely a whisper.

Herretus let out a long sigh. "Kiira, if this man loved you, as you say he does, why did he not come forward sooner?"

"He was going to speak to you during the Open Court a week ago at my insistence. It seems my instincts had been veritable since I will be trapped in this loveless arrangement." Kiira huffed in frustration.

"Do not be so quick to assume it will be loveless," Herretus said.

She turned sharply to her father. "This is nothing more than a political move to satisfy a war-prowling king that has been on the verge of making conquest on our kingdom for years. A temporary way to pacify a man who will never be satisfied with what he has been given!"

"Kiira!" Herretus snapped.

The reprimand was enough to set her lips into a thin line. She wanted to just be angry by this change in her life, and her father was making it impossible. It was within her father's right to arrange a marriage and her duty as his daughter to hold her end of the contract. She was years past the acceptable age for marriage as a woman of her standing, so why did he have to press this upon her now and with *Klynotia*? An earl of Lorea was by far the better choice, and yet he chose the Klynotian prince to punish her.

Kiira turned her gaze to the vivid windows filled with pictures of history. The quiet was palatable as she waited for him to speak again.

"Sweetheart, I understand you are upset and I respect your feelings. You need time; I know I did when my father arranged a marriage for me," Herretus said. His voice was gentle and kind, something she marginally appreciated. He may not like her current attitude, but he still loved her.

Too bad his love will do nothing to patch my shredded heart.

"How can you say that? You and mother were not under an arranged marriage, she told me."

Herretus nodded. "That is true, but my marriage to your mother was unique. My father still tried to arrange a marriage for me ... to a horrible young woman." A brief frown dipped his brow before disappearing again.

"Then why are you surprised, angry even, that I asked for something different? Why did you deny me the man I love when you yourself had a choice?" Kiira could hear the hysteric edge in her voice.

"You know why I made the decision I did. I might have been persuaded differently if you had not courted a man in secret," he replied.

"Why does that matter! No one would have known. It was out of desperation I even revealed the relationship to you."

Herretus' eyes narrowed and his face molded into the one he used when lecturing her as a child, fitting since, in many ways, this entire situation made her feel small. "You are independent and have been given a lot of deserved freedom, but you are still under my protection and responsibility. Your secretive actions with this other man you refuse to name were disrespectful to me, as your father, and I think you know that."

Kiira turned away. She had no argument.

"Now, pull yourself together for the evening meal. I need you to be the princess your mother and I brought you up to be."

His words were firm, and while they were merely pragmatic, they were salt in a wound.

Pull myself together ... easier said than done.

"I want nothing to do with them. With him."

"Your wants will not change the situation. I asked Liem repeatedly to find you so I could help you with this transition, but you avoided both of us. I was happy to give you distance, but my lenience is worn," Herretus replied.

Kiira sucked in a breath, holding it in place with her bottom lip. Distancing herself from her father, she let panic guide the fervent movement of her limbs.

My betrothed is going to be here tonight! Goddess—the pleading thought halted.

She did not know for what she should beg. An escape? A change of heart? Neither of those options was obtainable. A fresh wave of anger, hurt, and disappointment washed over her.

I have no control anymore. Never again will I be my own person.

"Kiira, I know this is not what you want, but we need to move past this wall between us. The distance is too obvious and we need to present a united front or King Grayten really will see this arrangement as a conquest," Herretus said.

She wrapped her arms tighter around her stomach. Being sick was a very real possibility for her at the moment. Herretus was quiet and tracked her with his gaze as she worked through the roiling emotions. Several moments passed and Kiira felt her time running out.

I need to say something.

"How can you know this marriage is the right choice? Can you really justify putting me so close to the clutches of a mad man? Will you say the same when you learn of my death because King Grayten discovers I am a magician?" She wished the warble in her voice was not so evident.

"Kiira, you will understand one day that some decisions are made with great difficulty, but to answer your doubts, I know this is the right choice. The gods will protect you."

"The right choice for you? The kingdom? Is that all I have ever been, a pawn for you to use at will?" Kiira shouted.

"Kiira, you know that could not be further from the truth," Herretus said, his words laced with more hurt than anger.

Pride belayed her regret. Kiira studied the detail of the window depicting the Mage War. Thick black lines connected hundreds of glass pieces. Without it, the image would be nothing.

I am those pieces.

When she felt like the appropriate words came to her, she set her shoulders and looked directly into her father's eyes. "Father, may I speak freely?"

"Yes, of course."

Kiira nodded. "Father, I respect you and I love you. You are an amazing father and king, but this, your actions in this matter are not the fair and just man I know you to be." Herretus raised his brows a fraction. She ignored it and continued. "I may be stubborn and willful, but unreasonable is not a part of my character. You know this. You should have told me about all of this sooner and given me a voice in the matter. I deserved more respect from you, not only as your daughter, but as a loyal advisor, commander, and an Elite Guardian of this kingdom." Her father's jaw firmed. "Be assured I will fulfill my part in this arranged marriage because it is a duty required of my position, but for now, that is all I will offer."

Her father was stiff and his gaze intense. It was the same look he had given her on the night of his announcement. She inhaled sharply.

If he doesn't like what I said, it was his mistake for giving the opportunity to speak freely.

His gaze softened a little, but there was still a hard edge in his hazel eyes that thread his words. "I understand your anger, however, arranging this marriage is my right as your father, *without your consent.* I have been incredibly lenient with you up until now about suitors and to call me unfair are the words of a rash child." His voice deepened and added a layer of seriousness. "I disagree that you could have been reasoned with in this matter. Be that as it may, I am pleased to hear you will fulfill your role in the arrangement; and I feel this bears repeating, your attitude *will* improve by this evening or you will find my patience truant."

Anger flushed Kiira's cheeks, and it took her a moment to reign in her emotions. She turned her back to him and studied another one of the windows above her. This one depicted the crowning of the first king, her ancestor ' generations removed.

King. The word was a sour one in her mind. Taking a deep breath, she looked back at her father with as much passivity as she could manage and said, "Everything will be done as you have requested." She curtsied, and without waiting for a response, walked away.

KIIRA WEAVED, twisted, ducked, pushed, and turned her way through the mass of bodies. Everything was chaotic, yet somehow still eloquent and precise; a dance floor with less structure. Spiced roasted meat, sourdough bread, and nectar-sweet drinks mixed with the crisp scent of hay, earth, and animals. It was a unique, heady combination only found in the marketplace and only this time of the year as a bevy of people gathered in the citadel to celebrate the year's harvest.

Shouts of merchants competed with one another as each demanded the attention from patrons milling the streets. Every class of person imaginable joined Kiira in the dance of commerce. Noble men and women strolled among the nicer stalls looking for a new trinket or jewel to add to their collection while upper-class patrons searched for paper, ink, or the latest material for a new dress. Mothers shouted at unruly children while bartering with sellers. Servants hurried around carrying baskets laden with fruits, vegetables, and grains; items needed to stock the pantry.

Kiira absorbed the chaotic energy, appreciating every second among the people of Lorea. The shout of a merchant and then another echoed around the busy marketplace, all trying to catch her attention.

"Princess! Princess! Come to my booth!"

"No, my stall! See what I have to offer!"

"Necklaces for sale, Princess!"

Kiira willingly gave a genuine smile to each of them. She made her way around the marketplace, stopping to look at glass beads, handcrafted dishes, small paintings, shawls, cloaks, food, and bolts of material; each seller trying to convince Kiira that what they had could not be lived without. She was not one for baubles and trinkets, usually preferring practical items. Still, she took her time at each of stalls, carefully examining the items handed to her and speaking to each of the merchants in turn asking how they and their families fared.

It was comforting, the simplicity of the moment.

This, this is normal. This is what my life should be.

Sadness pulled at her thoughts, but she allowed it to be quickly swept away in the clamor. This was the precise reason why Kiira had ventured into the market after leaving her father. She could hide in the open. Sometimes the best place to be alone with your thoughts was within the confines of a crowd.

Kiira eventually found herself standing before one of her favorite booths stuffed with bolts of silk and velvet cloth in brilliant colors. Every shade of an after-storm rainbow and others in between filled the booth. A vivid ruby cloth atop a bright plum caught her eye, and she touched the material fondly, appreciating the smooth texture beneath her fingers. Kiira knew she would not be able to walk away without making a purchase. The colors together would make a stunning dress.

Laurel peaked out from behind the curtain at the back of the stall. "I thought I heard someone breathing, thought it might have been Len. Little did I expect to find a beautiful lady standing before me." The booth owner stepped to the counter's edge. "A pleasant surprise that is. What brings you to my stall today, Princess?" Her voice was sweet, but strong and jovial as she clipped some words while forcing the consonants of others. "I saw you not but a few weeks ago. Decided you didn't like the colors for your Yielding dress?" Her wispy red hair framed her face, softening the sharp cheekbones. Her light blue eyes had a hint of lilac and glowed warmly lit by the sunshine. Kiira stored the joy it gave her in a corner of her heart.

"No, I just decided some fresh air was needed, and I cannot come to the market without stopping by to see you, but you have been holding out on me," Kiira said. "These colors are amazing!"

"You flatter me, princess. I just received some new bolts two days ago. You are the first to appreciate that ruby and plum." A sly smile crossed her lips. "I see that longing in your eye. How much will I be selling you today?"

Kiira tapped the side of her nose before giving a wink at Laurel. "I've already imagined a few dress designs. What would you do?"

Laurel's eyes lit up with the prospect of a new fabric creation and she began to gush about the possibilities. Kiira listened to every idea and commented with a few suggestions, each one starting with the merchant on another ideal dress pattern. Several minutes later, Kiira handed over a few gold coins for ten arm lengths of each color with a generous smile. "One of these days you will rob me blind, Laurel!"

"Hardly, princess, you are the one who insists on overpaying for my goods," she replied.

Kiira laughed. "Guilty, as charged!"

"Besides, when you come to my stall dressed in those hideous clothes," Laurel gestured and eyed warily at her outfit; a crimson linen tunic with worked-leather arm guards, her soft leather corset, dark-brown breeches, and riding boots. "Then I am required by law to make sure you own something feminine!"

"You don't think I am attractive in a man's clothing?" Kiira asked with mock offense.

Before Laurel could answer, a pitched whine tore through the air and the noise and commotion of the market ceased. Every eye fixated on the market entrance just a few yards from her. Kiira could feel the hair on her arms rise and danger prickling the back of her neck. This was strong magic. On instinct, despite the mass of people, she snapped her fingers and her bow and quiver appeared. The ringing was getting louder by the second.

"Laurel, get out of here and tell everyone as you go." Kiira climbed on top wooden slats for a better vantage point, and using magic, amplify her voice, she shouted, "Everyone, leave the market now! Guards to me!"

If the market was chaotic before, what happened now was tenfold. Masses of people didn't know how to think when danger was upon them. Kiira jumped across to a sturdy stack of crates and kept her gaze toward the sound origination. People were still running when an intense point of light appeared at the end of the deafening pitch before a brilliant flash stung her eyes momentarily. When she could see again, Kiira almost wished this was not real. She allowed her presence to be found, and within seconds, Liem was speaking to her.

'Kiira, where have you been, Fath—'

'Never mind that, I need you in the market NOW!' The mental shout was thunderous, but hoped that it would convey the urgency of her need.

'There's no need to talk—'

'NOW LIEM!'

'Why?'

'Did you not feel the...oh for god's sake...' Kiira sent him an image of the monstrous form in front of her. She was nothing in the presence of this beast.

Liem appeared by her side seconds later in a cloud of amber with his sword in hand. His sudden appearance removed the stunned veil over the Shade Demon's gaze. Sickening yellow eyes narrowed at them. A vicious roar erupted from the beast's maw, that left her ears ringing. Kiira dimly heard the alarm bells as she raised her bow and fired.

Twenty!—Twenty arrows and all I and my archers have done is turn the Demon into a poor imitation of a porcupine.

Kiira beat her skull against the wooden crate behind which she hid. She had only two arrows remaining in her quiver. She could summon more arrows, but it would be a poor waste of her energy. She was tired, thirsty, and wanted nothing more than a cool drink. The magic she had cast already dehydrated her to a dangerous level, and she was beginning to regret all the extra energy she poured into the spells in a desperate attempt to injure the Demon.

The water skin she always carried lay rumpled at her feet, bone dry and a page boy or girl had not been by in some time. She hoped they had fled out of fear and not suffered a more gruesome fate.

Kiira gritted out a frustrated breath. This battle had gone on long enough. Their physical attacks proved to be child's play. There was only one way for it to end; she and Liem needed to use whatever magic they each had left, and use it creatively.

I hate to be so open with magic, especially with the Klynotians due to arrive soon, but this thing will not die otherwise.

The Oranta—this particular Shade Demon—was nearly impossible to kill both physically and magically. The sleek, wolf-like animal towered eight meters above her head, well-above the height of the inner siege walls. Fur black as a moonless night with teeth as longer than her arm and as sharp as a new sword were stained with various shades of dried and fresh blood. Already, a single swipe of its massive paws, each thrice the breadth of a man's height, had killed several good and loyal men. Unmistakable intelligence glimmered in its menacing yellow eyes as it scanned its surroundings, looking for the perfect opportunity to attack. These beasts sowed fear into hearts. It's why they had been a favored instrument of destruction in the Mage War. They were lucky it hadn't decided to jump the wall to cause destruction to the kingdom.

It was an immediate death sentence to summon the creatures, so why was there one here now and who did it? Kiira hated to think of what it could mean. Taking a moment to sweep her eyes around the courtyard, she zeroed in on Liem. His face was an odd combination of horror, fear, and determination; like a painter had thrown all the emotions onto it without care just to see the outcome. As if he knew she was watching him, Liem glanced behind and briefly connected eyes with her. Mentally, she said to him, *'we need to end this.'*

He nodded. Barking out a few orders to the surrounding men, Liem retreated to her position. His breath was as quick as a frightened hare. Slick with sweat and drowning in fatigue, his normally massive build was much leaner. He, too, had poured extra energy into his spells in order to kill the creature. She felt for her twin. Liem would need to spend months recovering the muscle lost today because of the overuse of magic. She didn't envy him in this regard. Kiira gave him a moment to recover. Finally, he managed, "Do you have a plan?"

She was about to answer when a loud snarl came from the Oranta as it pounced on a group of men and women. Kiira had to steady herself from the shockwave the jump caused. She closed her eyes to regain control of her composure. The sound of bone and metal crunching threatened to turn her stomach more than any dying scream. A line of soldiers quickly replaced their fallen comrades, pushing the Demon back by stabbing at its paws. Kiira cringed alongside Liem, looking away for a moment as bright red stained the road beneath the flattened soldiers. She said a quick prayer for the fallen; so many would dine in Apelgo's Hall tonight. She took a deep breath to steel her resolve before saying, "I think the only way to kill it is if we can penetrate beneath the thick hide of that Demon. The slashes and nicks we create are just an annoyance to the thing."

"Where would you aim?" Liem asked. His eyes never leaving the chaos of battle as he calculated scenarios.

"The heart would be the swiftest."

"Yes, but do you even know where the heart is in an Oranta? Besides mother's death, a Demon hasn't been seen in centuries, and even then not much was known about them," he replied.

"Why do you have to be such a history nerd? And I did not say the heart was where I was going to aim," Kiira huffed.

Liem spared her the briefest of annoyed looks before going back to observations. "You also failed to make other suggestions."

She scrunched her nose and rubbed her forehead. "The only other target that makes sense is the eyes. It's small and on a moving target, but I am the best archer here. If anyone has a chance to hit it, I can." Kiira had already tried the eyes several times with minor success. The arrow sticking from the Oranta's snout was proof enough. Still, it was frustrating feeling useless.

Her brother nodded. His pursed lips and narrowed eyes were always the start of a master plan. "Piercing the hide in the hopes of hitting something vital is as you said, a waste. The eye or the open mouth is definitely your best bet. What casting were you thinking?"

"I had two thoughts; either a weighted and propelled arrow so it sinks in deep, or a poisoned tip," Kiira said.

"Why not both?"

"The casting of both would require more than I'm willing to spare. I am already dehydrated."

Liem nodded, face scrunched in thought. "I think both are necessary. I will augment the metal tip to penetrate upon impact and you handle the other."

Kiira sighed. "Alright, I will shoot the poisoned arrow first."

"No. Both of your remaining arrows should be exactly the same."

She cringed at the additional strain it would place on her body, but she nodded. At least the poison casting was within her school of magic, and would be less taxing. The same was true for Liem with the metal tip.

"Let's not waste any more time," he said, holding out his hand for an arrow.

"Liem."

"What?"

"I would rather not leave things to chance, any help you can give me to ensure my aim ... a distraction to steady the head, or something..." Kiira did her best to look contrite. "I know that's asking a lot from you."

Liem let out a heavy sigh. "You could have mentioned this sooner."

"You have seen how quickly it reacts!"

"Don't get short with me, Kiira, not now and not after what you are asking me to do."

"I'm sorry."

He jutted an open palm in her direction. "Apologize after we have survived this. Give me an arrow."

Kiira handed him the goose-feather missiles. Liem ran the fletchings through his fingers. Closing his eyes, he slowly moved his left hand along the shafts. An amber glow shone beneath his bracer, the magician's mark coloring as he used his magic. He shook his head and a new exhaustion lined his eyes, his chest and arms significantly leaner. When he handed the arrows back, Kiira felt a molasses sticky coating of his magic.

"What are you going to do to distract the beast?" Kiira asked.

Liem shrugged. "I'll figure it out when I get back to the frontline," he said quietly without inflection.

Before he turned away, Kiira caught him in a hug. Speaking into his ear, she said, "Be careful, I want to see you alive by the end."

His only reply was a quick squeeze and a grim frown. Kiira's gut twisted. Liem would protect the kingdom, and her, doing whatever necessary. Tears pricked her eyes as he moved away.

He'll be fine. He will be fine. Gods, please protect my brother.

The prayer felt small and weightless in the situation, but Kiira had to believe she was heard, otherwise her hope would crumble like the stones beneath the Oranta. Losing Liem would be devastating on top of the already-trying week. If he did, it might push her past madness. She shoved the morose thoughts aside and set her mind to the task at hand.

He can't die if I kill the Demon first.

Kiira focused on the arrows and poured as much energy as she could into casting a potent poison from a plant paste she stuck to the arrowhead. Leo had brought the various supplies she normally carried with her soon after the battle had begun. She could kiss him for his foresight. As the casting took its toll, Kiira briefly slumped against the crates, surprised she could keep her feet at all as waves of exhaustion rolled over her. She had just enough magic in reserve for one last large spell.

Hopefully, I won't need to use it.

She hated total blackouts.

Liem was shouting, and she heard him through a thick cloud of fog as her brain tried to catch up with reality. She needed to get into position but couldn't seem to shake the sleep pulling at her mind. All she wanted was water and a soft bed.

No! Kreshkt! I despise this feeling.

Her eyes blurred, and light punctuated the already painful blossom inside her head. Despite her efforts, her eyes drifted close and her legs laden. A hard jolt brought her to her senses. Leo stood in front of her, concern etched on every corner of his handsome face. "Leo?"

"Kiira, you need to focus!" His tone was stern. He thrust a skein of water into her hands.

Drinking the pouch dry, she shook the fog from her mind. "Yes, thank you, Leo." Taking a full breath, Kiira climbed atop a stack of crates, her stomach roiling with vertigo.

From this vantage point, she could see dark—nearly black—purple blood pooling under the feet of the Oranta. A constant growl came from the creature's bared lips. It seemed louder at this height. It caught sight of her and the calculating eyes of the Shade Demon studied her for several agonizing seconds. It felt as if the beast could read her thoughts. A shiver inched up Kirra's spine.

The Oranta refocused its attention on Liem and several soldiers as they moved synchronously toward the left front paw, though she was certain it hadn't forgotten her position. This was her moment. Kiira took shallow, steady breaths. Bow taut with the first arrow, she narrowed her vision to the angry yellow eye of the beast still meters above her head. Adjusting to account for the tremble of the crates, she waited, and loosed the first shaft.

The arrow sailed true. Time suspended as the Demon registered the strike of the missile. Rage erupted from the Oranta. The ground trembled in response. Whipping its head in agony, the beast sprayed yellow-green and purple ooze from the ruined eye. Soldiers tripped over one another, attempting to avoid the frantic movements.

The poison on the arrow was strong, and it was working, but if the fight was going to end, she needed to drive the arrow deeper or double the amount of poison in its system. Kirra knocked the second arrow. *'Liem,'* she called to him, *'I need one more distraction; a bigger one than the last.'*—he shot her a withering look from his prone position—*'I know and I'm sorry.'*

After a few swift commands, the surrounding soldiers scattered, and Liem stepped to face the Shade Demon. Intense shouts to protect the prince bounced around the marketplace. Nerves tingled up her spine. She felt the strong pull of Liem's magic as an amber glow surrounded him. The artificial light made him fierce and menacing. A small intensely bright orange sphere of concentrated fire between his palms banished all other shadows, and the power grew steadily in her brother's skilled hands.

The Oranta was a bee to honey. The one good eye steamed with malice as it focused on Liem. An earth-shaking step brought the beast closer to his position. Kiira felt her brother's frantic heart in her chest. Fear. A deafening growl compounded the feeling. She started losing the phantom connection she had with Liem.

Kiira sighted the ruined eye. Release. The twang of the bow paused her heart. Seconds were infinite. She waited.

The Oranta reared onto its back legs, roaring in agony as the second arrow embedded behind the first. It towered above the castle's outer defense wall. The Shade Demon clawed helplessly at its injured eye.

It's dead. It has to be.

The Oranta howled in pain, damaged, poisoned, and dying.

It was almost imperceptible, but Kiira could see when the Demon finally stopped struggling.

Liem, still near the animal, had kept his casting active, but reduced the destructive power. It was a smart move. Kiira was relieved he didn't need to use it. Liem looked as if he was about to release the flow of magic when the Oranta landed with an astounding thud. A massive shockwave of air and debris concussed across the marketplace.

The central road of the market rent open. Stones crumpled from the inner siege wall. Vendor stalls collapsed. Kiira wobbled on the stack of crates, jumping just before they toppled. A second rumble vibrated the earth. A bright flash lit the area, followed by a loud crack, then silence.

Horror gripped her as she saw Liem sailing through the air toward the stone walls. Her stomach dropped. "No!" The scream ripped from her throat.

Dread fueled her muscles as she shoved past soldiers, her eyes fixated on his flying body. He struck the wall head-first with a sickening thud and Kiira stumbled as a sharp pain pierced the back of her skull, shooting forward toward her eyes. Her vision dimmed. She sprinted even harder to Liem's side. Tears stung her eyes.

No. No. I will not let him die.

A pool of his blood soaked through her trousers and stained her skin as she knelt next to him. Inside him was a dimming spark of life. Drawing on the last reserves of her magic, she located the cracked skull.

Oh gods! Please. I beg you.

Focusing on repairing the skull, she used every last scrap of knowledge her old mentor taught about the body. Wrapping her hands around his head, Kiira knitted the damaged bone and tissue. Her lips cracked, welling with blood, tears vaporized as water evaporated from her body to fuel the magic. Kiira cut the flow of energy at the last possible moment. The sparks of her casting died.

Kiira slumped over Liem's chest and darkness flooded her vision.

It was up to the gods if they lived.

CHAPTER 12

ORDERS

"You are late," he said as his hired mercenaries slid onto the bench across from him. "Waitress, three ales and the specials."

"We're here in the allotted days," Ricker replied, twisting his mouth in disgust.

"I will give you a pass this time since you are to ill-mannered to know better, but two does not mean two, it means one. Do not disappoint me again."

The three men grumbled.

"What was that?"

"You 'ave our understand'n, sir."

"Good."

The waitress pushed three pints across the table and slid plates of rosemary-glazed roasted boar, garlic-onion bread, and aged cheese to his table addition. To his surprise, the three men actually waited, and he dismissively waved for them to eat. With his permission, they tucked into the food with abandon.

While they inhaled the proffered food, Zerrec leaned back to nurse his ale and run practiced eyes over each of the men, judging which he should send to Lorea to be his spy.

The fattest man was immediately out. He was too noticeable, but he smelled better and his shaved head actually improved his features because it no longer forced his eyes into a squint. He looked strong, though, so he'd keep him close and use him to begin construction of a new home for when he rescued Kiira. The thinnest one still had a pock-marked face, but at least his pitted skin was no longer filled with dirt and fish guts. His hair and breath odor, on the other hand, hadn't improved. Zerrec's first directive would be to have the corsair shave his head and chew on some mint leaves.

The last one—the only one he cared to know by name—was his best choice to send into Lorea. Ricker cleaned up better than the other two, and now his only defining feature was the scar from his right ear to lower left chin. Not ideal, but at least everything else marring his skin could be hidden by a well-made tunic. Zerrec never saw the point in tattoos, but to use his magic to get rid of them would be time consuming. He could heal the scar. Then again, if the origin story was good enough, no magic would be needed at all to get him a position within the castle grounds. An ex-corsair wanting to make an honest living would be enough of an alibi. Thanks to Ricker's muscular frame, he could gain a position as a garden attendant, a position always in demand. Inside the palace would be ideal, but all Zerrec needed was an ear to the gossip of the castle's staff.

Pleasantly filled, the three men leaned away from their plates to pat their stomachs.

"I have hired your services to assist in freeing someone dear to me. Do not worry, the killing will come later," Zerrec said. Handing the sickly one a Night Crystal, he said, "You will immediately depart for the road between Klynotia and Lorea that travels past Lorestan Lake. You will wait for the retinue of the Klynotian Royals, and more specifically the prince, before breaking that crystal to release the casting I've placed inside."

"How will I know it be the prince?"

"From the information I've gathered, he rides a gray mare and has the blue eyes of the Isokanii. It should not be hard to spot him." The pirate nodded. "Once you have completed that task, you will come find me, understood?"

"How will I find you?" He asked in his deep voice.

Zerrec slid a map across the table. "This will be our approximate location. I have yet to determine specifics. Ricker, you will go to Lorea and hire yourself as a castle gardener. You are brawny enough to pass as a worker. I'd prefer you inside, but I'll take what I can get."

"They will accept me like this?"

"Certainly not. You will need to acquire the right clothing and I will remove your scar." Zerrec ran a thumb over his skin from ear to chin.

"No one touches me scar."

"It is not an option. I have th—"

"No. One. Touches. Me. Scar." Ricker emphasized again.

Zerrec narrowed his eyes at him, debating on whether to push subject. He, of course, had the power to make Ricker do whatever he wished, but he could also see the genesis of resentment blooming if he touched the line marring the corsair's face. "Fine. The scar remains, but that is the last thing you demand of me. Understand?"

Ricker sneered at him, but didn't affirm. The stubbornness of the pirate would likely get him killed. Zerrec had no room for error in his plans, and he wouldn't hesitate to cut a loose string.

"As for you," Zerrec swept his eyes over the last hire. "You will accompany me to start other preparations. Do you know how to ride a horse?"

"We only have sea legs, sir," the fat man replied, his voice moderate compared to the others.

"Unfortunate. Learn quickly, we will not walk the entire way to our destination."

"I thought you Magics could teleport yourselves?"

Zerrec rolled his eyes. "I can teleport, but moving the two of us would be a poor waste of my power and abilities. We ride." Turning his attention back to Ricker, he said, "Since you refuse to remove the scar, I will put glamour casting inside a ring for you to wear. However, the power in it will only last so long, so make sure you take it off at night to preserve the time it works. You will not be in Lorea long, but the last thing I need is for my plans to be discovered and stymied because of folly. I will also give you a way to communicate with me quickly."

Ricker's frown deepened, but he nodded once.

Zerrec appreciated a man of few words, but it also made him suspicious. The corsair's body language conveyed his thoughts better than anything, even if Zerrec still preferred a talkative person over stoicism. Standing, he added, "Order yourselves another ale if you wish, but meet me at the stable yard in twenty minutes. We are on a tight schedule."

Two gold coins dropped—far more than needed—a low thunk as they hit the solid table. Wobbling. One. Two. Three. In perfect sync with his steps, coming to rest when his shadow no longer framed the door.

PREPARED

He eased into the comfortable sway of Tempest's walk and cast his gaze over the expansive Lorestan Lake to his left. The steady pace afforded him the opportunity to appreciate the sparkling waters tipped with bright yellow. A playful wind pushed tiny lapping waves to shore before tugging at his tunic and hair. The evening before, camping against the sparkling backdrop of the massive lake, had been the highlight of the journey. While he appreciated the unassuming grandeur of the Aria Bells, there was something indescribably different about the crystalline depths of the giant reservoir. Plenty of romancing ballads existed about Lorea's beauty, and the lyrics made sense now that he was seeing the kingdom with his own eyes.

> *Clothes of green sing to me*
> *illuminate Windrah's travail.*
> *I shall dance upon your hills*
> *and drink your sweet waters.*
> *Treasured Lorea, all my days*

It seemed as if the blessing of the gods permeated every inch of ground of the kingdom.

Terren wondered how often, if ever, the princess traveled to the lake, and if she appreciated the view as he did. Who was the woman he was to marry?

Variations of this question plagued his mind for the past week. Kamaria listened to each new adaptation of his inquiry and weathered all of his emotions on the subject. True to her nature, she was pragmatic about the entire situation; exactly what he needed in the midst of this chaos. Just thinking about his Bear made Terren wish he could be close to her, but the direct midday sun afforded no shadows for him to use as doorways into the Shade Realm. It wouldn't matter. She was on her way to the Shadow Dessert to inform his mother's family of the marriage. Her words carried faster than any letter he could send. Right now, their connection was nothing more than a faint whisper in his mind.

Talking about his puzzled emotions only helped some, and Terren still could not shed the bitterness caking his thoughts. Grayten ruined everything, just like he always did. The man cared only about his designs and his goals, sacrificing whatever and whoever was necessary to accomplish them. Terren's jaw ached. He needed to remember that his plans were just on hold, not shattered. This marriage would not stand in his way. He would marry the princess, somehow compose a stratagem so she wouldn't be a hindrance, and still free his people.

The only positive conclusion he identified about the entire marriage was Sairah having a female companion after they returned from the Lundemai. Few women desired to visit the court of Klynotia, and those around avoided his sister. Not out of dislike, but Grayten held a strange possessiveness over Sairah, and no one dared to tamper with the king's daughter.

A guttural laugh and a high-pitched squeal snapped his attention to the carriage a few feet ahead of him. Terren frowned and forced himself not to roll his eyes. Grayten insisted on bringing his favorite courtesans to Lorea, and the noises had been a nuisance the entire journey.

Thank Ny, we are almost there.

It was the last day of their travels, and he was ready to be done moving. Not that he minded traveling. Terren reveled in the adventure of something new, but this journey had tainted company.

He slowed Tempest to have her lumber alongside Sairah's carriage, several lengths back from Grayten's. Tempest flattened her ears and did a rather dramatic crow hop to show her displeasure. He didn't care for the slower pace either, but it was more bearable than listening to other sounds further ahead. Terren reached down to give her neck a good rub.

"I know girl, I know."

Tempest tossed her head and gave one last snort.

It was one of the rare moments—in her restlessness—she showed her personality. Terren couldn't help but smirk. "At least you are not stuck in a stable, you spoiled beast." The mare didn't react this time, but as one of his closest companions for years, he could tell she was brooding. Terren made a mental note to let her have a good run soon to appease the stormy attitude. He mused over the idea of offering to scout ahead.

Sairah poked her head outside the curtains of her carriage. "You know the horse cannot understand you."

Terren gave her an affectionate smile. "Oh, she understands, Tempest is just nursing a temperamental attitude. If I don't let her run off some of this energy, she will turn into the equivalent of an impetuous child."

"Terren, she's an animal. What kind of tantrum could she really have?" Sairah asked with a hint of disbelief. She had never been a horse person. Not that he blamed her. A traumatic experience like hers was plenty of reason to not be near one unless necessary.

"An animal with a personality like Tempest? You don't want to know. Once was enough for me," he said, cracking a smile.

Sairah gave him an incredulous look before ducking back inside the safety of her carriage. His smile brightened. In their week of travel, she had become more receptive to him. Most of their fireside meals were taken in silence, but the occasional small talk had been constructive and pleasant. Now it seemed their dialogue just graduated to another level. His sister had never been animated, but some of the fiery girl he remembered still hovered under her calm façade, glimpses of it showing now and then.

Thank you, Ny, for this second chance.

Terren cast out his gaze over the land. The lilting songs of brush-birds harmonized with the rough scratch of wind as it played with the stalks of grain. Sparse houses hid behind the swaying grains, built by the farmers who tended the fields, and every once in a while the harvesters popped up their heads to see who passed along the road. His party wasn't exactly inconspicuous. The ceaseless creaking of wheels and bright metallic jingle of harness and chain mail almost drowned out any natural sounds.

Terren took advantage of the comfortable lull to circle the retinue and talk with guards and servants. He kept each conversation hushed and limited, asking how each fared and if they needed anything. The small smiles given in return hinted at appreciation for his inquiries. He may not know many of the people well, but the least he could do during this journey was give them his undivided attention. Several incredulous glances from Grayten's loyal guard were directed his way, but Terren didn't care. If they told the king, he would deal with the consequences. He had a feeling his actions were not deemed important—more likely they were seen as odd idiosyncrasies, at least by the guards. Grayten could likely puzzle together what was going on, if he ever cared to give over two seconds' notice, but Terren remained confident the king would never find out.

The trek around the caravan was two-fold. Terren also used the circuit to check on the extra protection he had in place for the traveling party. It was the easiest way to keep tabs on his procured items during the day, making sure nothing had become visible without drawing undue attention.

Terren had taken Kamaria's advice seriously and attached multiple night crystals imbued with a deflection casting on every wagon and carriage in addition to crystals in the guards' saddlebags to cover the widest area possible. Procuring the crystals from the Magician's Cloister had nearly been an impossible task, but he'd managed. Noa, the Anibeytor Mage of the Magician's Cloister, hadn't been keen to let go of rare items. It was only his sincere promise of the crystals' return as soon as they reached Lorea and her faith in his character that convinced her to part with them.

So far, the quiet, well-traveled road made the precautions unnecessary, but he always preferred to err on the side of caution. That mindset saved him more than once in the past twelve years.

A grateful cheer from the front soldiers let him know they were within sight of the capital and, sure enough, the ghostly image of what must be an impressive wall wavered in the distance. They were making excellent time and would arrive in the capital well before the evening meal.

In just a few hours, I will be meeting the princess for the first time.

A sickening lurch in his stomach caused Terren to shudder.

Lucen, who had been walking beside him and Tempest, said, "Are you alright, my prince? Shall I fetch your cloak?"

It was a coded question. Should Terren have needed anything that was unfit for public eyes, Lucen could fetch it wrapped up in the cloak.

"No, Lucen, I'm fine. Just a sudden chill."

Terren set his sights back to the road to find a minute figure standing in the middle of the road. His generous eyesight affording him a clear view of the person long before the front guard would call a halt. He kicked Tempest to catch up to the lead. "Sir Bryn," Terren said, pointing, "there is a man up ahead, just standing in the middle of the road."

The knight raised a brow. "I see nothing, my prince."

"He's there. Call a halt and send a scout," Terren replied.

"The king would not like the unnecessary delay, my prince," Sir Bryn replied.

Terren stared at him, hiding his annoyance. He didn't want to be a nuisance, but unfortunately, the knight was leaving him with little choice. He would not risk his sister's safety and the entire retinue for the knight's disbelief.

He glanced back to the see his personal four-man guard trailing just behind. "Fine, my guard will accompany me while I scout ahead and you can keep the retinue moving." Before the knight could stop him, Terren kicked Tempest into a canter, and in a few short minutes, he found himself face to face with the lone figure.

Greasy hair hung in stringy clumps around a pock-marked face. It was a wonder this man had enough muscle to remain upright, odd considering he had the look of someone that spent time laboring outside. Based on the smell of him, Terren guessed he was a sailor and, more than likely, a mercenary.

"So, you're him," the man said in a deep baritone that did not match his sickly physique. "You look just like the master said."

"I'm sorry, sir, have we met?" Terren asked.

"For the first and last time," he replied. "The master says, 'you will not have her. Kiira is mine!'"

He knew the princess? Terren's skin prickled, and he urged Tempest to back away when the man dropped a black crystal and stomped to shatter it into pieces. The man in front of him was working for a magician! It was likely he could escape whatever casting imbued the crystal, but the guards did not have his immunity and Terren wasn't sure if the hidden deflection crystals in their saddlebags would be enough.

A loud snap and pop followed an odd burst of wind. Tempest and the other horses danced, ready to flee. At the same time, the crystal Terren slipped inside his boot shaft warmed and just as quickly cooled, serving its purpose. He darted his eyes around, looking for whatever should be directed at them.

"Kreshkt!" the man shouted. "No, no, no!" He glared at Terren. "The master will punish you for this escape." Grabbing hold of a pendant, he said something inaudible and disappeared in a cloud of crimson smoke.

"That was bizarre," Terren said to no one, but the guards still nodded their heads. None of the men let go of the death grip they had on the hilt of their swords.

Terren settled into a state of readiness. Several long seconds passed, and the urgent, frightened whispers of his guards touched his hearing. The retinue was nearing. Terren would dine in Apelgo's halls before he let any harm come to anyone.

There has to be something!

The plains and plowed fields remained frustratingly quiet. Terren would take anything over, not knowing.

A faint roar rolled across the plains from the direction of the Lorean capital. His eyes darted to the distant walls. He felt a brief flash of grief and anger raging within him from the Beasts of the Shade Realm.

That was all he needed to know.

Terren loosed the reins and Tempest jumped gladly into an all-out gallop toward the citadel, the shouts of surprised guards fading behind them as she stormed forward.

CHAPTER 14
AFTERMATH

The landscape blurred into a smudgy work of green, brown, and the occasional yellow. His eyes watered despite stooping behind Tempest. Caravans and other travelers quickly became tiny objects in his wake. Even the guards following him could not match his pace. His mare living up to her name.

Near the citadel walls, Terren slowed Tempest enough to shout to the line of entrants to move. The gods favored him and the loud beat of his mare's hooves seemed to be enough incentive to get out of his way. The guard's expressions turned from annoyance to shock outright as he barreled past the line of waiting people through the city gates. They didn't even have time to pretend to bar his path. The outcries from those behind him died through the clatter of shod hooves. His dramatic entrance might get him arrested, but he would deal with the potential consequences. If he could help kill the Shade Demon, that was more important.

Tempest skipped through and around crowded streets. She probably loved every second of this mad dash. Terren stopped long enough to glance around and gain his bearings. His heart beat heavy in his ears, but he still picked up whispers of the marketplace and Shade Demon from the mingling crowd. Even his hurried arrival did not compare to the current nearby danger. A compression of people indicated his heading. A crowd's curiosity always outweighed safety. Terren spurred Tempest through the crowd. Instinctively, people moved from his path, but not without complaint.

He reached the center of the city, only to find the massive oak doors to the market sealed. Thick and strong, they certainly made excellent defenses for keeping something out, or in this case keeping something in, though these oaken sentries would be nothing to the Shade Demon should it decide to break through. The guards standing watch wore fierce expressions and shoved away anyone venturing too close. Terren would have more luck negotiating with Grayten than trying to reason with these men.

Steering Tempest to the nearest shadows, Terren used his ability as a Shadow Walker to peer into the deepest shadows of the alley and into the Shade Realm. It was difficult, as it was just after midday, but again, the gods were on his side. Through the created doorway, he saw only lush, grassy plains and the occasional crooked tree. This did not bode well. He may not find a doorway back into the Sun Realm, near where he wanted to be, but he had to try.

A tremendous roar vibrated the air. Terren felt a crippling pain of loss from the Beasts of the Shade Realm before closing off as much of their connection as possible to remain focused. He was about to step into the Shade Realm when a bright light from the other side of the wall caught his attention. A new sense penetrated the air.

Death.

The Demon roared and a few seconds later appeared well above the wall with a thoroughly ruined eye. Terren heard the clatter of hooves and glanced to see his guard finally caught up to his position. They had yet to spot him, since they still fought through the crowd while trying to not also be enthralled by the towering beast. Terren used the distraction to slip into the Shade Realm.

His steps into the other realm were seamless. Terren looked at his hand as it turned from ghostly to solid. The transition still intrigued him, even though he'd been a Shadow Walker for months. It was slightly disturbing to watch his body change the way it did. The Beast's overwhelming anger and sadness hit him again with greater force now that he was in the same realm. He gritted his teeth. Pitiful keening would do nothing to make this situation better.

A hill from a long shadow had been his way in from the alley in the Sun Realm. At least he could go back to his original point. Terren took purposeful strides forward, estimating the general direction and distance that would allow him to gain access to the marketplace. He found a few darker shadows created by a cluster of trees. To his relief, this small stand connected him back to the Sun Realm and was inside the marketplace. He would have to crouch through the opening, but the gods really were on his side. His entrance would be quiet and obscure.

Terren's vision quickly adjusted to the brighter, harsher colors of the Sun Realm as he once again stepped through. It was times like these he was thankful to be the only Shadow Walker with the ability to travel in the day without eye covering. "My thanks, Grayten, for the one gift you never knew you gave me," he muttered.

Terren found himself standing in the shadow of some toppled crates. He took a few careful steps forward, keeping his movement unseen. Keeping to the darker areas would disguise his presence—another useful talent for being a Shadow Walker.

As he made his way closer, crushed merchant stalls and scattered goods made it look like a child had thrown a tantrum. The livelihoods of hundreds of people washed away by barrels of spiced wine and seasonal ales, all crushed beneath the beast's feet. Perfumes and other liquids flowed freely in the street to pool with the blood of the dead. The nauseating air was worse than the putrid smell of a tanner. To his heightened senses, the stench overwhelmed him, and Terren nearly gagged. It was the worst kind of toxic drink.

Staying in the shadows next to the wall, he crept closer to the commotion, avoiding the chaos of soldiers still trying to gain their bearings after the brutal fight. The harried men didn't need for him to be one more problem to handle. Plus, being caught and thrown in Lorea's dungeons would not go over well with Grayten. As it was, he would receive an earful for his flighty departure.

Terren spotted the Oranta lying in an unsightly heap. Closer now, he could clearly see the head of the Shade Demon and the mutilated eye that had been its undoing. Nothing about this situation made him happy. Shade Beasts were such brilliant and majestic creatures; for this Beast to be pulled from its home and twisted to serve an evil purpose, was deplorable. This act was ranked as one of the worst crimes by the Isokanii people, fueling their hatred of magicians. Every Shade Realm dweller knew the story of Shade Beasts being stolen from their realm and forced into slavery. And of all the magicians he knew, none would dream of summoning a Shade Beast. They found the act as terrible as the people of the Shade Realm and a dark use of their power.

So, why *this* master the sickly man served? Why was it connected to the princess? This Demon was summoned to kill him specifically. The thought sent a lead weight into the pit of his stomach. He silently thanked Kamaria for her urging to protect the caravan. Not that he was any happier the Demon ended up here for the Lorean soldiers to battle, but it would have been difficult to slay the life of a creature he loved, despite its twisted mind.

Terren was pulled from his musing when several loud commands issued and the echo of boots on stone rang as soldiers scrambled to do as their officer directed. Backing away from the wreckage, he slinked back into the shadow of the crates. With one last studying look at the scene, he made his way back to Tempest.

CHAPTER 15
AGREEMENTS

Hazy black turned into blurry shapes as Kiira tried to focus her eyes. The embers of a dying fire showed her the vaguest details of her bed. *Pop, pop, pop, ssss* accompanied the distant sound of crickets and bird chirps through the open balcony doors. Kiira blinked a few times, attempting to clear the fog from her mind. She pushed into a seated position and immediately regretted it as a heavy pounding reverberated behind her eyes. She groaned and the door to her room opened ever so slightly.

"My lady?" Jemma asked.

"Yes, Jemma, I am awake," Kiira whispered, still clutching one hand to the throb berating her skull.

A strong hand gripped hers. "Oh, Princess, I was so worried about you. How are you feeling?"

Kiira cracked her eyes to look at Jemma and tipped her lips at the maid's concern. "I feel as if I have drunk too much. My head pounds, a hammer on an anvil, and I am incredibly thirsty." She croaked, licking her lips, emphasizing the point.

"Well, my lady, you have been asleep for over a day. Gave the king a right scare you did," Jemma said, pouring a glass of water.

Taking a gentle sip, Kiira said, "I'm sure. And Liem?"

"The prince is fine, my lady. With the help of the royal healers he recovered by the end of the day and has been by your suite several times, a worried mother hen he's been. He had a few choice words for your decision to heal him and turn yourself all shriveled."

Kiira choked a laugh before cradling her head.

"Sounds like my brother. It wasn't his decision and he'll just have to accept that."

"Well, you can tell him yourself. I'll get a hot bath sent up for you and some food. It's been a while, but, if I remember, breads and plenty of water are the best thing," Jemma said.

"Yes, that will be perfect, and some fruit."

"Of course, my lady."

Just before she stepped away, Kiira asked, "Jemma, what time is it?"

"Three hours past mid night."

"Thank you, and I mean thank you for everything. The gods know that you did not need to stand over me as you did."

"Foolish girl. You are dear to me as any daughter and I am happy to care for you. You think I could've slept a wink worrying over you anyway?" Kiira smiled as Jemma gave her hands a good squeeze. "I'll inform the prince and the king that you are awake; after your bath."

KIIRA STEPPED from behind the screen dressed in a deep-orange velvet gown matching the color of the brightening day. She had already braided her hair into a simple pleat, and it took little time for Jemma to cinch the deep-red corset. As if aware of her father and brother's arrival, a rooster crowed just before a light tap sounded on the door. Kiira opened it to find the anxious faces of both men. She had no opportunity to greet her family before being sandwiched between them. Herretus murmured words of relief as he buried his face in her hair, holding her head against his chest, and Liem whispered reprimands in the most choked and half-hearted tone she had ever heard from him. "I love you both, too."

Herretus held her at arm's length but did not let go, studying her eyes. "Kiira, we were so worried. Never in my life..." He pulled her close again, cradling her head. "I prayed and prayed the gods would be kind to me and spare your life."

Guilt pricked at her. She'd noticed the dark lines of exhaustion lining her father's eyes. "It is not the first time I have overextended my magic," she said quietly.

Liem forced her to face him. "Kiira, I could not feel your mind. We only knew you were alive because you were breathing."

"Oh." Kiira cast her eyes down. "I am sorry to have scared you both, but I couldn't let you die." Tears glassed her eyes as she looked at her brother. "I couldn't ... I cannot lose you, too."

"We understand, sweetheart," Herretus said as he pulled her back into an embrace. Kiira found herself crushed between them once again and they stood in silence, with only the muted flicker of candles. It was the most peace she had felt in a week. The sun was pouring in through the open balcony when her father finally spoke. "Kiira, we need to talk about the arrangement."

She sighed and stepped away. The intimate moment could not last forever, but why did her father have to taint it with the off-putting subject? Kiira was still not ready to meet her betrothed, and she had managed—unwittingly—to avoid meeting him for an extra day. A minor victory, considering the price she paid. Anger coursed through her again and she wanted to pretend it had been nothing more than a horrible dream. Kiira could almost feel her father raise a single eyebrow in response to her dramatics, yet he kept his features impressively passive.

"Kiira, I know this is not what you want, but it is still going to happen. Be grateful it did not come sooner in life. Terren seems like an honorable man. From what I've seen so far he is nothing like his father."

"What a relief." There was no mistaking her dry sarcasm.

Herretus cleared his throat, letting her know that he did not appreciate her attitude.

"Father, I just woke from near death and you are already pushing a man I do not care to be anywhere near in my direction. How do you expect me to react?"

"I understand that, to you, this is not an ideal situation." Herretus held up his hand to prevent her from interrupting. "However, it does not change the situation, and you need to accept the path apportioned to you and let go of your anger. Now, I asked the prince to come early so you do not feel as if he is a complete stranger on your wedding day. Since you have been less than amenable to this arrangement, I am requiring attendance of various outings together, of *my* choosing. Am I clear?"

Kiira crossed her arms while rolling the words of retort across her tongue. Her father's lips were straight and his gaze unwavering, but he was more exasperated than angry. To her, this almost felt like a last resort on his part to obtain her full cooperation. He was kind enough to give her time to respond, but no amount of silent staring would diminish his resolve. Liem fidgeted, uncomfortable with the weight of the subject silently lingering between her and her father.

Herretus had always called her stubborn and said it came from her mother, but looking at him, stubbornness definitely came from both her parents. Of course, she would comply with his wishes. She had stated as much in the Grand Hall, but spending time with a man she wanted no relationship with was not a thrilling prospect. Kiira decided accepting her pre-volunteered participation in these outings was something she would only do if she could negotiate some measure of freedom.

Shifting, she set her lips and said, "I will do as you have asked and you can hold me to my honor as the princess that I will attend the chosen outings. However, I still want time to attend to my duties as a commander and to be given the opportunity to make requests regarding the activity of the outings."

"Agreed," Herretus replied.

Kiira raised her brows. "You agree so readily?"

"There is nothing to dispute. You have your wish and I have mine, we are both getting what we want."

"Not really."

"Stop trying to convince me to change my mind, Kiira."

She puffed out a breath. "Fine."

"Then we will see you for dinner."

"No."

"I beg your pardon?"

"No. I am not leaving this room today. I'll meet with the prince tomorrow."

"Kiira…" her father said through a rush of air.

"Father, I am not trying to be difficult, but I am not yet at my best, you can hardly argue against that."

Liem interjected. "Practically speaking she did just wake, Father. Kiira needs some more time to recover."

Herretus sighed. "Of course, I had forgotten." He glanced at the ceiling for an answer. "Alright, your first outing will be tomorrow. Terren will meet you in the stables for a ride."

The outing was perfect to lift her mood. "Agreed. The beach?"

"That is fine. Guards will escort you," Herretus said.

"Is that really necessary? I am only going to the beach."

"This has nothing to do with you, love. I know you ride to the beach often on your own, but this I have no control over."

Kiira raised her brows.

"Grayten, has mentioned he does not trust Terren. The prince has an assigned four man guard."

Liem snorted. "That's what the guard detail is about?"

Herretus looked at his son. "He has not said it outright, but several of his comments have made me suspect as much. Considering the prince disappeared for over a decade, Grayten's suspicion is not unwarranted even if his solution is outlandish."

Kiira could not keep the incredulous tone from her voice as she asked, "Even his own father does not trust him, and with evidence such as that you still want me shipped off to his kingdom?"

Her father scrubbed his face in frustration. "Kiira, I will not say this again. This marriage is the right decision."

Kiira stared at her father, really scrutinizing him. There was a deeper undercurrent to his words. She could feel it even if she couldn't fully describe it. She sighed and turned to study the fire dance in its rhythmic pattern. "I suppose I could take Terren to the Fire Falls."

"I'm sure he would appreciate that." Herretus smiled as he gave her another hug and departing kiss before excusing himself.

Turning to Liem, she scanned his frame. Sadness pulled at her eyes when she noticed how much muscle he had lost in the battle with the Oranta. "Liem." Kirra stepped into a hug. "I am so sorry."

He shrugged. "It's been worse, nothing I cannot recover. I'm thankful to be alive, even if I am livid you nearly killed yourself ensuring it."

"I refuse to apologize," she said.

"I wouldn't accept your apology anyway. It's nothing less than what I would have done.

"Then why are you livid, you dolt?" Kiira stepped away to make sure he saw the incredulous look on her face.

"Not totally sure, but it gives me a reason to be mad at you."

Kiira rolled her eyes. After a beat, she added, "Have you seen the prince? What is your opinion?"

Liem shrugged again. "I've not talked to him yet, but maybe tonight I will get the chance."

She sighed and nodded.

He stepped up next to her and threw a casual arm across her shoulders.

"Cheer up sis. If it's any consolation, at least you will get to be queen one day!"

Kiira scrunched her nose before turning to punch her brother in the stomach. "Oh, yes, Liem, that is an immense comfort. Thank you." He danced out of reach before she could jab him again, an especially irritating smirk on his lips as he fled the room, winking before he whisked out the door.

Alone with her thoughts, Kiira wondered what had her father so convinced of the trueness of this decision.

At least my first outing with the prince will be something I actually enjoy.

A small but happy smile graced her lips. Tomorrow she would be able to feel the wind in her face, smell the fresh salt air from the back of her beloved Starfire. She could already hear the hooves pounding and the sea crashing against the shore, and the view of the Fire Falls just before sunset would more than make up for the company. Kiira closed her eyes, already imagining the feel of sun warming her face and leagues of farmland leading to the ocean. There was nothing better than the freedom of open air!

MUSINGS ON A PRINCESS

*T*o be the sun. *To have the same purpose day after day and to know your purpose is important.*

A heated thought stiffened Terren's shoulders.

I had a purpose, and Grayten stole it from me.

Staring out the window from his room, he studied the landscape, still in deep shadow; the horizon turning a bruised color as the heavy night faded to a lighter purple. Soon yellow rays would skip along the edges of the sky. The land was beautiful, but it wasn't home. If only he could be in Klynotia.

The rolling hills and flourishing farms were the prosperity of Lorea. Generations of Klynotians couldn't remember true abundance. His own kingdom was not poor, not at all, the land's wealth sustained by the hundreds of mines existing in the Aria Bells, but the mostly prairie and rocky soil did not provide the conditions for growing food, leaving the kingdom dependent on trade in order to feed most of the population. Ostensibly, Grayten's desire to establish friendly relations with a wealthy kingdom, such as Lorea, Terren, supported.

To distract himself from his saturnine circumstances, Terren pondered the Shade Demon. There was so much to learn. The Oranta would have originally been a Shade Wolf. The distorted features of the poor twisted creature could not hide the beauty that once was. When he lived among his mother's people, he interacted with a Shade Wolf bonded to a cousin, one of the more light-hearted Beast that especially enjoyed speaking with Kamaria.

Thank the gods a bonded Shade Beast cannot be mutilated in such a way.

His heart still ached for the tragedy yesterday. He felt semi-responsible, since the attack was originally meant for him. Was there anyone he had angered recently or in his past that would attempt to take his life in such a way? He needed answers, preferably before his marriage. Terren made a mental note to begin with the castle staff and work his way through the guards. He was bound to learn something from the gossip.

One question, however, burned brighter at the core of his thoughts.

Who *was* Kiira?

She was clearly important to whoever sent the man from the road. She was active in the kingdom's military, a pleasant surprise, and definitely brave—readily facing a Shade Demon was no small feat.

He recalled meeting King Herretus the day before.

TERREN'S confident strides into the room caused a ripple of silence to fall across the courtiers. Compacted as he was between grumpy and sweaty guards, he groaned internally as all eyes turned in his direction, making him the center of attention.

He glanced up to where Grayten stood with Lorea's king. A controlled mask of fury pinching Grayten's face. Terren assumed the most humble look he could manage and walked directly toward King Herretus, every head moving in unison with his progress. Terren bowed before the king and said, "Your Majesty, I beg your pardon for not being here with the rest of the retinue. It was rude of me as your guest."

Herretus moved to shake his hand and with a clap on his shoulder he said, "That's alright, Terren. I'm just glad to see that you made it safely. Your father said you took off rather like lightning and your sister has been quite worried." Several released breaths chorused the room when everyone was reassured the king was not offended.

There was tension in the king's eyes, but he was hiding it well. Impressive considering the emergency at hand. "Yes, Sire, I heard the Shade Demon's roar and thought I might help." Terren said.

"Not," Grayten snorted, "with the way you handle a sword."

Terren clenched his jaw, but kept his face smooth. He was grateful when Herretus directed the conversation away from the derisive remark.

"That is kind of you. I apologize that my son and daughter are not here to greet you. They are both very involved in the kingdom's military and were the first to arrive at the market. At this moment we are all awaiting the outcome."

"I can tell you, Sire, that the Oranta is dead. Two well placed arrows in the eye," Terren said.

An interesting look crossed the king's face before he replied, "That's excellent news. How did you come by this information?"

"Just before the Demon fell, it reared and stood above the wall enough for me to see the damage."

The conversation was cut short when the doors to the grand hall actually burst open. Terren didn't think it was possible, as large and thick as they were. He moved aside to allow a young soldier, looking utterly frazzled, to deliver a message. He studied Herretus' reaction to the news of his children's severe injuries, but still alive. It always interested him how people absorbed information. He found a lot could be learned from the slightest reactions; it was why he took to looking and listening more than he spoke.

THE INTERACTION in the grand hall only provided surface answers, and though his curiosity about the princess ran deeper, it did nothing to take away his bitterness. This marriage was about more than the two kingdoms becoming allies. Grayten was too cunning for it to be that simple, yet Terren had no proof. Still, he could direct none of his anger toward the princess when his issues lay elsewhere.

His usually measured temperament was dangerously close to being swept away. Terren wanted to tear the room apart; he could feel it in his quickening breath and hammering heart.

Closing his eyes, Terren forced himself to relax with deep breaths, using the chants of the priest to calm his chaotic thoughts.

Even in the deepest darkness, Ny, Lord of Light, you are with me. You give me strength and guide me on the right paths.

After a few minutes, he realized he needed more than meditation. The tightness binding his chest refused to go away. Strapping on his various knives, he burst from the room and quickly strode past his sleepy guards, not caring if they kept pace.

The sun was a perfect half on the horizon, and the cool morning air filtered into Terren's lungs. He instantly felt better. The freshness of the harvest season brought a relief stifled by the thick walls of the castle. Energized, he propelled himself into a faster pace toward the outer wall. Terren stopped to take in the muted green fields and glittering river. The land hungered for the new light and strained for its colors to be vivid again. He inhaled a deep breath of salty air. The morning was pleasant, but thick, heavy moisture would soon invade, making it difficult to breathe. He didn't mind, but it was drastically different from the Shadow Desert, where the arid temperatures sapped the moisture out of everything.

His limbs strained for motion, and he soon found himself in the rhythmic pattern of a run. Each thump of his heel released the simmering tension coiled about him.

Terren slowed his pace as the exertion did exactly what he hoped. Grayten's scheme irritated him and inconvenienced him, but if his own plan for a coup was going to succeed, then following through with the marriage was the logical choice. The people of Klynotia would likely be more supportive of his rule if they deemed him stable, rational, and a loving husband.

That last one is going to need work.

Terren didn't easily trust women, except the priestess in the temple, and that's only because of their vows. Experience showed him women tended to be selfish and demanding. Even his own mother had left him and Sairah to years of Grayten's madness because of her lack of self-control. Terren would have eventually married—his position demanded it—but he had envisioned it on his own terms, further in the future, and with a bride of his choosing.

An hour's worth of running put Terren in a much better state of mind. The sun had burned away all coolness, but the building humidity still did not drive him inside. He ventured to the training yard. Luckily, on the way there, a well with a drinking cup was stationed to relieve his parched throat, his trailing guards satisfying their thirst as well.

Terren spotted a group of soldiers drilling with knives. He tilted his head, noting how they were actually quite skilled with a knife. Not as good as the people of the Veripoi, but still decent. Maybe it would be worth his time to find someone to spar with. Except, he still didn't trust the rotation of guards, acting as his second shadow, not to report his skills to Grayten. The leery king would see his talent as a threat.

Instead, Terren located a more secluded area of the training yard and practiced various basic drills with the knives and sword he always kept with him. A lone tree served as a practice target for his throwing. Halfway through his drills, the hair on his neck prickled. It was an ingrained feeling learned during his travels, and, sure enough, when he turned, a burly-looking man was studying him. Terren considered asking him to spar, but the mid-morning bells tolled and the man strode away without a word.

An angry protest from his stomach reminded him that food was important. Terren quickly made his way back inside. The cooler temperature of the castle was a welcome relief and the sweat quickly evaporated from his skin.

After exchanging the guard rotation at his quarters, he located the baths and relaxed in the hot water. The naturally heated mineral pools helped to promote healing and relieve sore muscles, or so the attendant had told him. It was easy to be jealous that Klynotia did not have such a luxury.

Clean and dressed in a linen cerulean tunic, chocolate trousers, and brown boots, Terren felt clean for the first time since arriving. His stomach protested loudly again at his delayed eating. Asking one servant to give him directions to the kitchens, he moved off in search of a meal.

Terren eased open the door to the kitchens, allowing a puff of steam to escape. Loud shouts of both rage and commands hummed in his ears. A chaotic battlefield of food. He almost received a rebuke himself from the Cook Master before the large, blustering man recognized him. Terren quickly asked for any spare food available to tide him until a proper meal. The Cook Master, Danel, a girth and jolly fellow when he was not yelling, obliged Terren by loading several loaves of warm bread, an eighth of a wheel of cheese, and a basket of fruit. It was an obscene amount, but the guards could feast with him.

In his suite, Terren studied the provisions, briefly debating if he should wolf something or take a portion of it and wander the castle. The idea of exploring the castle pleased him, so he tore off a third of the loaf, cut himself a chunk from the cheese, and stashed an apple in his pocket. He looked expectantly at his guards, who could barely control their wide-eyed drooling. "Do you really think me cruel enough to not let you eat?" Terren asked.

Lenden cleared his throat. "No, Your Highness, we already ate."

"That may be so but you are obviously hungry again. Take what you wish. Lorea is not short of food."

"It is inappropriate to eat while on duty. The king would be furious," Yven supplied.

Terren raised a single brow. "We will not be going anywhere near Grayten in the short time it will take you to eat some food. Grab something and let's go."

The guards ripped into the remains of his torn loaf and each took a piece of fruit. Terren gave a small smile, knowing he'd just won a measure of loyalty from the men. He may not like guards assigned to him, but they were still his subjects, and despite the rumors floating about, he cared for the people of his kingdom.

Terren led the leisurely walk through the halls, appreciating the quiet ambiance and the mousy eating noises of his guards. He explored many of the various nooks, crannies, and hidden doorways leading off the main passageways. He was also fascinated by all the artwork adorning the halls and stopped several times to study the different paintings.

A servant noticed him examining one particular piece and paused long enough to suggest he make his way to the castle's gallery, where he could find the prized collection of the king. Terren thanked the man and strolled in that direction.

Upon entering the brightly lit room, he had to let out a low whistle of appreciation. The large chamber was filled with thousands of pictures of the highest artistry. Large and small paintings alike covered every inch of the walls.

Eager to study each work, Terren began his journey through the gallery, each painting capturing his attention, some more than others.

He spent extra time on those depicting scenes of The Mage War. It had been eight hundred years since the land-dividing war, and many details had either been forgotten or distorted, like those depictions of Shade Demons. These images he had to turn away.

I know that Shade Demons are fearsome and must be killed, but to witness people in the Sun Realm hating something they have so little knowledge of sickens me.

His favorite paintings were of the unique landscapes. He admired King Herretus for having taken great care in selecting the pieces that adorned the gallery's walls. The renditions of the Glazefire Canyon and the Shadow Desert were surprisingly accurate.

Terren moved to the portraits section of the gallery. There were the standard paintings of the kingdom's lineage, as well as the current monarchy. Most subjects were jewel encrusted, displaying Klynotia's wealth. A steep reminder that the Lorean gem purchases were the only thing keeping his kingdom from collapsing. Terren shook his head before roaming to an older painting of King Herretus as a much younger man with his arm around Queen Jurica, who was holding the young prince and princess. It stood out prominently from among the others. Terren remembered hearing whispers of the violent death of the queen a few years after he left Klynotia. In this portrait, the royal family was happy, and a surprising ache settled in his chest. He couldn't help wondering what it felt like to be part of a love such as theirs. Terren was accepted by his mother's family, but it wasn't the same as being accepted and loved by your parents.

He sighed and progressed his gaze away from the idyllic scene. His eyes landed on a small portrait of the princess and he froze. Kiira sat at the base of a thick tree, one slender arm wrapped around her knees and sunlight through the leaves mottling her face. A silky, dark green summer dress hugged her athletic frame, and his lips curled into a smirk as he noticed bare toes peeking out beneath the hemline. She had just taken a huge bite from a pear and the juice glistened on her lips. Her smile radiated joy and her piercing emerald eyes hinted at mischievous delight. Loose braids piled into a haphazard knot contained her wild, honey-blonde curls, except for a few stray tendrils that loosely framed her face. He immediately loved this painting. He especially loved her eyes. The mischievous look held honesty, joy, love, and trust. This woman intrigued him.

One guard broke into his reverie. "Is that the princess, Your Highness?"

"I believe so, Harmend, at least the portrait matches the description I know of her," Terren replied.

"She's pretty," he said.

"She is definitely not what I expected."

Needing a distraction from his musings on Princess Kiira, Terren left the gallery and took a path towards his sister's suite. Her maid opened the door after a knock, and he found Sairah draped over a couch with a book shrouding her stomach. He covered a laugh with a cough. If his sister had a book in hand, she was bored out of her mind. "Sairah, would you accompany me for a walk in the gardens?" He asked, unable to hide the bemused tone in his voice.

She sighed in relief. "Oh, yes, please." She tossed the book aside like her hand would catch fire if she continued to hold it. At that, he could not hide a small laugh.

"What?" Her eyes were sharp and suspicious.

Terren cleared his throat. "Nothing. Sairah, you look radiant today."

She gave him an appraising glare.

"I absolutely mean it. You look as lovely as our mother," he said, offering her his arm. Sairah's lips curled ever so slightly as she took his offered arm.

They strolled through the shaded paths past the perfectly trimmed hedges of the queen's lush gardens, appreciating the artful arrangement of the beds and, every so often, stopping to examine the blooming flowers.

"You never really talked about her before you left," Sairah said, pulling a full rose toward her nose. She gave him a sidelong glance.

"Mother."

She nodded.

"I suppose I mention her more now because I returned from the Shadow Desert not long ago. The Isokanii are still fresh in my mind."

"I do not remember her."

"How could you? You were only three winters." A memory sprung unbidden to his mind of his sister, small and round-faced, screaming for her mother as he held her, trying desperately to give her some measure of comfort.

"Everyone compares me to her, you know. Should I consider the words a compliment? There are no pictures hung in the castle to preserve her memory. She's been gone almost twenty years and still I hear her name on the lips of the courtiers. Then there's the talk of how father changed so dramatically after her death."

Terren frowned. "Mother was very beautiful, that I remember, but you should not listen to rumors. Grayten was a different man even before he sentenced her to death, a death she brought upon herself. You're lucky to not have seen the change." A haunted look crept into his eyes.

"Mmm. Maybe I am, but I certainly felt the repercussions." She stopped to smell another flower. "These are so much prettier than ours back home. If only we could grow such beauty."

Sairah was deflecting the conversation. He didn't mind. Terren's own memories of his mother were scattered and inconsistent, but he would never forget the day of her execution and how it spun his world into darkness. He was relieved Sairah changed the subject.

Taking a dark green leaf between his forefinger and thumb, Terren gently rubbed the surface of the glossy green side, admiring how it glided beneath his fingers. He couldn't deny Lorea's soil quality seemed to grow just about anything, making it one reason the kingdom was so profitable. If Klynotia could grow quality food like Lorea and continue mining, the kingdom would be obscenely wealthy.

"What are you thinking?" Sairah asked as they once again took to the gravel path.

"Just an idea for improving farming in Klynotia," he said.

"Terren, you know as well as I that the soil is not hospitable."

"True, however, that does not mean that we couldn't make it so. The people in the Shade Realm grow tons of food in mostly rocky soil."

"Terren…"

"Sairah, it's just an idea. It's not like I can test it."

Sairah frowned at the ground, wrinkling her brow. When he asked her what was wrong, she smoothed her features and gave him a sweet smile. Obviously, the growing relationship with his sister was going to take baby steps.

Terren glanced toward bells ringing from the temple, signaling midday. A garden attendant found them and asked if they would care to take their meal beneath the shade of the Bosom Oak. The day was warm, but not unbearable, and it had been especially pleasant in the cool shade of the garden.

They ate dried cranberries and pineapple mixed with pistachios and walnuts underneath the massive oak. His favorite dish by far was a mouthwatering pastry slathered in fresh butter and stacked with a spicy smoked ham. Their conversation remained light and Terren spent much of the time animatedly describing his time as an apprentice to a surly blacksmith in the Shadow Desert. The man 'hated' every piece he created, even though his finished swords and knives typically sold for outrageous amounts. Terren's favorite part of the afternoon was Sairah's uninhibited laughter. Her delight in his tales warming his heart.

As the food dwindled, a pageboy came running up to them and bowed low. Breathless, the boy turned to Terren and said, "Excuse me, Your Highness, their Majesties King Herretus and King Grayten have requested your immediate presence. I am to escort you straight to the Meeting Hall."

Terren nodded. Giving his sister a hug, he said, "I will see you at dinner," and followed the pageboy towards the castle.

When they reached the Meeting Hall, the simplicity of the room took him by surprise. Everything in Lorea bordered on opulent, but this room seemed to be the stark exception. The sparse, utilitarian decor felt almost out of place. It was the most practical room Terren had seen since leaving Klynotia.

Grayten and King Herretus sat across from one another compiling and shuffling through an assortment of papers, probably all relating to the marriage, Terren guessed. It sickened him how this arrangement was nothing more than a political scheme, and he was being traded like a prized steed. Both kings looked up when he entered the room, and Terren gave a quick, polite bow to each.

Herretus broke the silence first. "Terren, how do you like your stay? I hope you have found things to occupy your time while my daughter is indisposed. I was told you'd been directed to the gallery and just this afternoon have enjoyed the gardens. Did you find them to your liking?"

"Yes, Your Majesty, I have found my meanderings through the royal grounds most wonderful. Everything I have seen is unique," Terren replied courteously.

Herretus smiled. "I am glad that you have found some measure of intrigue here in our kingdom."

Terren bowed in return.

"On to business then. When your father and I made our agreement, I thought it best that you and my daughter have some time to spend with one another before the actual wedding."

Terren acknowledged the statement.

"My Kiira, can be rather stubborn and I am afraid has been quite reluctant about the entire ordeal. So, I am hopeful various outings will help you two become more accustomed to each other." He paused for a beat and the seriousness in his eyes spoke volumes. "Kirra really is an amazing woman, once you understand her. I hope you are agreeable with this arrangement, your father said you have been amenable about everything thus far."

Terren glanced at Grayten. A clever ploy, making him look like the perfect son and, simultaneously, leaving him no option but to play the part or appear childishly belligerent. The princess did, to a degree, fascinate him, so he answered as honestly as he could, "I would be glad to be in the company of the princess, Your Majesty."

"Excellent," chuckled Herretus. "It is settled. Unless you have something else in mind I have arranged for you and Kiira to ride tomorrow. She is feeling much better and the beach is an half hour's easy ride. My daughter loves horses, and I have been given tales by our Horse Master of your amazing mare. You both should have a good time. Do you have any questions?"

"Where and when should I meet the princess for the ride?"

"Noon at the stables will be fine, the Horse Master will be informed and will have your mount ready for you when you arrive."

Terren bowed and left the room, hopeful that many of his questions about the princess would soon be answered.

CHAPTER 17
DO AN ACTIVITY TOGETHER

Cooing, Kiira stroked Starfire's muzzle as the charger covered her hand in saliva and juice, crunching on the ripe apple. The humidity clinging to the late fall air intensified the sweet aroma of the fruit as it mixed with the scent of fresh hay. Soft snorts and nickers from the other horses accompanied the occasional impatient stomp, reminding the hay runners to bring bags of milk oats. A few distant whinnies from the training yard filtered their way into the barn, completing the atmosphere. If Kiira could spend all of her time here, it would be no loss. This was paradise.

Wiping the sticky juices from her hands, Kiira touched foreheads with Starfire while stroking his soft muzzle, the motion soothing her mind. The charger snorted, eager for more petting. Mimicking him, Kiira made Starfire's ears flick. A giggle bubbled and escaped. If there was a prize for a horse with the biggest personality, Starfire would be champion. She tossed the reins over his head to fasten his bridle. His ostentatiousness was well known to the stable hands, and it was something she admired about him. With a few exceptions, most of the horses were docile, perfect for the nobles wishing to have a quiet afternoon of riding. Her feisty Starfire, however, made life interesting, and she doted upon him for his sometimes outlandish behavior. How could she not love a horse that shared her heart?

He was the perfect steed. Wickedly fast and oddly unique, Starfire stood out amongst his brethren. A perfect white oval covered the left side of his face, set against a coat as grey as a cloudy, moonlit night. His coloring faded to a lighter, mottled gray at his croup, and ended with a clean, snowy tail. Overall, the combination and placement of colors gave Starfire an unbalanced look; yet there was a strange beauty in the asymmetry, and he always reminded Kiira of shooting stars streaking across a clear night sky. Starfire preened and presented his sleek gradience to anyone willing to look in his direction. There were worse traits in a horse than vanity. Sadly, many who saw him for the first time feared they would be cursed if they came near or touched him. Superstitious fools the lot of them.

The only other person not afraid to be near Starfire was the Horse Master, and it took him months to move past the unwarranted fear. Once Jirrus did, however, he loved the charger as much as Kiira did—almost. From the moment Starfire was born six years ago, Kiira loved him. She had been in the stables helping to keep the mother calm, using her magic and other herbs to help the mare through the dystocia. The night of his birth would always be solid in her memory. There had been a different, almost static current to the air, and she had been the only one able to name the strange clinging feeling as magic.

As Starfire came further into the world, the magic turned soupy; as soon as he was out of the womb, the air immediately cleared and his all-ebony coat bleached and faded, creating his odd coloration. When Kiira first touched the sticky foal, she could feel the magic clinging to him. To this day, she still felt a tingle beneath her palms when she touched him. His connection to the god's gift was probably the reason she had bonded so intimately with Starfire. He was made for her. That night, she claimed the colt as her own. No one argued. Everyone present had been too spooked by the oddity to disagree.

Scratching his neck and muzzle, Starfire's eyes drifted closed in relaxation. She let his contentment flow through her. When his ears flickered a second before the clop of hooves drew her eyes to the entrance, Kiira turned to see Horse Master Jirrus leading a new horse. The blue roan equaled Starfire's eighteen hands, and her toned muscles showed strength from care and consistent exercise. The most striking feature was her pale blue eyes matching the undertones of her glossy coat. They were serene, calm waters, and Kiira found herself lost in them momentarily. Despite having a classic hue, there was definitely something special about the mare. Unable to resist, Kiira allowed the horse to smell her hand before stroking her muzzle. "Jirrus, she is absolutely beautiful, who did you purchase her from?"

"Well, Mouse," he said with a hearty smile, "I'd wish I did purchase this one, she certainly is gorgeous, but this little darlin' belongs to Prince Terren." His big voice resonated against the warm wood surrounding them.

"Really? I wonder where he acquired her, she is exquisite. There is something...unique about her that is enamoring."

"Thank you," said another male voice.

Kiira dropped her hands as if the mare's muzzle scorched and spun to face the prince. He looked different from what she expected, his dark hair crowned an angular jawline smoothed by a hint of a smile and gentle, crisp blue eyes compelling her to feel safe and at ease. Her heart staccato'd and her stomach lurched into a knot.

Kiira immediately admonished herself for gaping at the man, pulling her eyes away to examine an interesting knot of wood on the stable floor. Her thoughts were traitorous to Leo. She should not be so readily attracted to this prince. She wanted nothing to do with him. Kiira glanced at Terren, hoping he had not noticed, but luck was not on her side.

His mouth pressed into a grim line with an accompanying intense look told her sharp thoughts were being kept. Stroking the horse's muzzle, he said, "She was a gift many years ago from a friend and has been my companion ever since. You have quite the eye for a good horse."

"I'll say," said Jirrus, punctuating the words with a hearty guffaw. "This girl has been a stable mouse since she could walk. Sometimes I would even find her sleepin' on some of the hay piles next to a couple of the horses. Drove her parents mad, it did."

A hint of a smile crossed Terren's lips.

Kiira made an acute study of the floor, feeling the heat in her cheeks, and busied herself with releasing Starfire from his stall. "Jirrus, I hardly think the prince needs to know all of my exploits as a child." She said, teasing the man who was like a second father to her.

"Aw, well darlin' I only chaff 'cause I love ya so much," he replied and gave her an exaggerated wink. "You're my favorite Mouse after all and the only one I've allowed to scurry about my stables so freely."

Kiira blushed even deeper, but gave him a generous smile as he wrapped an affectionate arm around her shoulders and placed a quick kiss on her head.

She turned to see Terren watching; a small smile lighting up his features. It made him even more attractive. The prince's attentions quickly sobered the mirth pumping in her veins as Kiira remembered why she was standing in the stables with him. With an indifferent sigh, she said, "Just let me saddle Starfire and we'll get going."

KIIRA PLODDED beside Terren along the private road leading to the beach. Except for the few sentences in the presence of the Horse Master, they hadn't spoken. Uncomfortable, she fidgeted with Starfire's reigns.

This is so unlike me... I never feel flustered in front of anyone.

Starfire embraced her anxiety and fidgeted along with her. He was more unruly than usual and did several hops and lunges, trying to break into a faster gait to relieve the tension. She stopped the charger each time, but he was getting increasingly difficult to handle. He needed a hard run to calm him down, or her afternoon ride would be more miserable than fun.

She glanced in Terren's direction and was irritated to see Terren's horse was the exact opposite of her own mount. "Tempest, is quite calm," Kiira said, timidly trying to break the silence. "I would not have expected as much, given her name."

"She can be feisty when she wants to be," Terren replied.

"What inspired her name?"

"The snow storms in the cordillera. Her coloring is similar to the shadowed places of the snow in the mountains."

"Oh, the cordillera! I have never had the opportunity to venture that far north, those storms must be impressive." As an afterthought, she added, "We don't get snow here near the castle."

Terren nodded, and the thud of hooves became the only noise again.

So much for trying to start a conversation. If this is any indication of our future outings, I am already dreading them.

Terren's voice startled Kiira from her thoughts. Starfire jumped in response to her jerking. "We could gallop if you like. Tempest always enjoys a good run and it seems as if your Starfire would appreciate the exercise."

"What about your tag-a-longs?" Kiira motioned her head behind her.

Terren shrugged. "I'm not worried about them."

Kiira lifted an eyebrow.

He let out a weary sigh. "As long as we tell them what we're doing it will be fine."

She studied a rich patch of land in the distance for a moment and then nodded her consent. Kiira abruptly turned Starfire and trotted back to the guards.

It took some convincing, but they eventually agreed on the condition the prince wait for them at the end of the road. Kiira handed off the sack of food to the nearest guard and noted his surprise that she addressed him personally.

Without another word, Kiira spurred Starfire forward, but held him only long enough for Terren to match the pace. She gave the prince a playful smirk and then loosed the reins. The charger needed no other invitation. His powerful muscles bulged and heaved as he took off. His start was smooth and with each stride, his speed increased. The ground blurred, the rough dirt road turning into a lane of silk. Her heart soared as the wind rushed in her face. Being on Starfire's back was the same as having wings.

Kiira leaned low over his neck and let him gallop. His breathing was heavy, but not labored; Starfire was in his element. She pulled a little magic and connected with his mind, allowing his enjoyment of the gallop to seep into her bones. She absorbed every ounce of exhilaration rolling off of her steed. Glancing to her left, she saw, surprisingly, Terren and his mare keeping pace; but this was not the fastest Starfire could run. In the equivalent of a breathless whisper, within the charger's mind Kiira commanded, *let the magic take you.*

CHAPTER 18
PERSPECTIVE

Dust billowed as his boots struck the loose dirt path. Gathering Tempest's reins, he cooled her twitching muscles with an easy walk. Kiira and Starfire did the same in a steady looping oval ahead, waiting. Patting Tempest's neck, he said, "You did excellent, girl." Terren gave a smile at the huff of air she gave in response, as if to say, 'not good enough, though.'

Reaching the princess and her mount, Terren noticed a mischievous glint in her eye, the same as in the painting of her beneath the oak tree. He liked how Kiira continually surpassed his expectations of her.

"I have never seen a horse run that fast, and Tempest has some of the best bloodlines in the realms."

"Starfire is ... special," Kiira replied.

"That, princess, is an understatement. I would love to know what gives him his speed."

She tightened her lips and stared at the spot where she touched the charger's neck. "No need to stand on formalities; Kiira, is fine."

"Then I will call you Kiira, and you must call me Terren." He waited for her to say more, or continue on the subject of her horse, but she remained mute. It seemed inevitable that the afternoon would be awkward.

Terren turned his gaze toward the now not-so-distant beach, walking with the princess as she led them toward the surf, the horses creating a wall between them. It would be easy to keep quiet and 'be agreeable' as King

Herretus so aptly stated, but it would also make for a laborious afternoon. If he was going to be stuck with Kiira, he needed to at least attempt conversation. Taking a fortifying breath, he said, "So…"

"I will make you a deal, Terren," Kiira said suddenly, like she had been biting the words back and they had to all come out in a rush. "It is likely neither of us wants this marriage, and I think focusing on the idea of it will hinder our conversations, so how about we ignore that detail and try to just be friendly."

He was surprised that she spoke so bluntly.

At least she is not skirting the boulder between us.

Terren appreciated that. "I can work inside those parameters."

"Excellent. We already know the basics about each other, so tell me something about you I don't know and I will do the same," Kiira said.

Terren pulled his gaze to the princess, curious what exactly she meant by the basics. Obviously, his family, but what else did she know about him? He was not naïve enough to think parts of his journey throughout the realms went unnoticed. Even under a false name, he'd been recognized now and then. So what could he tell her without revealing the information he wanted to keep hidden? How wide of net should he cast on the things available to talk about? Did she want general, factual information, or something more personal? Finally, he said, "My favorite place to be alone is in the mountains. I like the cold, and I prefer the gentle feel of the Aria Bells over the sharp obtrusive edges of the mountains in the Klaroni."

Kiira nodded thoughtfully before giving him a serene smile. Gesturing before her, she replied. "I love the sea. The fierce unrelenting waters capable of eroding earth are the same waters to bring healing and life to that which is sick." She sighed happily. "There is a magic in the sea, not like magic from the gods, but … more. Something happens near the sea; time is irrelevant, moods flow with the plan of the tides."

"Poetic."

She smiled again, but kept her longing gaze to the glitter expanse of deep blue ahead. He'd only considering Reana a harsh mistress, but his view was tainted by his time aboard the *Surveysor*. Terren peered ahead as they continued, the gentle whoosh of the ocean getting louder with each step. The cool, salty breeze ruffled his hair and kept the sunny afternoon from being unbearable, and he agreed it would be easy to get lost in the lull of the waves. He appreciated Kiira's view, but still preferred the quiet only found in a thickly forested mountain buried in the clutches of winter.

Soon the road faded to dark, glittering sand. Terren bent, grabbing a handful and letting the black granules fall until only a small pile dusted his palm. The sand was interesting. It differed from his kingdom, where the sand was a pale brown; here, it bore a striking resemblance to the sand in the Shadow Desert. Upon closer examination, the small pile of sand held flecks of green and grey granules. Terren looked at his surroundings, trying to determine the sand's geological composition. To his left, he spotted dark cliffs and curiosity got the better of him.

"Kiira, do you mind if we stop by those cliffs?"

She glanced in the direction he was pointing. "Sure, those are the Slate Cliffs. We're headed there so you can see the Fire Falls, one of the wonders of our kingdom."

Terren squinted at the position of the sun, estimating it was an hour past midday. They were to be back for the evening meal. The sound of kicking sand alerted him to the guards joining them. Turning back to Kiira, he asked, "Are we close enough to walk? Should we ride the horses?"

"It is only about an hour's walk to the falls from here. We have plenty of time to meander." She looked wistful. "And enjoy the sea."

"Alright," he said, setting off across the sand, letting Tempest follow at her leisure.

They walked in silence, listening to the cry of gulls as each bird teased the surface of the water and the ever present *shhh, shhh, shhh,* of the waves pulling at the shore.

THE BRILLIANT MIXTURE OF RED, orange, and yellow from a lantern sun gave its last gift of light to the realm. The vibrant colors skipped across the shallow movements of the sea, deepening as they reflected off the dark waves pressing into the shore.

Popping a grape in his mouth, Terren fixated on the Fire Falls. The sun was reaching the perfect angle on the horizon, and the setting rays touching the very top of the tumbling water turned the falls blood red. As the sun continued its descent, it changed the water to a dark orange before fading to a lighter hue, bleeding into tints of pink, yellow, white, blue, and green. The blue and green coming from minerals in the Slate Cliffs. The play of colors reminded Terren of the extravagant strings of lanterns decorating a wedding feast in the Shade Realm.

This was a good end to a surprisingly pleasant afternoon. Terren had been apprehensive of spending time with Kiira, but since they both agreed to look past the uncomfortable knowledge of the arranged marriage, they held several decent conversations. He related a few of his experiences of the different places in both the Sun and Shade Realms and she described what it was like growing up with Liem and how she learned archery.

They had been quiet for most of the sunset, but now he looked over at the princess and said, "Thank you for bringing me here; this is spectacular. The paintings in the gallery did not do this justice."

The side of her lips tilted. "No, they certainly do not. Not even a drymera can capture … this."

"Kiira?"

"Hmmm."

"I have been curious about something; may I ask you a question?"

She shifted and cleared her throat. Hesitantly she said, "Of course."

"The day I arrived, your father said you and the prince are both active in the military. In what capacity do you fit into Lorea's military?

"Ah, yes. I am the Commander of the Archers, both infantry and mounted. Achieving the post was one of the greatest moments in my life," she looked down and smiled sadly. "I fought for the position as a way to honor my mother. It took a long time to convince the counsel and my father, but here I am."

"It is an honor, and you seem to bear the responsibility well."

Kiira fidgeted. "Thank you."

Terren waited a beat. "Was it you firing the arrows that killed the Oranta?"

Kiira studied him for a moment. He could see the unspoken questions in her eyes; determining if she could trust him. There was clear suspicion lacing her voice as she said, "Yes, and I have no qualms about killing the beast either."

Ok, defensive. Proceed with caution.

Terren smoothed over her bristling. "I'm surprised that the arrows did the trick. Usually magic is needed to give any attacks an advantage."

"There was … a mage on site."

"That explains it then," Terren said.

"Explains what, exactly?"

"How those arrows were buried so deep in the eye. I could barely see the fletching."

"You were in the market? How did you get past the guards? The gates were closed to prevent casualties," Kiira said, intensely interested in how he knew such details.

Terren cleared his throat. "Oh, I was outside the gates. I saw the arrows when the Oranta reared up at the end." Not a complete lie, but he didn't feel good about twisting the truth, either.

"Ah."

Silence persisted, as if they both knew there was more to the conversation but were unsure of how to continue. They each gazed at the Fire Falls for several minutes. Quietly, he almost didn't hear her speak. Kiira said, "Those monsters, even if they haven't been seen in years, are a blight on the realm. They should be eradicated once and for all."

Terren's throat constricted, and he could feel a thread of annoyance seep into his mind from Kamaria. She had returned from the oasis just this morning and was hunkered down on the sand in the Shade Realm, keeping a watchful eye over him. He tried to keep his tone as casual as possible, but even he could hear the edge in his voice. He needed to choose his words wisely. "You should not be so quick to judge. What do you really even know about Shade Beasts?"

Kiira picked at the blanket beneath them. "Should I not? I am an Elite Guardian, a protector of this kingdom. The lives of my people are more important to me than a senseless beast from another realm."

"Shade Beasts are not senseless animals, Kiira. They are intelligent creatures."

"Intelligent? You expect me to believe a beast that cannot be reasoned with and will kill mercilessly would be interested in negotiations?"

The atmosphere thickened considerably, causing the nearby guards to shift. Even Terren felt suddenly uncomfortable in his relaxed position on the blanket. He fought the urge to sit up, not wanting to ignite the confrontation in an already tense conversation. "Kiira, I do not mean to minimize what you had to do. Shade Demons' minds are perverse and those creatures must be killed; there is nothing else that can be done for them once they are taken from their place in the Shade Realm. I think you misunderstand me."

"All I seem to hear is your defense of them. That monster two days ago killed good men and women, and one of those Demons killed my mother. A Dyatro snapped her in its jaws, crushing her like she meant nothing." Tears gathered in Kiira's eyes. "A woman who valued life lost hers because of an easily manipulated creature. Anything that can be so readily misused should not exist."

It was Terren's turn to bristle. He nearly let a growl escape his throat as Kamaria's anger flooded his mind. Closing his eyes, he took a deep breath.

'Peace Kamaria, her anger is understandable, if not misplaced.'

Refocusing on Kiira, he carefully asked, "With that argument, should people not be destroyed as well? They can just as easily be manipulated by magicians."

"People, can learn to protect their minds or keep an amulet, and magicians today would never treat a human life with such carelessness," Kiira said.

"Agreed, and yet a powerful enough mage can destroy those protections in an instant, leaving even well-trained people vulnerable."

"That is my point, though; people have the potential to resist a mage's influence. These Demons must be weak-minded to be so readily pulled from the Shade Realm and turned vicious."

He sighed. "You speak of something you have no knowledge of. Shade Beasts are not weak, far from it. In fact, they are very difficult to pull into this realm. You should not blame a species that can no more control the evil intentions of a mage any more than a human can."

"You would side with them." Kiira set her jaw.

Terren narrowed his eyes. "What exactly do you mean by that princess?"

"Your sympathies are distorted."

His chest tightened, flaring at the callous blame she directed at him. He sat up and said, "If my sympathies are distorted, then so are yours. You are suggesting an entire species be eradicated simply because you hate the potential evil. Every word you have spoken about Shade Beasts is conjecture. If you really understood what you were saying you might actually be appalled."

"I doubt—"

"No. Until you really understand what a Shade Beast is, then I will not hear any more foolish arguments." His words came out harshly, even to his own ears.

Kiira glared at him. "DO NOT speak to me as if I am a child for you to reprimand, prince." She spat the title. Her next words hissed from a jaw so tight it was surprising she could still push them out. "I am not your wife yet."

Terren stiffened and felt his forehead crease, his eyebrows knitting together. Surprisingly, his voice was calm as he said, "If your arguments were founded upon fact, then I would not need to."

Kiira inhaled sharply.

"I understand you lost your mother to a Shade Demon and I will not pretend to know what it was like to lose her in such a manner. However, I find it appalling you speak of wiping out an entire innocent species, one you don't even fully understand, or for that matter, care to understand." He felt his passion for the magnificent creatures, including his love for Kamaria, pouring into his every word. "It would be like deciding every Wolfcat in the Sun Realm was suddenly evil because they kill anyone within their territory, but you make the decision unaware of this fact. What if, after eradicating the entire species, you learned the true nature of the Wolfcat? Would you call it evil then? Could you really live with that decision? The Shade Beasts are not evil because they can potentially be manipulated by the actions of magicians with dishonorable intention."

Kiira pressed her lips into a thin line as she glared at the blanket bunched in her fists. Abruptly, she stood, and mounting Starfire without her saddle, galloped away. Her sudden departure left Terren looking at the disturbed sand for several minutes before he sighed deeply, his shoulders caving.

Well, that is going to be a problem.

CHAPTER 19
A SHADOWED MEMORY

Pinpoints of light glistened behind her watery eyes. Gripping Starfire's mane, she buried her face in the silky fibers, letting the strands wipe away the beaded drops of water dampening her cheeks. If his mane did not catch a salty tear, it would be swept away by the cool stream of air. Kiira had given Starfire the freedom to set the pace, keeping only enough awareness to stay astride and guide his destination, though she was not entirely sure where she was going.

The ride back to the castle was over far too soon, and she found herself kneeling in front of her mother's grave. Kiira stared at the etched stone.

> *Here lies Jurica Lorestan*
> *Beloved Wife, Mother, and Queen*
> *Forever Remembered*
> *Rest in Peace*

Tears renewed as she read the words repeatedly. Under different circumstances, the inscription would soothe, but her emotions were too battered. At that moment, she didn't want to just remember her mother. Kiira wanted her there; to be held in her safe, comforting arms.

Behind closed lids, Kiira relived every second leading up to her mother's death, each tick forward in time, feeling agonizingly infinite. She had been frozen, shocked, and so terrified of the Shade Demon looming over her that no mental command could have persuaded her limbs to function.

Kiira buried her face in her hands.

Streams of salty tears crusted her cheeks as the dark memory occupied every corner of her mind. Picturing her mother's lifeless, bloodstained body, cold eyes staring back at her; the last moments of pain and fear etched in her pupils. Curling into the tightest ball she could, a cold numbness seeped into every limb as she let the black hole replacing her mother's vibrant light take her captive.

"Mother," Kiira choked, "I wish you were here. You would know just what to say, when to say it, and ... and you could have convinced father to let me marry the man I truly love."

"I have no doubt your mother could have convinced me, she was a fierce woman." Herretus' voice was soft as it reached Kiira's ears. "I loved her spirit; gave me a headache every time though," Herretus said, a sad fondness in his words.

Kiira slowly untangled herself and turned to look at her father. "How did you know I was here?"

He gave her a knowing smile. "The wall patrol sent me a message. Your hellacious flight was hardly unnoticeable. That, coupled by the fact that you were alone, gave them cause to believe something wrong. I know you only visit your mother's grave when you are deeply upset so I thought I had better come."

She frowned at the ground.

"The prince, Terren, he ... we got into an argument."

"What about?" To her immense relief, the question was only curiosity and not scolding. At least he would hear what she had to say.

Kiira played with her lip, working through the best phrasing of the contentious conversation between her and Terren. She sighed. Romanticizing what happened between them was futile, accepting that the authentic version of events cast her in a poor light. "We argued over Shade Demons and he told me I was being childish for wishing the extermination of an entire species; that my anger is biased." Her chest tightened, and she rushed her next words. "It hurts because he is right."

He joined her in front of the headstone, knowing full well his trousers would suffer for it. Kiira leaned into him when he offered the comfort of his arm.

"What kind of person am I to want vengeance on a creature that cannot resist the power of an Elder Mage any more than you or I?" It had been a long time since she had felt so small. A storm of emotions yearned to escape, and through all of it, Herretus simply held her. His presence and love were anchoring. She appreciated it more than words could express.

He hummed a long-forgotten tune, his mellow voice a warm summer breeze. It was a relief to have him so kind and understanding after their abating relationship the past week. Kiira felt even more emotion surge up within her.

Herretus gently stroked her back, patiently letting her coil through a jumble of emotions. After a while, he continued. "It is natural to feel anger against the monster that killed your mother. You are not a horrible person, you are just letting an awful memory influence the truth."

"He defended the Shade Beasts! It just felt so diminishing to her memory and he used Wolfcats as an example … and … oh, I don't know…" She sighed, the defeat weighing down her head.

"Kiira, I doubt Terren meant to offend you with his defense of Shade Beasts. He lived in the Shade Realm for a couple years. You know as well as I that their culture holds the Shade Beasts in high regard." Herretus paused, stilling his hand, and then spoke his next words with great care. "Sweetheart, heed my advice. If you cannot trust that your mother now dines in Apelgo's Halls, no longer feeling any more pain or suffering, then you will continue to find yourself in this spot; so consumed with bitterness that peace will elude you for the rest of your days. I know the pain you feel. I miss my beloved Jurica every day, but I also know that I will dine with her in Apelgo's Halls one day, and that is a peace beyond our current heartache."

Kiira was quiet for several moments, then she shook her head, letting the soft wool of his tunic brush the entire length of her brow. "Maybe, and maybe one day I will explain to him what happened, but right now I don't want to hear any more justifications for Shade Beasts." A heartbeat of silence passed and then she let a deep frustrated breath escape. "Really, after tonight I want nothing to do with Terren. Please do not make me be around him, father, I would rather be a spinster."

Herretus tightened his arms around her, probably squeezing a little harder than necessary. "Kiira…" The exasperation was clear as he drew out her name.

"Why?" she demanded, pushing away from him. "What is this arrangement really accomplishing? Clearly we are not going to get along."

Herretus searched her red, swollen eyes. "Kiira, I love you, but I have already given you my answer and I will not let you work your way into sabotaging this arrangement simply because the two of you have argued different views. Your mother and I had differences of opinion all the time. This will not be the last time you disagree with Terren."

Kiira squared her back to him. The truth of her father's words was suffocating, and the silence of the grave preferable company. She would confront her problems tomorrow. Trembling, she said, "Just, go away."

"I will leave you," Herretus said, his voice soft again, "but you need to come to terms with this. Don't let your anger follow you after tonight."

He turned to leave, then added, "You have more in common with the prince than you think."

With a conviction like she had never known, Kiira forced out a biting promise. "I will *never* have anything in common with him."

She clenched her jaw, curling and uncurling her fists as her father's retreating footsteps faded.

CHAPTER 20

HISTORY

The scrutiny of six guards prickled the skin along the back of Terren's neck as he gave a gentle knock on the door of the private study. A muted permission to enter floated through the thick wood. Stepping inside, he left the Klynotian and Lorean men to eye one another.

I really need to speak with Grayten about my guard detail.

As he shut the door, Terren barely controlled a grimace at the thought of them following him and Kiira on their Lundemai. He was making progress in terms of friendship and trust with the eight total men assigned to him, but even he recoiled at the idea of the additional bodies slinking along on a journey meant for the newly married.

Terren turned his thoughts to the present and his bride-to-be's father sitting before him.

"Ah, Terren, thank you for coming," Herretus said after a quick glance in his direction. "Please, have a seat. I just need to finish this while the information is fresh in my mind and then we will talk."

Terren nodded, settling into a plush chair in front of the large oak desk.

As he waited, Terren let his eyes explore his surroundings. The desk served as an anchor to the back third of the room and stretched nearly the width of the space. Roughly five feet on either side of the desk allowed just enough room to get by. Tidy piles of papers, scrolls, and books obscured the top of the polished wood. Two oddly shaped fist-sized rocks secured two piles, and Terren noted they had the same striations as the Slate Cliffs. They seemed odd trinkets to have in a well-kept space such as this. Possibly, they were objects given to the king by his children, albeit when they were much younger.

A window dominated the entire back wall—framed by thick, pale blue velvet curtains—filled the room with the natural light of late morning. Well-built shelves lined the two side-walls from floor to ceiling; brimming with scrolls, books, and a few knick-knacks. Behind the king, a comfortable chair with a small circular table secured the back right corner. Terren guessed it was used whenever Herretus had tea or food brought to him. He glanced at the grey temples of the king and could easily picture the lone man working through a number of meals and late into the night. For the first time since returning to his birthright, Terren imagined how lonely the position of king could be, carrying the burdens of thousands with no one to turn to.

Herretus shuffled some papers, tapping them into a neat stack before setting them to the side.

Terren sat up a little straighter.

Walking over to a knee-high cabinet, Herretus pulled a bottle and poured two glasses of a nearly black wine. Taking the proffered drink, Terren took a small sip and was pleasantly surprised to find it a product of the Shade Realm; a spiced beverage heavily sweetened with rock honey only found in the Night Crystal Quarries.

"This is not a drink I expected to find here in Lorea."

Herretus smiled. "Yes, it is my favorite. It is also expensive, so the five bottles I buy every year from the merchants I try make last. They never leave my study." A broad grin crinkled his eyes. "Normally, I wouldn't share, but I thought you might like some."

Terren returned the king's grin with a grateful smile.

I will have to make sure a large shipment is sent to him at some point, since there is an abundant supply in my family's cellars.

"Thank you, Sire, but you did not need to share such a treasure with me."

The king waved away the comment, turning a curious eye upon him. Terren kept the king's gaze and settled on his features to be as emotionless as possible. Typically, he did not care to be studied, a feeling that stemmed from spending a good portion of his years living inconspicuously, but in this instance he did not find Herretus' gaze uncomfortable. To Terren, it seemed the king was simply trying to decide where he fit into an elaborate puzzle to better understand him. If it had been Grayten sitting across from him, he would have found the observation irritating.

Herretus dipped his head as if confirming something for himself and took a sip of his wine. "Terren, I know of the argument you and my daughter had from her perspective. Please, if you can, recount for me what was said."

Terren cleared his throat and, shifting a little in the chair, repeated the argument as best his memory served. When he finished, he watched the swirl of wine as he gently tipped his glass back and forth. He wasn't ashamed of what he said to Kiira, but he was supposed to marry the woman soon and he could not deny her reaction concerned him. It plagued his thoughts most of the night and he spent many restless hours reflecting on how he could have handled the situation better.

"Terren, you need not be so worried, I am not upset. I only brought you here to give you a little history; to help you better understand my daughter and why she reacted the way she did."

"She mentioned a Dyatro killed the Queen."

Herretus nodded. "Yes, that is true, but there is more to the story, and Kiira has been told this, but she often minimizes the details of that day. I would ask you not tell her this, at least not yet. When you are married, if you feel the need to reveal what I have told you, then that is entirely up to you."

"Sire?"

"I imagine this makes you somewhat uncomfortable," Herretus said.

"You read my mind, Sire," he replied.

A small, humorless laugh escaped the king's lips. "That day was so traumatic for Kiira. She was very close to her mother. I encouraged her last night to find peace. Regardless, I think this history will help."

"I trust your judgment, Sire."

A few heartbeats passed before Herretus took a fortifying breath and, tilting his face to the ceiling, said in a low voice, "Ten years ago, I had an advisor by the name of Zerrec. Not only was he an advisor, but he was also my children's private instructor. He had been around since my children were no more than five summers and was considered a part of our family. My children loved him and I trusted him."

"I remember hearing of this advisor, but only in passing conversation," Terren said.

"I'm not surprised. Zerrec was very charismatic. A lot of people liked and adored him, especially my children. What most people do not know was he was also a magician, an Elder."

Terren stiffened, the wine sloshing dangerously close to the rim. The king's admission confirmed what Kamaria said about the twins. He was going to have to figure out a way to keep Kiira's gift hidden once they returned to Klynotia. Letting her be caught and executed by the laws of his kingdom would not bode well. He didn't need his plans interrupted yet again, and by a potential war.

A pox on Grayten for setting me up with a magician, the old fool.

Terren could not know if his father knew of Kiira's gift, but he forced himself to relax as Herretus continued.

"He was a brilliant young man, came to me when he was only eight and ten, though I didn't make him an advisor until he was older." He took a sip. "That is beside the point. Zerrec was the perfect instructor and I know my children are better off for having been tutored by him." He frowned. "However, when my children reached six and ten summers, as is traditional, Kiira became eligible and it was just before the celebration of their birth that Zerrec came to me asking for my daughter's hand."

"That must of have been a surprise to you," Terren said.

"Yes, it was. I had no idea that Zerrec felt so strongly."

"Your words sound hesitant."

"Let's just say I am grateful my wife intervened," Herretus continued. "When I told Jurica of his request, without hesitation, she told me it was not a good idea. She did not trust Zerrec's desire for Kiira and was adamantly convinced his interest bordered on obsession. She noticed changes in him I had been blind to. Of course, I doubted, and for some time considered the match. Ultimately I realized the truth of her intuition, thank the gods, though when I rejected Zerrec's request..."

"Zerrec was the one who killed the Queen?"

"Yes, and I can blame no-one but myself for her death." Herretus glowered at the dark liquid in his hand. "There was so much happening leading up to the celebration of my children's birth that I did not take a few moments to pull Zerrec aside and tell him of my decision. Unfortunately, he assumed my inaction was confirmation. During the celebration, Zerrec approached me asking when the announcement of the engagement would be. I proceeded to tell him Jurica and I had decided against it. Much was said, harsh words were exchanged, and, in the end, Zerrec lost his head. In his outrage he summoned a Shade Demon."

Quietly, Terren added, "That was probably not his first time."

"No, it was not," Herretus said as he shook his head. "Zerrec is much older than he looks, but his is a story for another time. I'm sure you can imagine the ensuing chaos. Common sense disappears in the presence of danger, and nothing spells danger like a Shade Demon."

Terren nodded.

"Before the Demon was summoned, my wife was trying to calm Zerrec and it was beginning to work. She did not like his obsession with Kiira, but she still felt sorry for him. Jurica was incredibly warm, loving, empathetic, and could easily persuade people, but she said just the wrong thing. I wish I could remember what it was, though it hardly matters anymore." The king deflated a little. "Zerrec completely lost control and, ultimately, he caused more damage and death than the Dyatro. He killed the creature himself before disappearing—only the gods know why—but it was the Shade Demon that killed Jurica." Herretus' next words were just loud enough to be heard above the ambient noises of the room. "If I could have taken her place..."

Terren nodded. "I know it's been ten years, but I am sorry for your loss. Shade Beasts are impossible to kill in the Shade Realm, so it's no surprise that, in a physical form, it is still very difficult."

Herretus acknowledged the statement and emotion roughened his next words. "I will be eternally grateful for what Jurica tried to do that day, even though I lost my other half."

Terren didn't know how to respond, so he let the statement filter into the air. He glanced at the king before diverting his gaze for respect. Though there were no tears in his eyes, he could see Herretus still dearly missed his wife.

"I am humbled you deemed me worthy of this knowledge. I will use it wisely."

Herretus looked back at him and smiled. It wasn't a sad or pleased smile, more hopeful. "Terren, I would be a fool to think you are genuinely agreeable with this arrangement. Kiira, obviously, is not. However, at least let me say this." He took a deep breath. "There are times, and one day you will understand, as both a king and,"—he smirked—"as a father, you have to make a decision based on what your intuition is telling you."

Terren's stomach twisted, and he found he couldn't breathe. Being crushed by a boulder would have been less surprising than the sudden feeling of having nothing to do with the idea of being Klynotia's future king. He would be a father one day. His position demanded it of him. Herretus continued, interrupting his quickly spiraling thoughts. Thank Ny. It was not a subject he was ready to consider.

"I know, without a doubt, you and Kiira are meant to be together. It is why I am so adamant about you two spending time with one another. This may come as a surprise to you, but I reached out to Grayten. I suspect if he had a choice, Grayten would forget your existence as his heir and attempt to try and live forever," Herretus said, ending the statement with a wry laugh.

Terren chuckled at the precision of his words. "You are very insightful, Sire."

"Not especially, but I think one must be blind not to see the truth about the situation in Klynotia." After a few heartbeats, he said, "You are nothing like your father, Terren. If I am being honest, and maybe recklessly bold thanks to this strong drink, I look forward to the day you are king. You are a good man from what I can tell, and Klynotia has suffered too much for far too long."

Warmth filled Terren at the praise. For someone like Herretus, to take the time to notice his character in such a stint of time elated him. Many people whispered he abandoned his duties in favor of chasing his own desires, and, while the assumption was partially true, he told no one the deeper purpose for his sudden departure. "I am humbled you even noticed me, Sire," he said, inclining his head.

Herretus lifted the corner of his mouth and Terren could immediately see the resemblance to Kiira, though in her features, she favored her mother. The king looked as if he wanted to say more, but after a slight shake of his head, he tipped the rest of his wine from the glass.

Standing, Herretus offered his hand. "Give Kiira time and I will speak to her again as well. Tomorrow she is scheduled to lead a hunt to gather meat for the Yielding Festival. I would like you to go with her."

"Am I to simply accompany or shall I join in the hunt?"

"Definitely join." Herretus laughed. "I doubt you carry those weapons for show."

"You would be right." Terren gave a genuine smile, unable to keep a hint of amusement from his reply.

"Thank you for coming. Oh, and one more thing. I was not pleased to learn of this, but before I announced my decision, my daughter was courting someone. She assured me nothing inappropriate occurred between them, but," he frowned, the stern expression revealing a burden that could never be expressed, "I thought it only right you know."

The information of her courtship stabbed deeper than he thought possible after so short an acquaintance. He stifled the rising emotions, determined to deal with them later, and bowed to Herretus. "Thank you, Sire."

He exited quickly and headed straight for his rooms. As he walked, he revisited the conversation and had the feeling Herretus was more aware of the surrounding activities than his demeanor let on. The knowledge the king had of things beyond his borders was extensive, and he used it all to make himself a better leader for his people.

Now, if only his daughter were as level-headed as he is.

HUNTING

A pained groan echoed through the morning as a large six-point buck thudded to the hard earth along with four doe disturbing wisps of mist. White fletched arrows protruding from the animal's chest. The remaining herd scattered, disturbing the otherwise peaceful forest with pitched squeals and the thud of hooves as they fled. Rangers rushed to field dress the deer for transportation, agitating the heavy mist.

Adding this kill to the mental tally she had, Kiira counted twenty-five deer and a growing mound of fowl and rabbits. The hunting party had done exceptionally well for the few hours spent in the Forest. They were nearly to the assigned number of animals needed for the first night of the upcoming festival, and if luck stayed with them, they would reach the citadel before the sun truly warmed the day.

A satisfied smirk tilted her lips as she left the Rangers to their activities, continuing further into the Forest to look for a new trail.

Kiira's practiced steps were quick, graceful, and muted enough to let her appreciate the conversation of the trees and animals. Walking among the historic copse, she listened for the gentle whisper of leaves and the strain of unwilling wind-moved branches. Louder than everything else were the chirps of hundreds of birds flitting through the oaks.

The air beneath the tree canopy cooled her cheeks as mist dallied about her boots, stubbornly refusing to dissipate under the rapidly warming day. The heady scent of damp wood lingered in her nostrils. Filtered sun mottled the mist with a pale mustard light, giving the forest a mystical quality as insects zipped erratic paths through the milky air, making it easy to see how fairy stories circulated the kingdom through the centuries.

As beautiful as it was, this creation of the gods should be paid due respect. Kiira was well aware of the potential danger lurking behind every tree of the Forest Wilds, but in moments like this, when everything under the canopy lay cast in a golden glow, it made each step amongst the old oaks worth the risk. Here, Kiira was alive, at home, with plant life surrounding her on all sides. Her blood hummed with each tree she touched. If not for the hunt, Kiira would spend hours sitting with the plants, coaxing them with her magic to be greener, grow larger, or bloom brighter.

Maybe I could be delayed while everyone returned to the castle. With Starfire, I could easily overtake the slow-moving party. The idea lifted a pleased smile to her lips.

A fading stir of air moved the mist, and Kiira pulled the cloak draping her shoulders. Stifling a yawn, she continued her hushed journey across the spongy floor.

Soon she spotted another herd of deer grazing in a sun-drenched clearing. She crouched low to stalk her prey, calculating how many arrows she could loose before the herd dispersed. If she managed to get close enough without disturbing the skittish animals, Kiira thought she could down three, at least.

A loud snap startled the deer, and they quickly scattered. She probably still could have gotten one, but her annoyance at the intrusion stayed her hands and she spun to face the offender, her jaw tight. "Terren, you just added an extra hour to our trip. How could you do that again? You have been snapping branches all morning!"

He raised an eyebrow and then gestured in the direction of where the herd had been. Kiira twisted to see the silvery fur of a Wolfcat disappearing after the startled deer.

"You would have lost your kill anyway." There was no malice or smugness in his voice, only cool logic. "I've been snapping branches all morning to keep this hunting party from danger. Would you rather your men be a Wolfcat's feast?"

"This is not our first time in the Forest." Her pitched voice echoed through the trees. Lowering her tone, she continued, "Why do you feel the need to play protector? Do you think us incapable?"

"Not in the least. It would, however, be completely foolish of me to act ignorant of danger when I can prevent it. This is not my first time in the Forest, either."

"Well, thank you, but your chivalry is gratuitous. You are obnoxious and loud and the hunting will never be done with you around. I don't know why my father thought you would be helpful!" Kiira stalked away, not caring about the murderous steps she took, leaving an obvious trail and the entire hunting party gaping at her.

It took several minutes of stamping through the forest for Kiira to remember where she was, slow down, and force herself back into a hunter's mindset. Without her wild footsteps drowning it out, the symphony of the forest filled her ears, the sounds soothing and soft. It took almost an hour, as predicted, but she came across another herd. Stalking closer for a perfect shot, she pulled her bowstring taut.

Four doe and a stag fell almost simultaneously before her eyes.

Stunned, she stared at the dead animals, her bow still drawn. Kiira's eyes landed on Terren as he strode to the kills, five knives missing from his belt. Slowly releasing the tension on the bow, she looked at the dropped deer again.

How in the ... when did he...?

She watched him with undisguised curiosity as he set about cleaning his knives on the lush grass. Rangers swarmed the dead animals. Terren sheathed his weapons and left the men at their work without a second glance.

He met her eyes and held them as he approached, his face blank, yet Kiira felt there was a strange heaviness about him. Terren gave a curt nod toward the frenzy behind him. "I believe that meets your quota, princess." Some emotion colored his words, but before Kiira recovered enough to question him, Terren retreated into the woods.

By the time the hunting party returned to the wagons, Terren was nowhere to be found. She looked for Tempest, but the cloudy-colored mare was gone. The prince's absence settled in her stomach and set it roiling. She wanted answers, and the one who held them had vanished.

KIIRA EYED TERREN throughout the evening meal, both irritated and fascinated. She had barely touched her food, too distracted by the desire to pepper him with questions. Terren studiously avoided her gaze, to her frustration, and the only words he spoke were indiscernible comments to his sister or when responding to a direct question. Palpable tension between them wavered, and based on the constant clearing of her father's throat, it was noticeable. The prince was the picture of ease, so the tell was her fault, which ultimately frustrated her more, since it put him in control of the situation.

Liem wormed into her thoughts. *'What about him has you so transfixed tonight?'*

Stabbing at the rosemary venison chunks, she frowned. *'He's not what he seems and I want answers.'*

'I could have told you that. There's a void about him that I do not understand. Even now my magic feels as if it is being leeched from me as I use it.'

Kiira gave him a quick side eye in which Liem responded. She hadn't noticed before, careful as she was not to use her magic around their guests. But now, made aware of it, she could feel the drain on her magic as well. She narrowed her eyes. *'Explain.'*

'The space around him feels similar to when the Isokanii merchants are around, but it is more than that. Terren only reveals what he wants seen. He's learned to control his expressions and emotions so well, the prince could be surprised by something and you would never know.'

'How do you know?'

'How do you not know, Kiira? You have spent years studying your opponents the same as me.'

She frowned, biting her cheek. Had she really been so blind? The tingle of being watched crawled over her arms. Kiira glanced up to find Terren's gaze sliding between her and Liem. Her brother was right. She had not studied her husband-to-be as she should have, masked by volatile emotions. Terren's glued attention screamed that he was definitely aware of something passing between them, but his expression remained as passive as always.

Feeling guilty for discussing the prince, Kiira pushed a pattern through the smashed potatoes. A jolt stuttered her smooth lines. Terren's obvious awareness was visible, because he allowed it. The truth that she knew only what he wanted her to know cajoled her stomach into unease. She discretely pushed her food away, avoiding Terren's eyes as she dabbed her lips. Kiira jumped at Terren, clearing his throat to speak.

"Sire, I would ask permission to escort Kiira through the gardens after the meal."

"Of course, Terren, the meal is almost over, you may leave now if you wish," Herretus replied. Her father's eyes burned into her skin, making her even more unsettled.

"Kiira?" the prince asked, gesturing toward the door.

"Certainly."

The men around the table stood as she rose from the table. Taking Terren's offered arm, she was now vividly aware of him, and his arm seemed to twitch involuntarily when she touched him. They strolled through the dim hallway and a strange heaviness fell on her.

Maybe I could feign illness to get out of this, or weakness after the morning hunt.

Wrapped up in her search for excuses, Kiira didn't notice they had reached the garden until a soft breeze tickled a hair across her cheek.

Away from prying eyes, Terren dropped her arm and moved away from her to casually lean against one of the many citrus trees guarding the path. His sudden coldness was more hurtful than Kiira expected. What was it about the prince keeping her on edge? Kiira breathed deeply, trying to calm her racing heart and crackling emotions.

When she finally looked at Terren, he hid in shadow and all she could see was the shine of his black knee-boots reflecting the soft moon and a faint blue glow from his eyes. The argument on the beach had been the undoing of a budding friendship, and this rigidity between them was exhausting. Why couldn't this be simple? Honest? Desperate for any inkling of the prince's thoughts, Kiira blurted, "What are you playing at, Terren?"

"What do you mean?"

"Earlier, in the forest, I know you were upset, and now ... now you are acting the disinterested gentleman. So, what game are you playing?"

"What exactly are the answers you are *hunting* for, princess?"

He emphasized the word just to rile her, and Kiira glared at him, wishing she had a dagger to throw. Not to kill him, of course, just to thud into the tree right next to his cold, staring eyes and force him to change that dreadfully composed face he always wore. "There, that is what I am talking about. Inside you were respectful like nothing was amiss, but out here—alone— you speak to me like I am nothing more than an object you are regarding. Distant ... undecided." Kiira bit her lip. Object may not have been the right word, but how often do the proper expressions leave the mouth when emotions coil through the mind? Now what must he think of her? The tongue was such a double-edged sword.

"Well, after being so clearly reminded the other evening you are not my wife, I thought it best to be objective."

"Being objective and treating me as an object are not the same."

"I do not view you as an object, Princess."

"Stop this! Stop it with these toying answers. I hate games." The force of her words started a pinpoint ache between her eyes.

Terren's voice softened, and his reply seemed almost thoughtful. "I am not fond of games either."

"Then give me honest answers, Terren. Where do we stand?"

"Where would you like us to stand?" He gestured to a spot further up the path.

Frustrated at his deflection, she gritted her teeth. "I do not believe you think I meant literally."

"No, I did not."

She growled, the sound pitching as she turned her back to the prince. A cool breeze floated over the flowers, every bloom danced happily in the moonlight. If only she could shrink and live among their petals. Then the only stinging hurts she would deal with were the attacks from misguided bees.

Unbidden, tears pooled in her eyes. Kiira pressed her lips to cast away the angry droplets, trying to hide the unsettled measure of her emotions, but her vexation prevented anything from sounding normal. "I thought we were trying to be friendly." Terren snorted. It was such an odd noise to hear coming from him. Kiira almost couldn't believe it had been him making it.

"So far, Kiira, you have made that impossible."

She shivered, from the temperature and from the truth of his words. Every ounce of her wanted to scream denial, but it would only double her guilt. She had been less than amicable toward... about everything. Warmth settled over her as Terren stood just close enough that they were not touching, but his body shielded her from the breeze. His kindness warmed her.

"I don't want to fight with you, Princess, so let's make a deal."

She nodded and waited for him to continue.

"This marriage is happening, it is set in stone. Since we are being asked to spend time together, we will keep the pretense and as long as we are in public I will stay by your side. If we are to be alone, however, I will disappear and leave you to your thoughts until we must return."

Kiira wrinkled her brow. His tone wasn't caustic, but his suggestion pierced her soul.

He thought she hated him.

She didn't hate him; she didn't hate anyone. Despising a situation was so different from despising the person involved.

How could I have ever let him believe I hated him?

Mother would be so disappointed in her actions.

"That isn't a solution, Terren." She finally understood what it felt like to be defeated. "I have been uncivil. Now, here we stand, making a deal to playact friendship." Clutching her throat, she paced away from him, needing the distance to think. "Under different circumstances I would have never treated you..." Throwing her head back, Kiira let out a weary sigh. "Gods above, this is not who I am." She inhaled a cleansing breath and faced Terren. "For all of the things I have done to make you believe I hate you, I am sorry. I will try to be more amenable."

The apology was pathetic and weak, but it was the only thing she could offer at the moment. Kiira walked away with the little dignity she could still grasp, leaving the prince staring after her.

CHAPTER 22
THE YIELDING FESTIVAL

'*T*his is what I wish to see in Klynotia. Joy, prosperity, peace; these are my goals, Kamaria,*' Terren said, spreading his arms wide. An overwhelming cacophony of colors and hundreds of indistinct conversations flooded the repaired market. Not a single drop of evidence remained of a Shade Demon's terrorization. He'd expected some sort of clean-up, but not complete repair in less than a week. The scene before him was remarkable, unlike any celebration he'd experienced. *'These people just suffered a tragedy and look at them, they dance and sing as though they had never known sorrow.'*

'Yepenzi, you know I share your dream. Do not be disheartened, this marriage has only delayed it,' Kamaria said. *'Klynotia will rise again.'*

'I know, but I am still not sure what to make of the princess. She will be a part of my life now and if this is the life she is used to, then Kiira will be sorely disappointed in my kingdom.'

'Why has this woman puzzled you? Why should you care about her feelings? From everything I have seen, she is spoiled, selfish, and not worthy to be tied to you,' Kamaria huffed.

'Your description of her is black and white, just as it is with my sister. I love you, Yepenzi, but even you must see the fault in such simple evaluations.'

'What is there to understand? The woman wants to annihilate my species, why should I have any respect for her?'

'Kamaria,'—he sighed—*'Kiira lost her mother to a Demon and you know people*

in the Sun Realm are not educated on Beasts. You can hardly fault her, or anyone else in this realm.'

His Bear was silent for several beats and he was unsure if she would answer or just sever their connection. He was touching on a sore subject. *'For you, Yepenzi, I will attempt to be more open minded.'*

Terren smiled. *'That's all I ask, thank you.'*

He closed his mind to Kamaria. He could trust she would do as she said, though it may take her a long time to come to terms with it.

Taking in the atmosphere again, Terren saw the Yielding Festival's charm exceed every description he heard as a child and, during the course of his travels; its delight and wonder reaching even those across the Reana. Joy was bandied about as freely as a spirited drink. Every stall in the market—except for food booths—had been removed to provide the space for the thousands of people in attendance.

The smell of roasting meats and warm bread imbued the air. Large casks of ale and wine teetered in every corner. The potent scent of charred wood mingled with the meat and alcohol to create a festive mood. His sensitive nose, thanks to his bond with Kamaria, picked up redolent hints of florals, spices, yeast, and sugars. Hordes of people gathered around the meat stalls waiting for their slices of meat and bread. The royal family paid for all the food and drink on the first night of the festival and the people took every advantage. It was no wonder Herretus was such a popular king.

Five massive bonfires placed in a row through the center of the market kept the space warm and bright. Smoke obscured the stars, and hundreds of special-made sconces hung from the top of the walls, shedding yellowed light on everything. Terren could feel beads of sweat forming on the back of his neck, and noticed most people had a slight sheen to their skin. Large swaths of crimson, gold, and green velvet draped in exaggerated arcs along the walls, and white velvet banners bearing the Lorean standard hung just beneath the peak of each arc. Stitched in gold, the crown of Ny encircled the trunk of an exposed oak tree root, the thread glinting in the dancing light of the fires.

Both Lorea and Klynotia were founded on a firm belief in the gods, and Klynotia's standard also featured the crown of Ny, only instead of the tree root, a stag reared within the protective circle of the crown.

Lively music from a group of passing minstrels drew his attention as a band of men and dancing women invited the crowds to join in singing. Terren smiled at the laughter, cries of joy, and chatter of those in attendance. How people could even hold a conversation without shouting mystified him.

Angling through the crowd, Terren looked for the area of the market reserved for royalty. To his surprise, there was none. Just one of the many differences between Grayten and Herretus. He made for a large stage erected in the center of the market, thinking it would be the most likely place to find the kings. Terren spotted his sister standing apart from the revelers. She was focused on removing something from the edge of her sleeve.

Sairah looked stunning in a deep plum gown, the hemlines stitched with amethyst and gold thread. It was an understated way to show the wealth Klynotia held in jewels. Her thick, raven hair fell in soft curls over shoulders and down her back with several small braids to keep the majority out of her face. Purple and cream flowers accented the delicate silver and amethyst circlet resting upon her brow. She looked up when Terren approached.

Genial, he said, "You look absolutely gorgeous. Every woman ought to envy you tonight."

"Thank you, you do not look so bad yourself," she replied with a teasing smirk.

Terren rocked on his heels, looking ruefully down at his own clothes. "This awful grass-green silk tunic was apparently the only appropriate thing Lucen saved from my wardrobe. I should have commissioned another set of clothes, or even borrowed something less ostentatious."

She wrinkled her nose at him. "I like it, but you would look better in a dark blue."

Terren gave her a sour look, but he couldn't hold it when she giggled, and he gave a chuckle of his own.

"And where is your show of royalty?" Sairah gestured to his bare head.

"I left it in my room. You know I have always despised wearing the thing."

She nodded. "Maybe so, but your opinions do not change the blood in your veins. Father will not be happy."

Terren frowned at the sudden mention of his father. His sister was right. He didn't care about Grayten's opinion, but he needed to stop acting like his place wasn't in a castle. He sighed. "I should retrieve it, though I don't know if I have time before the official start."

"Have one of your pups get it for you," she suggested, pushing her chin to the guards a few feet behind him.

Terren snorted. As funny and accurate as her observation was about the guard, he wouldn't treat the men like page boys. "I'll get it later."

Her smile fell, and they were quiet for a moment. Gently, Sairah said, "I've not seen you much. How is everything?"

Terren's amiable smile dropped, and he assumed a nonchalant expression. "It's been fine, but let's not talk about me. I would much rather forget our reasons for being here and just have some fun tonight."

She raised a sculpted eyebrow, but did not press for more information. At least she respected his desire to keep silent. Squeezing her hands, he continued, "I need to exchange pleasantries with Grayten and Herretus. After, you and I will dance the night away, while you laugh at all the steps I have forgotten in my absence."

Sairah giggled, nodding her agreement.

Terren approached the kings slowly so as not to appear rude and paused several feet away, waiting until either of the men acknowledged his presence. Herretus noticed him first and beckoned him closer. The king was in a jolly mood and it seemed already feeling the effects of the ale in his hand.

Herretus clapped him on the shoulder and said, "Terren, I am glad to see you! I was just about to officially open the festival. Join us on stage?"

"I am at your disposal, Your Majesty," he replied, though an uneasy feeling stirred in his stomach.

"Wonderful! Now, I know you didn't see Kiira today in preparation for the festival, but did you cross paths on your way here?"

Terren was about to answer when Kiira's voice came from behind him.

"I am here, Father," she said. "I apologize for my delay. I had some last minute details that needed attending to, and you know how Jemma gets about my hair on special occasions." A teasing smile tipped her lips.

"Well, as always, she did a fine job fussing." Herretus gave Kiira a warm smile. Terren glimpsed pure love and admiration in the king's eyes and a fleeting memory of his mother smiling at him the same way flashed before him.

Kiira stepped into view, and Terren nearly had to pick his jaw from the floor. He caught the embarrassing expression just in time. Perhaps it was because he was used to seeing Kiira in a tunic and breeches, but her current dress and radiant smile made him briefly forget he was forced to know this woman.

The fitted silk gown was a similar green to his tunic, only hers a shade darker. The tight sleeves, made from a sheer deep green material were stitched with gold thread starting at the wrist in a small clusters, dispersing as it traveled up the sleeve to her shoulder, the pattern replicating on the bodice, impressed the idea of dandelion seeds floating on a gentle breeze. By far, the most extravagant part of the dress was the lower half because of the several layers of solid and sheer material in gradient shades of green. The gown flowed smoothly as she shifted from one leg to the other, giving the illusion of the swaying feathery grasses. Kiira's honey curls had been braided and pinned in a loose gathering on the right side of her head, cascading over one shoulder with several tendrils still framing her face. She, too, wore a circlet of fine woven silver, and guilt pricked at him for not wearing his.

What he noticed more than anything else, what he always noticed about Kiira, were her sparkling emerald eyes.

She glanced at him quickly, something like uncertainty flashing in the look, before returning her father's smile. "Father, you are dashing this evening. King Grayten, I am pleased you are able to join us for our yearly festival. Terren, same to you. It seems we share a fondness of color." A small frown wrinkled her brow. "Are you well? You look as if you have seen a spirit."

Kreshkt. To think I would act the fool over a pretty dress.

Blinking from his stupor, Terren covered his shock with a flattering reply. "Not a spirit, princess. A vision." He bowed and gave her a light kiss on the hand.

She thanked him, laughing uncomfortably, unable to hide the small blush coloring her cheeks.

'Snap out of it, Yepenzi,' Kamaria growled in his mind.

The sudden intrusion of her voice sobered him. Clearing his throat, Terren stepped back, dropping Kiira's hand and clasping his own behind his back.

Rubbing the side of her neck, Kiira said, "Father, shall we begin the festival?"

A whirlwind of movement ensued and Terren found himself standing at the back of the stage between Sairah and Grayten as Herretus gave an opening speech. The address summarized how well the agriculture and live-stock produced in the last year. The abundance was astonishing, and for everything mentioned, the king gave thanks to the gods, and especially Ny, for the blessing. The crowd roared, clapped, laughed, or cheered in all the right places. He ended the oration by thanking the people for their hard work, reminding them this kingdom could not function without their dedication and loyalty, and how humbled he was to serve them as their king. The resounding cheer resulting from Herretus bowing to the people made it sufficiently clear how respected the Lorean King was.

A small measure of jealousy whipped at Terren's mind. It was not the adoration creating the thought, but the desire for his people to know the fortune of having a good leader and abundant yields. Once again, he felt frustration bubble in his chest that this marriage put his plans on hold.

When the cheers died, Herretus added, "This year we have an even grander cause for celebration!" Terren's ears perked. "At the end of the Yielding Festival, two kingdoms shall be united through a bond deeper than friendship. I am pleased to announce the marriage of your princess!"

This cheer was even louder, even more forceful than all the others. The people were beyond thrilled. Terren clamped his teeth together till his jaw ached and forced a cheery smile. This had to be the most miserable moment of his entire life.

If only the people knew how much she disliked me.

Stealing a look at Kiira, he expected to see a grim happiness, but her expression was the same one depicted in her portrait in the gallery. A bright, easy smile. It was definitely not because of marriage to him. Did she really love her people so much she could fake such a genuine smile? It would be impressive if that were the case. In his brief moments with Kiira, her love of Lorea and its people was always evident. He suspected it was one of the many reasons she hated the arrangement; it would take her away from here.

The crowd's elation of the impending marriage soon turned to a chant of *'Kiss! Kiss! Kiss!'* and Terren found himself instantly uncomfortable and his smile fell. Ignoring the crowd would reflect poorly on him, but he had no desire to be publicly affectionate. He glanced at Grayten. The expectation from him was obvious. Looking at Herretus, he saw only hopeful encouragement.

Wonderful, he thought. At least Kamaria was the only one to hear his epithet.

He wouldn't kiss her, but the people wanted a show, and he would give them one. Leading Kiira to the front of the stage, he faced her, holding both her trembling hands to his chest. Her eyes pleaded that he not bend to the crowd's demand and he could see her heart trying to leap from her chest. Kiira must feel like a frightened, trapped hare. She would never openly object. They were betrothed, and the kiss would not be out of place.

A charged hush settled over the people and, as he leaned toward her, a real flash of fear glazed her eyes. He gave her a gentle smile before placing a chaste kiss on each hand. He gave a reassuring squeeze to her fingers as relief filled her features. Putting space between them, but holding her gaze, Terren raised his voice for the crowd to hear. "I dare not kiss so lovely a lady until she has asked me herself." Giving a bow to Kiira, Terren exited the stage, slipping into a shadow as the ensuing roar deafened Herretus' declaration: the celebration had officially begun.

CHAPTER 23
DESIRE

Zerrec eagerly focused on the miniature image of Kiira within the seeing crystal, hungrily consuming the flow of her wild hair despite efforts to tame it, and glowing smile as she laughed with those around her. She was radiant in a custom green silk dress as she danced through the crowd, patches of firelight enhancing the gentle curves of her feminine figure. She was dazzling, breathtaking.

As always.

His eyes closed, envisioning the first time he watched Kiira dance the Pavane. She had glided across the floor with lithe precision, a bird soaring upon a steady current of air. Her eyes were alert with joy and her smile radiant. He sighed.

Grace, pure grace.

Looking to the crystal again, Zerrec loved the way erratic flames from the bonfires reflected off of her honey curls, deepening the natural golden color.

She is the most gorgeous creation, so like my Loralyn.

His pulse quickened.

As had been his habit since shedding the self-imposed seclusion, Zerrec checked on Kiira every day, drinking in her countenance, letting the sight of her soothe the ache he felt for companionship. Normally, he would have considered it pointless to view Kiira on the first night of the Yielding Festival, but he needed to see her. He longed to touch her once again. The ghostly images of his memory were smut compared to watching the princess in real time through his crystal. He craved her, and the need to be at her side overwhelmed him.

Frustratingly, he couldn't go to the festival. Not without causing alarm and finding himself in chains, but it didn't matter. Soon she would be with him forever. Zerrec touched the uneven surface of the crystal and the image closed in on Kiira's face so he could stroke a gentle finger along the curve of her cheek, the rough edges of the crystal a poor substitute for what he knew to be supple skin.

This small bit is enough for now.

Smiling at her happiness, he was reminded of the moment he fell in love with Kiira. She had come to him crying from something Liem said; confiding in him, allowing him to sit with her and hold her while she shed broken tears. She was far too young then, but it was in that moment he knew he wanted more; more moments to wipe the tears and to comfort, but even more moments of laughter, dancing, and building a life with Kiira.

He let his past dreams take hold of him now. Their future would be perfect. She was beautiful, intelligent, and a magician. Their two children—a boy and a girl—would play in and out of the trees surrounding their home nestled in the Forest. Kiira would tend a garden, using her gift to grow the largest produce of anyone near, and he would sell potions and healing services. A serene life in which he could look into her eyes each morning. Eyes the same as Loralyn's; unending emerald green, like the rolling hills of Lorea on a summer's day. Those eyes were his passion and life. His attraction was more than physical; without a doubt, she was his soul mate, the perfect replacement for what he had lost so many years ago.

Kiira was the only woman he would spend the rest of his life with. Any effort, great or small, was worthwhile if it meant seeing her free of the Klynotian prince. Zerrec let his lips turn into a rare smile.

Panic crossed Kiira's face, jolting him from pleasant thoughts. Zerrec pulled back the image to show the wider picture. He gripped the rough rock ledge, bruising his hands. His nostrils flared, indignation lighting his anger. The Klynotian whelp was about to kiss the woman he loved!

He has no right to touch her because of a crowd's frenzy!

The scene unfolded slowly in his eyes and the rock sliced into his fingers, blood seeping from around his grip. He couldn't watch, but to look away distressed him. The prince would pay for that mistake, and his death would be exceedingly painful.

Releasing the magic, Zerrec stepped away from the crystal, breathing deeply to calm his galloping pulse. He needed to rescue Kiira soon. The longer the princess stayed near that lout of a prince, the more it would break her spirit.

Maybe, with Ricker's help, I could steal her away before the wedding.

Zerrec shook his head at the idea. That would be senseless. Why fight a kingdom, possibly two, when it was far easier to fight a single man? Why have an army on his trail when he could slit the throat of the prince and be done with it? By the time anyone discovered her missing, he could have her safely tucked away where they wouldn't be found.

He blackened a spot on the cave wall with a spout of fire, the sandy pieces pooling on the floor as a fist-deep hole appeared in the wall. He loathed that his plans to free Kiira were delayed, but he needed to wait until the Lundemai. It was less than ideal, but it was his best chance.

He took another cleansing breath.

Once he had Kiira in his arms again, all would be set right. She would see how much he loved her and agree to be his. Until then, he needed to be patient.

Zerrec looked longingly at the crystal.

Until then, my love, I shall have to watch you from afar.

CHAPTER 24
STOLEN MOMENTS

The quiet of the cobbled main road felt weighty as she and Terren walked together from the castle towards the joyous glow of the market. A few stragglers rushed past, eager to join the celebrations. If Kiira had just been able to convince herself quicker to go with the prince to the last night of the Yielding Festival, they wouldn't have been late. She had groaned, a very un-ladylike noise, according to Jemma, when he knocked on her door that evening. If only shutting the world out with a suffocating pillow would have worked. Attending the festival with the prince every night had been one of her father's stipulations, so she complied. However, Kiira had a loose interpretation of the word 'attend' and, upon entering the marketplace each evening, always found an excuse to escape the prince's side as soon as possible.

Every moment in Terren's presence was a reminder of their wedding day looming and the reins of freedom removed. The constant congratulations and well-wishes lavished upon them by the people were an irritation. She genuinely loved her people's felicitations, but each happy word made marrying Terren less appealing. Each passing day, each outing, Kiira mustered a brave face and stuffed down the misery circulating through her. The brave face was for her people, and the prince knew it.

Every night, as the daily festival celebrations ended, Kiira found solace in being nestled against Leo's chest - the only person who grasped the depths of her sorrow. The first time she went to him, they stood in an awkward silence, their eyes darting around, avoiding any direct contact. With a simple act of opening his arms, Leo shattered the spell, and she was drawn to him by an unseen and relentless force. Regardless of their complete innocence, as a woman betrothed, she should be nowhere near him. If her father discovered these secret meetings, he would erupt, but Leo's presence offered solace amidst the silty turmoil within her. Her rational mind screamed at her, labeling it as a terrible idea. Visiting her second in command each night was ultimately hurting both of them, but Kiira felt more drawn to him than ever. Leo was the man she couldn't have, and that made her cling even more desperately to him.

Still, this did not stop the slow wedge pushing them apart. Her desperation encouraged reckless public displays of affection that continually put them in danger of being caught, and it was a dilemma she did not care to resolve. If only her supposed relationship with Terren could be so fluid. It would make this whole miserable experience tolerable.

The hostility from the garden confrontation a week ago lingered, making her exchanges with the prince reluctant and uneasy. The tension between them so thick it could be sliced and served as a main course for dinner. Seeing the obvious strain, her father's dissatisfaction grew, yet Kiira's will to try harder abated with each passing day. Terren's constant temperance during their required outings made them unpalatable, leaving her unsure if his detachment was fueled by anger or an inability to find the right words. Though he was never unkind, getting him to talk was akin to extracting water from a rock, and the tolling of the noon bells each day sent shivers down her spine.

Mostly, Kiira felt like she hovered on the precipice of Terren's awareness, that he barely registered her existence. The loneliness she felt because of his rejection was more painful than she wanted to admit. Something about the prince both attracted and repelled her. The conflicting emotions drove her to understand the prince through observation, trying to pick out details that might help her make a connection. Once, she even stooped as low as using her magic to enhance her hearing and listen to one of his private conversations with his sister. She managed to learn of a burgeoning relationship with his sister and immediately felt guilty for the invasion of his privacy. Other than that, he kept a schedule as unvaried as his facial expressions.

It frustrated Kiira that she could not seem to make her relationship with Terren blossom. She had tried—at least she thought she had—to not be so off-putting, yet it didn't seem to be enough. Besides her sour Aunt Liane, Kiira could charm anyone. She'd done it for years. But Terren maintained a stony exterior throughout all of their interactions, and nothing she said or did seemed to affect it. If only she could figure out how to break through, but he was a puzzle she was trying to solve without all the pieces.

The worst afternoon by far was their time in the library two days past. Kiira spent the afternoon hours wishing she were with her archers and Leo. Instead, she was stuck reading an advanced text on plants, one she had studied before, and frequently sent glances in Terren's direction, hoping, praying for something to be said, though she didn't know what. At each of her stolen looks, Terren's face remained as impassive as ever. Kiira found it difficult to believe *The Smade Guide to Growing Fruits* was more intriguing than a conversation. She had read that particular text and it was not a page-turner.

Now it was the last evening they would spend together, and they stood for a moment outside the glow of the bonfires. The reality of how her life would change in two days made her drop Terren's arm in favor of adjusting the unruffled cuff of her tunic. She let her eyes dance over the people enjoying the last night of the Yielding Festival. Even with the dark cloud hanging over her, she loved seeing the pleasure and ease filling every corner of the Market Square. Despite everything, seeing her people so happy made her smile. She needed to absorb every moment of this night and treasure it. This was her last Yielding Festival. Just like that, the black cloud came back in full force, pulling the corners of her mouth downward.

"Kiira, is everything okay?" Terren asked.

Taking a deep breath, she plastered on a pleasant smile. "Of course! I shall see you later, for a dance, yes?"

"Yes. When would you like me to find you?"

"Oh, no need. I will find you." She waved, leaving Terren on the semi-darkened road, looking as unresponsive as ever. She could feel his eyes upon her back as she slipped through the hundreds of people.

Kiira scanned the crowd for Leo, wanting to be near him. It took nearly a half hour, but she found him sitting with several of the archers enjoying the cinnamon spiced ale; a well-loved staple at the festival each year. Kiira grinned as she looked at the mixture of men and women in various stages of inebriation. Everyone in the kingdom's military took advantage of the festival's relaxed schedule and allowed themselves to be a little more reckless with their alcohol consumption.

Stepping up to the group, she plucked a mug from Hayla's hand.

"Well, this is the sorriest, laziest, most worthless group of slugs I've ever seen! I'm going to have to double your routine just to make up for it. Cheers!" Kiira downed the rest of the drink before slamming the empty vessel cheerfully onto the table.

Coran raised his mug. "I'll drink to that, Commander!" His words so slurred it was difficult to understand him, but the group still cheered to his reply and each took a long drink before giving the table a hard rap with their knuckles.

Kiira laughed. She was not serious, and they all knew it. She snagged a couple of full mugs from a passing Drinkier, tossing the young lad a gold coin. He smiled at her and stuffed the coin in his pocket, the weight of the gold adding a skip to his step. Keeping one, Kiira handed the second mug to Hayla, who smiled shyly at her; the young archer was new and had yet to warm up to the boisterous group.

When she was comfortably seated, Larkin was the next to raise his drink.

"To an irreplaceable Commander!"

"Here, here."

"Here, here!"

Leo gave a mock frown. "Hey now! I am just as capable as our lovely princess."

"That's true, Newly Appointed Commander Leo, but you're not so pretty to look at while taking orders," Larkin said, giving him a wicked grin.

The table broke into riotous laughter and jeers. It took several minutes before anyone could gasp enough air to speak again, and most had tear streaks reddening their cheeks from the joy.

The hours ticked by as Kiira and her archers recounted embarrassing or witty tales, interspersed with the occasional drinking song. More archers found their way to the group and soon almost the entire company surrounded her. At one point, a fiddler joined them for a few tunes, giving rise to an impromptu dance around and on top of the crowded tables.

Every passing minute lifted Kiira's heart.

When the bells of the temple marked two hours past midnight, Kiira glanced around and noticed the market area was quite empty. If this was to be her last night to be wrapped in Leo's arms, she wanted the cabin's esoteric interior to absorb the rhythm of his breathing and for time to turn into molasses. Standing, she raised her mug and waited for everyone to be silent. Kiira held the gazes of several archers for a moment. "I am so blessed to have had the privilege of being your Commander. I will miss all of you and will think upon the good and tough times we have shared, always. To the best division in the military!" Giving them all a bow, Kiira threw back her drink, finishing it with three hard taps on the table to emphasize her toast.

Instead of the expected cheer, the response to her toast was somber. Each man and woman, under her command, stood, placed a fist over their sternum, and bowed. It was the highest respect they could give her, a salute to their commander and a bow to their princess. Kiira blinked away the water building in her eyes. Holding tight to her lower lip, she nodded, acknowledging the gesture. Before they could see a single drop, she spun and hurried away.

"I'm here, Leo," she said, grabbing his hand to guide him closer.

He wasted no words in greeting, pushed her against the wall, and allowed the rough, top-heavy, half-timbered house to shelter them from view. Far from the center of the city, someone would have to physically walk down the narrow space to see them. It had been their meeting place all week. In the safety of the darkened alley, Kiira let her guard down and wholly concentrated on Leo's lips against hers. The uneven surface dug into her back, but she didn't care.

I am going to miss this … him.

She deepened the kiss, closing the already tight space between them.

Several minutes later, Leo rested his forehead against hers and they breathed in each other's quick breaths.

"I need to catch my breath," he said through a small laugh. "You're too overwhelming."

"I am not," she quipped with half-hearted indignation.

"In a good way, love, in a good way."

When their breathing had slowed, she said, "I was afraid you missed my signal."

"Believe me, I was looking for it," he replied. "It just took me a while to get away inconspicuously."

Kiira gave a wry laugh before resting her cheek on his shoulder. Leo folded his arms around her. With her face buried in his neck, Kiira took a deep breath and lost herself in his scent: cedar and warm wax.

"Promise me you'll come later. This will be the last night I can hold you," Leo said.

She sighed. "We walk a dangerous line as it is, even now I must return to the festival to keep up appearances with the prince."

"I don't care how late you are, please, just come," he whispered, tightening his arms.

Kiira imagined the pleading look in his earthen eyes. Denying him was impossible. Again, the rational part of her mind screamed she was being foolish. Guilt reminded her this was not at all how a princess should act, but Kiira needed this last night as much as he did. She agreed to meet him with a deep kiss; savoring, memorizing the moment and the feel of his lips. Breaking away, she swiped at hot tears.

My entire world is being ripped from my grasp; the only things I have ever wanted, gone because of some ridiculous arrangement. Leo should not have to beg for one last night with me.

Leo didn't ask what the tears were for, he knew. He'd heard it from her lips on more than one occasion, and he had repeated the same sentiments to her. Kiira let him hold her a while longer. Finally, in a broken whisper, she said, "I must go."

He held her hand as long as possible as she stepped into the brighter part of the moonlit alley. Even though she would see him later, she refused to look back. Using the distant music of the festival, Kiira navigated her way back to the flooding lights and cheerful conversations. She pasted on a smile. Terren soon appeared by her side with a deep frown, though she had said she would find him, and held out his hand.

A lively song started, and her feet directed while her mind drifted to other things. Kiira startled at a tighter squeeze of her hand. "I'm sorry, what did you say?" She asked, her cheeks burning.

"You seem more distracted than usual tonight. Is everything alright?" She didn't miss the edge darkening his voice or his emphasis on the word distracted.

Something was off about him, especially if he was showing emotion. Kiira would consider the implications of his actions later. She shrugged. "Oh, yes, I'm fine. There is much on my mind."

Terren narrowed his eyes, looking like he didn't believe she was telling the whole truth, but luckily, he didn't push the subject. Doubtless she could lie convincingly enough, and the last thing she needed was him discovering what she had been doing. There was no justification for her time with Leo. At the song's end, Kiira excused herself, drifting toward the market's exit; she really was no longer in the mood for the surrounding happiness.

Kiira was just about to leave the bailey to return to the castle grounds to meet with Leo one last time when a disembodied voice startled her. She jumped, whirled, and was shocked to see Terren leaning casually against a house. The moon revealed an emotionless profile, his eyes glowing in a haunting shade of blue, as if he were a spirit, watching her intently. "Terren, what are you doing here?"

CHAPTER 25
DARK ACCUSATIONS

"I should ask you the same, princess," Terren replied. Without the bright sounds of music, the frustration lacing his voice was evident. Not how he wanted to begin the conversation, but his patience with Kiira had been pushed to the edge.

"What do you mean? I was going to the quarters of my second, we have much to discuss before I relinquish everything to him." Confidence colored her voice, but he could easily see her features in the sliver of moonlight available, and the flash of guilt she quickly covered did not elude him.

Closing his eye, Terren let go of the last threads of hope he'd been harboring with a heavy sigh. He should have known better than to trust her.

I should have known better than to believe she might be different.

How could Kiira lie so readily with such damming evidence? He watched her slip away somewhere each night, thinking she just needed space from the chaos of the festival. Gods knew he did, but what Herretus told him about her secret courtship turned into a nagging suspicion. He tried to snub it, give her the benefit of the doubt, but when he saw her disappear from the festival this evening he needed to know for sure.

Following Kiira through the dark streets had been easy. As a Shadow Walker, night was no hindrance to his vision. What he wanted to find was a woman needing respite and instead stumbled upon a woman easily stepping into the arms of another man. The moment had sent painful streaks through his chest.

Only I would be so foolish to hope for something like love from a woman.

His heart beat angrily as he clenched his hands. A woman's heart was fickle and could not be trusted. "I know he is succeeding you, but that's not why you're going to him tonight."

"What other reason would I have to be here?"

A battle of wills waged between them. The faintest hint of music twirled in the breeze. His lack of response was the prodding she needed.

"Say it, Terren." Kiira snapped. "Whatever it is you're thinking, speak plainly. I would hear the truth from you." She crossed her arms, defiance lifting and squaring her shoulders.

He took a few steps closer. She was not intimidated, but at least now she could see exactly how much her actions insulted him.

Mimicking her defensive stance, he said, "I know being forced to marry is unsettling, that is one thing we agree upon. What I'm not pleased to see is how easily you ran into the arms, and bed, of a man to whom you are not betrothed. Will that be your default when we are married? Run away? Run to someone else? Whatever I have done for you to dislike me, I did not deserve your disrespect." Terren kept his tone even, but it didn't match the frantic pace his heart pounded out behind his ribs.

Kiira gaped at him for several seconds, then clamped her mouth to flex her jaw, controlling a torrent of words. The fire in her eyes spoke volumes. Terren was not happy with her actions, yet a minuscule part of him couldn't judge her in them, either. Many of his nights were spent with Kamaria in the Shade Realm seeking comfort, except his Bear was a friend, not a lover.

Kiira narrowed her eyes. "Let me make the situation clearer for you. I am not *sullied* as you are suggesting, Terren. You wish for the truth? I have kissed him, I have lain next to him these past nights, and I almost did give myself over to him."

His chest tightened at the harshness of her words.

"Lucky for you"—she spit the three words at him like venom—"Leo respects me enough to not treat me like a lady of pleasure. I love Leo, and ours is a love that existed long before you stepped into my life."

Terren clenched his jaw, and he could feel the anger tightening the muscles in his neck. "You think you are the only one who is losing in this arrangement?"

Kiira leaned back from him with raised brows. When was the last time he had raised his voice? He couldn't remember.

A humorless laugh escaped her lips. "Now you show emotion! If you had not been an impenetrable fortress, I wouldn't have been so miserable and compelled to seek out comfort from Leo. Smiling, even just acknowledging a person's existence goes a long way in building a *friendship*, Terren. I could have better conversations with a rock, and that's exactly what you are; a boulder in my way."

"That is such a selfish point of view," he said.

"Selfish?" She laughed, incredulous. "I am giving up the man I love to follow my father's decree. That's called sacrifice."

"That is not an act of sacrifice."

"No?" She stepped close enough he could feel the warmness of her breath. Kiira narrowed her eyes. "I could change this whole situation if I truly wanted to, and make you nothing more than a horrible memory. Be glad for my restraint, prince. I *hate* this arrangement, but I respect my father and will pay heed to my duty as the princess."

Terren matched her gaze. He didn't appreciate the threat. Not that she could actually hurt him, magic or otherwise. He had too much knowledge on her for it to happen. He gave her a bitter laugh. "Going to see Leo each night is the furthest thing from respecting your father."

"Do not presume to think for my father, Terren. You don't know his mind," Kiira spat.

"You are naïve if you think I am mistaken about your father's thoughts." He lowered his voice, making sure his next words would be received exactly as he intended. "Right now, in this moment, I have every right to go to your father about this." He gestured toward the small living space behind him. "All of the evidence is in my favor. How do you think your father will respond?"

Kiira scoffed, pushing past him. He let her go. She needed to release her anger, and he needed to meditate. Pinching the bridge of his nose, he willed the enmity pounding at the back of his skull to be caged. He hadn't been this agitated since leaving the priesthood in the cordillera years ago. Terren wanted to go immediately to his rooms, but his guards were likely beside themselves looking for him at the festival. Opening a door to the Shade Realm, he made his way back to the market square.

TERREN WAS NOT NORMALLY one to brood, but the conversation with Kiira left him unsettled. After his meditation, he crawled into bed, exhausted from the abrasive momentum of the festival and the confrontation with the princess. It hadn't occurred to him until this morning what felt so off as she stalked past him.

I felt magic being used. It was subtle, but it was there.

Why it unsettled him, he couldn't say, but the notion simmered in his mind as he watched the shadows of the furniture creep across the floor. Even Lucen, who could usually get him to talk, received only an acknowledging nod and limited words in response to questions.

The sun was setting when a loud banging startled Terren, and he pulled his eyes to the door. Grayten usually just barged in without the respect of notification, which meant it had to be Herretus or Liem. He'd put a gold coin on the latter, since Kiira's feelings toward him seemed to have transferred to her twin.

Terren heaved himself from the chair and drug open the door. Stepping out of the way, he was interested to see Grayten, King Herretus, and Prince Liem enter his room. All three of their expressions held varying levels of anger.

At least, if the king is upset with me, Herretus is the most level-headed.

"Terren, have you seen my daughter today?" Herretus asked.

"No, Your Majesty, I have not," Terren said.

Grayten growled. "If I discover you in a lie, boy."

The growl would have been intimidating if Terren had any amount of respect or fear for Grayten, but the low rumble came across as merely annoying. Terren locked eyes with him. "It is no lie, sir. I've seen naught but the interior of my rooms today."

Herretus sighed. "I thought that might be the case."

"Kreshkt, Terren, then where is she?" Liem butted in, pouring blame into the question.

Terren looked pointedly at Liem, but said nothing. His mind whirled with the information. Kiira was missing?

I didn't imagine the magic then.

"Did something happen last night I need to know about?" Herretus asked.

Terren shifted his gaze back to the king before giving a quick glance toward Grayten. If Kiira really was missing, then he could not hold back any information. A small part of him didn't have the heart to disgrace her with the information he possessed. He knew too well the sting of being discredited before family. Still, her absence was his fault.

Reluctantly, he nodded his head. "I confronted Kiira last night as she was going to see..." He was not really sure how to finish that statement. Her lover? No, she made it quite clear that was not the case. "When we were done, I am not sure where she disappeared to."

Grayten's scowl deepened, his eyes murderous. If he'd had the freedom to speak, there would, no doubt, be shouted remarks about his incompetency and threats about what would happen if Terren ruined the arrangement. Herretus gave a deep frown, but it was not directed toward him. Liem's expression rivaled that of Grayten's, protective of his sister to the bitter end.

Abruptly, Herretus said. "Everyone, please leave, I would like to speak with Terren alone."

"Give me a few minutes alone with him. I can get my son to talk," Grayten offered. Terren cringed internally, knowing his time would be wasted on senseless yelling if Herretus agreed.

"That will not be necessary, Grayten. Terren will undoubtedly give me the answers I'm looking for," Herretus assured.

With one last displeased look, Grayten stalked from the room, the dismissal making him furious. Liem grudgingly followed.

Before the prince shut the door, Herretus turned to his son. "And Liem, if I find out you listened to our conversation, you will not like my punishment." Once the door had shut, he said in a calm voice, "Please tell me everything that happened."

Terren summarized the conversation from the night before and waited patiently for the king to answer. Finally, Herretus spoke. "Kiira hasn't been found in any of her usual hiding places or anywhere inside the citadel." He glanced out the window. "If she disappeared, as you say, then we need to send a search party into the Forest, but I fear it may be too late for that; night has nearly fallen."

"The Forest Wilds, Sire? She would go in there alone?"

Herretus nodded while he gazed unseeing at the stone floor, his mind working.

Why would she go there? Kiira knew the Forest well, but it also wasn't the safest place to be alone. Terren would have liked a little more information, but King Herretus seemed lost in the pace of his fervent steps, making the atmosphere in the room tense. Terren wished he could say something to be helpful. He liked the king. His daughter was a different story. The thought of marrying the restive woman left a bitter taste in his mouth. Yet Kiira would soon be in his care and he could have handled the situation better last night. "Sire, I would volunteer to scout for her. I have the skills to track at night. If there is a trail, I will find it."

Herretus stopped and studied Terren. An unhappy smile picked at his lips but didn't hold. "I imagine you feel responsible, yes?"

Terren hesitantly nodded.

"Do not. Kiira is to remain accountable for her actions."

"I would still volunteer. We may not get along, Sire, but I do not wish her harm; especially if my skills may aid in finding her," he said.

Herretus paused for a moment. "Very well, but you and I are the only ones that are to have knowledge of this. Will you need any Huntsman to join you?"

"Yes, Sire, and no." Terren wanted to know why the king was giving such a command, but he wouldn't question it. If there was one thing that he had learned in his time here, Herretus always had a reason.

Herretus laid a hand on his shoulder, and his eyes softened. "Terren, if you lose the trail, don't stray too much further, I do not wish you to put yourself in danger for her. If that is the outcome of this venture, Kiira will need to find her own way back."

Terren bowed as Herretus exited, his mind lingering on the cryptic request.

CHAPTER 26

RUNNING

Heated tears dampened Kiira's cheeks and fell onto the soft loam of the misshapen trail made by her insistent stride. Her heart beat fiercely, the sound reverberating in her ears, a thunderous sensation in her chest. Reckless, Kiira ran through a narrow tunnel of winding trees, her pounding footsteps echoing off the trunks. Wild limbs etched her skin, grabbing hair and clothing, but she ignored the external pain, anticipating the exertion to shed the weight of her burdens.

It didn't. If she looked behind her now, the fetters of her anger would lay in a thick trail. Just the thought of trudging through them again to return home sent a plummeting sickness through her stomach.

No. Run, Kiira. Don't think. Just run. Run.

Despite her attempts to clear her head, the memory of Terren's confrontation doggedly followed her every step, never letting her forget the truth. Why did he have to ruin her joy? Why couldn't he have just acted oblivious? She would have stopped seeing Leo once they were married. How could he think so little of her? Terren had known her barely a week and he thought to judge? What was the harm of spending time with the man she loved before losing him forever? Hurt, resentment, anger; every feeling she had been burying beneath a practiced smile leaked down her cheeks. Anxiety, frustration, and bitterness fought for space within the confines of her mind. Only running seemed to keep the chaotic feelings from completely overwhelming her. Maybe she could run from her problems, never looking back.

Liem was the heir to the throne, anyway. Born first, he had the right to everything; she was just the spare; it didn't matter what happened to her. So why couldn't she marry the man she loved? When her brother married, she would no longer be useful in the court. His new wife would fill the role her mother left vacant with her death.

Kiira was tired of it. Tired of being the odd orbiting piece no one needed, tired of the false smiles and making sure everyone was pleased. Did no one notice how much she had sacrificed already just so she would remain important? Why did she have to sacrifice the things she loved to marry a stranger? She really should just keep running. If she could have disappeared years ago with just her bow and Starfire—

No! She swiped at red, watery eyes. That's my hurt talking. I could never leave my family, the people, and the archers so carelessly. I love them, too.

Kiira forced herself to focus on the muted thud of her feet striking the ground. She didn't need to spiral into apocryphal thoughts. It wouldn't solve her problems.

When it happened was unclear, but eventually every collision of her foot with the ground chipped away flecks of the bleak emotions encasing her heart. The tense knots bunching her shoulders eased, a wonderful freedom let her breathe. The weightlessness she felt sent a fresh burst of energy through her limbs and a bubble of wild laughter slipped her throat. Where had that come from? Kiira hadn't thought laughter was possible, but it didn't matter; this was the best she had felt since learning of the arrangement.

Calmer, she slowed her headlong pace. Except, the lesser exertion allowed for black ideas to crawl into her thoughts.

My pretending the wedding isn't coming has no more allowed me to keep Leo than a tree can resist shifting upon a breeze.

Deep sadness occupied the space of anger as reality washed over her. Leo was the only man she had ever truly loved, and he was the same for her. He was her best friend.

An overwhelming ache for her mother sliced through her chest in a clean, swift movement, a glowing knife through butter. Fresh droplets gathered in her eyes. In the ten years of living without her mother's wisdom, guidance, and love, never had she faced a problem that could not be overcome, relying on herself, Jemma, or her family to see her through. Now, more than ever, Kiira desperately wanted to speak with her. Her mother would have known exactly what to say and do in her current situation. She would have listened, understood, and advised her through every part of this arrangement, and she would have been the bridge between what was and what would be.

Stupid, useless tears. Pull yourself together, Kiira!

Hiccupping sobs sent her stumbling.

Snap!

She slowed as the loud crack dissipated through the reverent trees. An all-encompassing fatigue absorbed her will to stand. Knees buckling, she landed—hard—on the dirt path. Wincing, Kiira rubbed the sore spot on her backside. Only then did she notice how labored her breathing and cognizance had become. That wasn't good. She needed a clear head if she wanted to make it home. Kiira squinted through the scant light filtering through the trees. The forest here was dense, something she'd never seen before. Some trees grew no more than a few inches from one another, vying for prominence. The dim and gloomy surroundings gave the rough trees an ominous quality.

Is it … morning?

Alarm spiking, Kiira shot to her feet. Holding out her palm, she bloomed a small, flameless orange lily with a deep-red center. The light did little more than cast an eerie glow on everything as she twisted, studying her surroundings. Nothing was recognizable. That really wasn't good.

I am definitely lost.

Needing a better vantage point, Kiira snuffed the flame and scaled the nearest oak. The low branches made it easy to quickly climb to the crown of the forest. Above the safety of the boughs, she saw only a sea of dark green in every direction. The sun was softening the horizon in front of her.

How in the world did I run all night and this far without noticing?

Normally, she wouldn't be worried about finding her way home, but without a doubt Kiira was deeper in the Forest Wilds than she had ever been. Fear formed a knot in her chest.

Get a grip! Just descend the tree and form a plan to get home.

Securely on the forest floor, Kiira took a deep breath, letting the lilied light bloom again in her hand. She glanced around. Getting home was important. Her family would be concerned and the Forest Wilds were dangerous to travel alone. Sure, she had walked through the thick trees many times before, but she had always remained in scouted areas where it had been deemed safe, and with a bow. What in the realms had made her come here? Was it the draw of plant life? That made little sense, though there was something special about the trees surrounding her. Kiira blew her lips, contemplating her situation.

The only defenses she had were magic and a couple of knives in her boots. She had kept her weaponry to a minimum during the Yielding Festival. What she wouldn't give for her bow and quiver. Having a familiar weapon would give her a small sense of security, even if it didn't make her any less the easy prey. Except her distance from the castle prevented her from summoning it. The only thing benefiting her was that it would soon be daylight and with her core magic she could easily find fresh water, one benefit of being what many called nature gifted, though officially she was a learner of the Green School. Kiira preferred the common name since the other fell flat on the tongue.

A protesting growl erupted from her stomach, distracting her thoughts. "This was so foolish of me. Goddess please help me out of this predicament." Kiira pressed a palm to her forehead; maybe the pressure would produce a plan. Her stomach just grumbled again.

Finding water and then food is priority number one.

Closing her eyes for a moment, she concentrated on the god-gifted magic coursing through her veins. Directing her thoughts, she used it to locate fresh water. It was close. Snapping her head around, Kiira looked in the direction she needed to walk, except it was the opposite way she had come. Walking toward home would be more beneficial. "I'm not really that thirsty," she said, denying the truth with a hard swallow.

Kiira started retracing her steps, but a gnawing feeling centered on her breastbone compelled her to turn around and continue toward the water. At first she ignored the sensation, but it took only a few steps before the feeling gripped her heart and mind like a vice, overwhelming every other thought and sensation. She stopped and stared curiously down the path leading towards the water. Was it worth it? Water was important and she might find something edible near fresh water. She could easily backtrack. Kiira worried her lower lip in consideration. With a laugh of disbelief, she took a step and prayed she was not making a horrible choice. The new heading washed a wave of eagerness through her, cramping her stomach with eager energy. It could be the lack of food, or maybe it was the goddess answering her prayer.

As Kiira wandered deeper in the Forest, the natural deep brown of the oaks turned into a minacious black, though Kiira felt no fear from the ominous trees. These oaks were simply unusual. Touching one, extraordinary life exploded under her fingers, as if special water coursed through their roots. These trees were foundational, the ancestors to the outlying trees, and the true heart of the Forest. Kiira kept a light hand touching the rough bark as she continued, enamored by the magic pulsing through them. It filled her mind, erasing all other thoughts, and her core magic seemed to glow brighter in the presence of these special trees.

Focusing on the richness surrounding her, Kiira missed a sudden drop in the path. Her stomach drove into her throat as she tumbled down a steep embankment. Head over foot, she landed in a breathless heap, her nose smashing into the dirt.

Ouch!

Groaning, Kiira pushed herself up to scowl at the malicious hill.

As if falling wasn't enough, why shouldn't there also be a few twigs in my hair? Serves me right for not paying attention.

It made her feel slightly better to grumble as she rubbed a pulsing spot on her elbow. Taking in her surroundings, she noted how the trees along the ridge grew in a perfect arc. Following the gentle curve with her eyes, Kiira turned to be met by an enormous oval clearing bathed in elegant morning light beaded in shining dew. Her jaw slackened of its own volition.

This was The Lieta Springs, the name springing to her mind instinctively. She shivered.

Kiira's eyes darted madly to the various wonders decorating the springs. Seven flawless pools made of smooth ebony rock dominated the center of the clearing, glistening as water trickled and cascaded from one circle to the next. The soft burble of moving water lightened her spirit.

Scrambling to her feet, Kiira took tentative steps toward the predominating water feature. Springy earth beneath her feet made her look to see lush grass cushioning her steps, the vibrant green inviting her to remove her boots and feel the feather-soft grass tickling her toes, and she did just that. Her chest tingled like effervescent wine as the magic within her swelled from the contact with such healthy plant life.

Free to enjoy the sensuous verdure, Kirra inched her way closer to the ground-level pool. It was the largest of the seven and at least ten meters in diameter. Peering into the depths, the crystal clear liquid still held the soft glow of the moon as it swirled a few times before flowing into a wide, loitering stream and disappeared into the trees.

Taking deferential steps, she edged her way around to the six other pools. The perfectly stacked spirals reminded her of the nautical shells she often found on the beach. Examining each of the pools in turn, she stepped to the smallest and tallest of the seven. It stood to her height and was the source of the water for the entire system. Peeking over the edge, Kiira couldn't see anything but a black abyss.

Mumbling, she said, "The water is flowing against nature, strange." She tapped her chin. "Though, I suppose it is not that strange considering the density of magic here." Kiira was surprised by the pools. Based on legends, she expected the springs to be ... grander. These were impressive and beautiful, definitely, just not visually imposing like she'd imagined. This called for corrections to the records in the royal library when she returned.

Curious about the temperature of the water, she stirred the surface and a pure bass note sounded.

Laughing, she blurted, "Now that is a wonderfully strange discovery!" Touching the water again, this time with a little more force, another low note resonated in the clearing, this time louder.

Fascinating.

Kiira tapped multiple pools in succession, running between them. A delighted grin stretching a smile as the meadow filled with the most beautiful harmonies. The various pitches, light and lilting, held joy and love for the world that could only be expressed in nature. The chorus faded and she couldn't stop herself from touching the pools again. This time the layered tones melted every care away and Kiira found she had no desire to leave.

Reluctantly, she turned from the pools. There was too much here to let her time be monopolized by the intoning waters. A glimmer at the north edge of the clearing caught her attention and a large patch of Star Fire lilies shimmered with a dusting of water, each tiny water bead holding on to the last remnants of a silver moon. Kiira reached out, whispering her fingers along one of the soft petals.

To her dismay, the imperceptible touch not only removed the water droplets but wiped the color from the lily as well. A pure white streak now marred the surface of the once flawless petal and a bright orange stained her finger. Instantly the flower drooped, turning a black so dark that an irreplaceable void had been created amongst the thousands of gorgeous flowers. Kiira's heart wrenched at the accidental destruction. The unwarranted death sent a stabbing pulse of regret through her chest.

Goddess, forgive me.

She backed away from the delicate creations, afraid to disturb anything else.

Safely away, she studied a haphazard pile of maroon rocks. Approaching, a comfortable heat radiated from the area and she saw several reptiles lounging in the safety of the shadows. Her eyes relaxed from the soothing warmth.

Shaking her head, Kiira forced herself to step away. She couldn't fall asleep when there was still so much to explore.

The new sun highlighted a cluster of ripe berry bushes. An angry growl from her stomach forcibly reminded Kiira how long it had been since eating. Making her way to the fruit, she hoped there would be no ill effects from her touch as with the lilies. Picking one to be certain, she popped the ripe blackberry into her mouth, letting the delicious juices coat her tongue with a sweetness unlike anything she had ever tasted.

Even the castle gardeners would be envious of the quality.

The royal gardeners were always trying to improve last year's harvest. A devious smile quirked her lips; here she had found the perfect berry, and the gardeners would never know. Using her tunic, Kiira collected a generous amount of blackberries, raspberries, and blueberries. There were a few other berries, but not ones she recognized. She refrained from plucking the ripe fruit. Though she was dying to have a taste, it would do no good to poison herself simply to satisfy curiosity.

Kiira settled next to the largest crystalline pool, dangling her feet in the cool water. The length and distance of her run was finally seeping into her bones and the cooling water felt wonderful on her tired feet.

Morning had come in full force, signaling her need to return home, especially before her muscles protested any additional movement. Popping the last berry into her mouth, Kiira tried to stifle a tremendous yawn as a deep weariness settled over her.

In my current state, trying to find my way home would do more harm than good. I'll just take a short nap.

Crawling to the maroon rocks, she stretched out beneath a low hanging one. Lying on the soft grass, she let her eyes lazily wander around the clearing. A secure peace filled her mind. Kiira closed her eyes. Any concerns she had lay far beyond the edges of the meadow.

CHAPTER 27
WORRY

"Kiira's fine. She's fine. Kiira's fine. She's fine." Panic itched at his throat and he rubbed just below the small knot where the feeling seemed to generate. He needed to solve this before his love was seriously hurt, but how? He didn't know where she was and he didn't have the tools to attempt locating her. Getting the supplies he needed to locate her could take days, days he didn't have, not to mention the-less-than-ideal distance from her supposed location within the Forest. His heart beat a stuttering rhythm as his inability taunted him. The best he could do was continue to fuel magic into his seeing crystal and hope for results. Zerrec glanced at the seeing crystal, still void. Pieces of this tattered hope fraying more.

"No. No, stay focused. You can find her. You must find her. Kiira's Fine. I will not lose her. Focus." Zerrec took several murderous steps as he paced between the cavern walls. "That pathetic prince did this," he muttered. "I know he caused this. He's made her afraid. I'll kill him and then Herretus for making her go through this debacle. He will regret denying me my rightful place by her side."

The solid opaque void wavered in the crystal. Zerrec pounced toward the pedestal. Nothing. He banged his fist against the wall, sending shooting pain to his elbow. He shook his hand to relieve the pain.

He'd been in this state of unrest since discovering from Ricker, his eyes, and ears within the citadel, that Kiira was missing. How long had she actually been gone? The gossip in the castle had only begun this morning. The last time anyone had seen the princess was at the last gathering of the Yielding Festival, celebrating with the other archers.

Now, hours spent funneling various amounts of power into the crystal to find Kiira did nothing to give him what he wanted, just bleak cognizance of no information. It filled every corner of the cave system he currently called home. Draining energy pulled at his limbs. Zerrec drooped for a moment before readjusting his resolve. He paced faster to keep feeling in his limbs. Maintaining a casting outside his school of magic was not doing him any favors. He wanted—needed—to eat and sleep, but refused to give in to the temptation. He needed to see with his own eyes she was safe; the lack of results was eating away at his crafted self-control. "Kiira, why would you run into the Forest? You know it's difficult to track people in there."

Which is exactly the reason why she did. The thought slapped him with reality.

"Stupid, reckless girl." An ache bloomed at his sternum. "I can't lose you, my love. I can't." He glanced at the crystal again. Opaque black continued to fill the jagged crystal.

This would be a perfect opportunity to rescue her if only he wasn't blinded by the magic penetrating the Forest. Wherever she was within the boundaries of the thick oaks, Kiira was surrounded with permeating magic, negating his vision casting. Old lore from before the realms broke flitted through his memory. A place no mortal could find without the help of the gods. A sanctuary of some sort, but he dismissed the notion. It'd been decades since he'd heard anyone talk of it, and the gods were not active in the world as they once were.

The gods would never deign to answer us. We're nothing to them.

Hunger gnawed at his stomach, chasing away his thoughts. Zerrec pushed the feeling aside. He would starve before releasing the magic fueling the vision cast in his crystal. His stomach did not agree.

"Kiira, I have to know you are safe," he said to the void within the jagged rock. "Please. Give me something. An entire day has passed my love." He stepped over to the crystal and—knowing it was futile—tried to force an image to appear.

His stomach churned as a headache bloomed behind his eye.

The logical part of his mind whispered he needed to stop, to rest, but it was not nearly as convincing as it should have been.

I'll just sit for a while and if I become tired, I can stand.

Zerrec sank into the nearby chair and forced alertness into his eyes, focusing on the crystal.

Blinking bleary eyes open, Zerrec raised his head to see the crystal lying dormant. Instantly on edge, he flew from the chair.

"No! No! No!" Zerrec berated himself as he poured magic into the crystal. How could he have slept?! Faint grey swirls like smoke twisted through the uneven surface and his fury turned to excitement. It was working! She was alive! He touched the crystal with greedy fingers. Kiira appeared with sharp clarity, though, shadowed within a darkened room. She had fallen asleep next to a dying fire. His love was alive and whole. A relieved breath passed his lips. Joy-weakened knees had him slumping in the chair just behind him. "She's fine. I haven't lost her." A smile covered his lips.

Standing, Zerrec moved closer to the crystal, directing the image to scan over her entire body, making sure she was truly well. Peace flooded his system. "She's fine and perfect as always."

The casting slowly moved from head to booted toe as he directed. Zerrec caught a glimpse of white fabric clutched in Kiira's hands, reflecting the yellow and orange of the dancing fire. Curious, he zoomed out to see more of the room. A snake's warning escaped his teeth. Smashing his fist against the stone pedestal sent a jolt through his elbow to his shoulder. The gown was a loud reminder of her unchosen fate, one he was suspended in waiting to rescue her from. It was a slap in the face.

Herretus will pay dearly for this! They will all pay for this.

CHAPTER 28
DIVINE CONVERSATION

Groaning, Kiira stretched the rest from her limbs before rubbing wakefulness into her eyes. She turned her head to move from beneath the sheltered rock and froze. A queen Wolfcat lay before her, staring intently with glowing lilac eyes. Meeting the gaze of the massive creature was a death wish; but stupefied by the proximity of the large feline, Kiira lay frozen as her mind arrowed into wakefulness.

The Wolfcat tilted her head, waiting for her to do something, and the longer Kiira held the female's gaze, the more it seemed like the cat was curious and had no intention of harm. Tentatively, she moved to kneel before the amazing creature. The Wolfcat's piercing lilac eyes tracked her cautious movements, but otherwise, the magnificent creature did not move.

Settled, Kiira darted her focus elsewhere and found she was surrounded by a semicircle of all manner of creatures. Deer, mice, raccoons, bears, wolves, raptors, songbirds, all rested, waiting in reverence to the queen Wolfcat. There was unnatural intelligence to all the creatures gathered. A seed of uncertainty made her question whether she should attempt to leave the clearing or simply wait. While none of the animals took notice of her specifically, Kiira still felt on edge.

The twinkling of floating fireflies captured her gaze as the insects mingled amongst other happy little bugs zipping and darting a few feet above her head. The buzz of dragonfly wings and the chirps and trills of cicada all blended into a soothing night song. If she wasn't so alert to her surroundings, the sound would easily lull her back to sleep.

The half-moon brightened her face, and the longer she peered up at it, the more vivid it became. So much so that Kiira squinted before being forced to cover her eyes.

Well, that was odd.

Lowering her chin, the queen Wolfcat no longer sat before her, replaced by the most striking woman she had ever seen. A well of beauty radiated from the woman. No words could ever give justice to the sight before her. The simple kneeling posture of the lady with demure hands resting in her lap, her large, and gentle lilac eyes, it was all so simple and yet so wonderful. The barest hint of a smile graced the woman's features as she studied Kiira for several seconds.

"I do favor the Wolfcat to other creatures we created, they are so majestic. I am pleased to see Skehtra grow under your nurturing," the woman said.

The lady's voice, a warm honeyed tea, melted over Kiira, and she couldn't help but think there was something incredibly familiar about the woman. Then she foolishly realized why. She had seen this image all her life in the temple, though a much less radiant version than the one before her. Immediately, Kiira fell prostrate and said, "Goddess Windrah, you honor me with your presence. I am your loyal and humble servant."

A touch on her shoulder invited her to peek at the goddess, who encouraged her to kneel comfortably. "Sit with me as a companion, Daughter."

Kiira complied.

"Now, Kiira, I have much to discuss with you. Listen well for it is imperative you heed my words with care, this is the reason I have brought you to my sanctuary," Windrah said.

Kiira trembled. She attempted to still her hands with pressure to her thighs, but the excitement of the moment was too much and the nerves traveled to the rest of her limbs and tied her tongue. All she could manage was to nod again.

Windrah smiled. "My Daughter, I have heard your prayers and the anguished cries pouring from your soul; a love lost is not easy to bear. Take heart for you need not bear it alone."

The implication of the goddess' words crushed Kiira. "There is no hope for me to be with Leo, then." The statement came out more like a question; a small part of her wishing the goddess would contradict her.

"There is always hope, but that does not mean it will be realized."

Kiira frowned, biting the inside of her lip.

"It is imperative you marry the Klynotian prince for the future of the broken realms," Windrah continued.

Kiira's eyes darted back to the goddess. "What real value is there in a political arrangement?" Kiira tried to keep the bitterness from her voice but knew she had failed the moment the words left her lips.

Windrah smiled knowingly. "Terren is destined for you, My Daughter, and though you do not see it, he needs you as much as you need him."

"Need him? I already had everything I needed," Kiira said before she could control the disrespect seeping into her words. She should not be speaking to the goddess in such a manner, but the direction of this conversation was clear, and she didn't care for the destination.

"Do you not trust the wisdom and plans of the gods?"

Hesitantly, Kiira replied, "Of course I do, but why does that make my love for Leo insignificant? I was content—happy—with him. Why Terren?" It was a question she needed answered.

Windrah tilted her head slightly and glossy chocolate waves fell over her shoulder. She gave Kiira a patient smile and said, "Your love for Leo is not insignificant. It has shaped him profoundly, but he has a different role to fulfill in the future of the broken realms at the side of another."

Kiira grimaced at the words.

"Kiira, trust is not always easy, especially in the midst of hurt. Find peace in this; your marriage to the prince is not an arrangement of men but of the gods. I promise a love like you have never known will be found with Terren. However, it will take effort from both of you. It will strengthen you, challenge you, and comfort you. Seek first the will of the gods and it will always be so. Trust these words."

Looking at her laced finger, Kiira mulled over the words of the goddess. Words spoken by the deity she had devoted her entire life to serving should not to be taken lightly. But that did not change the uncertainty and the pain still settling deep in her heart. "Goddess, I just don't see how we will work. Terren and I...we do not work well together."

"You do not mesh because you do not wish to."

Kiira winced at the sharp truth, then glowered at the tufts of grass between her knees.

"My Daughter," Windrah continued, "you have always been self-reliant. An admirable quality that has gotten you far in life, but it is also your greatest hindrance. Learn to relinquish control and give Terren a chance to support you in this life. You will find his heart is as fragile as your own, though he hides it well. He needs your respect and your unrelenting love."

Kiira released a long breath to unbind the tension in her shoulders. This was not what she wanted to hear. The lightest of touches had her looking to the goddess again.

Quietly, Windrah said, "Love is chaos and calm, joy and pain, laughter and sadness; the strongest of these is the one you choose to pursue. Love is never static. It will change, grow, or weaken as you choose. Terren can be the husband you wish, if you open your heart to let love heal the hurt that divides."

Kiira clamped her hands together, making the knuckles white. She released and studied the color flooding into her hands. "Windrah, I acknowledge what you are saying and I will put effort into the relationship with the—Terren, but how do I just let Leo go?"

"My Child, obedience is not always easy and does not always result in immediate changes, but obey my instructions and my promise to you will be fulfilled," Windrah replied.

The goddess' words created a hole of sadness in her soul, though it left her with a small measure of comfort as well. She loved Leo, but the path before her was set: she would marry Terren. She did not have to obey the goddess, but divine wisdom was never wrong. It was at times like this, when the gods' desires did not align with her own, that Kiira selfishly wanted to abandon faith, except there was always a still, small voice reminding her the gods had never failed her before. She just wished obedience made her situation less painful. Tears pooled in her eyes. Looking back up, she softly said, "You have my promise. I will be obedient and do all you have instructed; but I would be lying if I said your promise gives me hope."

Windrah's smile brightened and her beauty increased tenfold. "Sometimes hope seems lost, My Daughter, but it is an anchor for the soul and will never leave you, always to be found again."

A blinding light radiated from the goddess, and Kiira had to shield her eyes. Blinking back her sight, she stood on a colorless plain. Smooth and white in all directions, but her footing was sure. In the distance, two figures moved toward her followed by the colors of nature, though the surroundings here were unidentifiable. Kiira blinked, and Starfire pulled to a sudden stop near her. She stumbled back in surprise and complete confusion. Tempest followed just a few seconds behind.

What in the—

The thought was cut short as Starfire's head moved and she saw a duplicate of herself laughing from the horse's back. The perfect copy twisted in the saddle, biting her lower lip to hold in the laugh threatening to escape. This couldn't be real. Terren—other Terren—pulled Tempest closer to other Kiira and gave her a playful pout, trying very hard to look disappointed.

I didn't think he was capable of more than a flat stare.

The expression had the desired effect on other Kiira because a snort escaped her.

Jemma is right. That is such an unladylike noise.

Other Terren said, "I would have won if you had not cheated."

"I did not cheat," duplicate Kiira replied in mock offense. "I simply used your weakness to my advantage." She flashed him a brilliant smile.

Can I really be that cocky?

"Hmmm," duplicate Terren replied, "I am not the only one with weaknesses." A sly smile tipped his lips before he pulled her from her saddle into his lap. Starfire snorted with a couple of stamps and walked through her. Suddenly Kiira found herself not watching, but living the moment.

It was so real. The hammering of her heart, shallow breaths, the heat of Terren's body as he held her close, his soft breaths against her cheek as he kissed her jawline, and especially the dryness in her mouth as he neared her lips. Before she could untangle herself from the situation, Terren kissed her. Not a gentle peck on the lips, but like a man in love who wanted every part of her.

This is so real.

His lips were sweet, gentle, and lingering. She felt his love pouring from the intimate touch and her heart forgot rhythm. When he pulled back, the softest touch of his calloused thumb stroked her cheek.

Terren leaned his forehead against hers. "I love you, Kiira."

This is too real to be a vision.

The goddess whispered in her mind, 'The revelation awaits the appointed time ... though it lingers, wait for it; it will certainly come to pass and will not delay.'

This would be her reality? The intensity of her dormant relationship with Terren scared her. She had never felt this, whatever it was.

Before she could process what she experienced, the same brightness as before pierced her eyes, forcing her to squeeze them shut.

ADJUSTING to the dim light of a fire, Kiira twisted to see the flower-laden interior of her suite, and Jemma sleeping in the rocking chair next to the warming flames. Darkness still shrouded everything. She needed to speak with her father as soon as possible. Stepping toward the door, a glimpse of white caught her attention. Kiira looked down and gasped.

'The revelation awaits the appointed time. A gift, My Daughter.'

CHAPTER 29

APOLOGIES & EXPECTATIONS

L etting out a long, tired, frustrated breath, Terren raked a hand through his wet hair, creating chaotic spikes before attempting to scrub some of the sleep from his face. He muttered a few heartening words, tempting himself to stay awake long enough to make it back to the soft, comfortable mattress in his suite. He'd already dozed several times in the castle baths, the warm water soothing his aching muscles from the hours of constant movement.

Ten hours and all I find is a perfect trail that completely vanished. He huffed, banging a soft fist against the stone wall.

It had been nearly midnight after a full day searching before Kiira's trail went cold. What drove the princess to enter the Forest in the first place? When she ran off, he thought little of it, assuming she was going to lap the outer wall. It was one of the few things he really knew about the princess. She loved to run. Still—into the Forest? The woman was mad to go in there alone, at night, and so deep.

Hoping to give a good report to Herretus, Terren almost avoided going to the king's study to deliver his dismaying news. Purely out of respect, the king was not a man Terren wanted to disappoint. Still, honor demanded he go, and to his relief, a nightly patrol informed him the king retired some hours prior. At least now he could gain a clear head before meeting with Herretus. He just had to bear the knowledge of the frustrating news for a few unconscious hours.

Seriously, what was Kiira thinking?

This question drove him to find the answer. Their argument left both of them hurting. True, but to disappear? Kiira's reaction didn't seem to match the resilient spirit within her bones. It was only after Terren lost her trail that he noticed how far he ventured into the Forest Wilds. Then he worried.

Kamaria, to his annoyance, refused to help him in the search. She reasoned foolish people should not be helped out of foolish situations, her typical black-and-white philosophy. She wouldn't even hold a conversation to keep him company during his scouting because she thought so little of the princess. His Bear needed to learn more compassion.

The grandest sight in the two realms was finally seeing the door to his room, and he could almost hear the bed calling his name. He greeted the two guards standing attentively outside, each acknowledging him before he pushed past. Terren was glad he convinced Grayten to remove the guard detail constantly following him. It was nice being able to move about without a four-man shadow, but the postings outside his door still indicated how little Grayten trusted him.

Opening the door to a roaring fire, he immediately appreciated the warmth it gave.

I hope Lucen didn't stay up for me.

The thought vanished when he noticed the shadow of two feminine legs clad in trousers outlined by the snapping light. Terren found it interesting she chose to have her back to the entrance. He almost questioned how she entered the room without his guards knowing, but quickly dismissed the notion. Kiira lived in this castle her entire life. She was bound to know the servant passages well.

Shutting the door, he pretended not to notice his guest and made for the small table meant as a personal eating space. Terren methodically removed the knives and sword he carried as protection. He wasn't ready to speak to Kiira yet, needing a moment to not let his frustration bubble to anger. He spent so long looking for her and now here she was in his rooms, unharmed. Why did she seem to bring out the worst in him?

The rustle of fabric preceded quiet steps as she came up behind him. He turned. Leaning against the table and crossing his arms, Terren said, "I have heard of people running off before their wedding due to nerves. Never did I think it would happen to me. You really hate the idea of marrying me that much?" He tried to keep his words light, but the lack of sleep blurred the barriers he usually kept.

Kiira anchored an elbow to the tall chair nearby. "I do not hate you,

Terren. I told you as much days ago, and I left because I needed some time alone to think."

"Time alone I can understand, but three leagues into the Forest?"

"You were looking for me?" She asked, tilting her head. The slight movement made her honey curls glow just a little more golden in the dim light.

Terren scoffed. "Believe it or not, Kiira, I care what happens to you as my betrothed. I am not without feeling as you seem to think. Your safety will soon be my responsibility and I respect your father far too much to not at least help."

She winced, eyes darting away because of the words. Concentrating on a dark corner of the room, she said, "I am sorry you went to such lengths to find me. I have no desire to be a burden to you. I was safe. The goddess took me to her sanctuary and cared for me."

Terren straightened. "You met the goddess?" He forced relaxation into his muscles upon noticing his open eagerness.

"Yes, and she is even more beautiful than the paintings depict. An artist could never really do her justice." Kiira smiled, but her expression was more of an odd mixture of worry and awe.

The wonder on her face was far too genuine for her to be lying, Terren decided. Kiira wouldn't look at him, waiting for permission to continue. Finally, in a much softer tone, he said, "Your family is worried about you. Do they know you have returned?"

"No, I have not been to see them. I was going to see my father when something spurred me to speak with you first," Kiira replied.

"That was foolish," he chided. "You could not have known when I was returning. Your father needs to know you are well."

"I knew I would not have to wait for a great length of time and have been here only a few minutes; long enough to stoke your fire. I needed to speak with you first." The insistence in her voice reminded Terren how stubborn his bride-to-be was.

Terren sighed and rubbed a hand over his face before pushing his hair back. Crossing his arms, he nodded to the princess. "Alright, what did you want to talk about?"

Kiira let out a shaky breath and rubbed the back of her neck. She still wouldn't look at him and he wondered what had her so on edge. She was by no means timorous and the nervousness was completely out of place from her earlier assertiveness. After a deep breath, she finally said, "I came to apologize. Since learning of the engagement, I have acted dishonorably toward Leo, toward my father, and most especially toward you. I have come seeking your forgiveness and to learn if it is not too late to still marry."

Terren roamed her downcast features for several minutes. She was sincere, but what really dug at his thoughts was why she was saying these words now. Could he truly forgive her? His biting anger toward her the night before stemmed from deep-seated resentment. He admitted to this fault while scouting the Forest. His issues didn't give him permission to be unkind, which meant it didn't give him permission to not accept her sincere apology. It was more than his mother had ever done. Whatever happened at the Springs definitely impacted the princess.

Despite this truth floating through his mind, he still found it difficult saying what was needed. The longer he delayed, the more agitated Kiira became. At last, she closed her eyes and released a defeated breath.

With a sad smile she said, "There is no blame, Terren, I hope with time I can mend what I broke." She started for the door.

"Kiira, wait."

She paused, her posture hopeful, but didn't turn. Terren moved to block her exit and continued, "I accept your apology, and as for being wed, I don't think either of us have a choice in the matter."

Relief flooded her eyes, and she instantly relaxed. For the first time since meeting him a week ago, she gave him what he thought was a genuine smile. "True, but that's not really what I meant."

Terren raised a single brow.

"I know we must marry, but I am not as resentful of the arrangement. Honestly, it will take me some time to ... let go, but I am hoping you still find me worthy enough to work at having a genuine relationship beyond the mere demands of diplomacy." Giving him a tentative smile, she continued, "I was hoping we could go into this without bitterness."

Wow!

Terren nodded slowly. "I can agree to that." He couldn't offer a smile, but some weariness lifted from his shoulders and he felt a measure of hope for the first time since leaving Klynotia.

Kiira's eyes brightened briefly before her eyes found sudden interest in a dark corner. She seemed even more uncomfortable than before. "This may be odd to talk about beforehand, but I want you to know that I will consummate the marriage, but afterwards I—"

"Kiira, stop right there," Terren said, holding up his hands. "I am too exhausted to properly discuss what you were about to say. We can address all of it later, during the Lundemai."

Her relief was palatable. "Thank you."

Terren nodded, finding he actually agreed with her hesitation. His years as a priest made it almost as uncomfortable a topic for him as it seemed to be for her. A few more awkward seconds passed. When Kiira didn't move or say anything else, he asked, "Was there something else? Not to be rude, but I would really like to sleep."

"Yes, I suppose the ceremony is near..." she trailed off and remained standing where she was.

"Kiira?"

"If we are going to move forward, as friends, I think there should be complete honesty between us. That being said, I need to tell you something else important."

"Alright." Terren gestured for her to continue. He appreciated her desire for openness between them, but a pinprick of trouble came to mind. He agreed with having a foundation of honesty, but he knew telling Kiira about his connection to a Shade Beast right now would not end well. His heart beat a little faster, knowing he would, in a way, be lying by not being forthcoming. However, the two of them were standing on fragile ground and he was worried about being the one to disturb it.

Instead, he watched as Kiira cuffed the sleeve on her left arm and held her wrist out palm up. There, just below her palm, was the Mark of the Mage. She snapped and an orange-red flameless lily bloomed in her palm and the mark glowed a pale green. Now, he could see the symbol perfectly; a palm-sized circle with a coin-sized hole in the center. Odd symbols and swirling lines decorated the inside. From his time in the Magician's Cloister, he knew it was a compacted phrase from within the text of the gods. The script on Kiira's wrist read *Individual of One*. When not channeling magic, the mark looked like an odd discoloration on the skin.

Terren wasn't surprised she was a magic wielder. He and Kamaria noticed it early on, but he was surprised she revealed it to him so soon. Kiira didn't openly reveal her gifting. In fact, if his Bear said nothing or if she never touched him, he would have never known.

"I thought it only fair I tell you, rather than you finding out. You don't seem surprised." Kiira released the casting, and the space between them darkened.

Terren shrugged. "I had my suspicions, but assumed you would tell me when you were ready."

"You're not upset? I figured since..."

"Since Grayten is a magician hating monster who kills gifted ruthlessly that I would be the same?" Terren asked, trying to keep the bitterness from his voice. He glared at a spot past Kiira's shoulder. If there was one thing he hated most of all, it was being compared to Grayten.

"No, you are not anything like him," she waved her hand dismissively, seeming not to notice the malice in his voice, "but I did not expect you to be amicable toward the idea."

Her brazen honesty about his character softened him. "I actually have many friends who are magicians and I have a great respect for the art. What level are you?"

"Oh, good," Kiira said, relieved. "I am a Prime Mage."

"That does surprise me."

Kiira smiled. "Thank you for your time, and your understanding. Sleep well, I will see at the wedding."

She gave him a mischievous smirk, then disappeared in a cloud of leaf green smoke.

UNION

Lifting the coronet from his brow, Terren turned the etched metal band over in his hands, attempting to find a way of relieving the vice it created. A useless endeavor.

Replacing the royal adornment, he adjusted the sleeve of his white silk tunic, straightening the pristine material. The gleam of his boot caught his eye, and he twisted his heel to check again if any scuffs marred the well-shined surface. The cursory check led Terren to spot a white thread clinging to his black dress trousers. Bending to pluck the rogue strand seemed to tighten the collar of his tunic, making his neck feel as if stood in the stocks, and he couldn't help but run his fingers under the edge, lifting the material from his skin.

"Your Highness, you look fine," Lucen said.

He turned to see the manservant making great strains to contain a grin. Draped over his arm was the Klynotian royal mantle. Terren grimaced, knowing he would have to wear the wretchedly obnoxious velvet cape for the entire ceremony. The sapphire blue cloak stitched with the kingdom's standard felt more like an eyesore and a target upon his back than a mark of royalty. As much as he loved his kingdom, he didn't take pride in wearing it. To Terren, it represented generations of murderous men—his ancestors. He might seriously consider designing a new familial crest once he became king. Turning his back to Lucen, Terren took a deep breath and waited for the heavy mantle to rest upon his shoulders. "I have never been this out of sorts, Lucen. I shouldn't be, especially for a marriage that is nothing more than a political move by Grayten."

"While that is true, it is still your wedding. There is a permanent change happening in your life. It stands to reason you should be nervous," Lucen replied, arranging the mantle on Terren's shoulders.

"I have had many permanent changes in my life and none of them have ever caused me to feel this way."

"Maybe you have more feelings for the princess than you are willing to admit?"

Terren huffed and rolled his shoulders, adjusting the weighty cloak. The only thing he would admit is appreciating Kiira's efforts to apologize. Taking several meditative breaths, he recited the prayers of Ny to calm his mind.

Be strong, be courageous, all you that hope in Ny.

Terren relaxed as the words Naanel used to say each morning before meditation came to him. They were words he needed to hear at the time, and he was glad they were so ingrained in his memory. The simple phrase was a reminder he could handle any situation, any predicament.

Clanging bells jolted him from his moment of reverence and Terren opened his eyes to take one last look at, for the last time, a space of his own. Everything of his would become hers; theirs. That thought alone sent a pain through his sternum. What was it about sharing a life with the princess he found so difficult to accept? He just had to ignore it.

Be strong, be courageous.

He took a fortifying breath. Terren nodded to Lucen before striding confidently from the room.

Entering the grand hall from a side door, he avoided the multiple stares roaming over his skin and took his place on the steps of the dais. The Master Priest gave him an encouraging smile. Terren acknowledged the holy man before looking for his sister. He spotted Sairah whispering to her lady's maid, standing along the aisle about three people back from the front. She was wearing a lovely sapphire blue matching the mantle he wore. If only he felt as grand in the color as she looked. Sairah must have been sensitive to his gaze, because she turned to look at him. She studied his attire for only a moment before a rich smile washed over her face, accompanied by an affectionately wicked gleam. She would poke fun at him later, he knew, but he returned her smile with a small one of his own. Terren would endure whatever teasing she gave, thankful for each little moment bringing them closer to a healed sibling bond.

On the opposite side of the aisle from his sister, an older woman did her best to wrangle a Wolfcat kitten. He'd seen Skehtra following Kiira around the castle, the picture of calm. Today, however, the silver furred hellion refused to remain still. Terren cleared his throat to keep from smiling and lifted his eyes to give attention to the grand hall.

For a kingdom as rich as Lorea and for a princess as adored as Kiira, the décor was fitting. Crisp white silk highlighted the dark stained wood of the large space, the grand hall undergoing a drastic change since he first saw it upon his arrival. Every detail had been considered, down to the pristine white flowers with glittering gold centers crowding every space people were not already occupying. It was like standing in a sea of clouds at sunset; the sensation intensified by the sun crawling toward night. Sunbeams pierced the colored glass, lighting up the white silk with vibrant reds, pinks, yellows, oranges, and minute hints of blue, giving the impression of the sun setting within the Grand Hall and not outside.

Above the heads of the people, standing on a tight balcony on either side of the massive main doors, eight horn players stood poised with long gilded brass trumpets jutting out over the assembly, ready to play heralding notes at a moment's notice. The highly polished metal glittered from the hundreds of candles illuminating the room.

Those in attendance spared no expense with their own clothes, the room full of opulent attire. Variants of green, blue, red, yellow, brown, black, orange, and violet all stumbled over one another, vying for attention. The handful of Klynotian noble families in attendance were all dressed in the same blue as the mantle, weighing his shoulders. The commonality was too perfect for it to not have been an order from Grayten. Seeing others dressed similarly made Terren feel less conspicuous.

He caught Grayten's eye. The king was scowling at him and mouthing something Terren couldn't quite make sense of when a dazzling melody filled the Hall, stopping whatever useless remark Grayten was trying to convey.

In unison, every guest turned to see the massive doors swing open to reveal the princess. Kiira clung to her father and brother as her eyes darted about the room before she locked her gaze to his. The three royals stepped into the full light, and the entire room let out a collective gasp. Terren might have been one of them. Stunning stuck to the forefront of his mind, obstructing any other potential words to describe Kiira. He thought she looked exquisite the first night of the Yielding Festival, but today far exceeded anything he'd ever seen her wear.

The white shimmering silk of her bridal gown clung to her and brushed the ground before trailing a few feet. The gauze and silk shifted as Kiira walked toward him. Sheer sapphire fabric layered the back two-thirds of the skirt and came to a point at her waist. An ornate hand-width belt glittering with white pearls, blue glass beads, and silver thread separated the skirt from the simple white silk bodice. The wide neckline stitched similar as the belt enhanced the delicate curves of her collarbone and gracefully transitioned to white sleeves fitted to the elbow before widening into bells of the same sheer blue material layering the skirt. The cost must have been outrageous. People would talk of this dress for years, and Terren wouldn't be surprised if replicas were attempted.

A single strand of miniature pearls fit snug against her throat, weighted in place by a teardrop sapphire resting perfectly in the hollow of her neck. Matching earrings dropped from her ears, dancing as she walked. Most of her loose, voluminous curls had been pinned to the side before draping over her left shoulder. Thin strands of sapphire, silver, and gold wire twisted through her vibrant honey hair, adding a whimsical touch to the refined wedding outfit. A simple silver circlet shaped to mimic the rolling waves of the sea marked her place as royalty.

As beautiful as she looked in the dress, what really made Kiira exquisite was her smile. It wasn't forced. She was genuinely smiling—at him. His bride. Terren felt his heart stutter as his stomach decided to lodge in his throat.

As she moved closer, he noticed subtle nervousness beneath her mask of joy, and hidden beneath the brightness of her emerald eyes was a glimmer of hope.

Hope.

He didn't know how much of it existed, didn't know where it came from, and he didn't care. This was a fresh path, and it was what this rough relationship needed for them to not be miserable. He would take any measure of hope that existed. Nervousness flooded his system as Kiira mounted the steps of the dais.

This was surreal. This was actually happening.

Kiira flashed him a brilliant smile as if to say she had successfully made it to him without tripping. He bit back a grin. How had he not noticed this side of her personality before?

Because I didn't want to see it.

A cough from somewhere reminded him they were not alone and Terren forced his attention to her bright eyes and, annoyingly, he felt his heart trip. No matter how beautiful she was, he should not have feelings for a woman he reconciled with such a short time ago. Yet something in him changed; a new gravitation toward Kiira.

Hope.

Giving her father one last hug and her brother a kiss on the cheek, Kiira let go of Herretus' arm and slid her hand into Terren's for assistance up the remaining steps. Her grip was tight, and Terren could feel her nervous energy through the fabric. The trumpets ended their fanfare as he and Kiira faced the Master Priest of the Nyan Temple in Lorea.

The priest wasted no time.

"My Lords and Ladies, we are gathered here in the sight of the gods to join together this man and woman. There is no cause for absolution by the law of the gods we faithfully serve or by the law of the realm." The priest's words, in a rich, deep timbre, settled with authority as they bounced around the wood paneled hall. Fixating on Terren and Kiira, he continued, "If either of you know of any impediments as to why you may not be joined, then confess it now, lest the wrath of the gods be upon you." When neither of them spoke, a jolly grin broke the priest's stern demeanor. "Excellent. Terren take Kiira's hands, right with right, and left with left."

He did as the priest instructed and held Kiira's gaze. A beat of silence passed before the priest continued.

"With your clasped hands you have formed a symbol of infinity. This link and the placement between you is purposeful, symbolizing the never ending commitment you must have to each other and to the gods."

Kiira's grasp tightened. She was stronger than he imagined.

The Priest said, "Terren, of the royal line of Mythieres, will you have this woman to be your wife, to live together under the divine ordinances? Will you love her, serve her, honor and keep her, in all circumstances; and forsaking all others keep only her, so long as you both live?"

He gave Kiira a reassuring smile. "I will."

The priest then turned to her to ask the same. Before replying, she held his gaze for a drawn second and said, "I will."

The priest took a cord of three colored ribbons. One white, representing the gods, one sapphire blue for Klynotia, and one pine green for Lorea. The Master Priest wrapped the cord twice around their hands before knotting the strands.

Focusing solely on Kiira, Terren repeated the words to bind himself to the woman before him permanently. "I, Terren, take you Kiira, to be mine, to have and to hold through trial and joy, to love and cherish, till death takes us, by the gods ordinances." As he spoke, her breath shortened. Could she tell the sincerity of his words? Was it fear? Or hope? Her eyes smiled at him.

When Kiira repeated her vow, Terren could have sworn she stressed the word love, but it was so fleeting he could not be sure.

While untying their hands the Priest said, "To proclaim to the world the two of you are bound, rings will be given and received. Please pass them to me."

Terren pulled his from a hidden pocket and a sharp breath from Grayten made him smirk inwardly. He was sure to receive a verbal lashing from the king later for the small circular object. As far as Grayten was aware, the ring, now in the officiate's hands, had been lost nearly two decades ago.

After taking his and Kiira's rings, the High Priest raised his chubby hands above his head and loudly proclaimed, "Bless these rings, O merciful and loving gods, Ny, Windrah, and Apelgo. Let those who wear them, given and received, be ever faithful to one another and to you. With authority, divinely given to me, I declare these rings shall not depart their hands unless death takes them. A symbol these shall be of the promise made here today."

Terren took the ring, and it now felt sticky. Magic. Would his connection to Kamaria void the casting placed on the ring? It was something he would mull over later. The priest cleared his throat, waiting for him to continue. Terren slipped the band onto Kiira's first finger of her right hand, saying, "With this ring, I am yours. I will honor you. Everything I have, I give to you. Let it be known among men and among the gods."

Kiira's eyes widened, and she took in a sharp breath; staring at the ring curiously before somewhat fumbling to do the same for him. Grasping his right hand, a gentle smile tugged at her lips when she noticed his trembling fingers. Terren cleared his throat and forced stillness into his limbs. She repeated the words while sliding the ring onto his finger. A tingle shot up his arm and warmth settled in his chest. The shock must have registered on his face, because he noticed Kiira's smile grow even bigger. Whatever magic the priest used was stronger than the immunity he had as a Shadow Walker. The casting had to be nothing less than the pure magic of the gods.

The priest directed them to kneel, finishing the ceremony in prayer. Placing his overly warm hands on their heads, he said, "Let us give thanks to the gods! O Creator Ny, Loving Windrah, and Emissary Apelgo, givers of grace and life; bestow your blessing upon this man and woman, your servants. May they perform all vowed and made known to others today. This pair, wondrous gods, whom you have joined, let no man separate. They have given their pledge, therefore, I Gresher, Master Priest, divinely appointed by the gods, pronounce you man and wife. In the names of Ny, Windrah, and Apelgo." Smiling, the priest said, "Stand, prince, and kiss your bride!"

Helping Kiira, his bride, his wife, to her feet and before losing his courage, Terren wrapped his left arm around her, trapping her right hand against his chest, and planted his lips firmly on hers. This close, he could feel her heart beating as rapidly as his own. To his surprise, she threw her free arm around his neck and returned the kiss.

The crowd's gladsome roar deafened the hammering of blood in his ears. When Kiira giggled, her lips tightening into a smile under his own, he ended the kiss. Drinking in her bright green eyes, Terren smiled at her small bubbles of laughter.

They stood only a moment in front of everyone before Terren guided Kiira down the central aisle. The melodious trumpets marked their exit as white petals showered them and filled the room with a sweet scent. Covered, they left a trail of the petals in their wake as he guided Kiira to a small room set aside for them while guests exited to the garden.

Alone, he looked at Kiira, taking in the moment. Then it truly hit him.

Gods above, I'm married!

MAN & WIFE

Standing in the quiet space, Kiira bit her lip, taking in Terren's regal outfit. He was handsome in his tunic, trousers, doublet, and varnished boots. The sapphire mantle made him look dignified and the burnished coronet stood out against his thick, dark auburn hair. Seeing Terren like this gave him an air of authority he usually suppressed. Her heart fluttered. For the first time since meeting the prince, Kiira actually noticed the details of his features.

Terren had naturally darker skin that she imagined bronzed with sun. He had a strong square jaw, definitely from Grayten, but he inherited the eyes of his mother. With the blood of the Isokanii in his veins, Terren's eyes were a striking pale grey-blue that faded to nearly white toward the iris. Faint lines of darker deep-ocean blue and sea glass green streaked intermittently from the outer edge. The mottled coloring of snow-capped mountains contained within his eyes.

"Kiira?"

"Hmmm?"

"You have been staring at me for several minutes," Terren said.

Kiira blushed and turned toward the flames. "Oh, I apologize." Playing with the newly placed ring on her finger, she twisted it and experimentally tried to remove the band, but it was useless. The magic embedded in the ring was powerful and, as the priest said, would never leave her hand. At least she would never have to worry about losing such an exquisite ring; she had not expected so much from Terren. Thin silver and gold wires wove around a dark blue opal holding a piece of the night sky. It was not what she ever pictured for a ring, but it was perfect.

"Kiira, I know this is all overwhelming, but are you alright? You do not seem to be yourself."

She laughed. "I am fine, really." She waved his question away. "This ring is stunning. I absolutely love the design; it must have cost a fortune. I did not expect..."

"It cost me nothing. It was my mother's wedding ring," he said with a sad smile. "I hope you do not mind."

"Oh, not at all, I am flattered. The ring I gave you does not compare."

"It is simple, I like simple," he said. "I was wondering what message has been engraved into it."

Kiira reached out a hand toward the slow burning fire, letting the heat seep into her fingers before settling into a nearby chair. "The inscription is a promise; written in the dead language of magicians from before the war. I have a copy of an old reference book and have always appreciated the design of the script itself, but found it useful this time as well."

"What does it say?"

Kiira studied the flames, hesitant to tell Terren what she engraved. It had been difficult for her to willingly put the message on the band. She had stared at the smooth polished metal for hours, wanting to be absolutely sure of her decision, otherwise she would only cheat herself and Terren even more so. Ultimately, she stood firm in her belief of the words and the vision given to her by the goddess. "I'll tell you, but know that not much has changed since we spoke earlier. I am still heartbroken over Leo."

Terren nodded.

"I thought long and hard about what I wanted to engrave on the band and, when I did, I performed a Resolute casting, making the promise secure, for a magician must speak the truth that is in the heart."

That caught Terren's attention. "Kiira—"

She held up a hand. "No, Terren, I did it intentionally. The script says, 'My Love Will Never Be Static'. It is a promise to you, and to me, that I will not compare you to my love of the past, but will only pursue the love that will be unique to us, that I choose you."

He frowned at the band in thought, twisting it as he tried to piece together his words. Hesitantly, he asked, "You think you could love me, despite the circumstances?"

It was not the question she had expected. Did she also hear a note of hope? Quietly, she replied, "Yes, one day."

He nodded to acknowledge her answer, but took a moment to process her reply. "I do not understand. Why the sudden change?"

She tipped the corner of her lips. "Let's just say the goddess and I had a very eye-opening heart to heart."

"Will you tell me?"

Kiira looked at the ceiling and bit her lip. "Perhaps in the future."

Terren twisted the ring, studying the flowing script. "Thank you. It was not—"

"It was; because I did not want to resign myself to a loveless marriage, and neither should you," she said.

Three rapid taps disturbed the conversation. Kiira sighed, looking toward the source of the disturbing noise.

Oh, gods, here we go; time to be drowned in congratulations.

It's not that she disliked the well-wishes or the number of people. For the occasion, it was appropriate. Her hesitation was more about how dry her throat would be by the end of the night from constantly speaking. A selfish reason not to brave leaving the room.

When the knock came again, this time more forcefully, Kiira glanced over at Terren and he nodded his agreement before giving permission to enter. She was surprised to see Liem, expecting another servant or even Jemma.

Before she could ask why he came, Liem teased, "I am surprised to not find you two love birds snuggling on the couch ogling over each other."

"Like how you and Ariella make eyes at each other when you think no one is looking?" Kiira retorted.

He gaped at her briefly and then sputtered, "How do you know about that?!" Clearing his throat, he calmed. "Besides, I have been courting her for a time. I deserve a few stolen glances."

"Stolen? Liem, you are terrible at hiding things, and at least if we were ogling over each other, we're married. What's your excuse?" Kiira held back a laugh. Liem's glare was comical.

Before he could answer, Terren interrupted. "As entertaining as your sibling squabbles are, we should not keep guests waiting."

Liem's affectionate glare turned sour as he looked at Terren. While she had come to a compromise with her new husband, her brother still had a long way to go.

This will require a long talking to, knowing Liem.

Kiira was relieved to see that Terren's expression remained placid, patiently waiting, and she wished she could fix the issues between them now.

"Yes, I suppose we should not," Liem spat.

Kiira jumped in before words could turn ugly. "Why did you come? Why not send one of the servants?" It was a pathetic attempt to soften the tension in the room.

Liem relaxed some and sheepishly said, "I wanted to see you, since..." He glanced away, focusing on where the wall met the floor.

Kiira smiled as she scanned his face. Her brother would never say what he was really feeling for fear of appearing weak, which was ridiculous, but she would respect his silence. Gracefully, she crossed the room and wrapped Liem in a hug. He was recovering his muscle nicely after the Shade Demon attack. His crushing hug only abated some after she let out a faint squeak, but he was still reluctant to release her. Kiira whispered, "You act tough Liem, but your insides are mush. I love you and will miss you too."

Liem responded with a huff that tickled her ear.

Stepping away and turning to Terren, she asked, "Shall we go present ourselves as man and wife?"

Terren gave her a simple smile. "We shall."

THEY STEPPED into view and the cheering crowd verged on the side of riotous as hundreds of people packed the garden in celebration of the marriage. White silk linens with smatterings of gold droplets hung between the trees, sparkling in the light of candles and small fires. Each gentle breeze rustled the fabric, creating an ethereal feeling. Strings of candles in glass jars crisscrossed over the white and gray polished stone floor, giving a warm glow to the bright full moon shining down. Soft, lively music played from the stringed quartet stationed on the far end of the rectangular space, the cheerful notes sinking into her bones and she felt lighter.

Terren led her to the place of honor and declared the wedding feast officially begun. Servants poured from the shadows, filling drinks or platters of food. Kiira took a grateful sip from her goblet. The heavily spiced wine coated her tongue with the taste of rich earth before turning sweet as honey; the start to a magnificent meal. Her nerves for the ceremony had stifled any desire to eat today and with the main excitement over, hunger clawed at her stomach.

Cook Master Danel and the entire staff had outdone themselves in the preparation. Plates of fish and forest game were presented for her to choose at preference; and a number of amalgamate dishes using traditional cooking techniques from Klynotia and Lorea to celebrate the uniting of the kingdoms. Since seafood was her favorite, and Danel's specialty, Kiira leaned toward selecting those dishes, but did make a few choices that favored Klynotian cooking.

Her first selection was a small plate of cucumber slices topped with chive and lemon whipped crab salad. The soup course was a delectable venison simmered in a coconut cream sauce instead of the traditional bone broth. It was so good, Kiira attempted to swipe some of Liem's share. Luckily she failed, otherwise she wouldn't have been able to stomach the delectable main course of lemon, pepper, and basil scallops wrapped in strips of tender quail served on a bed of mixed chilies and mango.

At first, the pairing seemed odd, but at first bite, Kiira fell in love with the combination and would be sure to request the meal whenever possible. After the scallops, a chilled stuffed artichoke stood in its place. The garden grown vegetable, roasted to perfection, pulled apart easily, the herbed bread and goat cheese stuffing clinging to the leaves. She was so full that looking at the salad nearly made her sick, but the first bite was all it took to convince her that a dish this heavenly should be devoured. By the end, her stomach protested the amount of food she had eaten, as did her dress.

Conversations ebbed and flowed. Despite her earlier reservations toward this evening, Kiira enjoyed each second. When dessert came into her line of vision, she vowed to make room for the special sweet, though her belly cramped thinking about it. The intricate creation set before her was almost too beautiful to eat. Rich chocolate, molded into the shape of an oyster shell, was arranged to reveal a luminescent 'pearl' inside. It seemed criminal to destroy such a labor intensive creation. Did Danel really have his crew make hundreds of these? Looking around, she saw that only she and Terren had the honor of eating such a special creation. Still, it took several minutes for her to decide that taking the first bite would be worth it.

The edible oyster was the highlight of the wedding feast. Breaking open 'the pearl', the fresh white cake easily split and a tart raspberry filling spread over the sweet chocolate. She didn't stop the moan escaping her throat.

The sound caused Terren to look at her. She grinned sheepishly at the suppressed humor in his eyes, and color flooded her cheeks. He gave the barest hint of a smile and said, "I completely agree."

Kiira finished her meal with the last sip of her third glass of wedding wine, letting the pleasant warmth it gave hum in her limbs. She pressed her chilled fingers to her face, attempting to cool her cheeks. Her head spun pleasantly as she watched the twirling couples on the dance floor. Colors blended and faded as ladies' gowns whirled and men leapt through complicated twists and turns. Soon, the frivolity was too much to simply watch. Kiira wanted to dance!

Terren must have sensed the change, for he squeezed her hand, gaining her attention. "I would like to dance with my wife, will she do me the honor?"

Kiira nodded, eagerly gliding beside him to the dance floor just as the musicians ended a lively tune. Other couples parted to allow them the center, and Terren readied the opening position of a fast-paced dance. The musicians started without hesitation. Bowing his left foot forward, she replied with a deep curtsy before the soft notes of a flute whispered through the breeze. Holding his arm vertical and palm flat, Kiira placed her right palm on his and they turned six steps before switching directions. Stepping away from one another in a half-circle, they came back together before spinning a complete turn. Terren lifted Kiira by the waist to place her at his side for the next sequence of the dance. Encircling each other's waist, they took larking steps in a circle before ending with two long strides in a straight line. As each new instrument added to the melody, the tempo increased to a frenzied pace. By the start of the fourth repetition of steps, the entire ensemble was active in attributing to the feverish beat. Terren moved with confidence through it all.

Kiira smiled at him when she heard a small laugh escape. The quickness of the dance let them move as one. It was thrilling!

The music ended.

A slight breeze blossomed chills across her shoulders. Kiira glanced at her hands, still clinging to Terren's waist, her grip tighter than necessary.

How long have we been standing like this?

Her awareness expanded to hear the crowd cheering for a kiss. Gazing at Terren, she saw subtle curiosity and could almost hear the silent question whispered. It was her decision. At the Yielding Festival, he refrained from kissing her so openly and she definitely had not wanted him to. Now? They were married and to deny him, especially on this day, seemed cruel.

Her heart tumbled in an off rhythm and she knew if she agreed, this would not be like the kiss at the ceremony; one performed out of the necessity of the moment. This was more.

Would it be leading him down a path that I am not fully ready to walk?

They had been standing still for so long that anticipation silenced the crowd. Seconds felt like minutes as indecision warred in her mind. She wanted to kiss him. This was her husband, after all, yet a small part of her still resisted. Terren's hands tenderly squeezed her waist, letting her know he wouldn't pressure her and the reassurance made her heart sink. Why though? She tried to imagine how it would all play out, the feel of his lips on hers, the exultation in her heart. But when she looked into his face, it was Leo that she saw; Leo she still thirsted for.

Yet, I promised that my love would never be static. Is this the first step to mending my broken heart?

It seemed like a logical explanation, but Kiira could not in good conscience bend to the crowd's expectations, not when her mind and heart were focused on another.

To compromise, she tiptoed and kissed his cheek. The crowd's disappointment was palatable, but this was her day, not theirs. Understanding flashed in Terren's eyes, and he smiled at her. He stepped away, awaiting the start of another dance. As the music began, Kiira reminded herself of the promise she engraved on his ring and upon her heart.

A JOURNEY BEGINS

Rolling to his side, Terren found the large bed devoid of the one person who should be there. Only the residuals of mussed bedding showed Kiira slept next to him; that and Skehtra curled on her pillow. He was surprised the little cub remained since she typically remained glued to her mistress like a second shadow. She purred loudly compared to the languid morning. It was what had awoken him. Terren reached over to scratch the silver fur ball, earning himself a lazy wink of violet eyes. For some reason Skehtra had taken to him, and if she was not with Kiira, the cub was near him. He was one of the few people she allowed to touch her.

He continued to scratch her ears while taking in the room. Muted blue light filtered through the window and he wondered where the princess, no, his wife, had wondered off to so early. Their wedding suite was on the west side of the castle and Terren silently thanked whoever had the foresight to put them here. A gentle throb behind his eyes reminded him of just how much he consumed last night.

Her cup was as overflowing as mine. How can she already be upright this morning?

Struggling to keep the pounding in his head from getting worse, Terren moved carefully to a sitting position, a groan escaping.

The morning air was already thick and wet, strange for the cooling season. He stretched stiff muscles, popping a few vertebrae in the process as he walked toward the sitting room; still no sign of Kiira. Terren attempted to talk with Kamaria, tell her good morning, but she seemed fixated on the practice of ignoring him since his search for Kiira in the Forest Wilds.

The soft twang of a bow came from the cracked doors of the balcony, where he found Kiira, and a small wave of relief washed over him.

You are overreacting, Terren. He rubbed his forehead. *I blame it on last night's drink.*

A part of him admitted he took the responsibility for her safety seriously. Terren glanced down at the ring on his finger and fiddled with it for a moment before slipping through the gap of the door. Without disturbing Kiira's practice, he leaned against the cool stone of the castle wall, just off-center enough to see some of her profile.

The never-halting rain of arrows toward an unseen target fascinated him. He could fire an arrow from a decent range with accuracy, but Kiira's smooth and flawless form was the work of a Master. She used a hip quiver, uncommon, but it allowed her to fire more rapidly and with more grace. Shifting his head a fraction, Terren looked through the baluster to see her target in the distance. Except for a few off-center arrows, which were probably starting shots, her clustering was perfect. Waiting until she released an arrow, he quietly said, "That target looks about ninety meters away, am I correct?"

Kiira whirled and had an arrow aimed at his heart with an amazing speed. Her skills with a bow were whispered amongst the soldiers, and he wanted to see for himself if her reflexes were worthy of such admiration. She did not disappoint. Since he expected her reaction, Terren remained casually leaned against the wall with his arms crossed, but he was lucky she didn't fire.

"Great gods, Terren, you scared me! How long have you been standing there?" She wrinkled her brow. "And how did I not notice you?" Kiira lowered her weapon.

"I have a way of going unnoticed," he replied, "and not long. I've only seen you fire a few arrows. So, am I correct?"

He repeated his question, and she confirmed the target was approximately the distance he thought. After hooking the bow across her chest, Kiira leaned stiff armed against the balustrade and they studied each other for several drawn seconds before he asked, "How is your head not hurting?"

She smirked. "Magic. I can clear the effects of alcohol but I also drank plenty of water last night."

"Lucky."

"I can do it for you as well."

Terren held a hand up. "No, I'll be fine as soon as I drink some water." He did not need to go into the specifics as to why her help would be fruitless. More specifically, he didn't want to lie to Kiira. It was bad enough he was stalling about being a Shadow Walker.

She nodded and then studied the stone wall several feet above him.

"What are you thinking about?"

"I was thinking about the Lundemai. We never got around to talking about it, since we," she paused, "since I wanted nothing to do with you."

Terren shook his head. "Kiira, we are both at fault."

"That may be, but you still made more of an effort than I did."

"I would not necessarily agree."

"Well, we can agree to disagree then," she said.

After a few moments of unsettled silence, Terren asked, "So, where were you thinking to travel for the Lundemai?"

There were so many options, and he was eager to hear her response. The sooner they came to a decision and left, the better. The longer they lingered, the more of a crutch would develop; hindering their relationship and defeating the whole point of a Lundemai. A tradition established before the Mage War, it forced arranged couples to learn how to live with one another away from family, friends, and familiarity. Everyone participated in some manner, even if it wasn't for a full year. Terren hoped she would be inclined to hide away, but based on what he knew of Kiira, she was adventurous and appreciated new experiences, so he put the last thought from his mind. She would no more hide than he.

His headache increased. Traveling would mean they would likely encounter friends and possibly enemies from his past. Plus, he would also have to clue her in on the multiple identities created over the years. He rubbed his temples to ease the tension gathering behind his eyes.

He was making a mental list of some less-than-desirable places when Kiira asked, "Truly, you wish to know my thoughts?"

Glancing her way, he said, "This Lundemai is not just for me, why would you think I not care?"

Biting her lip, she replied, "I was hoping you would agree to show me the places you supposedly visited during your years of travel."

He gave her a wry smile. "I am not surprised, although that is exactly what I was hoping you would not say." A cloud covered her previously smiling face, and she focused on her moving toes, probably coming up with a way to convince him to agree with her.

Curious of her reasoning, he asked, "Why?"

Her pleading eyes met his, and his heart ached at the sadness he saw in them.

"I have never been outside the borders of Lorea and I have always dreamed of visiting the places you are rumored to have been. My responsibilities here never allowed me more than a few weeks of reprieve and always within the borders to ensure that I could return quickly if needed."

Terren studied Kiira for several seconds. The sadness of being tied to the kingdom was evident in her voice. There was no question she loved Lorea and serving the people, but her sincerity and longing made him realize just how blessed he'd been to visit so many places. He would have to place his earlier qualms aside; she deserved to see the realms, and he was confident he could avoid any real danger.

Pushing off the wall, he moved to her side. Now that they weren't at odds, he found his body humming in pleasure at her nearness. When she wasn't being feisty, she was like bottled sunshine, though right now her demeanor was darkened by a raincloud of disappointment.

"Here is my suggestion then. We travel north to the Nyuten Temple and stay there for a while. You will love the library and I have not seen the priests in many years, they will house us for a time. We should not stay long or the cold season will hinder our travels. Afterwards, we can travel east, down the edge of the Glazefire Canyon, before crossing the bridge and making our way to the capital in the Shadow Desert. I would like to introduce you to my mother's family. They were made aware of my marriage, so meeting you will be important to them. On the return to Klynotia, we should make our way via a passenger ship that can carry the horses. It would be the fastest."

The final words had barely left his lips before Kiira flung her arms around him and squeaked with delight.

"Terren, do you really mean it?" Joy and eagerness bubbled out of her.

He smiled and slid his arm around her waist, saying, "Yes of course, on one condition."

She sobered.

"In many of the places I visited, I went by a different identity to keep myself safe, I only ask you do the same. If I give you an instruction, even if it seems odd, please do not question me. Anything I say is for our safety."

The sunshine returned.

"Oh, Terren! I will do anything if it means I get to travel!" She squeezed tighter. "I will find Jemma now to help me pack, so we can leave before first light." She kissed him on the cheek and then rushed out the door.

Terren placed a hand over the spot where her lips touched and gave a small chuckle at the exuberant contact. Kiira's joy left him feeling light and airy, but as the door closed behind her, trepidation entered his heart. A small voice in the back of his mind told him he needed to be hyperaware of his surroundings on their travels, that something would happen beyond his control. He hoped it was nothing more than imagination getting the best of him.

Shaking his head to dispel the ill thoughts, Terren went inside to dress and gulp down several measures of water.

THE MORNING to midday passed quickly and Terren found himself buried beneath calculations as he worked out the exact details of the Lundemai journey.

The few hours of work got him halfway through writing down all the specifics. He accounted for distances between destinations, the time it would take to cross those distances, where they would stay, persons to contact, and how much money they would need. It was a boring task, but necessary. An ill-planned trip was not something he wished to experience again. Knowing what to expect would help keep him alert to anything out of place, but writing all of it down on paper was giving his hand a cramp.

The door to the suite burst open, and immediately his free hand went to his side. Liem's bulky form shadowed him, and the deepening scowl on his brother-in-law's face did not bode well for the ensuing conversation. Terren sighed and dropped his quill, stretching his fingers while leaning back in his seat. "What can I help you with, Liem?"

"I found out you and my sister are leaving in the morning to go traipsing across the two realms. I came to *inquire* if you even attempted to convince her otherwise. Do you have any idea how dangerous your journey could be?"

"I am aware of the danger, *definitely* more so than you, but Kiira wished to visit places outside of her home. How could I deny her? This is her Lundemai as much as it is mine," he replied, his voice edged, but polite.

Liem growled and leaned across the desk, getting as close as the hindering furniture would allow. The prince was close enough for Terren to notice the veins of emerald green spiking through his caramel eyes. He narrowed his eyes at Liem's obvious display of dominance.

"Simple, Terren, you say '*no*' and then walk away. I do it all the time."

Terren kept his face neutral. He could think of a few choice words, but kept silent. Kiira was not easy to simply say 'no' to, and he doubted Liem was as good at saying the word as he claimed.

At his lack of response, Liem continued, "Danger can change location and form in an instant. I have attempted and cannot convince Kiira to let go of this lunatic journey. Since you will not be swayed either, understand this; if anything happens to my sister—*anything* at all—I promise you will not live long enough to regret not being able to protect her."

I am done playing games.

Splaying his fingers on the desk, Terren rose out of the chair, forcing Liem to lean back. There was a brief flash of uncertainty in the prince's eyes. Terren was not even slightly intimidated by Liem and made sure it was evident in his reply. "First, I care for Kiira and will do everything to protect her. Second, and I repeat, I am well acquainted with the dangers this trip poses and am taking every precaution with the planning. I am accustomed to being aware of my surroundings and am always on alert. Third, be careful with your *threats*, Liem, should you ever decide to follow through on your promise, I will not go down without a fight."

They glared at each other for several tense seconds before Liem growled, "As long as we understand one another."

Without another word, he turned and stormed out of the room, slamming the door in his wake. Terren dropped his head into his hands and rubbed his eyes in an attempt to burn away the image of Liem's glare. The last thing he needed or wanted was to have Kiira's brother as an enemy. He knew the prince did not like him, but he did wonder why the man thought it necessary to make such a fierce threat over her safety.

Sighing, he resumed his calculations. One day, he would have to address the strained relationship between them for Kiira's sake, but right now, there were other things to worry about.

CHAPTER 33
AT AN END

Kiira barely registered Jemma's skittered jump as she banged open the doors to her suite, racing to her clothing cabinet. Bouncing on energetic toes, she surveyed the clean, pressed items neatly hung and stacked on the various shelves. Packing was the number one priority.

It's really happening!

Kiira mentally listed off the items she might need, tossing tunics, trousers, and boots into a haphazard pile on her bed, smushing the perfectly fluffed covers.

"My Lady, what in the realms—"

"Jemma, did you know in the plains there are hares twice the size of Liem's hands? They can grow so big because they're only hunted by the Veripoi, and such a small predator group has allowed the Lepu to thrive so much that the females can be selective breeders and the whole species has become stronger and more resilient."

"My Lady, what in the—"

Kiira tossed a comb from her dressing table to the growing mound occupying her bed.

"Oh, and did you also know the Kettletail Leopard hunts at night, relying completely on its perfect night vision? I hope I see one while we're near the cordillera. They hunt the Season Owls roosting in the lower part of the mountains."

"My Lady, please, I beg you to tell—"

"I suppose I ought to pack a few dresses as well. Traveling only with tunics and trousers is probably—oh and we're also going to visit the Shade Realm! Isn't that exciting?" She spared a glance over her shoulder. The room was beginning to look as if a storm had passed through. "I'll definitely—"

"Kiira!"

She stopped mid-step and stared; her maid rarely ever used her birth name, but that's not what had caused Kiira to pause. It was the distress in Jemma's voice. Red-rimmed eyes immediately overshadowed the frantic need to pack. She'd been so focused on the journey of their Lundemai, Kiira overlooked the slumped shoulders, trembling hands, and tear-stained cheeks of the woman who had been her confidant, friend, and faithful servant for decades.

Kiira rushed to Jemma to envelop her in a hug.

"Oh, Jemma! Do not cry for me, for I shall return before you know it and of course you will join me in Klynotia."

"It's not that," she burbled, though it was difficult to understand.

"Then what is it?"

"I've been here since you were just a babe, and since your mother died, well, I have—and you're just not a young girl anymore…" Jemma fell into choking sobs.

That was the chisel agin Kiira's joy. Seeing and especially hearing the emotions of the woman who had been there for her in the most difficult and the most joyous moments of her life made her own tears flow to reach past the haze of her previous excitement. Embracing each other, they melted to the floor, allowing the ebb and rise of joy and sorrow to wash over them; for the excitement of the newness to come, and for the end of a normal way of life.

Curled by the low fire, Kiira rested her head on Jemma's lap like she had as a child, savoring the gentle, loving touch of the woman who had been a constant in her life. Though she was not losing her maid, everything was going to be different.

Eventually, the tears dried and they could look at one another again without distress. Suddenly, their emotional outburst seemed unbelievably ridiculous; after all, change was the way of life. Uncontrollable giddiness melted into breathless laughter. This time joy trickled down their faces. As Kiira pushed herself up, a little breathless, she said, "My stomach and cheeks have not ached like this in so long. Jemma let us not forget to laugh in our new home!"

"Aye, my Lady, love and laughter will be the cure to all we face."

KIIRA SAT AT A SMALL, round wooden table under the shade of the Bosom Oak, glaring at her brother. The guaranteed destruction of their meal and the scowl from their father were the only thing keeping her and Liem from casting magic at one another. Kiira had been considering plastering leaves to her brother's face. His sour attitude and vehement disapproval of her Lundemai plans was burrowing under her skin. She had only taken a few bites of her lunch before Liem launched into a heated tirade at the stupidity of traveling outside of Lorean or Klynotian borders. Rendered mute at first, Kiira refused to let him win this argument, and now their staring contest had become a battle of wills.

"Kiira—" Liem started, but she sliced her hand through the air, cutting him off.

"Liem, when it is your Lundemai you can go anywhere and do anything you like. This was our decision and no matter what you say, I will not change my mind."

"Kiira is right," Herretus interjected. "I am as concerned about her safety as you are, but this is their decision. I trust her abilities and I trust Terren to protect her. You should do the same."

Ignoring their father's words, Liem slammed the table with a fist, rattling the metal plates and utensils.

"Kiira, this is madness! You know the Shade Demon attack had to have been the work of Zerrec. At least within the kingdom you have the protection of our gift and access to other magicians." Liem gestured wildly. "Out there you are an easy target. He could kill you!"

"Enough!"

Liem clamped his mouth shut. She rarely lost her temper with him, but he was taking it all too far. He focused on the rosebush near his knee, working his mouth while his face turned as red as the roses he eyed.

She lowered her tone. "You are acting as if I have not heard your concerns. The problem with your arguments, Liem, is we do not know for sure if Zerrec had a hand in the Demon attack. The realm has had peace for ten years, if it is him, why then the sudden appearance? There are too many questions and not enough answers, nor reasons to stop me from going."

Herretus said, "Again, she's right, Son. There is no real evidence of his return, no matter how suspicious the appearance of the Demon might have been."

Liem glared at her and then at their father. "That does not mean Kiira needs to go purposely traipsing into danger."

"I will keep in mind the potential danger, but nothing has changed," she softly said. "You know better than anyone. I have dreamed of seeing more, and this is my opportunity."

There was a sad acceptance on her father's face, but Liem's anger was not diminished. "If you will not be convinced, then I will go to Terren, he needs to know."

He stood to leave, but Kiira froze him with a snap of her fingers, a faint glow peeking out from beneath her wrist guard. Kiira squeezed her eyes and contorted her lips. Liem was not going to like what she was about to do, but she'd accept the consequences of her actions later. "Warn him if you wish, but I forbid you to tell him anything about Zerrec. You are not to give him specific reasons to change our plans. Remember, your anger is with me and not him. This is my decision. The embargo casting I placed will wear off in a few days." With a wave, she released him, avoiding Liem's eyes as he stormed away.

An uncomfortable silence settled around the table.

Herretus cleared his throat and said, "Do you really believe that was necessary?"

"Yes," she whispered. "He would have said something and I desperately want to travel outside of Lorea, Father. I will tell Terren but at the right time. He was already reluctant to take me to the places we are going; I do not wish to add fuel to the idea." She pressed her lips together. The decision between right and selfish had no contest in this situation.

"Kiira, your mother and I raised you to be honest. Do not think I haven't noticed you have been different these past weeks. This is a dangerous path you are walking. You and Terren are barely standing on solid ground. The possibility of encountering Zerrec should not be kept from him. I think he will be more understanding than you give him credit for."

"I promise I will tell him, but only after we have left," Kiira said.

Her father gave her a piercing gaze. There was so much knowing in his caramel eyes that she wanted to squirm.

"I will not contradict your decision, but you should know Terren is already aware of Zerrec. I spoke with him after the incident at the beach, so telling him of the present situation would only be half of a surprise to him."

She stiffened. "What! Why?"

"He needed to know why you reacted the way you did to his comments about Shade Demons."

"What did you tell him?" Kiira asked.

"What he needed to hear," Herretus said.

She pointed a fork at him. "That's not an answer, Father."

"What we spoke of is not important; just know he is not unaware." He covered the accusing utensil, forcing her to lower her hand.

Kiira bit her tongue to keep from saying something else. She really wanted to know more about this secret conversation, but when her father did not want to speak, nothing would convince him otherwise. Instead, she stabbed at the food on her plate.

CHAPTER 34

EAVESDROPPING

"So, they will be traveling to the High Temple. Interesting choice, it is not where I would go if it were our Lundemai," he mused. The destination did not entirely surprise him; the priests and priestess of the High Temple were known for their eagerness to learn and housed the largest library in existence. His Kiira loved to read, and unless the rules changed, the Nyuten welcomed any travelers who sought them. The entrance was difficult to locate, the priest believing some nonsense about the hardest paths being the most rewarding. If they were going to the temple, the prince must already know where the entrance was or had a connection to someone inside. It was a new and interesting bit of information.

Lounging in an overstuffed, high-backed chair, Zerrec sipped from a pewter mug half-full of pear and apple cider. He grimaced as lukewarm acidity from the apples coated his tongue. Ciders were always better cold. Resting the base of the metal mug in steepled fingers, he cast a thick layer of ice across the bottom and up the sides, avoiding the handle. Satisfied, he returned his attention to the conversation between his love and her family.

Ricker—to his credit—managed to hide his communication crystal near the royals while working in the garden, allowing Zerrec to listen with ease to the conversation. He couldn't see anything, but it was easy to imagine the scene. Closing his eyes, he focused on letting the soft rustle of leaves as they twirled on the occasional breeze transport him to the royal park, where the warble of songbirds and loud buzz of insects filled the air. He could almost feel the mild harvest sunshine warming his face. Zerrec would have loved to be there now. Memories of walking the gardens with Kiira floated behind his closed lids—perfect afternoons drifting by while he demonstrated foundations for her school of magic. Those years were some of the best in his existence. He truly missed the gardens, but mostly her, and her enthusiasm, curiosity, and joy.

"Out there you are an easy target. He could kill you!" Liem barked.

Zerrec choked into his goblet. The liquid surged down his throat with an icy vengeance, forcing him to beat his chest with a fist. Anger boiled in his stomach and he glared at his seeing crystal.

"Danger, from me? She has nothing to fear from me!" Zerrec's next words came out softer. "Empty headed fools, the lot of them. I have only ever loved Kiira and would not harm a hair upon her head. She's brilliant and an excellent magician. I would never be careless with something so beautiful belonging to me. I have already learned the cost of negligence; it's a price I will not pay again." A flash of Loralyn's beautiful smile tore at him.

"I will accept your anger at me, but as I have said, this is my decision … the embargo casting I just placed will wear off in a few days."

Kiira's voice interrupted his thoughts. A slow smile crept up his lips and Zerrec snorted derisively. "Liem should have known better than try and manipulate Kiira." A tingle of pleasure ran up his spine at her ruthlessness in forcing her brother to keep quiet. She had become bolder in his years of absence, and her newfound confidence was attractive.

After Liem stormed away, Zerrec cut the flow of magic into the crystal. Thanks to his eavesdropping, he knew the general route of the Lundemai and knowing it would greatly assist him in rescuing Kiira. This would be the easiest mission he ever planned, and by far the most rewarding.

Killing the pathetic prince would be a pleasurable experience, and he envisioned the fiercest pain imaginable on the Klynotian whelp. Manipulation of the body was his core magic and the prince would feel every ounce of his wrath for marrying Kiira before being sealed in the ground—permanently.

He needed Ricker to help him execute his plan. The other two idiot pirates-turned-mercenaries the man called friends had become more than useless. Zerrec left them to be sentries and cooks. Ricker was quiet, ruthless, and smart, the perfect combination for what he planned to accomplish. The mercenary would be here in a matter of days, having been given the order to return once the prince and princess left the citadel, and they could ambush the newlyweds before they entered the temple.

"No, wait. perhaps not before the temple," he mused, his frown deepening. The newlyweds would be on high alert after leaving the borders of Lorea. He didn't want to fight the skilled prince and Kiira's magic together. It was possible to win against them, but he worried Kiira could get injured. Plus, she may not want to be married to the prince, but that did not lessen the soft heart she held for everyone around her. She certainly wouldn't wish for his death despite her negative feelings toward the prince. He needed to separate them first. "Cooped up in the temple, my love will realize just how much she loathes the prince. Afterwards, when their bond is weakest, is when I will step in to rescue her."

Waiting was not ideal, but he was patient. If he could wait over a decade for this opportunity, he could wait a few more months, and it would not do to make a mistake because of his haste. He long ago learned the value of patience, and to distract him from rash ideas, turned his thoughts to the thankfulness Kiira would display once he set her free.

The prince will be dead, and then she can marry me.

CHAPTER 35
WIND POWER

A light breeze teased the hair on Terren's arm as it lay draped across his eyes to block the dim early light. He didn't want to wake, however; they needed to leave soon to make it to their first destination before nightfall. A few quick rubs across the bridge of his nose brought a modicum of wakefulness. Terren turned his gaze to find Kiira wrapped tightly in her saddle blanket, sandwiched between Starfire's flank and the dying fire currently sending pinpricks of glowing embers into the air to swirl momentarily before winking out like sleepy fireflies.

Kiira definitely ensured the cooler air would not be a bother, just as she promised. He shook his head at her stubbornness. She'd never been this far north, and the temperature was unexpected to her, even layered with wool. The previous night had been the first time she could not sleep due to the cold air, and he'd awoken to find her shivering, with deep shadows under her eyes nearly falling over from exhaustion. That morning had ushered in their first argument since the wedding.

Before then, a steadily growing friendship was the only thing between them. The solid months' worth of travel served them well, giving plenty of time for laughter, stories, and enjoying each other's presence. When Terren spoke, Kiira listened attentively, appreciating his opinion and respecting his thoughts. He gave the same courtesy to her and the change from their interactions in Lorea was dramatic. Terren definitely never expected so much from her so soon. Then, yesterday morning came a grievous reminder of the old Kiira when she made it incredibly clear she was not comfortable sleeping next to him, even for warmth. Terren hadn't thought such a small idea would upset her so much, the suggestion merely practical. His blunt observation of her stubbornness, however, ended communication, reducing easy conversations the day before to quipped replies.

Last night, Terren ventured to bring the subject up again, still thinking her hesitations ridiculous. After all, there was nothing romantic about his suggestion. He just wanted to make sure she stayed warm, except she took the comment out of context, demanding if he believed women to be weak, helpless, and subservient. Shocked by the horrid misrepresentation of his words, Terren spent several heated minutes clarifying his intent. Exhaustion from traveling finally pushed them to sleep separately again, still terse at one another.

Pushing to sit, Terren shook away the last vestiges of sleep. Looking at Kiira one more time, he sighed, hoping eventually she could one day let go of the man she left behind. He knew Leo was the underlying reason for her vehement refusal. She made a promise to him, and he believed her promise, but last night he pressed too much.

It has only been a month; he reminded himself. And I also scorned the idea of an unwanted spouse. Who am I to judge her emotional progress?

An especially bitter breeze sliced through the temporary shelter and his thoughts. Concerned, Terren moved so as not to disturb Kiira and hoisted himself to stand on Tempest's back to gain a more unobstructed view. If that slight icy breeze was any sign, he did not like what was coming their direction. To be sure, he needed to get closer. Settling on his mare's back, Terren leaned low, letting the warmth of her engaged muscles relax him.

He ventured just beyond sight of the small campfire, trying to get a clear view around a stand of trees. Standing on Tempest's back again, he was glad he spent the effort to train the mare. She was perfectly still despite the stiff heel of his riding boots digging into her spine.

Squinting, he analyzed the blue-gray grass of the Burning Plains and his worst thoughts were confirmed. A cooling season wind storm was pushing its way off the mountains. He'd considered a wind storm a possibility in their travels, but truly hoped to avoid the nasty piece of weather that ravaged the plains a few times a year. They were difficult to predict, even for the plains-dwellers.

Terren frowned. Another icy breeze stung his face, and he shivered. It was confirmation enough. He lowered onto Tempest and urged her back to camp. They didn't have the supplies on hand to wait out a wind storm. Kiira could probably do something with magic, except the casting would be outside of her core gift of Nature, and he didn't want to put that much strain on her. It would be better for them and the horses if they got to the nearest town as quickly as possible.

Terren thundered to the very edge of their camp and, in his haste, startled Kiira awake. Her wide eyes took in his wild approach and fierce expression, and the soldier in her immediately scanned their surroundings. He would have liked to be gentler, especially after last night, but lingering for niceties was not a luxury they had time for.

"We need to move, now."

Kirra stood and pulled her blankets tighter.

"Why?"

"A wind storm, coming off the mountains. We are not properly supplied to wait it out." He thanked the gods when Kiira didn't fight him and instead began packing without a second of hesitation. That was something, at least.

"How far is the nearest town?" She asked.

A slightly stronger frigid breeze cut through his clothing, and he noticed Kiira shiver violently. Terren prayed for the gods to give the horses strength for a hard ride today. Maybe they should ride together for warmth and switch horses to keep them from overtiring? No, they would move faster if they didn't have to stop to switch horses.

"Terren, you're scowling. Is everything okay?"

"Fellos is a day's easy ride up this river, so if we push the horses, we can make it before the wind storm is at its worst," he said. "Hopefully."

Nodding, Kiira finished packing without another word. They were efficient and only one other stinging breeze swept over them before they broke camp. Terren instructed Kiira to put on as many layers of clothing as she could spare. She took longer than he liked, pushing his anxiety up a few notches. He experienced several of these storms both with and without the proper protection and he was not looking forward to experiencing one again.

As soon as she put on her last garment, he mounted, urging Tempest into a quick trot. She tossed and snorted as he turned her into the now slow but cold steady wind. He forced the mare to obey. Getting to good shelter was as much for the horses' benefit as theirs. Terren was a good distance away before realizing the sound of a second horse wasn't behind him. Turning, he saw Kiira still at the camp and standing in front of Starfire.

This is not the time for a love session with the horse!

Exasperated, Terren turned around and galloped back. "Kiira, what in the gods names are you doing!? We need to go, now!"

She glared at him, saying nothing, but stepped toward Tempest to stroke her muzzle as she had Starfire. He was about to interrupt her when she cut him off. "Peace, Terren, hold your tongue; I am helping, just give me a minute."

Terren did hold his tongue, hard and between his teeth. As irritated as he was at the moment, if he'd learned anything about Kiira in the last month from her stories, she did not take needless actions when the situation was important. However, her deliberate and sedate pace did not help his nerves. When she finished, she mounted and spurred Starfire forward, Tempest following without encouragement. Surprised at his horse's willingness to move, curiosity crept into Terren's thoughts. What had Kiira done?

Pulling up next to her, he was about to voice his question, but she anticipated his curiosity. "Our scrambling made the horses nervous. I impressed upon them our need for urgency and they have agreed to push as much as possible."

The morning went by quickly as they varied between gallops, easy trots, and walks. The wind gusts were not unbearable, and the horses continued through the steadily increasing stream of air. About three hours into their ride, Terren saw what would be the first real blast of powerful current heading their direction; the flattened stalks of tall grass were difficult to miss. Just before it was to hit, he turned Tempest so her rump would face the onslaught of icy wind and tightened the clothing around him in preparation. Kiira, paying attention, copied.

A loud howl preceded the frigid wind, and Terren heard a faint squeak from Kiira just before the horses reared in protest. It was a good thing they would reach Fellos in the next few hours.

Terren despised the entire situation, but there was no time for sympathy, so he urged Tempest forward once more, determined to make it to their destination. Terren kept his eyes on the horizon, waiting for the next force of air to come. When it did, he repeated his earlier process.

There was nothing.

An increase of cold air and the pitched whine of strong wind greeted him, but the angry blast did not accompany its brothers. He glanced to see Kiira with her hands out and pointed in front of her like the prow of a ship. The blast of air passed, and she drooped slightly. Terren stared at her.

"Kiira! Those wind blasts are at least fifty knots and are only going to increase! You will exhaust yourself if you do that every time."

She matched his tone. "The horses will not continue if I do not manage to divert the current! When will we reach the town?"

He narrowed his eyes at her and frowned. Never in his life had one person been so much trouble. "If the horses can keep up what they are doing now, just after midday; but Kiira you can hardly expect to keep doing this all the way there!"

Her eyes pleaded with him to understand as she leaned forward to divert another blast. "The horses will not continue otherwise, they have made that clear to me," she said flatly. "I made them a promise and I will keep it. The best we can do is to get to Fellos."

Terren took a deep breath, tempering his frustration. Finally he said, "Kiira, I do not like this at all. You should not have"—he rubbed at his wool cap in frustration—"this is exactly what I was trying to avoid by racing to our destination. It could kill you! If I had known you were going to make such a promise, I would have found a way to make a shelter instead."

Kiira channeled another blast, and visible lines of exhaustion started showing. Concern shot through him.

"As if I don't already know how difficult this is going to be, Terren, but after that first blast of wind both horses refused to go further without my assistance. My promise to help was the only way to keep them from bolting." Kiira gave him one of the most honest expression he'd ever seen from her. "I know my limits. My promise to you is that I will not let it kill me."

Terren clenched his jaw. What he preferred was to lecture her on the stupidity of this decision, but she was not a child. She was his wife, and she was doing her part to help with the circumstances they had been given. "Alright, but never do anything like this again without talking to me first. This is exactly what I mean when I say you're too independent and stubborn. I cannot protect you to the best of my abilities if I am unaware of your intentions."

Kiira gave him a long stare, pride and annoyance flashing in her emerald eyes. She opened her mouth to reply but quickly snapped it shut again, nodded, and turned to redirect another howling wind.

Terren wasted no more time. He kicked Tempest into a hard gallop, his urgency twofold, for now Kiira's life was at stake.

TERREN GUIDED the fatigued horses toward the inn, their lame walk a thudding drum against the hard-packed main road. The air, now painfully cold, was reduced to a heavy breeze inside the walls of the town. At least they would find a reprieve next to a warm fire, and hopefully, Tanan would have some warm spiced wine available. Utterly spent, Kiira slumped so far forward it was a wonder she hadn't fallen out of the saddle. The very last blast struck near the main gates of Fellos, taking the last vestiges of her energy with it across the plains. They reached the safety of the protective walls before another gust rolled off the cordillera.

Inside the stables, Terren paid the attending lad well to give good care to the mounts before pulling Kiira from the saddle. Her weight surprised him. It was the first time he held her so intimately. Even in her lifeless state and with several layers of clothing, he didn't need to strain to carry her. Cradling her to his chest, he felt the gentle rise and fall of her breaths, easing his worry. The best thing he could do was to get her warm and have some food and water ready for when she awoke. Now, more than ever, he was thankful for the years he lived in the magicians' cloister; at least he had some idea of how to help her recover.

Pulling the door to the Starbryt Inn and Tavern, Terren entered a large cheery room and almost groaned in gratification at the inviting and immediate rush of oppressive heat, cacophony of rough singing, and boisterous conversation. A welcome change from the oppressive, whistling wind. The roaring fire sizzled in the center with a Klaroni Boar glistening over the dancing flames. The scent hit his stomach and reminded him angrily of its emptiness.

Every table brimmed with patrons escaping the biting weather. Bar maids bustled around the room in a frenzy, shouting food and drink orders while smacking away the hands of men attempting to be too friendly. Bar tenders dwarfed by huge casks filled orders and chatted with patrons. A group of minstrels played a vivacious melody only to be nearly drowned out by all the voices singing along. Mugs of ale floated around the room and sailed across the bar in rhythm to the madness.

Terren's gelid entrance sent a wave of hush across the room and a sea of faces turned to stare him down. He could not blame them. He must certainly be an odd sight, wrapped in layers and carrying an unconscious woman. Scanning the room, a hearty laugh pinpointed the inn's owner near the kitchen entrance.

Pushing through the tightly packed patrons, the jolly man came toward him, clapping Terren on the shoulder. "Ceress! My good man! I din' think I'd ever see you again!" At the innkeepers' welcome, everyone in the room instantly forgot his presence and went back to their drink and song.

"Tanan, 'tis good to see you," Terren shouted back to him.

"Same here ma' boy. Same here! What brings you back ta our corn'r of the world?" Tanan asked, as he glanced down at Kiira's prone form.

Terren gave the innkeeper a rueful grin. "This is my wife Kessa. She wished to visit the temple, so here I am."

Tanan let out a hearty guffaw and took a minute to control himself before chuckling. "Oi! Well the gods be praised, n'vr did I think I'd see the day a Nyuten Priest be married! Couldn't handle the vows, eh boy?"

"How could I keep such vows in view of a beautiful lady like this? I will tell you the story over a pint of ale or spiced wine, yes? Can you also have a portion of whatever smells so divine, a loaf, and a pitcher of water sent to our room?"

"Ah, a pint of ale for an autumn tale, I shall be glad ta have tha' with you! And certainly, I'll have the missus send it up shortly. Y'ur old room just happens ta be vacant and I've recently added a double bed to it," the innkeeper winked at him knowingly, "must ha' been the gods givin' me foresight."

Terren ignored the implications and took the room key as he headed for the stair. "Excellent, thank you, Tanan. I will be down later for that pint."

Laying Kiira on the bed, he started a fire in the hearth. The room wasn't frigid, since all the buildings in Fellos were double walled, but it still was cold enough to be uncomfortable. Once a crackling fire danced across the logs, he removed the layers Kiira had worn. Stripped to her tunic and trousers, Terren arranged her beneath the covers and stared dazedly at her prone form. Her display of power today impressed him. It didn't match her petite frame.

Stray locks of golden, wind-blown curls covered her features. He brushed them aside to reveal her sleep-heavy eyes and dehydrated lips. As upset as he was with her hasty actions, what she did today was selfless, a quality he could appreciate in a wife, and he liked her all the more for it. The last month of travel showed him that he could easily grow to love her, if they could keep from arguing long enough for it to be an option.

A knock interrupted his thoughts. Terren placed a kiss on Kiira's brow, knowing he would not have the opportunity again for some time, and opened the door. The owner's wife stood there with the biggest grin and the biggest portions of food he'd seen since leaving Lorea.

"Maireen, I am honored you stepped from the kitchen to deliver this yourself."

"Well, I just had to see with my own two eyes. I dinna believe that beguiling man when he said Ceress was back an' stayin' in our inn! Look at you handsome, come give us a hug!"

Avoiding the tray of food, Terren stepped into the jolly woman's embrace to be crushed by a powerful arm. Just when he could not breathe, Maireen let go and handed him the tray of food.

Wagging a finger at him, she continued, "I wanna hear all 'bout this pretty girl of yours, so don't you dare start talkin' to Tanan without me!"

"I wouldn't dream of it Maireen," he said with a smile.

She gave him a jolly wave and bustled back down the stairs to meet the demands of raucous patrons.

THE ART OF CONVERSATION

Kiira bolted upright, heart thudding as her body begged desperately for air. A meager part of her rationale knew she was safe, but blurry vision and an unfamiliar space made her thrash, frantically trying to connect the unknown pieces before her. The fire crackled, a bright hiss preluded a loud pop. She jumped. Taking several deep breaths in through her nose and exhaling through her mouth, Kiira willed her heart to stop beating a manic rhythm. A clear mind was needed before anything else.

As everything came into focus, she slumped in relief. A well-loved plush chair nestled next to the hearth, mirrored by a small table topped with something edible. Tucked against the wall in front of her feet, she could see the dark, familiar shapes of their packs and sleeping gear.

Oh, thank the gods we made it.

Unfortunately, as Kiira's heart calmed, a pounding headache surfaced, sending the room into nauseating undulations. She covered her mouth and closed her eyes, attempting to keep from being sick. Her only relief would be food and water, and Terren was not here to ask for help, as she would have expected. Was he still angry at her? She fought another wave of nausea. Alone and desperate, Kiira stumbled toward the table, her clumsy movements making her vision darken. She lay on her stomach for several minutes, dry-heaving, before finding the energy to ease into a sitting position. Not caring if she made a mess, Kiira pulled the tray of food from the table, sloughing off most of the stew onto the tray. At least she could use the bread to soak up the spilt liquid.

The stew was cold, but she chewed unhurriedly, appreciating every bite. When it was gone, Kiira felt infinitely better, but her body cried for a gallon of water.

And I could devour an entire loaf of bread.

Despite what she thought might be a late hour, the callings of her stomach were more important and she prayed the innkeepers wouldn't mind if she snooped around the kitchen. She could always pay them extra gold for the trouble. Painstakingly, she pushed up the wall, using it to support weak limbs.

She inched her way down the hall to a flight of stairs. A new wave of exhaustion hit her just thinking about the effort it was taking to raid the kitchen. After a deep breath, Kiira made wearisome progress down one step at a time. After forcing herself to traverse six steps, dizziness twisted her stomach and her heart attempted to leap from her chest as air came in agonizing gasps. Maybe she should have just stayed in bed. This was definitely the worst experience she'd ever had after taxing her body. At home, Jemma always cared for her, but this time she was facing the frailty of her body alone. Kiira had told Terren the truth. She did know her limits and would not have killed herself, but knowing where she could draw the line didn't change the after effects. Still, she did not regret her choice.

I'll admit diverting the air may not have been the wisest decision, but I'm not a Weather Mage and it got us safely to Fellos.

Once she felt semi-functionable again, Kiira stepped to make her final decent. However, she misjudged the strength of her legs, and with the dark stairwell skewing her already hazy vision, she mis-stepped and tumbled down the last flight. The racket was painful to her ears as it rattled in her mind, increasing the knife point of pain boring through her skull. Tears leaked from her eyes. Kiira had hoped to avoid drawing attention and her clumsy descent was sure to have woken someone. Attempting to push up, she groaned, knowing she would sport several bruises.

"At least I made it down the stairs," she mumbled. Seconds later, someone was by her side and carrying her back up the stairs.

Panicked, she weakly cried, "No, No, No! Please, I need water and food."

"I will bring you both, but you should not be out of bed," Terren's gentle voice answered her.

It was difficult to tell in the dark hallway, but Kiira thought his expression seemed pinched. Still, she was relieved it was her husband and rested her head against his shoulder.

Her lento pace down the stairs was undone quickly and soon she was back under the covers, this time propped up with pillows. Terren helped her get comfortable, but he was tight-lipped and focused. She figured he must be upset at her, but he left before she could so much as breathe a word.

The length of his absence seemed infinite. Rationally, Kiira knew he was not gone for more than a few minutes. The skewed understanding of time was her weakened mind talking. To keep her thoughts from straying negatively, she undid her braid and combed through the mess with her fingers before tying it back into a plait. As she finished, Terren entered the room carrying a tray laden with an array of food, a pitcher of water, and, bless him, a lot of bread with butter.

Sitting on the bed and without looking at her, he said, "I was not sure what you wanted to eat, so I asked for a little of everything, I hope that is alright."

"Terren," she whispered, touching his arm, "I have upset you. I am sorry."

He stared at the knotted wood floor.

"Kiira, I understand you know your limits and can handle your magic. You are a Prime for a reason. But I'm upset you made the decision you did without me. If I had known the horses were too stubborn to move, I would have found a way for us to be sheltered and you would not be here now barely able to stand." Terren ran a hand through his hair and focused on the edge of the blanket. "As I said, I cannot protect you if you act without telling me, You have to trust me."

"Terren," she said, and waited for him to look at her. "I do trust you. If I have learned nothing else about you this past month, I at least stand firm in the knowledge that I can trust you. However, you were so insistent on leaving this morning, I assumed there was not another option and we needed to make it to the nearest town. I did what I thought necessary." She released a heavy breath. Quietly, she added, "Is it so unreasonable to believe that I wanted to protect you as much as you did me?"

Terren started to speak, but paused. His brow wrinkled, and Kiira couldn't help but let her lips curl up a fraction. He was actually rather adorable when he was deep in thought. She sobered when he cleared his throat, not wanting to give him the wrong impression.

"You're right. I made a snap decision and you didn't question me. I still have to learn how to include others in my decision-making as well. Living the way I did for so long, it is not my strongest personality trait." A rueful smile touched his lips.

Kiira laughed. "Well, you are stuck with me for another three seasons, so we still have some time to get the hang of it."

"We have much more time than that."

She dropped her gaze. This was getting too personal for her. She changed the subject. "I'm starving, thank you for bringing this!"

Terren nodded. While she ate, he filled her in on the cover story given to the innkeepers. She was the daughter of a wealthy merchant and they had met while he was acting as a guard for the caravan. They ended up eloping because she didn't want to marry the intended baron. Kiira wrinkled her nose when he said her 'name' was Kessa. "You are no longer allowed to pick names for me."

If Terren had a pouting face, this was the closest she was ever going to see. "What's wrong with Kessa?"

She laughed. "That is the name of one of my brother's dogs."

"Fair enough, I am no longer allowed to pick names." He smiled briefly and the last of the tension between them melted.

Terren continued to detail the plan for the next few days. Once the wind storm completely dissipated, they would make their way to the Temple of Ny. Terren described what to expect; everything from customs to schedules, the architecture, and a brief history of the priesthood. Kiira also learned they would be housed in separate sleeping quarters, since men and women were always kept separate within the confines of the temple, no matter the relationship. Lastly, he mentioned that he might be asked to instruct initiates for the duration of their stay.

Kiira was so absorbed in what Terren was saying she did not realize all of her food was gone until she blindly grabbed for something and grasped the empty air. She looked down in surprise at her empty plate. The bed shifted, and she looked up to see Terren attempting, and failing, to suppress a laugh.

"Why are you so surprised?" He asked, still trying to conceal his mirth.

"I have never eaten this much food in my life! Seriously, I just ate a Liem-sized meal and did not even notice." She playfully narrowed her eyes. "I blame you and your fantastic tale of temple life. You distracted me. If I get fat from this it's your fault."

Terren let out a hearty laugh. It was the first time he had been really tickled by something she said. Kiira liked the sound of it and laughed with him. It was rather amusing. Liem could eat a lot of food, and she was a third of his size. With her stomach now heavy, sleep pulled at her eyes. She tried to stay awake longer, but Terren encouraged her to rest and as soon as she lay back, sleep claimed her.

KIIRA BLINKED her eyes open to a cheery stream of morning sun and the tantalizing smell of bacon and yeasty bread.

Bacon and beer bread.

Her stomach grumbled in anticipation of the salty and fatty foods. Quickly changing into a clean traveling dress and washing her face, Kiira raced downstairs, stopping short at the bottom step. Lines of empty tables, sure to be crammed later, were dotted with a few sleepy travelers. Terren stepped up to her side and pulled her close. She leaned into him, grateful for someone familiar to be near. She liked the experience of a new place, but a small part was uncomfortable since she had never been outside of the kingdom. He whispered good morning as he led her to an empty seat.

"What's with the dress?"

"Well, I thought outside Lorea, I should probably appear more like a lady." She lowered her voice and hissed, "plus the merchant's daughter you described would not be caught dead in trousers except for riding, maybe not even then."

He chuckled and leaned back in his chair. "Glad to see you are accepting your role with grace."

Kiira rolled her eyes and caught sight of a well-rounded man and woman carrying four hefty plates of food in their direction. Terren introduced the owners, Tanan and Maireen. Standing, she offered a hand, but was swept into a crushing hug, sandwiched between them. Kiira stiffened at the unexpected gesture. They released her with a laugh and Maireen chattered as if she had known Kiira all her life.

The next three hours flew by as Tanan and Maireen dominated the flow of conversation. All the stories they had to tell were wonderful, and she learned more about Terren in the few hours than she had all month. The owners knew him during his time as a priest. His job for a solid year had been to bring any communications and supplies back and forth between the town and the temple. The Starbryt Inn is where he stayed each week. Even after the position was passed to another, he still came to visit the couple. Terren became a beloved adopted son in the three years he lived at the temple. Neither she nor Terren could hardly say a word as Tanan and Maireen kept a stream of stories. Most were hilarious, and Kiira's stomach ached from the constant laughter. More than once, she caught Terren hiding a bemused cringe behind his drink.

After a particularly long span of laughter, the couple abruptly declared they needed to stop lazing about and get to the day's chores. As they busied themselves with their work, a comfortable silence replaced their energy. Kiira could not keep the grin from her face as she looked at Terren. He responded with a smile and a shrug. For the first time since they met, the man sitting before her felt real. He wasn't the broody and sullen prince she had first met. Out here in the world, he had friends, embarrassing stories, and an easy smile.

Kiira wanted to see more of the real Terren.

CHAPTER 37
THE PATH OF THE PRIEST

The towering peaks punctured wispy orange and pink clouds. The snowcapped purple-blue pastry cream peaks stretched east to west as far as Kiira's eyes could see, each mountaintop defiant against the preceding plains. Kiira briefly remembered the rise of the land a few days prior as she battled the windstorm, but nothing could prepare her for the silencing power the mountain range created. All the stories, poems, songs, paintings, and descriptions of the majestic Klaroni Cordillera were nothing in comparison to what her eyes beheld.

Shadowed in early morning light, the imposing landscape was luminous, proud, and bold, in complete opposition to their gentle, inviting, and sloping cousins, the Aria Bells.

Sitting astride Starfire before the massive mountains made her feel small, insignificant, but not inadequate; only humble. Kiira felt far more blessed than she ever had in her life. A few soft tears of joy rolled down her cheeks as she absorbed the significance of this moment; a dream come true. Reverently, she whispered, "They are amazing, Terren. I cannot begin to describe…"

"Just wait until you see the view from the temple. Even if we bypassed the priests and took the path east through the cordillera it is still spectacular," he replied.

Kiira swiped at her cheeks as she turned to him and caught a quick glimpse of unease slipping behind a controlled smile. In the last month, she'd picked up on the nuances in Terren's face and voice. He was far more expressive than she originally believed, if you were quick enough to catch it. His initial discomfort at visiting the temple had been vague, but something was evidently bothering him. As reassuringly as possible, she said, "Terren, why do you sound so nervous to visit the temple? I thought you had friends there that would be happy to see you?"

He relaxed ever so slightly as his eyes darted back and forth across the peaks, looking for something only he could see. "Many will be happy at my return, but since leaving the temple I have experienced much and some of which I fear will not be agreeable to the Doyen." He turned his gaze to give her a worried smile.

"Well, I cannot say it will be fine, as I know little about the priesthood, but if it does not turn out well, at least you still have me." Kiira mustered the biggest grin she could, trying to lighten his mood.

It wasn't the happiest expression, but Terren did smile. "I could not ask for a better companion." He glanced at the sky again and said, "We should begin moving. If we are going to visit the temple, I want you to experience it properly. It will take us most of today to reach the rest point."

She nodded and pushed Starfire to follow Terren's lead.

KIIRA STUDIED the cave entrance from a safe distance. Scrutinizing the rough circular opening, she felt thick ropes of magic guarding the unassuming cavity.

Why in the world would the entrance be so plain? How are travelers supposed to find this? For that matter, why is there such a heavy magical wall if the temple is supposed to be open to all?

Looking at it was mildly discomforting and dissatisfying. After an exhaustive early morning of winding along the mountain, she had expected something more inviting as an entrance.

Bitter air stung her throat and lungs. The shock sent shivers through her limbs, and she rubbed her arms to dispel the chill. Dismounting, Kiira ran a practiced eye over Starfire, making sure he had not strained or injured anything while climbing the semi-steep and soft terrain paths before entering the belly of the mountain. She stood just behind Terren, waiting for him to take the first steps into the swallowing darkness. He gave her one last questioning look, as if to say 'there's still time to decide not to go', but she encouraged him forward. With a sigh, he set his shoulders and took confident strides into the blackness.

If Terren had not warned her previously, Kiira would've panicked, as he completely disappeared from sight. It was disconcerting, but she trusted him. She smacked Starfire on the rump, encouraging him to enter, and then echoed her husband's steps.

The passage was fine until Kiira realized she couldn't move and she couldn't see. Her heart picked a faster tempo when her feet held fast, refusing to budge despite her commands. Instinct kicked in and she tried to fight the compressing weight of magic, but the more she squirmed, the thicker the magic became. The utter blindness did not help the situation. Panic seized her breath.

I just want to leave. Please, just let me leave.

Terren's soothing voice came from somewhere beyond the blackness. "Kiira, stay calm and let the magic examine your intentions for being here. It will not hurt you."

His familiar voice eased some of her fear. Taking a deep breath, she willed her thoughts to think of home, some place familiar and safe, allowing the magic to complete its purpose. Tingling shocks ran the length of her body. A spark of intelligence pressed her senses, digging into what Kiira thought was the most intimate and safest part of her mind. The presence was both terrifying and thrilling. No sooner had she surrendered to the magic than her freedom was granted once again. Blackness melted away, and it felt as if something gently eased her forward. Blinking, she stood in a brightly lit, very wide tunnel with Terren busy tying cloth over Tempest's hooves.

Scowling, she asked, "Could you not have warned me about that?"

"No, I could not. It is a part of my vows as a priest to reveal none of the magic surrounding and permeating the temple. It is the protection of Ny to keep those with ill intentions from entering." He looked at her side wise and seemed sincerely sorry that he hadn't been able to prepare her for the invasive ordeal.

Kiira decided to give a lighthearted response. Rolling her eyes, she said, "Oh if that is all…"

"Did you just roll your eyes at me?"

Apparently, that was not the right time for a joke.

She bit her lip and did her best to look apologetic, but then she saw his sliver of a smile. He was teasing? Fisting hands on her hips, Kiira asked, "So what if I did?"

He laughed as he led Tempest on a slow walk forward. "We are about to reach the hand-carved reliefs depicting the entire history of the two realms. The Sun Realm is on the left and what is known of the Shade Realm is on the right. I know all the stories well, so if you want me to narrate any, just give the word."

"Is that part of the training for priest?"

"Yes. Initiates are required to memorize the stories before they can move forward with their training. The priests believe having a firm grasp on history is but one key to several levels of understanding."

Kiira nodded, the statement ringing true. It was a lesson drilled into her during her own studies and sadly; she had not valued the teaching as much as she should have; the ultimate cost of her disinterest being her mother's life. If she had even been the slightest bit more attentive in the history of the realms and the Mage War, she would have known the truth about Zerrec.

It was a shortcoming she would never forget.

Around a corner, the rough edges of the reliefs took shape into an exquisite picture. Kiira couldn't rein in the gasp escaping her lips. Great care had been taken to accurately portray every defining event in history. The carvings lining the tunnel pulled away from the rough rock, shaped and smoothed to perfect detail. Reverently, she stepped toward the wall to caress the cool stone, needing to touch the surface for her mind to accept the carvings as real.

Kiira lovingly stroked the gradient textures, fascinated to see her numerous history lessons as a child come to life in the dimensional drawings. Whoever placed the oil lanterns in the tunnel had done so with such care that even the shadows cast by the light seemed integral to the reliefs. The skill it took to create such fine work without the aid of magic awed her; she had no skill in the fine arts. Kiira envied those that did.

As they pushed forward, she stopped often to study the reliefs as individual depictions flowed together to create one continuous story. She was pleased to readily recall the stories, and every so often, a picture of a priest or priestess who made a significant impact on the world diverted her steps so she could study the portrait in detail. These renowned warriors and protectors, up to this point, had just been stories to her, but seeing images of their dedication and selflessness inspired even greater respect for them.

Her favorite scene, by far, was that of the survivors from the Mage War meeting the Isokanii for the first time. From opposite sides of the tunnel, two hands stretched toward one another, seeking the other in friendship. So much sensitivity had been etched into the gesture, into the faces of the men, Kiira could almost feel the timid and fragile friendship forming between the people groups. Before her was not just the Realms history but her family lineage, and now it seemed to have come full circle with her marriage to Terren, a son of the Shade Realm.

Kiira became so lost in this realization that she did not notice how far Terren had gotten ahead. She hastened past the remaining carvings, longing to spend more time studying them, but it was wise he stayed in the lead. If she set the pace, they wouldn't have gotten far.

KIIRA SHIELDED her eyes as she exited the tunnel behind Terren. Her eyes adjusted and she realized any descriptions she knew of the temple would not do justice to the sight before her.

A warm sun illuminated the large, circular courtyard as priests and priestesses mingled or scurried in and out of the peristyle. Broad, towering columns twisted gracefully a few meters above her head before smoothly transitioning to a polished dome carved with the Nyan glyphs for unity, service, and faith. The vast opening of the vaulted cupola, topped with crystal clear glass in one half, kept the ever present cold of the mountains at bay. If she had to guess, they were standing in what had once been an enormous natural cavern, the founding priest shaping the temple to move with the natural grace of the mountain.

Kiira turned in a complete circle, absorbing everything as anticipation flooded her core. This was only the courtyard!

A strange voice startled her out of her reverie. "Brother Terren! What an unexpected appearance! Have you brought us an initiate?"

Kiira turned to see the speaker.

"Brother Johsh, it is good to see you." Terren bowed to the slightly older man who had appeared before them. "Unfortunately, I have not brought an initiate, this is my wife, Kiira." He gestured in her direction and Johsh cast a cool look her way, his face pinched.

Unsure of how to respond to the ill reception, Kiira gave the bespectacled, balding man a pleasant smile and wave. In return, the priest gave her a critical eye and pursed lips. She immediately felt wary of him.

Johsh turned his accusing eyes to Terren. "The Doyen will not be happy you have broken your vows, brother, and have returned to flaunt them so."

"The Doyen agreed to change my vows, Brother Johsh, nothing has been broken."

The man narrowed his eyes further at Terren and then looked at Kiira again. She suppressed a shiver. The priest's gaze truly did make her uneasy. Kiira wanted the man gone, so she employed her favorite court trick. "Did I hear correctly? Brother Johsh is it? I remember Terren mentioning your name. You serve in the library, correct?"

The priest looked uncertain for a moment, then stood a little straighter, "That is correct, I am second attendant to the Master Librarian."

Kiira clapped her hands with dramatic enthusiasm. "Wonderful! It would be such an honor to receive a tour from someone so knowledgeable. I am very much a bookworm and would be pleased to hear everything you know. As second attendant, your understanding of such a vast collection must be incredible. Under your vigilant care it must be thriving." She tilted her head to give him a glowing smile.

Johsh regarded them, his eyes darting between her and Terren. She continued to smile comfortingly and give the priest her most hopeful expression. Finally, he gave her a slight bow and a restrained smile. "It would be my delectation to give you a tour of our library. You shall be my honored guest whichever day you so choose."

Placing a hand over her heart, Kiira deepened her smile. "Johsh, you are most kind. I shall not wait long and very much look forward to our time together."

Bowing one more time, the priest regarded Terren again before his long strides carried him quickly away.

"What was that all about?" Terren asked her, giving her a hard look.

Kiira waved a careless hand. "I know his type. He thinks himself better than others, so I played to his entitlement. 'A fool's flattery' my mother called it. I forced him into a position where any refusal would have been damaging to his pride, and on the tour he has to humble himself enough to agree you were right about the library." She shrugged.

Terren closed the space between them with the barest hint of a smile. Her heart ticked faster at his nearness. She willed—uselessly—that the traitorous muscle in her chest would remain steady as he lightly kissed her knuckles.

Quietly, he said, "You, my lady, are a force to be reckoned with. I am glad to have you with me."

A deep blush colored cheeks and the longer she held his gaze, the more charged the air became. Uncomfortable, she asked the first question coming to mind. "Are you not allowed to marry if you take the vows of priesthood?"

Terren must have sensed the change, for he stepped away, rubbing Tempest's neck as the mare rested her head over his shoulder. "That is normally the case. Every priest or priestess you meet here has agreed to stay in the temple for the remainder of their lives and to abide by celibacy. It is a core part of the vows and I'm the one exception because of who I am."

"You mean since you are a prince?"

"Once I accepted my role in this world, yes. Grayten may not think much of me, but he would despise passing the throne to a cousin or my sister."

Kiira studied him. It sounded as if Terren would have walked away from his birthright. Yet that didn't seem to fit his character. He struck her as loyal, not the type to abandon those he cared for, and she could not picture him forgetting the people of his kingdom.

"You would have renounced your title?"

It took him a moment to respond.

With downcast eyes, he said, "I was very broken and lost when I came to the temple. I was desperately looking for an escape from my past and I found peace here. Yes, I would have left it all behind, except my mentor advised me otherwise and was an active voice in the restructuring of my vows."

Kiira could see the pain of his past surface briefly before he hid it once more. Here was yet another side of Terren she did not expect. The more she learned about him, the more of a mystery he became. She reached out, giving his hand a gentle squeeze. "I am glad, then, for this mentor's encouragement; otherwise I would have never met you."

Terren smiled and kissed her knuckles again. "Come, let's see what you think of the temple."

CHAPTER 38
LOST

"Kreshkt!" Kiira's step into the cavern entrance immediately turned his seeing crystal black as an impenetrable wall erected between him and his love.

Zerrec increased his flow of magic with a flickering hope he could bypass the protective spell she now was under. Nothing. Why did he even try? Until his love stepped outside the magic protecting the temple, he could bleed himself of energy, as he nearly did a few weeks ago, and never see a flicker of Kiira's image in the uneven surface. This was one more reason for him to despise the gods. He'd been waiting for this moment, anticipated it, but the sudden loss still wrenched at his heart as if it was being pulled from his chest. He let out a strangled moan, knowing he could not keep a watchful eye on his beloved.

Since the temple was built seven hundred years ago, not long after the Mage War ended, the Nyan Temple was deemed a refuge for any who sought the reclusive mountain sanctuary, and it remained as such. Unbidden, faded memories filtered through his mind, the images appearing as nothing more than an artist's sullied painting ruined by heavy rain. Distorted recollections of the courtyard, the meditation gardens, and sky-blue robes dim behind closed eyes. A few good memories subverted by the disappointment he found inside the mountain sanctum.

Zerrec opened his eyes. He did not need to dwell upon negative thoughts in his mind's eye.

He rubbed his hands through his hair, mussing the plait as he paced the cavern, toying with the idea of going to the temple and forcing his way past the magic just to ensure she was safe. The need to know spiraled an ache in his chest.

He missed her so much, missed knowing he could view her at any time. However, the mere thought of approaching the temple sent a shiver of disgust from nape to sacrum. He hated the gods and wanted nothing to do with them. Nor did he fancy being around the hazy, blinded notions of their followers. No, he would never go near the temple again as long as he lived.

All he could do was be patient—again. If he was honest, it was a virtue he was tiring of upholding. This moment was so much worse than when she had disappeared into the Forest. He might know her location, but he didn't know when he would see her again. How long would they be in the temple? Zerrec thought back to his afternoon of eavesdropping.

What did she say? What did she say?

Striding toward the crystal, he channeled his memories through the rectangular spires. He listened to the conversation three times before resigning that Kiira didn't know the length of their stay, meaning he would never know. With a growl, he pushed away from the pedestal.

I just want her with me, where I can watch over and protect her.

The complete lack of control of this situation kept Zerrec pacing and sent his heart into a double beat. Right now, the only thing in his control were the details of his rescue plan.

I'll keep it simple and act as soon as she is outside the temple. She has spent too long with that whelp as it is.

Until then, he would plan her rescue to the minute. It would be perfect. Truly, Kiira deserved only his best effort, so he would give it. She always gave her best effort for him as his student, so he would repay her in kind. Zerrec would check the crystal religiously, enduring until he could see her again.

CHAPTER 39
CURAVAILED

The dimly lit audience chamber choked any fresh air following him in from outside the grandly carved doors at his back. Terren wished he could reverse his steps for a final breath of something other than the stifling atmosphere weighing the space. He wasn't afraid, but the tempo of his heart didn't seem to agree.

Arrayed before him, the five Doyen priests and priestesses undoubtedly watched his approach, though he couldn't see their eyes. In the exact center of the circular room, five perfect beams of natural light filtered down, dramatically illuminating the Doyen. Heavily exaggerated shadows masked facial features, save for their mouths. There would be no mistaking the words coming from their lips.

The room was designed to make attendees uncomfortable—small. Not a single priest or priestess would call him foolish for feeling some sort of fear and reverence.

The three men and two women sat perfectly straight, arranged alternately, covered in swaths of cloth to form elaborate robes of blue and white. The occasional glint of gold shimmered along the hems in the threadbare light, each stitch in a unique pattern to designate their rank as Doyen.

Terren savored a deep breath and confidently walked toward the small cushion that served as the judgment seat. The brush of his borrowed robes muffled any sound his boots made on the grey marble floor. It was strange wearing priestly garments again. Once comforting, the clothing now felt unyielding. He had learnt much and grown since his time in the temple. Terren still practiced many aspects of the priesthood, never fully forsaking the order, but he didn't keep the minutia of strict details as a way of life, nor did he want to. If he never left these mountains, he would have missed out on many life-changing lessons, taught to him by people of both realms.

Kneeling, Terren prepared for a long wait. The Doyen would speak when they pleased, evidenced by the time it took for them to summon him. He and Kiira had been here nearly two weeks before they 'requested' his presence, and most of those two weeks were spent ruminating on when the moment would come. It made him poor company. Thank the gods Kiira was understanding of his solemn state and left him to his solitude while she explored the temple on her own. When the requisition did appear, in the form of a small square paper scrawled with tight script, he relaxed. He despised wasting time waiting for the inevitable. This audience with the Doyen would prove to be no different. It could take minutes or hours depending on how deep their questions delved.

A dense silence enclosed the chamber except for a low hum of wind brushing across the symmetric holes in the ceiling, recalling his times on misty shores during half-moon nights. He shifted slightly to get a more comfortable seat, and the rustling felt startling in the hushed space.

Terren needed something to distract him from the deadness. He began to silently translate passages from the book of Ny to Isokanii, which proved a difficult enough task to be effective. The time of quiet before the Doyen was endless. As he finished translating his tenth psalter, words and phrases jumbled uselessly in his head, at which point he switched to Sunlander to continue reciting chants and prayers, focusing all of his memory on the passages for wisdom and patience.

The deep melodic voice of the High Doyen penetrated his thoughts.

"Brother Terren, welcome back to the High Temple of our great creator Ny. We see your patience has not been drained since your departure."

"It is by Ny's favor I can so easily rest," he replied.

"That is true for us all." The High Doyen paused, thickening the tension. "You have been summoned to determine if your presence here will continue to be welcome. Do you have anything to say before we begin?"

Straight to the point, then.

"No, please ask the questions you feel necessary." The evenness of his voice surprised him, since a disjointed knot of worry tangled itself around his heart. His concern was mostly for Kiira; she'd barely explored the temple, and he didn't want to ruin her visit.

The priest farthest to the left spoke next, his voice tinny. "It has come to our attention that your heart has been tainted. Your vows did not keep you on a straight path. Do you expect us to treat you with the same regard as before?"

Cautiously, Terren said, "My highest regards to you leaders of the faith. No, I do not expect any here to have the same regard of me. I have experienced much in the last nine years and experience is the root of wisdom, knowledge, and growth."

"Then you would agree we should no longer allow your stay welcome within the walls?" The furthest right Doyen asked.

"If you so choose for me to leave then I will respect the decision, but I humbly request this not be considered. Is it not in the foundational creed that all not of ill intent are welcome to the temple? I have brought my bride here so she could experience the wonders of the temple. I would dislike pulling her away from a place she has so recently come to appreciate."

"The temple is not a tourist destination, Brother," the left priestess said, her heavy accent punctuating the warning.

"Forgive me if my words betrayed otherwise, I have never believed as such. I respect the temple as a place of peace, learning, and safety. Kiira requested to come here to learn from the vast library, I am merely a conduit for her to achieve that goal. If I was mistaken to bring her, then please correct my understanding."

"Brother, you are admitting to bringing your wife here. You have broken your vows as a priest just by doing this," the priestess to the right stated, her voice raspy and strained.

Terren took a fortifying breath, ensuring he would not speak in haste. "I have broken no vows, wise leaders. I know two on this council agreed to have my vows specifically altered because of the obligations I have to Klynotia."

"He speaks the truth, let the matter of his bride be at rest my brethren," the High Doyen replied. "Brother Terren, our grandest and main concern, and the reason for this summons, is not your bride, but what the magic revealed when you entered the sanctuary."

"I will admit I disregarded my vows for a period of time. I became unsure of myself outside the safety of these walls and I did things I am not proud of, nor wish to repeat again. I stole, lied, cheated, and was entirely selfish. I have since repented and returned to Ny. Becoming a priest of Ny was one of the greatest joys in my life. If it is not too bold to ask, I pray you find the gods' grace in your hearts toward me. I am not the same, but I have no doubt where my faith lies."

The left priestess said, "Brother, we are not concerned with your past transgressions so much as we are unsettled by the darkness etched on your heart. You have been touched by the Shade Realm. Your choice to accept and attach to the darkness is something we cannot welcome here in the Temple of Light."

Terren turned his eyes downward and squeezed them shut. He needed to form his next sentence carefully. It was important to appease the Doyen, but he could not let them continue with a false understanding of his bonding with Kamaria. He would never regret choosing to bond with her. It was in his blood to be a Shadow Walker. She was his Yepenzi, and their bond would be a comforting rhythm in his chest until the day he died.

Lifting his head, he straightened his shoulders, channeling the confidence he had in his Bear. He sent a silent, thankful prayer to the gods for the clarity they gave him.

"Leaders, I understand my acceptance of a bonding could be considered negative; however, my bond with a Shade Beast has not destroyed my heart or faith and has only served to deepen my understanding of our creator. I chose to complete the Ermyjek because it is my maternal inheritance. To be a Shadow Walker is a gift passed down through the generations and it is a lineage I am proud to continue.

"The darkness of the Shade Realm is not the same darkness every priest and priestess prays against. After living there for several years, I stand firmly in the conviction that the Shade Realm is simply another domain of Ny. Do not the history texts mention he is the purveyor of both light and dark? I believe Ny formed and shaped both the realm of Sun and Shade. The Shade Realm is not evil, it is a misconception benighted after the Mage War. As a Shadow Walker, I consider myself fortunate to live and experience both realms of the gods' creation.

"The darkness you rightly reject is not embodied by the Shade Realm, nor is it what you see etched upon my heart. That blackness has no single location, it always surrounds us and we cannot escape it without the intervention of Ny himself. The gods' grace is for all."

Silence absorbed his words, and the echo of his voice faded from the stone. Air charged between Terren and the high priest, the tension a taut rope connecting them. He may have upset the Doyen by disagreeing with their views, but he refused to let lies continue when he could speak the truth. The Isokanii did not believe in ternion gods, but their unbelief did not mean the Shade Realm wasn't a creation of Ny, and Kamaria a beautiful product of the god's hand. It was only by Ny's will that Terren survived the bonding with his Bear. If his connection to Kamaria was so evil, then why did the gods save him from dying during the Ermyjek? Peace settled in mind and soul. Terren knew where his heart lay and what he believed. Anyone too narrow minded to agree did not deserve his anger.

Soft whispers fell too delicate for him to hear as the council discussed. After several minutes, the High Doyen rendered council's judgment.

"As the Doyen of Ny, we do not agree with your assessment or your choice to create an attachment with the Beast. Ny is the purveyor of light over dark and the Shade Realm has and always will be the opposite; the negative to the Sun Realm. As his priest and priestess, we sit in the chosen realm of Ny and your reluctance to renounce this darkness forces us to one choice. Terren, as of this moment you are no longer to associate with the priesthood. Your rank as a Nyuten Warrior Priest will be stricken from our records.

"Despite our disagreement, you may stay in the temple with your bride for as long as desired. You were correct in stating that we have no right to turn away those whom Ny has given entrance. You will always be a welcomed guest and friend. Should you choose to challenge our decision—"

"I accept the conclusion reached by this council and appreciate the honor of being called friend of the Nyuten Priest," Terren said. He clenched his fists and jaw as a piece of his identity was summarily stripped away. Logically, he knew he was more than a title, yet the judgment still stung. The temple had been his first stop after leaving his kingdom, and the structured life here helped him to begin the path to restoration.

The High Doyen interrupted his thoughts. "Very well, then you are free to leave."

Quickly, Terren rose and exited, eager to be away from the council.

CHAPTER 40

THE SEAMSTRESS

The faint whisper of air trailed Kiira's padded steps down the dimly lit hall. Until Terren returned from his summons, which he warned might be lengthy, she was on her own. The only option then was further exploration. Kiira had tried not to grin too broadly when given the news. The prospect of discovery danced electric sparks across her skin.

The Nyan Temple was beautiful, and the library, oh the library, was a learner's dream. Like all areas of the temple, the marbled granite had been coaxed into delicate representations of nature. Finely sculpted statues filled numerous alcoves and dusty passageways. Spiraled pillars and brocade bookcases towered over her, and the wide foundation of the conical library constantly glowed a warm orange, the smell of wax and worn paper permeating every spare inch. The buzz of turning pages and scratching quills hovered about the room as priests, priestesses, and visitors sat amongst the hundreds of tables, chairs, and over-stuffed pillows, studying or reading for pleasure.

All the library's beauty, however, failed compared to the thousands of texts filling sleek shelves cut into the hollow mountain in a never-ending spiral of ledges and walkways. Kiira had nearly wept with joy upon seeing the collection for the first time. This was beyond her wildest imaginations and she could easily become lost in the repository.

Which is exactly what she was doing at this moment. With Terren typically by her side, she had spent most of the last two weeks working through the various lower levels, poring over texts not in the Lorean Royal Library, but knowing unexplored levels existed near the top remained a constant itch at the back of her mind.

The particular hallway she now traversed, Kiira found upon one of her few trips to the mid-levels. Hidden behind a large twisted pillar and potted fern, it piqued her interest because someone had evidently taken care to hide the entrance. As she stepped softly toward the bright glow at the end of the hall, her senses tingled. She focused on being noiseless and alert.

Kiira paused at the rim of shadow outside the door, positioning herself to have a better look into the room.

Well, that's definitely not what I expected to find.

Warmth rolled into the hallways from a sun-drenched room made almost entirely of glass. Heavy curtains hung from floor to ceiling, silent sentries protecting stacks of cloth from the sun's rays. She squinted to better see the materials deemed worthy of protection, and unless her eyes deceived her, colorful bolts of silk, leather, and cotton were mounded against every mountain wall.

The steady *creak, clunk, creak, clunk* of a rocking chair caught her attention. It conjured memories of hours spent at her mother's side, her soft voice telling stories while embroidering. Kiira would sit at the base of the chair, absorbed in the tales weaved to life by her mother's steady voice, watching as she made perfect stitches into the fabric.

As she crept closer to the door, the rhythmic bob of snow white hair pulled into a neat and practical bun came in and out of view. Kiira longed to walk into the room and examine everything, but she didn't want to invade the old woman's privacy.

"Well are you just going to stand there or are you going to come in?" The priestess' soft, papery voice surprised Kiira so much that she obeyed immediately and stumbled into the room.

Circling to face the woman, Kiira explained, "I apologize, it was not my intention to spy, but this hidden nook was too much of a curiosity not to explore."

"Oh, that's quite alright, dear. I've been praying you would find your way to me."

Kiira smiled. "Have you? Curious indeed. Is that how you were aware I was in the hall?"

The little old woman looked up from her work. "Now if I told you that, Kiira, I wouldn't be the mysterious old woman you found at the end of a darkened hallway." Her dark green eyes sparkled.

Kiira smiled. One feisty response and she was endeared to the slight woman. Her smile grew into a generous grin and a bubbling laugh.

The priestess returned the laugh with a small chuckle of her own before turning back to the delicate lace handkerchief she was stitching and began rocking again. When Kiira remained unsure if she should stay or move, the old woman said, "No need to be rooted to one spot, dear. Feel free to walk about the room. Come sit down and have a chat with me when you are done."

Having permission, Kiira meandered around the bolts of cloth, brushing her fingers across them. Stacks of finished items lay scattered about the room, the embroideries as exquisite as her mother's. Kiira stroked the threads of one of the folded pieces.

This room feels like home.

Taking a seat on the floor next to the old woman, she praised her work. "You have some of the most exquisite work I have seen. My mother used to embroider. The times spent with her are some of my most treasured memories."

"I think that is the highest compliment anyone has ever given me."

Kiira watched as the old woman turn an unassuming green thread into shimmering leaves and curling vines. "How did you know my name?" She eventually asked.

"I know everything and everyone in this temple. Nice to finally meet you, dear. My name is Tereyssa."

Kiira smiled. True to what seemed to be her nature, the old woman had not really answered her question. "The pleasure of meeting you is all mine." Kiira watched the smooth, quick stitches for a moment. "Would you like some help? I am terrible with thinking up designs but I can stitch. My mother taught me and I still keep at it, though not as much recently."

"Really?" Tereyssa peered at with thoughtful eyes, then nodded once. "I would adore your help, dear. Just select something from that stack over there; I already have designs drawn on them. Thread and needles can be found in the basket."

Kiira sorted through the rather impressive stack of unfinished items and settled for embroidering a sky-blue silk shawl. Tiny sparrows sketched along the hem, flitted in and out of budding tree branches. Selecting bright green thread for new leaves, Kiira pulled the fine threads in and out of the material. The first few passes were neat but done with clumsy movements. Soon enough muscle memory kicked in and she, too, had a steady rhythm.

"Tell me a bit about yourself. How is it that you came to be married to Terren?" Tereyssa asked after a few moments.

"How much do you know about Terren?" Kirra countered.

The priestess chuckled. "I like you, dear. I know he is the prince of Klynotia. His mentor was one of my dearest friends before his death."

Kiira nodded. Naanel was the first person Terren sought upon their arrival. The news of his death put a rain cloud over her husband for a few days. She felt for him, losing someone so impactful wasn't an easy burden to bear. "Well you might as well know I am the princess of Lorea." She pursed her lips. "Although, now I should say I will be the crown princess of Klynotia." The acceptance of the idea sent a worming sensation through her stomach.

"Oh, how wonderful! I always prayed he would find the perfect woman."

"I'm not sure about that, Tereyssa. Terren and I are friends, sure, but I cannot say I am the perfect woman. It was an arranged marriage and neither of us warmed quickly to the idea."

"Nonsense," the priestess flapped the extra fabric of her work at Kiira. "I can tell things about a person, and my intuition tells me you're perfect for that boy. It'll all work out so long as you both choose to make it work."

Kiira smirked. "The goddess told me the same thing not so long ago. I suppose you *and* Windrah cannot be mistaken."

Tereyssa laughed deeply. "I really do like you, dear. We'll get along swimmingly while you're here. Now, tell me more about this meeting with the goddess."

Kiira obliged, recounting the events leading up to her confrontation with Windrah, all while working diligently. Between focusing on her work and conversation with Tereyssa, the day slipped away from her, and it wasn't until her neck ached and her eyes strained to see the threads in the dimming light that Kiira realized the hour.

Rolling her shoulders, she looked out the glass wall at a sea of blue-grey light. Scrutinizing her work in the candelabra's light, she was pleased to find she had not lost her touch. Clean, even stitches forming dozens of leaves were just the beginning of the larger design. She held it out for Tereyssa to examine and the old woman snatched it from her hands. Several muted seconds passed as she ran her fingers over the stitches and moved the fabric.

She looked at Kiira with bright eyes, her tone full of enjoyment. "Well I should say, dear, that your mother taught you well. This is excellent work. Come back and help me anytime during your stay."

Kiira released a breath she didn't know had been stopped in her throat. For some reason, a deep-seated desire had settled in her mind to please Tereyssa. Smiling, she said, "Truly? I would love to come help you. How often do you work?"

"I am here every other day. As much as I like to think I'm a spring flower, these old bones cannot handle more than that."

"Then I shall be here every other day as well." She gave the priestess a sincere smile. "I quite enjoy your company."

"That remains to be seen, dear," Tereyssa grinned, and tapped the side of her nose.

Kiira chuckled, and she helped the old woman from her chair. After lighting a lantern, Tereyssa took the lead, shuffling from the room. Leading the way back to the women's sleeping hall, Kiira decided the earlier comment about a 'spring flower' didn't seem entirely genuine. For an older woman, the priestess was incredibly spry and walked at a rather hurried pace. Not that it bothered Kiira; the brisk pace helped her to keep warm from the bitter air.

Nearing the building, Kiira spotted Terren outside her door in a meditative kneel. How was he not freezing? They hushed their conversation as they neared his position, but he must have been expecting their arrival, for he opened his eyes, their icy blueness glowing softly in the moonlight. She had been married to him for over a month now and still they pulled her off-center.

Terren's eyes held the barest hint of humor. "I see you have met the *famous* Tereyssa."

"Don't be tart, Terren, your wife and I have had a lovely afternoon, haven't we, dear?"

"Absolutely!"

His smile broadened into an ornery grin. "So you are allowed to give me a hard time, but I cannot return the sentiment?"

"Precisely. I am allowed to get away with anything at my age. You, young man, have a long way to go before you have the right to be cantankerous like me."

Terren let out an honest laugh as he stood. Kiira could not help but laugh as well. Not only had Tereyssa put him neatly in his place, but Terren had an infectious laugh. She liked it quite a bit. He drew near her and wrapped a light arm around her, gently rubbing her arm. She hadn't noticed how cold she was until that moment, and she leaned into his warmth.

"How did your summons go, Terren?" Tereyssa asked.

His mask slid into place and a cool, cordial smile replaced the genuine mirth previously radiating from him. "We are allowed to stay here as long as we like. It is what I was hoping. Kiira has only just begun to access the wealth of knowledge available in the library which is the main reason for us coming to the temple."

Tereyssa narrowed her eyes at him. "What are you not telling me?"

Terren sighed. "How do always know?"

"When you get to be my age..." She left it at that, as though it was explanation enough.

Terren shrugged his shoulders, trying to act nonchalant. "I have been Curavailed, but remain a friend of the priest."

Shock transformed Tereyssa's face. Concerned, Kiira peered at Terren, but as always, his stoic expression revealed nothing. The only hint he might be agitated was the increased pressure he applied to her arm. She suspected he betrayed that much only because he was less careful with appearances around friends.

"Kreshkt!" Tereyssa hissed. "Those fools! Blinded by their swollen importance! Hypocrites!"

Kiira never would have pictured Tereyssa using such a vehement curse. Feisty, yes, but the old woman was a devoted follower and one of the sweetest people Kiira had ever met. Such wild emotion should not have been possible for the old woman, yet here she was condemning the Doyen for what was obviously a serious decision.

Now her curiosity had to be satisfied. Looking up at Terren, she asked, "What is Curavailed?"

He returned her gaze. "Curavailed means I am no longer considered a priest."

"What! Why?"

Tereyssa answered, "It has to do with his connection to the Shade Realm, dear. Those stubborn fools think it has somehow spoiled him. I ought to go in there and give them a piece of my mind!"

"Tereyssa, please do not. They are already upset with me for agreeing to disagree with them. I can fight my own battles."

Kiira was genuinely confused. If it was because his mother was Isokanii, then why had they let him enter all those years ago? "Terren, what does she mean your connection to the Shade Realm?"

He pulled her closer and squeezed tightly. "A tale for another time, at which point, I will want to know how Tereyssa discovered my connection since it was *after* I left the temple." Terren narrowed his eyes in suspicion.

"When you get to be my age…" the priestess replied, waving her hand to dismiss him.

A STAFF INTRODUCTION

"*I cannot* take this anymore," Kiira said.

Terren looked up from his book as the loud snap of a swiftly closed cover ricocheted from wall to wall of the cavernous library. She cringed at the loudness of her declaration. An uncomfortable hush settled over the room as everyone peered in their direction, many of them with narrowed eyes and exaggerated frowns. Resettling his gaze on Kiira, she visibly shook and not from any chill. At least she looked contrite about the disturbance she caused. Gently, he closed his own book and laid it on the table before leaning closer. He said nothing, but raised his brow and waited.

Taking a deep breath, she continued, "We have been here a little over twelve weeks and I have become plump and lazy. I need to do something besides meditate, read, and embroider. I'm not used to being this ... static." She extended a general gesture to her surroundings.

Terren gave a brief once over and definitely didn't agree with her assessment of plump and lazy. In fact, since being in the temple with a strict no-meat diet, he would bet she lost some weight. Still, he understood how the lack of activity could leave her restless. Since being curavailed and no longer allowed to spar with other priests, he felt the same itch to do something besides sit around.

If he was honest, his activity level dropped, not because he could no longer exercise, but because he had been sulking. If Kamaria had been near enough for them to speak, she would have told him to stop brooding and move past the decision, bluntly reminding him the excommunication was ridiculous. He would agree with her, too. It was not as if the knowledge of the priestly teachings suddenly disappeared at the change in his status. What did the title matter now? Terren smirked as an idea came to mind that would be beneficial to both of them. Quietly, he said, "I may have a solution. Meet me at the stables in one hour? Wear something comfortable."

Kiira looked skeptical, but agreed. She grabbed both their books and hurried to shelve the texts. He watched her walk away and felt his eyes wander her form. She was the picture of beauty.

Abruptly, he stood and made his way from the library; hopefully the man he sought would be in a favorable mood today. A few lefts, a right, and through a rarely used back door, Terren entered the soft, comforting wood and hay scent of the temple's stables. A deep, satisfying breath brought the barest smile to his lips. He could live in a clean stable and be satisfied. Walking past the forty other mounts, a combination of temple bred and those belonging to visitors, he stopped at Tempest's stall to find her blissfully asleep. Since returning to the temple, Terren often found her like this. She was enjoying being home.

He had not stood there long when he felt a hard, warm, semi-damp snort cover the back of his neck and he turned to see Starfire reaching as far as he could from the neighboring stall, trying to lip him. Terren laughed, and the gelding sent another snort brushing across his face. Kiira didn't lie when she said her horse could double as a court jester. He hadn't believed her at first, since the horse disliked him, but with his consistent presence around Kiira, Starfire eventually deemed him trustworthy, and the horse's colorful disposition became more and more obvious.

Terren turned and pressed his brow near the white spot on Starfire's muzzle and gave his cheek a good rub. Before long, the gelding snuffled through his clothes, looking for a treat.

Spoiled rotten horse.

Kiira brought him an apple each time she visited and, by extension, Starfire expected it of Terren as well. Smiling, he pulled one of the two swiped apples and held it out for the gelding. "Are you happy now?"

The Horse Master answered the rhetorical inquiry. "Don't encourage that beast, Terren, gives me the cricks, stubborn equine."

Terren spared a gentle smile for the bent, grey-haired priest. The man looked ancient, but there was a sturdiness to his limbs that hinted at great strength. While he didn't take care of the daily maintenance, the grumbly old man knew horses and how to care for them. He was the one who had begun the horse breeding for the temple over seventy years ago, and with Terren's affinity for horses, the two men had been easily drawn together.

"Starfire certainly is quite spirited, but he's loyal. I've grown to love him, even if he is spoiled." Terren reached up and scratched the gelding behind the ears.

"Bah!" The priest swatted the air in exasperation. "He is a nuisance, and I shall be glad to be rid of him!"

"Now, Sartenn, he cannot be all that bad."

"Oh can't he? I can't tell you how many times I've found that horse out in the pasture when I know I locked him in his stall. Yet I can't seem to catch him in the act, it's like he magics his way out. I shall say it again: he is a nuisance; I'll be glad to rid of him!" His old voice cracked with the exclamation.

Terren laughed. "Starfire, a magician? That would be quite a sight."

Sartenn pruned his wrinkled face with an angry glare. "You sayin' you don't believe me?"

"Quite the opposite, it fits his personality. How about in exchange for a favor, I relieve you of him for a few hours?"

"Aye, and what would you be offerin' me in return, young Terren?"

"For the remainder of my stay, I will care for the stables in your stead if you allow me to have use of the paddock on those same days with no disturbances between morning meditations and the noon meal."

Sartenn narrowed his eyes as he studied him. Terren tried to look relaxed and maintain an unassuming expression. What he intended to do was not necessarily wrong. He was exploiting a loophole, but the Doyen would be displeased if they found out.

Finally, the old man replied. "What are you up to?"

"I just need the space to do some physical activity since I'm no longer welcome to spar with the other priest, and it has been strongly suggested I not use the training space provided for guest." It was the truth, mostly. "So, do we have a deal?"

The old priest scratched his chin and studied the ceiling, taking a full minute to consider the proposition. "Alright, I don't see anythin' wrong with it, and I trust you'll keep your end of things. No funny business, mind you! I don't wanna come to find you and that pretty lady of yours were in here doing things not allowed in the temple." If there was one sure thing about Sartenn, he was a stickler for following guidelines. It was this aspect of his personality that made Terren sure he and Kiira would have use of the space without disturbance.

"Sartenn, I can *guarantee* there will be none of what you are suggesting." Kiira hadn't so much as initiated a kiss, much less hinted at a desire for anything beyond it.

The small man nodded his head, sharp and quick. "Good. Now, when did you want this deal to start?"

"Today, if you will allow."

"Today?" He asked with a new suspicion. "You've only got a couple more hours until the noon meal, why not the day after next?"

"It's been several weeks since I have done a proper routine and lethargy is taxing."

"Okay then … I suppose I'll just shuffle away. It'll be a good thing, you helping me, I had some projects what need attending."

"Thank you, Sartenn. I will be back after midday to make good on my promise."

The old priest waved a casual hand with his back still turned and left the room. He was not a swift fellow, but at nearly a century in age, it was impressive he could still walk without any assistance. As soon as the old man was out of sight, Terren pulled out the staffs he'd hidden in Tempest's stall and made his way outside to the paddock.

Bright sunlight forced him to squint. Rich, bright green grass stretched out for a distance before stopping abruptly by a wall of glass. Beyond, the blue-grey-white sharp slopes of the cordillera surrounded the paddock like a fortress wall. The paddock was a true engineering feat. It still fascinated him, even after all this time, the structuring of this place. The entirety of the valley needed to be kept warm all year round and was enclosed by thick panes of glass to insulate the space from the bitter mountain air. A magic casting on the glass allowed for just enough of the penetrating sun to keep the space at an optimal temperature. The enclosure was a generous twelve acres and the soft ground ideal; the only danger was forgotten manure piles, something he could easily alter. This made the paddock the perfect place for sparring. Plus, its isolation from the rest of the temple meant no one would stumble upon them.

Soft footsteps approached, and he turned to find Kiira looking incredulous. He could not help but smile at her expression.

When she was close enough, Kiira asked, "So, I have an idea of why we are here, but care to give me the details?"

"Certainly." He tossed a wooden staff in her direction, which she easily caught. "We have use of this space every other day between meditation and the noon meal to use for sparring. I made a deal with the Horse Master." She narrowed her eyes. Her questioning gaze told him everything she was thinking. "Do you want to use the time or not? I'll gladly make use of it with or without you." It was a blunt answer, but Kiira didn't always care for gentle conversation.

She sighed. "I am dying for something, so I will play along, but you are already not in good graces with the Doyen, I'll be sorely disappointed if us being here becomes an issue because of this little *arrangement*."

"It will be fine, I promise."

She softened. "Terren, I don't want anything to happen to you because of this."

"I know, but we'll be fine. I trust Sartenn to keep people away." He appreciated her concern.

Kiira weighed the staff in her palm as though considering what to do, then swung it experimentally overhead and behind her back.

"So, what do you think?"

"It feels similar to a long bow in length but definitely heavier. I would likely be more comfortable if this was cut in half and I fought with two pieces," she replied.

"You mean short staffs," he said.

"I suppose, but I'm willing to give this a try. I had been thinking about learning a new close-range weapon, so this is as good an opportunity as any."

Terren nodded and then hesitated. Should he simply instruct Kiira or physically guide her through the movements? In the past, he would show his students what to do and have them mimic, but these sessions were much more intimate and provided the perfect opportunity for him to try to break down some of the physical barriers between them. Since entering the temple, their friendship had blossomed as they spent countless hours discussing a wide variety of subjects. Everything from political structures and battle strategies to faith experiences, even simple likes and dislikes. He could recall her favorite color—green—but seemed to continually hit a wall with attempts to move past friendship with Kiira. He had no desire to push her into something she was unprepared for, but they were married. It was a little antagonizing. She still held feelings for the archer, more so that those feelings were holding her back from him. Terren knew Kiira had loved Leo deeply, but the last few weeks made it clear to him he was ready to move forward.

Kiira interrupted his thoughts by asking, "Terren, is everything alright?"

"Yes, of course, I was just determining the best way to instruct you."

She searched his eyes, for what he was not sure, since it had been an honest answer. "Since this weapon is so unfamiliar, it might be best if you helped me move through some of the basic motions."

Terren felt his stomach tense. Was there an underlying meaning to her words? There did seem to be a new hesitation in her stance.

Was that an invitation to be closer? Gods above, I hope so.

Clearing his throat, he said, "Hold the staff in front of you with your dominate hand, palm down, but not too tightly, feet shoulder width apart and slightly askew." Nodding, he circled Kiira to check her alignment and smiled. She had an archer's stance, good for firing arrows but bad for hitting someone with a stick. Stopping behind her, he gently adjusted her hips to be more squared and wondered if her heart adjusted a few beats at his touch. His certainly had. "Excellent, now grip with your other hand, palm up, and anchor your dominate hand to your waist." Circling to the front, Terren studied her for a moment. "You've just learned the antipode grip. This is the first basic grip of the staff."

Kiira smiled. At her encouraging expression, he continued with the mountain grip; a double overhand hold on the staff with hands just slightly wider than shoulder width. These two basic grips were the parents for a variety of other hand positions. He took the time to show her the other respective grips, gently moving her hands, shoulders, hips, or feet to the proper position. Each time he made contact with her, the tempo of his heart spiked. He was being far more intimate in his teaching than necessary, but he also hoped it would result in a positive outcome.

"Perfect, Kiira," he praised, his quiet voice near her ear. There was no mistaking the shiver she attempted to hide. Stepping back, he said, "Now, let's move to the basic movements so the staff begins to feel more comfortable."

Terren moved her through different spins and handling techniques, explaining which ones to use in different situations. As the movement of the spins became progressively more difficult, the concentration painted on Kiira's face intensified. The last spin, the double underarm infinity spin, required her to send the staff around her body. She struggled to move through the skill, but Terren remained patient, knowing she wouldn't give up until the movement became natural.

There were a few stumbles, but for her first time working with a staff, Kiira did well. It helped she was athletically inclined, with exemplary command over her body. He easily imagined them sparring at their next meeting.

"So, how are you feeling about the staff thus far?" He asked, ending their lesson and settling on the grass to rest.

"Surprisingly, I really like it. There are similarities to knife fighting in how my body moves, though the length of the staff feels odd in my hands. I never have been one for bulky weapons. It's why I have always preferred the recurve bow and knives."

"Understandable, but the staff can be a very elegant weapon. Knives feel like a natural extension of the arms, but a staff is used perpendicular to the arms, making it harder for it to feel natural in your hands. You'll get the hang of it, though. You've already made an excellent start."

She nodded her thanks and stared at the intricately designed long thin piece of wood.

"It might burst into flames if you keep staring at it like that," Terren said after a few seconds, teasing.

Kiira smirked. "With as much lacquer as there is on this thing, it wouldn't take much."

He laughed, and Kiira returned his smile briefly before standing with an easy grace. She offered a hand. Unfolding his legs, he clasped her forearm and, with a heavy tug, she pulled him to his feet. Instead of letting go, however, she stepped closer and wrapped her arms around him, resting her head against his chest. The embrace was so unexpected that it took Terren a few startled seconds to return the gesture. When he did, a soft sigh escaped her lips. This was the first genuine show of more-than-friendly affection she'd given him since beginning their Lundemai. Seems he hadn't misunderstood her comment earlier. When she released her arms, he was a little reluctant to actually let her go, however; he promised to give her time, and with matters of the heart, he desired to tread carefully.

"Thank you Terren," she said, smiling again. "I will see you at morning meditations?"

He nodded and watched Kiira walk away, twirling the staff, leaving him standing with an unsure heart beat and the smallest glimmer of hope.

CHAPTER 42
FIGHTING ATTRACTION

A wicked grin commandeered Kiira's lips as she advanced through a series of speedy attacks, forcing Terren to step back as he blocked. Anchoring the staff, she wheeled her feet overhead—a skill she'd mastered remarkably quickly—putting some distance between them for a much-needed respite.

Today was a good day. She was making Terren earn this win. Taking his advice to heart. Over the last five weeks, Kiira had worked to make the staff an extension of herself. Twirling the staff, she casually side-stepped, studying her partner.

She had been exceptionally clumsy during their first sparring sessions, ending most of them frustrated. Terren, forbearing as ever, thankfully, never showed his easy wins and continually encouraged her to try again.

With conscious effort, and additional solo practices, she improved her skills. Small victories became regular and her appreciation of the staff grew. The first time Kiira truly felt a connection to the weapon in her hands, the transition had been so smooth she actually managed a bruising hit on Terren. Her win was short-lived as he took advantage of her shock to disarm and ground her. Yet, in that brief moment, she finally knew what the long, thin weapon should feel like in her hands. After that, her skills with the staff increased by great strides and now, five weeks later, she was actually a viable sparring partner; and it was her favorite method for thwacking people.

Her rapid advancement was a blessing and a curse. As she triumphed,

Terren would reveal more of his skills and once again be difficult to beat. The colorful bruises and sore body she could handle, but the losses were a mark to her pride. Kiira couldn't be too upset. Truthfully, Terren proved to be the perfect teacher, knowing when to increase his efforts to force her into the next level of learning, and when she did have something incorrect, he would stop to adjust her stance or grip, his touch sending tingles across her skin every time.

The sparring strengthened their friendship, opening a door for engagement in new and different conversations. Terren relaxed more when his body was busy. He talked easily with her, showing more of his tempered humor, compassion, and intellect. She found herself respecting him deeply, and more than that, she felt the beginning threads of a connection.

It had been difficult to admit how her feelings for Terren reshaped because of their staff sessions, since it was both joyous and distressing. She had been connected with Leo, too. Kiira did her best to disguise her turmoil, but her husband was observant. He gave her space, yet never let her skip the sparring that forced her to be in close quarters with him. Tereyssa also helped her muddle through the gradual shift of her affections, giving Kiira gentle reminders that love is always a choice, and one she could make without regret.

"Your relationship is sealed by the gods, dear, don't forget that. To love him is to do their will." The old priestess' words had comforted Kiira. Her sadness over not marrying Leo ebbed until she finally was able to enjoy Terren's presence without reservation.

Sparring with Terren allowed Kiira the opportunity to stop fighting her attraction to him, and the more she let him romance her, timid as it was, the more she could see he was beginning to love her, too.

He offered her affection in small ways. His favorite was an embrace after the execution of a dizzying move that should have grounded her, and instead wound up tucked safely in his arms, looking into amused ice-blue eyes. His easy, sometimes impish grins would speed up her already rapidly beating chest. Occasionally, he would leave soft kisses on her cheek, the feel of them lingering long after he released her from his embrace.

Today, however, his 'special' move would not work. Kiira took a few cautious steps, studying her prince, determined to disarm him. They were in their third round, and per usual, he held the advantage. She wasn't naïve, Terren wasn't giving the fight his all, but she could confidently say she wasn't making it easy on him either. Lunging, Kiira engaged him in a swift series of attacks, forcing him back a few more steps toward the glass wall of the paddock, trying to press his back to the wall to prevent him from effectively using his staff.

Patience rewarded her this round, and after a few minutes, she finally had Terren where she wanted. He gave a sly smile, causing a seed of doubt to bloom in her mind. It was a tiny thing, but the fact that he was getting beneath her skin irritated her more. She studied him critically. He either knew her intentions or he was trying to make her *think* he knew her intentions.

I have to make a decision.

Squelching any doubt, Kiira pressed forward again, waiting for her opening. Victory was almost in sight! The strikes were planned in her head. She made to execute her strikes—and found herself short of breath, looking at a diffused sun through the tall glass roof of the paddock. Dazed, she lay there a moment, attempting to picture what Terren had done. As her breathing steadied, his gentle and teasing voice tickled her ears.

"Thought you could back me into a tough spot to win?"

"Yes," she groaned, picking up her head to glare at him.

"Did you forget I am a master at the staff. There is still a lot for you to learn." Tilting his head, Terren leaned over her and smiled, but it was more of a contained grin. "I guess this means I win, again."

If he hadn't grinned, Kiira would have accepted her loss. He was about to learn to not engage her competitive nature. As sweetly as she could muster, she replied, "Who said I was finished?"

She quickly swept up her leg, swinging it in an upward arc directly against the backs of his knees. The shocked look on his face as he thudded to the ground, his legs crossing hers, forced a bubble of laughter from her throat. Soon he was laughing with her, and when the merriment subsided, Kiira wiped the water brimming in her eyes.

Terren scooted around to lie next to her and they relaxed into a companionable silence, enjoying the quietness of the space, the bright sun, and the soft grass. Her heart stuttered when he reached over to hold her hand. The gentle stroke of his thumb over hers sent a riot of excited nerves along her arm and straight into her stomach.

I love him.

Not just in the deep friendship way that had been their standard for some time, but she was completely, irreversibly, and madly in love with him; a love that had unconsciously blossomed. His romantic pursuit of her helped, but Kiira loved his gentle manner, so opposite to her frazzled, worried, and busy nature. He was solid and steady to her constant need to be part of the solution.

It surprised her how a few months of marriage could take her from reluctance to love, though she supposed that was the expressed purpose for the Lundemai. Admitting this not only filled the hole in her heart left by the loss of Leo, but it now felt full to bursting. There were parts of her she didn't know were incomplete until Terren had burrowed into her soul. He was her better half, her best friend, and her love. An unconstrained grin took hold of her lips as she realized just how much she loved the man holding her hand, subtly stroking her skin.

"What are you grinning about?" Terren asked, interrupting her thoughts.

Rolling to her side, she propped her head on a bent arm. "I was just thinking about how truly happy I am, here with you."

He mimicked her actions and studied her for a moment. "Truly?"

"Yes, do you doubt my sincerity?"

"Not at all."

Kiira smiled, absorbing the joy reflecting in his eyes. Suddenly, the desire to kiss Terren overwhelmed every thought and sense and her chest thrummed with desire. Her focus zeroed in on his lips as if invisible cords led her. He sensed the change in her demeanor, for he leaned closer and she was about to give in to the desire when, oddly, she remembered Zerrec and her family's warning that he might be loose. Why now?

The previous delightful tension tingling in the air between them drained away, and Kiira sucked in a breath. Deep down, she knew she needed to warn him about her old mentor before moving forward. Secrets never served those you loved; they were selfish things that picked at the threads binding relationships. Terren deserved complete honesty, and she had waited longer than necessary. She started to pull away, and he stopped her with a gentle hand to her cheek. She looked into his eyes as he searched for the reason for her hesitation.

Sitting up, she played with the grass at her crossed ankles. "Terren, I have to tell you something. It's important."

Knee to knee, he grasped her hands and gave them a gentle squeeze. "You know you can tell me anything."

Taking a cleansing breath, she said, "Do you remember the day you arrived in Lorea?"

"How could I forget?"

She gave a humorless smile. "Well, to keep this simple, we believe the Demon was summoned by my old mentor and powerful magician, Zerrec.

My brother did not want me to leave the kingdom because of the possibility of encountering him. It is the first time we have seen him active in over a decade." Kiira took a hesitant breath, gripping his hands tighter. "I didn't tell you about my family's reservations because I didn't want you to change your mind about traveling."

Terren gripped her hands a little tighter, and his eyes narrowed.

Hurriedly, she said, "I didn't tell you about him then and I should have and it's plagued me ever since. I'm so sorry. It was selfish and—"

"Kiira," he said, "it's alright." Tipping her chin to meet his gaze, Terren gave a reassuring smile. "I'm glad you told me."

Surprised by his unusually calm reaction, she wrinkled her brow. "You're not upset?"

"I wish you had talked to me, but I also understand why you did not. Fear is a powerful motivator to stay silent when we think it will destroy something valuable to us. I should know. At least this explains the angry lecture I received from Liem before we left." Terren quirked the side of his lips for a moment before catching her eyes, serious. "Promise me this; no more secrets between us. Be honest with me even if you believe that whatever you say may be hurtful. I don't want our relationship to be built upon constantly appeasing one another. I spent the majority of my life giving into others' demands or wishes; it is a miserable way to exist and I never want that to be the foundation for us. I love you too much for that."

Kiira's heart stopped, lodged in her throat, dropped to slosh in her stomach, and then found its proper place in her chest to somehow start beating again.

"Do you really mean...?" she trailed off as Terren squeezed her hands.

He nodded.

"I love you too, Terren," she whispered. As the moment washed over her, every nerve tingled with joy and she gave into a broad grin. Then it was swept away with the midday bells in the distance, signaling the end to their uninterrupted window. Kiira sighed and sent a glare toward the chimes.

Just my luck.

Kiira moved to stand, but Terren held her in place. "Terren? What is it?"

"There are some things I have kept from you."

She nodded. It was understandable. There was still much she didn't know about his past. What was important was that he was telling her now. Terren was quiet for so long that Kiira thought she might have to urge him to speak again.

"What I have to tell you must wait until we leave the temple." The words looked like they were lodged in his throat and he had to force them through.

Something was really bothering him, but she had learnt not to push him. Terren always said what needed to be said—it just took him longer. Kiira gave him a timid smile. "Okay. I trust you."

Terren tried to return the smile, but it fell weighed down by the heaviness gathered around him. "In the meantime, I have someplace special I would like to take you. Would you do me the honor of your company?"

She didn't care for surprises, but something about his demeanor beckoned to her sense of adventure. "Yes, of course."

He smiled. "We will leave after meditations tomorrow."

CHAPTER 43
KLARON POINT

Breathing in the crisp morning, Terren stretched the sleep from his muscles before blinking his eyes open to the solemn dong, dong, dong of the waking chimes, indicating meditations would begin soon. Meditations. He rubbed his chest at the slight pang of the reminder.

Months later and it's still difficult to wake up knowing I have no responsibilities as a priest.

A three-month span should have at least tempered the idea of being Curavailed, but the temple held too many reminders. Priests and priestesses he considered friends now shunned him, favorite haunts within the temple were now off-limits, and hundreds of text were banned from his view. The most painful reminder of his excommunication was the clacking of wood whenever he passed close to the training areas. Losing the staff fighting was especially difficult, since it was through the trainings he first found peace in his life. The Nyuten fighting methods were about more than combat; it was finding harmony through movement, using the physical to focus the mental. Terren still remembered the day he earned the title of Warrior Priest and deemed worthy to pass the knowledge to others.

Staring at the ceiling, he attempted to stave off disappointment and anger, but the feelings swirled, hazing over everything else. He was not one to succumb to emotions easily, and he said he was at peace with the decision of the Doyen, but lying here now, he admitted it wasn't the truth, no matter how much he tried to convince himself. Every morning he prayed Ny would give him the strength to forgive the Doyen for their closed-mindedness.

The Nyuten leaders were supposed to be the most exemplary priests in the order, as they had obtained godly enlightenment. Yet their lack of compassion was so opposite to the god's teachings. Their condemnation shocked him to the core and left his insides a knot of slowly-scarring hurts.

He'd known the Doyen would speak to him about his connection to the Shade Realm when he first stepped through the entrance, but for them to demote him because they believed he no longer represented Ny was offensive. Having lived in both realms, he understood the creator in a way the Doyen never would. As enlightened as the High Council was, they didn't know his heart and where his faith resided.

If only Naanel were here. He would have known exactly how to guide me through this valley.

It was for Kiira's sake he endured the daily torture of being in the temple. He hid it; for her joy in being there helped to keep the bitterness at bay. It was easy to ignore the whispers and stares when he focused on her.

A satisfied smile appled his cheeks as he thought about yesterday and her reaction to his declaration. It was amazing how quickly their relationship progressed; from dislike to love in a matter of months.

'*Yepenzi?*' Kamaria's voice echoed unexpectedly through his thoughts.

'*Kamaria!*' He immediately arose and opened a portal into the Shade Realm from the darkened corner of his room. He found himself on the side of a mountain with several wide ledges spanning below him. Leaping from ledge to ledge, he shucked the heavy wool of his outer garments as he went to combat the drastic temperature change between the two realms. Logically, the mountains here should be just as cold, with it being near the dead of winter, but the surrounding air was much balmier than that of the Sun Realm.

Kamaria's large, sinuous form emerged from the opaque rock around her. Here in the dim morning light, his Bear was nothing more than a suspicious shadow. The relief of seeing his bond partner flooded him with inexpressible joy, and Terren took two large strides, burying himself deep within the soft yet bristly fur of her paw.

'*Oh, Kamaria, I have missed you.*' She hummed in response to his attention. '*I have been miserable with our link being only the ghost of something more. How have you spent your time?*'

'*I traveled the two realms doing much contemplating, but I spent the majority of time with my brethren in the Shadow Desert. Your family is eager to meet your bride,*' she replied, and he heard the slightest hint of bitterness at the mention of Kiira.

Terren pulled away to look squarely into one of Kamaria's large black-and-grey pupils. *'You came back because I told Kiira that I loved her, didn't you?'*

Kamaria remained silent.

'Oh, Kamaria…'

'Do not reprimand me, Terren.'

'Kamaria … Yepenzi, you must know I still love you. You are forever my bond partner. Nothing will change that.'

'No…'

Terren could sense her reluctance. *'If you know that to be true, then what is this about? I thought time away would help,'*

She remained silent. It was disheartening for them to finally be this close, only for her to feel more distant than before. Not even the barest hint of emotion passed between their mental link. Avoidance and distance would not make things better. Her sulking had gone on long enough. *'Kamaria,'* he said, *'she is my wife. You had to imagine love would be a possibility. Do not tell me it wasn't even the smallest of considerations when you chose to bond with me.'*

'It was a consideration,' she said hesitantly.

'Then, tell me, what has you so bothered by my love for Kiira?'

Reluctantly, Kamaria let a spark of emotion flicker and Terren felt himself smaller than the tiniest ant, and insignificant.

His heart ached for how belittled Kamaria felt by the new love bringing him so much joy, and he wished she could share it with him. He would need to be careful in the future not to let her or Kiira feel this kind of insignificance. The last thing he wanted was to alienate either because of a misunderstanding.

A spark of amusement seeped between their mental link as Terren considered the juxtaposition of her feelings compared to her physical size.

'You find this funny?' She growled.

'Dear friend,' he said, reaching out to stroke her, *'not in the slightest.'* Terren rested his forehead on her prickly fur and let every feeling he had, everything words could not adequately describe, flow between them. As Kamaria came to understand his feelings, a deep elation rolled through her chest, vibrating every bone in his body.

'It is a relief to know your heart, Yepenzi, and to find my doubts unfounded.'

'No one will ever have a connection like ours,' Terren said.

'I did not want to be forgotten.'

'How could I forget you? You are a part of me.'

'It has happened before,' she reminded him.

'Yes, but I will not allow it to happen to us. Love is infinite and there is always room for more. Just because I love her differently, doesn't mean I love you any less, and I need you to be open minded about Kiira. Be willing to accept her, for she is now a part of me as well.'

Kamaria growled.

"Don't do this, Yepenzi. She needs to accept you as much as you need to accept her. Give me time, she was deeply hurt by a Demon. You have my memories of how difficult it was for me to lose my mother. Kiira was much older and much closer to hers," Terren said aloud.

His Bear sighed, as much as a Beast could sigh, and he felt the reluctance through their mental link.

'Promise me,' Terren said, putting an extra push behind the mental words. They were partners and part of their bond meant sacrificing for one another, even if they were disagreeable.

'I will do what I can to help her trust me, you have my word.' Kamaria finally said.

'Thank you.'

Kamaria hummed again, and he could feel true contentment radiate from her for the first time since his marriage. Terren spent the rest of the time allotted for morning meditation conversing with his Bear, learning of all she'd done since he entered the temple. Through a combination of images and words, he retold his meeting with the Doyen and the subsequent feelings.

'Well, I say you are the one who is correct,' Kamaria stated, so matter-of-factly, Terren couldn't help but let a smirk touch his lips.

"I appreciate the support, but you are biased. I should not be so angry. I have other special things in my life besides the title of Nyuten Priest, but I am still struggling to find a reason to just let the feelings go," Terren replied.

'It's okay to be angry, Yepenzi. It sounds to me as if you have been fighting the anger. Maybe you need to give yourself permission to be angry before you can let it go.'

"I can't," he whispered.

'Why not?'

Softly, almost with a touch of fear, he said, "I've told you how I was … before. You've seen my memories of that time. I have no desire to be that person again."

'Terren,' Kamaria said with a gentleness he seldom heard from her. *'You are not that person anymore. Allowing yourself to properly grieve over something important to you will not damage the peace you've found.'*

"How do you know?" He asked, his voice catching on his lips. The young servant girl—terrified—after he ruthlessly hit her upon seeing she brought him an unfavorable dinner often still flashed through his mind and drove him to be a better man. An involuntary shiver rolled across every inch of his skin. He never wanted to succumb to that darkness again. He never wanted to be a byproduct of Grayten.

'I know because you have something your monster of a father does not,' Kamaria reminded him.

Terren let the thought soak into his soul. She was right. He had a grace Grayten never would. He chewed on her words, still unsure, but hope lay its gentle hand on him once again.

TERREN GRIPPED Kiira's wrist as her fingers lost the tentative hold on the slippery rock. Denton's Ascent was known for its precarious surfaces being slick with condensation, especially just before the final tunnel. This may not have been the wisest path to reach Klaron Point. The near vertical incline was almost impossible to climb. It had taken them the last hour just to make it up the steep rock face. But he knew Kiira was strong, and he purposefully chose this route because it was a challenge, guessing Kiira might enjoy the vigorous stretch.

Kiira grumbled, "Does the path to get here have to be so difficult?"

Maybe not my best idea.

"The path to clarity is often arduous, but the end reward is always worth the journey."

Reaching with her other hand, she clasped his forearm and scrunched her nose at his philosophical response, causing him to chuckle. Terren easily lifted Kiira up the rest of the rock face.

"How are we going to make it back by a reasonable hour? It has taken us a day to get here," Kiira said.

"There are several paths to reach Klaron Point, some are more direct than others," he replied.

"You mean we could have taken an easier path?!" She sounded indignant.

Definitely not my best idea.

"We needed to arrive here by a certain time, and I wanted to spend the time with you without the watch of prying eyes."

Kiira's outrage melted into a blush, and she gave him a sweet smile.

Terren pulled at their clasped hands, tucking them between their chests. He smiled, staring at her while both of their breaths returned to normal. Keeping one of her hands firmly in his, he turned toward the fading light ahead.

"So, have we finally made it?"

Terren nodded. "Almost, we should hurry so we don't miss it."

Kiira tilted her head to the side, her eyes pleading for a hint.

"I'm not telling you, that would spoil the surprise," he said.

She sighed emphatically and genially tramped after him into the tunnel's darkness.

The last walk was short and soon he had Kiira wrapped in his arms beneath a warm blanket, watching the sunset. Wisps of white breath floated in front of them for a moment before being whisked away on thin, icy breezes.

Terren rested his chin on top of Kiira's honey curls and small strands danced in and out of his vision as they soaked in the last rays of a muted winter sun. Hundreds of mountain peaks stood as dignified guardians between them and the distant Seas of Reana. Shadows jutted in and out at odd angles all along with tall sharp spires, lengthening as the sun disappeared behind the peaks.

Darkness pushed ever faster at the clinging rays; pink, red, yellow, and orange gave way to purple, blue, and black. One by one, stars sparked into existence, re-lighting the dimming sky. Soon the heavens would be alight with millions of the distant blinking lights, and here, standing on the edge of the world, it was almost as if he could easily stretch to pluck each one from the sky.

Terren pulled Kiira closer, and she buried herself as much as possible into his embrace. He sighed, happy with how natural it felt to have her in his arms. He never dreamed of such a moment.

"Terren, why me?" It was a heavy question.

"Oh, well you see, Grayten made me." She turned to glare at him for jesting, but he just pulled her closer and pressed his lips to her head, chuckling. "There are many reasons, Kiira, but if I had to pick one thing, it would be your courage." She shifted enough to look at him, and this time he nudged her to completely turn to face him.

"My courage?"

"Well, you faced a Shade Demon, ventured outside of your kingdom because you knew there was more, battled a wind storm to protect me and the horses, and made a promise to love me; just to name a few. Every one of those things, especially the last, takes courage."

"You give me too much credit." She turned her face away. "Facing hard challenges or the unknown is a part of life and, you're easy to love, Terren."

"That was not the case five months ago, if you remember, and it may sometimes not be the case in the future. But you've still chosen to love me, and you didn't have to bind yourself to that promise, Kiira, you chose to, and that's courageous."

She contemplated his words, focusing on a distant mountain peak. Terren studied his bride in the light of a swollen moon. Her captivating, bright emerald eyes darkened and her curls swayed in the wind.

Finally, she said, "I suppose there's some truth to your words."

"You don't sound convinced."

Kiira took in a shuddering breath. Looking back at him, a hesitant fear shone in her gaze. "Terren, I love you, more profoundly than I have ever loved anyone ... yet, I need you to understand that a small part of me will always care for Leo, just not—"

"I know," he said.

"Doesn't that bother you?"

This was the perfect opportunity to present a nascent thought upon his relationship with Kamaria. He wanted to tell her everything, but this wasn't the right time to tell Kiira about his Bear. He could, however, be understanding, hoping she would be the same later. "No. I couldn't ask you to stop loving someone that had such a profound impact on your life." He echoed his words from his conversation with Kamaria. "Love is infinite. It can change, be redirected, grow, or cease; it all depends on what we choose."

Kiira laughed and turned her face to the sky, shouting, "Alright! I get it!"

Terren wrinkled his brow.

"I'll explain later," she said, still laughing.

Terren pulled her close, tightening his grip, and pressed a long kiss on the top of her honey curls before resting his cheek against her crown.

"Terren?" Her muffled voice floated to his ears.

"Hmmm?"

"Is Klaron Point still considered temple grounds?" Kiira asked.

"Yes."

"Oh," she said, turning her gaze down.

"What is it?"

"Well, I was hoping that part of the reason you brought me here was to kiss me. I mean our first true kiss." She bit her lower lip and he could feel the stiffness of nerves flowing through her muscles. "I suppose that's not possible since—"

Terren guided her lips to his, cutting off her doubts. His heart felt as if it stopped and pounded at the same time, leaping in joy. Kiira smiled beneath his lips and eagerly leaned into his embrace as he deepened the already fervent kiss. Terren memorized every second of this moment, lingering on the taste and feel of her mouth on his. This was not like the kiss at the wedding, a momentary brush of a touch that tingled with excitement. This kiss was bedrock. Knowing Kiira deeply loved him made this kiss better than he dreamed.

Terren pulled away briefly to drown in the joy electrifying her eyes. Her smile melted him into nothing, but before he could devour her lips again, a burst of light flashed, catching their attention. Intense, dramatic, green and purple lines snaked overhead, seeming to moving with excitement. The silhouette softened into muted pale green clouds, still restless, but an ocean of light against dazzling stars.

Kiira gasped. "What is it?"

"I've heard it called Ny's Beckon by the people in Fellos, sent to guide the deceased to Apelgo's Halls, though, the priest do not think of it that way," Terren said.

"What do they believe?"

"The priest think it is because of the rotation of the world since it happens so often."

"There is no record of this in the Lorean Royal Library. It's beautiful. How could I ever describe this to an artist to paint?"

Terren pulled her closer to stave off the chill. "I'm glad you could experience this. It is never guaranteed to see them."

They stayed upon Klaron Point late into the night, kissing as softly and continuously as the lights. They only paused when the lights changed and were brighter with harsher lines—twisting, pulling, and moving, in vivid red, purple, and green. Time really meant nothing, and it was only after Kiira shivered sharply in the icy wind that Terren picked her up to move them into the shelter of the cave system.

She laughed. "You did not need to carry me!"

"No, but admit it, this was more fun."

Grinning, she said, "Yes, it was."

Resting his forehead against hers, he said, "I have to admit, this is not at all how I imagined our first kiss, but it was absolutely perfect."

Running her fingers through his hair, Kiira added, "I couldn't agree more." Then she kissed him again.

After some time, Terren pulled just enough away to whisper against her lips. "It's very late, we should start back."

She nodded, and reluctantly, he turned to guide her to the exit. Kiira stopped and held him in place with their grasped hands. "Terren, I'm ready to leave."

There was an odd light in her eyes and a cautious smile. He stared for a moment, then cleared his throat as realization set in. "Okay, give me a few days to make sure everything is in order and then we'll go."

She smiled, and they moved forward together.

CHAPTER 44
GOODBYE

"Stop fidgeting, dear, it's distracting," Tereyssa scolded.

"No sitting position is comfortable," she complained, adjusting again before wiggling deeper into an oversized plush cushion, one that had been long term borrowed from a reading room in the library.

"Mmmm. I can't imagine why, you've always found the cushion acceptable in the past."

Kiira pulled thread to create little knots for the bud of a flower. Currently, she was attending to the last stitches on a design of thumbnail yellow roses around the cuff of dark leather riding gloves. "It's because I know I'm leaving," she mumbled. Kiira always looked forward to her days in the embroidery room, but today was a more subdued occasion, even though her afternoon had already been scattered with pieces of laughter.

"What was that, dear?"

"It's because I'm leaving, Tereyssa. I'm eager to continue, but ... I am going to miss you," she sighed. "I have so enjoyed our afternoons together."

"Dear Kiira, I shall miss you as well. Your presence has brought much brightness to my usually simple days, and you have helped to advance my orders to a manageable number again! But we both know this temple is no place for you and it's time to continue your journey."

Kiira smiled, returning focus to her stitches. A few moments of companionable silence passed as she studied the decorated gloves, loving the idea and wishing she had more time to complete a pair for herself. She would have made her stitches on a lovely dark green, the color of healthy leaves, with lighter tinted thread, the color of fresh shoots as they emerge.

Tereyssa interrupted her thoughts. "Did I ever tell you about the first time I trained Terren with the staff?"

The priestess' colorful words painted a picture of a clumsy young man who tripped over the long stick falling into an ungraceful heap time and again. Kiira could only imagine the sight of such a tangled knot of limbs, especially since Terren was anything but clumsy now. She delighted in the tale, making sure she memorized the sound of Tereyssa's soft, papery, and gentle voice, wanting the sound to be forever etched into her soul. There was something about the old woman that refreshed Kiira and made the world seem a bit brighter.

"I expect regular letters updating me," Tereyssa said.

Kiira looked at the old woman and grinned. "And I expected you to say as much! I promise to write every spare moment. I believe the first town we stop in is Albea and then we will pass through the plains to Forchid."

"Really? I am surprised that he is taking you through the plains. It's safer along the root of the mountains."

"Terren says he has something to show me and that our bearing is important."

Tereyssa chuckled. "Knowing that young man, I'm sure he does."

"And I am sure—with little to no information—you have puzzled out my intentions, which would prompt me to ask you not to say anything," Terren said, as he entered the room and casually leaned one shoulder against the frame.

"Now Terren, just because it seems like I know everything, doesn't mean I do," Tereyssa chided.

"I'll believe that when there is evidence to prove as much," he replied.

Tereyssa snorted and pushed her rocking chair with a little more enthusiasm.

Looking at Terren, Kiira gave him the most dejected look she could muster. "I cannot even have a little hint?"

"I told you already, I no longer want to keep things from you."

"That's not really a hint. Please? You know I am terrible at guessing things anyway."

"Absolutely not and if you continue to pout, I will kiss it from your lips," Terren said.

Kiira's eyes dilated as she reined in her surprise. "You will do no such thing! Especially in front of Tereyssa!"

"Will I not? Care to test me?"

She almost believed the truth of his words, but the overly seriousness of his tone didn't match the playful glint in his eyes.

Tereyssa cleared her throat. "As much as I enjoy watching the two of you be in love, I can say that as a Rabbi Priestess, I do not approve of your lip locking … any of it." She kept a straight face, turning a serious eye on each of them.

Kiira colored a deep shade of pink from her neck to cheeks. "How did you know? No, wait, let me guess … when I get to be your age…"

It was the old woman's turn to let out a hearty laugh. Terren grinned, and Kiira found herself laughing softly as well.

When Tereyssa finally caught her breath she chuckled, "Dear Kiira, yes, I shall miss you very much indeed."

Kiira sighed. "And I you."

"Well, don't be so melancholy about it, I'm not letting you leave without a token to remember me by," Tereyssa chided. She tied a finishing knot and snipped the threads of the piece in her hands. Holding it up, the full length of the shawl was revealed. "This is for you."

Standing, Kiira lovingly stroked the completed piece the priestess held. The dark green wool, adorned with intricate stitches in varying shades of green, gave the fabric a vibrant appearance. Tereyssa read her mind. The monochromatic color, with its subtle variations, added a depth that was exquisite. The priestess had beautifully brought together the most significant aspects of her life. Artful, delicate designs portrayed her regal lineage, adoration for archery and hunting, unbreakable bond with Skehtra, extraordinary magical abilities, affection for animals—especially horses—her undying passion for running, and, most importantly, her profound love for Terren. The depictions flowed smoothly from one to the next, creating a harmonious blend of images with no standout. It was her story described in thread, the intricate design molding together in one cohesive pattern.

The shawl slipped through her fingers, appreciating the velvety texture on her skin. This would soon become her favorite garment. This was more than a token; it was a treasure of the old woman's craft. Overwhelmed with gratitude, she couldn't help but burst into tears of joy while embracing Tereyssa, unable to utter a single word.

"Careful dear, hug me any tighter and you'll choke me," she chuckled.

Stepping back, Kiira wiped the tears from her eyes and mumbled an apology. She reverently wrapped the shawl around her shoulders. As instructed, she kept a length covering her left arm and wrapped the fabric around the entirety of her back before buttoning it closed on the left shoulder with the remaining material draping in easy folds. The lightweight wool was surprisingly warm; already she could feel heat rising to her cheeks. Thankfully, the shawl did not include a hood. She preferred to not cover her head since it was a hindrance to her as an archer. Pulling her arms back into a firing stance, Kiira found that the design of the shawl was loose enough for her to move freely, but not so loose she would be cold on a mild day. Tereyssa could not have given a better gift.

"It is absolutely perfect and I shall treasure it always," Kiira said.

"Well, I'm glad you like it, dear. I have these items for you as well." She handed over a pair of gloves, stitched with a vine of plumeria flowers around the cuff, and a hunting belt dyed in the same dark green as the wool. The soft leather of both items supple in her hands.

"Tereyssa, this is too much. How can I repay you for all of this, it must have cost you a fortune," Kiira said.

"Don't be silly, dear. I can spare some money for a few little gifts," Tereyssa replied, adding, clicking her tongue for measure.

"I can vouch for that, I used to make her deliveries and trades when I was here last," Terren interjected.

"Hush you," Tereyssa scolded, "or I shall not give you your gifts."

The surprised look on Terren's face would have been comical if Kiira was still not so awed by the items in her hands.

"Tereyssa..." Terren's countenance darkened.

"Hush, I said."

The priestess handed Terren a woolen cloak in a dark grey, nearly black. He examined the embroidery with care before putting the item around his shoulders and fastening the front. The long material draped to mid-calf. Terren lifted the hood of the cloak and, after situating it on his head, it concealed his face without hindering his forward vision. If it had been night, he would have completely disappeared into the shadows.

Kiira looked up from her own gifts long enough to study the stitches of monochromatic threads on his cloak. There were so many different images that it was almost difficult to discern what seemed to define him. A flood of new questions came to mind, especially about the ebony she-bear that connected the designs. As much as she had learnt about Terren, he was still a mystery in so many ways.

He dropped the hood and Tereyssa handed him a pair of leather gloves and a hunting belt in the same dark shade as his cloak. There was no doubt these gifts cost a fortune, but bringing it up again would only offend the old woman.

Reverently, Terren grasped Tereyssa's hand between his palms and bowed over their hands in the traditional sign of respect for an elder in the priesthood. Looking into her eyes, he said, "Tereyssa, your kindness will never be forgotten, by either of us, and I want you to know that you are more of a lady than many of the royal women I have ever known. You have a beautiful heart and it abundantly shows in the thoughtfulness of these gifts."

"I couldn't agree more," Kiira said. "Thank you for being a person I will never forget."

Tears sparkled in the old woman's eyes. "Now you two, don't go making a big deal out of something so small. Just consider these items a wedding present." She waved a casual hand. "Besides, I did it for selfish reasons. Whenever people admire your shawl and cloak you can send their business my way." The words were dismissive, but the old woman couldn't hide the tremor in her soft voice.

"Tereyssa," Kiira said, "I will not let you deny how much you care for us. These gifts are priceless and I shall consider it an heirloom given to me by family." She stepped over to the old woman and hugged her again.

Embracing the two of them, Terren said, "Kiira could not have said it better."

"Oh you two..." Tereyssa blubbered out before succumbing to soft whimpers. When she could speak again, she said, "You have brought me more joy in these last months than I have had in many years of my living in the temple. You are the grandchildren I could never have, and I will miss you dears something fierce."

Kiira and Terren spent the dying hours in Tereyssa's company before going through another round of tearful goodbyes. Terren didn't cry, but he was openly sad. She, on the other hand, was a mess, and it took her minutes to choke out a goodbye to the old woman. Leaving Tereyssa's sewing room in the dim evening light, listening to the dying *click-clack click-clack* of the wooden rocker, made it difficult to breathe. Terren put a comforting arm around her shoulder as they walked away, and Kiira let sadness envelop her like a cocoon.

CHAPTER 45

THE PLAN

Red eyed, he watched the small, distant image of the worthless fool and Kiira as it was projected through the jagged edges of his crystal. Finally, he could see his love again, feel close to her again. Months passed, his anxiety growing with each day, and here she was, picking her way down a steep section of the eastern path toward Albea, smiling. The scene before him licked at his control on anger, but adjusting his shoulders, he took a deep breath, keeping his feelings in check.

Kiira's hand slipped into his as she took a big step down from a boulder. Too much momentum sent her into the whelp's arms and heated jealousy coursed through his veins as the prince kissed her knuckles. Zerrec's teeth ached, and he consciously mocked a yawn to ease the tension shooting into his cheekbones. Those were hands he should be kissing. Zerrec moved the view to his beloved's face. There was a change, a light deeper than friendship in her eyes. Being in the temple had the opposite effect of what he expected. He'd seen the expression—given to him—by other women throughout his centuries.

No, no, no!

He would give anything to see Kiira look at him the same way. The way Loralyn had looked at him.

She still will, he reminded himself. *I need to act quickly. She deserves more than what the prince can give. She deserves what only I can give her!*

Zerrec estimated their progress down the mountain. They would reach the city of Albea by nightfall. His preparations were in such a place that he could expedite the rest to rescue Kiira now, and he desperately wanted to go after her. Forchid, though, was more conducive to his overall plan; with the hundreds of twists and turns in the massive city and countless people, it gave him a key advantage. He might cause a stir that was talked about for weeks, but he could remain nameless. Albea, in comparison, was a simply planned town with few alleys and not nearly enough people to cover his tracks from anyone who might come after her—namely Liem. It would be better to wait, even if every regenerated cell in his body hummed with anticipation, ready to take action. How much longer he could contain it he didn't know.

Taking wide strides to the left and to the right, he repeated the pattern until he could properly focus. Zerrec reviewed his plan—though he knew it by heart.

Get to the city. Cause a stir. Silence and Rescue Kiira. Kill the Whelp. Leave the city.

He wanted to leave nothing to chance. If there was one thing he knew, the smallest detail left abandoned could have the most damaging consequences. The pacing soothed his mounting anxiety enough for him to think more clearly. Confident his plan would go smoothly, Zerrec shouted, "Ricker! We need to leave immediately!" The faithful mercenary appeared beside him in an instant and followed him like a shadow, waiting, listening, ready. "Get your two idiot friends to ready the horses, we leave for Forchid tonight."

As the tattooed man walked away to fulfill his bidding, a slow smile curled Zerrec's lips. He had no doubt Kiira would soon be his.

CHAPTER 46
A UNION COMPLETE

A strip of light flickered in his eyes from the not quite closed curtains of the spacious room at the Snowdrift Inn. He blinked and squinted at the annoyance. Unwilling to rise, he shifted lower in the bed, causing Kiira to stir. Once comfortable, Terren attempted again to find slumber, but his mind, having already acknowledged the sun, refused, so he allowed the cobwebs of sleep to be dusted from his mind.

His eyes traced the inconsistent patterns in the grain of the log walls. Restless contours stretched all along the beams, forever straining to reach something but never quite able to connect; frozen in motion. Built with resilient mountain trees, the inn had a basic and rough construction, which he loved. The sturdy walls could withstand the chaotic storms sweeping over the cordillera from the harvest season through planting season, and the timbers could easily bear the burden of wet snow.

Lying comfortably in the enormous feather bed, Terren relished the comfort provided by additional coin. Not only had he gotten excellent rest after trekking through the mountains in winter, but it also provided a pleasant place for the two of them to be together for the first time. Terren looked at his wife, contentment seeping through him. He smiled.

She was pressed against his right side, her head resting on his shoulder and an arm draped across his chest. Her beautiful long honey curls fell erratically all around her head, both above and underneath the covers, the glossy strands glowing in the sunlight. The covers moved gently with her soft, even breaths. Terren closed his arm and curled his fingers across her biceps. The softness of her skin sent tingles up his arm. His smile deepened as memories of last night came to mind. The consummation of their marriage had been nothing spectacular, it just happened, and it was perfect.

Terren traced lazy circles on Kiira's exposed shoulder and enjoyed the moment. In the stillness, he could hear the stirring of new day preparations, the soft, happy chirps of winter red throats, and the muted *tink, tink, tink* from the blacksmith a few buildings away. This was one thing he missed about living in the cordillera; the peacefulness accompanying a gentle snowfall. The world was always a little more hushed in its daily conversation, respectfully trying not to disturb the clean, glittering white landscape.

Kiira shuffled, pulling herself closer, bringing his attention back to her. It was surreal. The woman lying next to him was his wife, and most importantly, she loved him. A fierce love Terren knew he could rely upon for the rest of his life. Kiira didn't do things partially, as in everything, she was completely devoted to him; a gift he would carefully guard. Terren swallowed down thick emotion as the idea of unconditional love washed over him. It was a feeling he never really hoped to find in a woman buried long ago, refusing to even entertain the notion, until Kiira unexpectedly crumbled his defenses.

Thank you, Ny. You have blessed me.

Terren let one small huff of humor escape his lips, thinking about the course of his life. He had returned to Klynotia with one goal. To free his people from the tyrannical rule of his father, only to be blindsided by the devastating news of an engagement. He was still bitter toward Grayten; despite that, he would change nothing about the past five months. Headstrong and disagreeable, Kiira also was caring, graceful, and easy natured. All of her was both beautiful and unique. She was perfect for him. He thanked the gods again for the unplanned blessing of her in his life.

Kiira stirred, starting with a deep yawn and a stretch reminiscent of a waking feline, then glanced at him. Her sleepy eyes and lips smiling, as brilliant as the rising sun. Terren sighed in contentment and placed a long kiss on her brow. When he pulled away, her emerald eyes sparkled in delight and love.

She curled into him a little more and they stayed wrapped in each other's arms for several minutes, enjoying the moment. He wished for adequate words to describe how much he appreciated the woman beside him, and to stay suspended in this moment. Yet, the day was progressing without them and they needed to continue their journey. He promised to show Kiira the realms and, with nearly half of their Lundemai past, they could not be as leisurely as before. He was about to say something when she spoke.

"Terren, do the tattoos along your left side mean something?" She traced her finger over the lines of his stomach. He had to control a flinch from her tickling touch. "I noticed them last night."

He paused, not entirely sure what to say. Terren expected the question, as it was not a design easily missed, but what would be a proper explanation? He still needed to tell Kiira about Kamaria.

A seamless design decorated his left ribcage and arm as it moved around the side of his abdomen, back, and arms. The pointed and sweeping lines inked into his skin transitioned into three distinct motifs, each with its own meaning. The materializing bear on his shoulder blade was the least noticeable image, but it marked him as a Shadow Walker. A tribal bear's paw on his pectoral caught the eye first as it gradually transitioned into an artfully crafted depiction of a bear standing tall on hind legs. Taking up most of his left side, this primary image—given to him after Kamaria chose him as her partner—extended from his ribs down to his hips. The bear's aggressive stance was contradicted by the curious tilt of its head and soft expression. It was his favorite.

Terren needed to tell her about his abilities as a Shadow Walker. It was a key part of his identity and one he had no desire to keep hidden from her. Not anymore, but his hesitation always stemmed from how he should approach the subject. All of his misgivings arising from the conversation they had about Shade Demons on the beach.

The longer I wait, the more difficult this will be. She deserves to know before we travel into the Shade Realm.

He restricted his jaw, frustrated at how difficult he was finding it to speak of such an important subject.

"Terren?" Kiira asked.

"It is a symbol of my family history on the maternal side."

"What do they mean?"

He sighed. "I promise I will tell you everything, but only as we are crossing the plains, not before." She was about to protest, but he stopped her. "Please, it is not a simple explanation and not one to be made within civilization. I am sure your questions will be plenty once you hear what I say. You have my word you will know everything before we reach Letra Mera."

"Alright," Kiira replied. She was disappointed, but trusting. The knowledge curdled his stomach.

She settled back into a comfortable position again at his side. The silence this time felt almost unbearable. He wanted her to be understanding. He wanted her to love him and to be generous with her forgiveness when she realized he kept this from her for so long, but all he could do was pray for a favorable outcome.

Terren decided to speak with Kamaria. Now that she wasn't as uncharitable toward his wife, his Bear might have some good ideas on how to present the information. That was something he would work on as they crossed the plains today. Unwillingly, he said, "Kiira, we need to keep moving. It takes two days to cross the plains and it is almost a full day to cross the expanse of the canyon." She muttered something into his chest. "What?"

Looking up at him, Kiira repeated, "Do we need to begin moving this minute?"

"I suppose we could stay a few more minutes."

"I was thinking we could stay a little longer than that," she said, moving her eyes away and looking uncomfortable.

"Why? Is the bed truly that comfortable?"

"Yes, well and..." Kiira bit her lower lip. Her eyes glowed hopefully when she glanced up at him.

Understanding took him, and a thrill crept across his mouth, turning the corners into a pleased smile. He liked this suggestive side of Kiira. Rolling so she was now underneath him, he trailed kisses along her jaw, starting at her ear. Her breath shortened and when he came to the corner of her mouth, he whispered, "Is this more what you were thinking?"

Kiira nodded, still breathless as she held his gaze.

Terren's eyes sparked with hunger. A humorous breath of air escaped his lips as he kissed just below her ear. Then, in a low rumble, he said, "I think we can manage to be delayed for a little while longer."

He didn't give her a chance to respond before devouring her lips, pushing aside his worries for a time and completely losing himself in his wife.

CHAPTER 47
SHADOW WALKER

The unbroken landscape stretched endlessly as vibrant tints of red, orange, and yellow set swaying winter grass ablaze in the fading light. Tempest and Starfire pushed through stalks, creating a steady *shhh, shhh, shhh,* prompting fond memories of lazy afternoons by the shore.

Kiira's shadow extended a long diagonal before her as she rode just behind Terren, traveling southeast, their ultimate destination, Byloraan, on the other side of the Kilunys Bridge to stay with his uncle for a few days before venturing further into the Shadow Desert.

She sighed, glancing over at her husband. He'd been silent most of the day, not keen for any subject, and the forced silence left her to puzzle through hundreds of questions and supposed answers with nothing more than his cryptic remarks to go by, which merely catered to her curiosity and anxiety. Why did he seem so nervous? Did he not believe she was trustworthy? She wished he had something, anything, to say.

Though Terren is not one to speak aimlessly. Goddess, give me patience. He'll tell me when he's ready.

Focusing on the horizon, Kiira tried not to think about anything. Not of the intriguing tattoos—rather attractive against his brown skin—nor of his tenebrous attitude about whatever was on his mind, and despite her efforts to clear her mind of these distractions to focus on other things, the enigmatic questions persisted to consume her thoughts. She was so introspective, Kiira nearly passed Terren, who had wordlessly dismounted and began setting up their camp for the evening. Following his lead, she took to the task of caring for the horses, a labor she could meticulously focus upon to find a few blissful minutes of silence in her contemplations.

The smell of a rabbit stew aromatized the gentle breeze with a delightful smell. Kiira's stomach complained profusely at the enticing scent, pulling her back to the present. She hadn't even noticed Terren leave the camp to hunt. Briefly connecting with the horse's minds, she impressed upon them not to wander and left them un-hobbled to devour the abundant plains grass. Making her way to the fire, Kiira settled comfortably onto a blanket as Terren handed her a steaming bowl of the chunky stew and situated himself on another neatly folded blanket to her right.

She absently poked the vegetables and meat with her spoon, knowing the dish would be delicious. Terren was a proper cook, but as hungry as she was, she couldn't find the will to eat. She startled, nearly dropping the steaming meal when Terren spoke. Looking up, Kiira asked, "What?"

"Will you cast a protective barrier around the camp?" He asked. "What I have to tell is for you alone."

"Terren, there's no one out here."

He gave a small smile. If she didn't know him better, Kiira would have considered the expression condescending. She shrugged and snapped her fingers; the languid breeze shifted, creating a perfect circle of tall grass like sentries. This was not a casting she could maintain for long, but for a while at least any words spoken in the dead air would not leave the current of wind circling their camp. Faint shimmers of pale green caught in the light as the breeze circled them, the only sign of something different.

Satisfied, he said, "Tell me what you know about the Mage War."

"I know the history like anyone else," she replied. "Before the Mage War everyone had the gift of magic. Like today, skill depended on study. No government structure existed and people lived in both nomadic and settled groups. People abided by a natural order of rules and everything was fine until Elders of the Mage Schools believed there should be a hierarchy. Many didn't agree, but thousands were still persuaded and convinced those more powerful should govern those beneath them."

Terren nodded. He gestured for her to keep going.

"This started the Mage War. It divided the realm; sons were against fathers and daughters against mothers. Cities and towns were constantly destroyed and rebuilt. It was a never ending cycle because both sides were strong. The conflict continued for a nearly thirty years until what was intended as an ultimate act by hundreds of Elder Mages didn't go as intended and it physically ripped the realms. Instead of the intended Shade Demons, the Shade Realm was pulled, bringing the two lands together, killing nearly everyone in the Sun Realm and scarring the land."

She noticed Terren sober slightly, but continued.

"That act brought access to the Shadow Desert and the Isokanii people. It also created the Glaze Fire Canyon. The contrast of the Shade Realm to the Sun Realm forced together is what produces spectacular flames." Kiira finished. "Why did you need to ensure I knew the history?"

"It's foundational to what I am going to share with you. What do you know about the Isokanii?" Terren asked.

"I know what Gettii of the Eshalahee has told me when they come to the citadel. He and I have been friends for many years."

Terren smiled. "I know Gettii. I only met him once when I was living in the Shade Realm. He came by to purchase weapons to protect the caravan from the blacksmith I was apprenticing with."

"You should tell Liem you were a blacksmith apprentice," Kiira said, abruptly changing the subject. It was something she had been thinking since Terren had first told her about the surly man.

Terren raised a brow.

"It might give you and my brother common ground ... never mind. It's not important."

Terren looked thoughtful for a moment, nodded, and then gestured for her to continue.

"Oh, yes," Kiira said. "You mentioned your mother was the from the Daswadii tribe."

"Yes, the Daswadii tribe is also the largest and the ruling tribe over the others. My mother more specifically comes from the Chausekkii family, the main royal family over the Isokanii," Terren confirmed.

"I didn't realize one tribe was more prominent than the other, I just thought each tribe had their own leaders and rulers," Kiira said.

"Each tribe has a leading family. One person is elected from that family to sit on a high council to help guide the decisions made by my grandfather, the Mafelbno, or Emperor."

Kiira nodded, taking in the new information. Gettii had taught her much over the years, even some conversational language, but he never mentioned this. "Okay, but I still do not understand how this relates."

"You will. I am assuming you know the specialty trade of each tribe?" Terren questioned.

Kiira nodded and said, "Of course, and I remember the merchants said a tribesman is not forced to learn the tribe's specialty, and members can learn other trades if desired, but most are content."

Terren acknowledged her statement. "True for all except the Daswadii tribe. As royalty, we are the only Isokanii who can choose to be a Stietii Tetsa, or more commonly referred to as Shadow Walkers."

Kiira looked at him skeptically. "Shadow Walkers? That is a children's tale."

He shook his head. "I can assure you Shadow Walkers are real. All Shade Born are adept at diverting the attention from the Daswadii tribe's 'trade'. It is the Isokanii people's most valued secret. We let outsiders believe they are nothing more than stories."

Kiira studied him for a moment. There was an intensity in his eyes she had not seen before. Terren seemed to be willing her to understand, to know, and to accept the truth of his words. "So … acknowledging the direction of this conversation, you are trying to tell me you are a Shadow Walker? That is what your tattoos signify." She gestured to him noncommittally.

Terren let out a restrained breath, and confirmed hesitantly with a small nod, as if any sudden movements might frighten her.

Quietly, she replied, "Exactly, what does this mean and why are you nervous to tell me?"

"I am bonded with a Shade Beast, Kiira," Terren said.

She paused. "Which you emphatically told me before is not the same thing as a Shade Demon."

He nodded. "Stietii Tetsa is a choice and initiates train for years before they are allowed to attempt the Ermyjek Ceremony or 'The Forging'. The process is extremely taxing on the body and it has the potential to kill the man or woman, but if successful, you are bonded to a Shade Beast for life."

Kiira felt sick. "You knew it could kill you and attempted it anyway?"

"Yes, deciding to be a Stietii Tetsa is not for the faint of heart. It is a part of my heritage, and while I lived in the desert I learned my mother was training to be a Shadow Walker before she married Grayten."

"What was it like, the bonding?"

"Excruciatingly painful," Terren said, grimacing. "It felt as if my entire body, mind, and soul were being stripped away layer by layer." He lowered his voice to a reverent timbre. "Truthfully, I had to be willing to die to complete the Ermyjek. Once the process was complete, my physical form changed and I took on qualities of my Shade Beast."

"This sounds so much like magic, yet it's not?"—Terren nodded—"I don't know what to make of it." She shook her head. "So, being a Shadow Walker makes you invincible?"

"I can be killed, it's just … difficult." A humorless smile touched his lips.

Kiira focused on the fire. She wanted to believe Terren. It was not like him to lie, but his tale was rather incredible and yet she had seen stranger things with magic than his claim to be attached to a Shade Beast. "What else can you tell me about being a Shadow Walker?"

"When the bond is established, I was mentally linked to my Beast but the connection runs deeper than that. As a Shadow Walker, magic has less of an effect on me. I am not invincible to castings, but the connection to my bond partner makes me more immune to magic than most. Shade Beast naturally negate any magic cast upon them. I also have heightened senses."

That's why my magic feels suffocated when I touch him.

Kiira gave him a curious look, and almost asked more, but decided she really didn't care to know. His intense gaze was so hopeful, desperately wanting her to accept his words and not think less of him for it. She turned her eyes again to the fire and watched it dance in an undecided pattern between white, yellow, and blue, the hypnotic flames helping her to focus and process everything Terren explained.

This is almost too fantastic to believe.

Being able to merge your identity with another life force was of the Elder echelon of magic and here sat a man with no magical abilities, telling her he could. Kiira had a hard time believing this was not magic, but Terren was clear on that point, and none of the Isokanii merchants possessed the gift of magic. Sorting through his information, something still bothered her, but she could not put it to words. Instead she asked, "Why is the knowledge of the Shadow Walkers kept secret?"

Terren released what seemed a sigh of relief. "Shadow Walkers are the ultimate protectors of the culture, people, and the Shade Realm. Since The Mage War their—our job is even more important. If others, especially mages, knew the power we possessed, it could be devastating for the Isokanii."

"If Shadow Walkers are the ultimate protectors, then why are there whole tribes of warriors?"

"While we are powerful, there are few of us who have actually made a connection with a Shade Beast. There are roughly two hundred in total."

"That's quite a few," Kiira said.

"Not in tribes of thousands," Terren replied.

She nodded, conceding to his point. Kiira waited for him to continue, but it seemed he was allowing her to direct the flow of conversation. "How intelligent are the Shade Beast?"

Leaning forward on his knees, Terren said, "They are very intelligent, though Kamaria only learned to communicate with words because of our bonding. She still prefers to interact with sights, emotions, and scents. It can actually be really confusing at times."

The knowledge about the Ermyjek Ceremony bothered Kiira more than ever. His connection with Kamaria, if she understood the bonding process, put the two of them on intimate terms. A sliver of doubt nudged at her thoughts.

They are more intimate than I could ever be with Terren.

Sadness pulled at her brow.

How am I to compete with an attachment to the very core of who he is?

His connection to the Shade Beast was on an even deeper level than her attachment to Skehtra.

Kamaria would always be a deep-seated part of who he was. A mixture of anger, a deep sadness, and regret filled her as she realized her position was second place.

I gave him my heart, and this is what it cost me. I have to share him with ... with an animal.

She looked at him again, and there was a shimmer of hope in his eyes. Hope that she would accept this part of him. How she could continue to love him?

No! I cannot think such thoughts. I love him ... I do. Maybe that's why this hurts.

Needing a few more minutes, Kiira turned back to the campfire, letting the light sear her vision and dry her eyes. The bonding was permanent. Terren would always have a 'shadow' about him.

Maybe seeing this Bear would connect missing pieces within her mind, change her perspective. She was terrified of meeting a Shade Beast. It was small hope she did not entirely expect to work, but it was worth at least trying. "Would Kamaria be willing to meet me?"

Terren nodded and his gaze becoming unfocused and distant for the space of a breath before he returned and said, "She has agreed to reveal herself." Straightening and looking over his right shoulder, he said, "Alright, Kamaria."

A low swishing sound started behind him just outside the illumination of the fire. A heavy presence created a void in the protective barrier. The first thing Kiira could see was an enormous nose and thick snout, seemingly formed by the darkness itself. Then a massive head materialized like mist coming together to create a solid shape. The Bear's eyes were all black, with a light gray ring for the iris. The intelligence was immediately obvious; the Bear looking at her in a knowing, distrustful way. The mighty trunk-like neck followed, leading to the fully formed towering body. Kiira stood abruptly in fear. The she-bear was even larger than her encounter with the Oranta.

Backing away slowly, never taking her eyes off of the animal in front of her, she quivered, "Terren, that is ... that is a Shade Demon." Without thinking, her bow and quiver appeared in her hand.

A rough snort came from Kamaria, making Kiira jump. Terren stepped in front of her gaze, breaking her eye contact.

Holding up his hands, he said, "Kiira, I promise Kamaria is not a Shade Demon. Remember what I said at the beach? A Demon's mind is distorted, and bent to the callers will. It's why they are so vicious and hostile; it is not an accepted bonding by the Beast. Please trust me; I would never put you in danger."

Kiira stopped and glanced between him and Kamaria several times before focusing on Terren. His relaxed features and calm posture helped her to release her pent up breath. She let her bow fade from her grip. Grasping her hands, he stepped backwards, beckoning her closer to the enormous figure. Kiira's feet haltingly followed. He whispered words of encouragement as they neared, probably because her hands were trembling so badly he thought she needed it. She did. Stepping behind her, Terren guided Kiira's hand toward the Bear. Her large wet nose was twenty times that of her hand and ice cold to the touch. After a few seconds, Kamaria snuffled, causing her to jump again and clutch her hand to her chest.

"You're doing great, Kiira." Terren moved around from behind her, but still kept a hand on her waist and scratched the she-bear's snout. Kiira's heart tripled without his comforting warmth at her back. Kamaria reveled in his attention, closing her eyes in bliss, and pushed her snout into his hand it nearly knocking him over. A soft, deep chirping growl-like sound emanated from her throat. Kiira could hardly remain upright, watching their interaction. This was not just a friendship or loyalty between them. They were fused together body, mind, and soul. Everything Terren said crashed in an enormous wave, crumbling her already disturbed emotions. Devastated and overcome with grief, Kiira did the one thing that comforted her in times of stress. She spun out of his grasp and ran as fast as she could away from them.

She didn't care where she was going; her only intention was to be as far from their intimacy and camaraderie. She let heartache stream in rivulets down her face as betrayal fueled her stride. The slight rational part of her mind knew betrayal to be a dramatic description of her emotions; yet it was the only word coming to mind. She wanted all of Terren, his mind, body, and soul, things that should have been hers immediately as his wife. Kiira never wanted to be second, not to her husband, but because of Kamaria, she was the 'shadow', the one destined to always be in the background.

She ran faster as images of Kamaria and Terren flashed in her mind. Tears blurred her vision, making it even more difficult to see in the inky darkness pressing in on her from all sides. The energy of despair surged through her limbs as her heart thrummed in her ears. Suddenly, a heavy weight trapped her arm, and she was forced through a stumbling arc, straight into Terren's chest. Kiira tried to pull and push away as sobs racked her frame, but he locked muscular arms around her, unmovable as siege walls. Giving up, she cried into his chest and, as upset as she was by the whole situation, she found more comfort in his presence than through the hard pounding of her feet. Loosening his hold slightly, Kiira braved a lookup to see deep concern etched into his features as he examined her tear-streaked face.

Patiently, Terren held her, stroked her hair, and every once in a while placed a kiss on the top of her head. Eventually, the tears slowed, and she melted further into his arms. He picked her up and cradled her in his arms as he walked back to the fire. The heat of the fire to one side and he on the other melted the cold, penetrating her emotions.

He came after me ... that is the second time.

It was a profound realization for Kiira.

He was silent, but held her tightly. Leaning away from him, she dared to look into his eyes and they expressed everything he would not say. He was hurt, but he still loved her, and he wanted to know why she ran. Focusing on her laced fingers, it took Kiira several minutes to acutely describe what she was feeling. He placed a gentle hand on her twirling thumbs, stilling her fidgeting hands. She took a shuddering breath and released it long and slow before beginning her explanation.

When she finished, Terren let the easy night breeze carry away her words. His firm hand pulled her chin, forcing her to look at him, and he searched her gaze. Tears were already forming as she briefly glanced at his ice-blue eyes before focusing on his shoulder.

I can't look at him ... I just can't.

Shame for her actions, turning her gaze away.

"Kiira, look at me please," Terren gently said.

Reluctantly, she looked at him again and prepared to see a whole range of emotions, and all she saw was compassion. Kiira sucked in a breath to keep herself from crying.

When Terren seemed sure that she would not look away, he said, "I will not deny there is some of me belonging to Kamaria, it is an unavoidable part of the Ermyjek Ceremony. However, you need to understand our bonding is more a partnership, comparable to a longstanding friendship. She only has access to me, and I to her, when allowed."

"That is not any different than your relationship with me. I am considered your partner as well." She added bitterly, "and not by choice."

"Kiira, I don't ever want to hear you say those words again." His words seared with anger and frustration, and his grip tightened painfully over her hands before he relaxed after a breath. "How we came to be is of no consequence, you are my choice. You're my wife and that makes you more than just a partner. You are my Ishaiio."

Kiira choked back a sob at the word. There wasn't a perfect translation into Sunarian, but Terren essentially said she was the missing half of his heart, a sentiment not commonly uttered amongst the Isokanii.

Terren continued, "Kamaria, as wonderful as her friendship is, can never fill the voids in my life only you can and have filled. She is intelligent and comprehends much, she is able to hold a conversation, but she is still an animal. I will always care for her, but she will never have access to the place in my heart and soul reserved for you alone."

"Terren—" He placed a finger over her lips.

"Kiira, you and you alone have been the caretaker of my soul since the day you told me you loved me and it will remain as such until the day I dine in Apelgo's Halls."

Terren pulled her in for a fervent kiss with gentle passion, holding her head securely in his hands. A sob of joy bubbled in her throat as she realized the depth of his words. Relieved, she returned his kiss as Terren's love for her flooded her soul, healing her previous doubts and worries. With as many barriers as there had been in their relationship, there was no hesitation in Kiira's mind about where they were now. He loved her far greater than she ever thought a man could.

Ending the kiss, she pulled back and smiled at the love gazing back at her. She threw her arms around his neck and kissed him again, pouring every ounce of her love into it. Terren gripped her waist tightly, as if he was afraid she would disappear again.

Kiira pulled at his shirt with an intense urgency.

He slowed her movements and whispered, "This, I want to savor."

Tears dotted her vision as she let him, with the utmost gentleness, remove every layer. This time, every touch and heartbeat felt more real and special than the first. This time, she understood the truth of their relationship. It sealed the gap between her soul and his, stitching her permanently to him. A music as sweet as the first life-giving breezes of spring seemed to vibrate in the air. For the first time, she felt complete; a half made whole.

FORCHID

"Terren! The bridge!" Kiira's exuberant smile held the wonder of a child receiving a present as she stood in the stirrups to gain a better view.

He supposed this was a gift for her, considering she had never been outside Lorea. They were still some distance away, but he drank in her enthusiasm. Her joy at something so simple lit a fire inside of him he'd long forgotten, and he looked forward to when they actually crossed the bridge; she would likely be speechless. He smiled affectionately at Kiira.

Looking at the position of the sun, Terren determined they would reach the western city, Letra Mera, also known as Forchid, by late that evening. The warm, bright disc was already beginning its descent toward the western horizon. This was their third day on the plains, the journey taking longer than he intended. Once again, a night filled with Steasi Storja, or Star Stories, caused a morning delay. The Veripoi, a small nomadic people, were by far the best story tellers ever to cross his path and Terren enjoyed passing along their history to Kiira. He dug deep into his memory and exhausted his familiarity with their culture just to satisfy her thirst for knowledge. Kiira sat down again in her saddle and Terren could see her smile had only grown wider in the short time she viewed the bridge.

"I'll race you!" She said, and spurred Starfire before the sentence was even complete.

He laughed and urged Tempest to follow the trail of her glee. The walls of the city came into view after a few hours of alternately galloping and walking. Kiira won their initial 'race' and a smug grin accompanied her laughing eyes.

Oh, how I love this woman.

He smiled back before returning his attention to the low, sprawling city.

Forchid stretched for miles in an enormous circle, protected—for an unknown reason by a thick stone wall with a constant patrolling guard. There was nothing to threaten the city. This stretch of land was the most peaceful area of the Sun Realm. The massive barrier seemed overkill, but the city's designers apparently thought otherwise.

Terren led the way, passing through the first gate as the setting sun behind them turned the smoke-blackened stone into an odd mottled design. Tiny sections of white—more like less-blackened stone—attempted to peek through. He imagined that at one point the white gleaming walls were a sight to behold, but after hundreds of years of exposure to the smoke created by the Glaze Fire Canyon, the mired and pitted surface was nothing more than dreary and depressing. The constant soot made the city one of his least favorite places to be. The miasmic air clung to everything and everyone.

The line through the portal gate came to a near stop as the last of the stragglers hurried through before guards barred entrance for the night. The throng of people made forward motion a tedious affair. Once they were in the city proper, just to have a reprieve, Terren led them off the primary thoroughfare to allow some of the crowd to disperse. He watched, studying every detail of his surroundings, looking for signs of danger. He didn't tell Kiira, but the closer they had gotten to Forchid, the more his senses suggested something bad would happen. There wasn't any evidence to suggest the thought had merit, it was just a feeling, and he didn't like the growing intensity, which became especially stomach turning inside the walls. Terren looked past the hundreds of roofs to the governor's castle at the easternmost edge.

One night and then we'll cross. I'll feel better once we're in the Shade Realm.

The creaking gates closed with a shuddering boom and the main road cleared enough for them to navigate without issue. Taking Kiira's reigns, he led her through the maze-like streets toward the heart of the city. She chattered while pointing at unique structures and dozens of shops, entirely fascinated by the sprawling city.

Her constant stream of words kept him from dwelling too much on his dislike of having to navigate the twisted pathways. Terren's first time trying to traverse the city had been two steps past a disaster, as he was lost for several hours because of wrong turns and dead ends. His usual good sense of direction abandoned him, even with a compass in hand. He'd finally become so frustrated he paid one of the local urchins to help him. The twisted orientations of the roads made for a formidable defense; soldiers familiar with the city would have a great advantage against those that did not know the layout. He still considered commissioning something similar for the fortification of the citadel of Klynotia, but it didn't mean he had to like it.

The passage of an hour finally saw them to the front of a well-kept but soot-covered inn close to the central market district. As one of the larger and more popular spots visitors frequented, they would be lucky if there was a room. Winter was not a favorite season for travel, so his hopes were high.

Terren looked up at the wooden sign carved in the shape of two ringing bells and painted a bright gold, the eye-catching color dimmed by the soot and appearing brassier. It was a losing battle for the shopkeepers and tenants to keep things clean. A wonder they still gave the effort.

Having gotten the horses groomed and stalled for the night, Terren led Kiira into a boisterous tavern; their entrance unnoticed by the cheery and inebriated crowd. He held tightly to her hand, weaving through the compacted bodies to the bar. A stooped and sickly looking bald man poured drinks to expectant patrons. Terren waited patiently until the barkeep turned to him to take his order, and it took him only a moment for the man to recognize him.

"Jayan! Well, I never," Torrel said.

"Torrel, it is good to see you." Terren smiled. "Do you have a room to spare for a night?"

"For you, my friend, anytime." Torrel turned and disappeared beneath the surface of the counter momentarily before popping up again with a key spinning around his finger. "Room fifteen."

"Thank you, and a bath too, please," Terren said.

"Certainly, but it'll be at least an hour with as busy as I am tonight."

"Not a problem, we will have some food first."

Terren pushed his way to the stairs and ascended to the third floor. He opened the door to a small but nicely furnished dust-free space. The outside of the buildings may be despairing to look at, but the citizens of Forchid long ago learned the secret of keeping grime from invading their homes. A double bed swallowed the room—crammed next to a tiny table with two chairs near the fire. After relinquishing their packs to the floor, Kiira gave him a wry smile.

"Seriously Terren, how many people do you know?" She asked.

He shrugged his shoulders. "I have always easily found friends wherever I go."

"That is putting it mildly."

He laughed and escorted her back downstairs for a hot meal.

CHAPTER 49

THE MARKETPLACE

The smell of fresh bread and the day's roasted meats filled her nose as Kiira stepped onto the main thoroughfare of the marketplace. Breathing deeply of the enticing flavors, she decided convincing Terren to stay one more day was infinitely better than missing out on seeing such a different culture from her own. There was only so much she could experience from atop a saddle. The people of Forchid were an uneven mixture of gruff to mildly happy, and everyone seemed to be so industrious. Loreans were much more relaxed, focusing on friendship while still completing their work on time. Staying longer was definitely worth Terren's sour mood and lengthy lecture to not leave his side before escaping the confines of their miniature room.

Following her nose, she wandered into the open door of a bakery right as an errand boy darted past carrying trays toppling with well-wrapped loaves, likely taking his fare to the nearest taverns. The warm air inside welcomed her with the tangy aroma of yeast, a reliable smell regardless of where she traveled. Kiira pulled in a deep breath, savoring the air as she languidly worked her way around the shelves of bread, examining each roughly written label and trying to decide what would delight her tastes.

As she was browsing, a shadow darkened the door, catching her attention. A starved beggar entered the shop with a hopeful look. Terren tensed beside her as the baker, a plump man with red-orange hair and beard, stepped from behind the counter to gently lead the man from the shop. The small shoulders and despairing pale blue eyes of the piteous man as he walked across the street wrenched at her heart. There were few beggars in Lorea's capital, thanks to her father's efforts, and she couldn't stand to see such hurt painting the withered old man. Kiira watched him sit heavily against the wall before turning around and immediately requesting two loaves of the seeded honey bread. Walking over to the old man, she handed him a full loaf.

"Make this last as long as you can." Kiira smiled at him gently so as not to frighten him. This close she could see he was rather old, and he had a similar eye color to Terren's, though his were milkier, as if they had been bleached by the sun.

The beggar's distant eyes stared at her in disbelief and uncertainty for several long seconds before warily taking the loaf from her hand. She smiled as he ripped off a piece, devouring it in seconds.

He gave her a half-toothless grin, making her giggle. Holding the smile, she said, "Mag jou tafii ke ya nagligte gaan." The old man gaped at her as she stood to leave. Kiira gave him a final wave before turning away.

Terren brushed the small of her back. "May your journeys go by the lights of night. How did you know he was Isokanii?"

Tearing off a section of her honey loaf, Kiira handed the piece to Terren. "I didn't know for sure, but I guessed based on his eye color, and he seemed to understand me." She ripped a small piece and took a bite of the still warm bread.

"He is Isokanii, and he did," Terren replied.

Kiira nodded before returning her attention to the ever-bustling market-place. She meandered forward, enjoying the hastiness of the people and owners peddling their wares. A grimy sign carved to represent piles of fabric caught her attention. Glancing inside the window, she saw hundreds of bolts of cloth of all types of materials and colors. Intrigued, Kiira pushed her way into the store. The small shop allowed for only the barest amount of room to maneuver, and as chaotic as it looked, there was a surprising amount of order. A few women, mostly upper class, chatted while analyzing the colors and quality of the materials. The women laughed and bickered as they decided what to purchase, or who would look lovely in which color.

This is so normal.

Kiira smiled at the idle small talk. Another thing she had noticed in her travels, people changed little, despite the culture shifts. They still had thoughts, opinions, and feelings as each person trundled from one day to the next.

Kiira fingered the fine materials, looking for a colorful fabric to turn into something beautiful, maybe even something she could embroider to send to Tereyssa. Terren stayed near the door and leaned casually against a stack of wool. The tinted blue material he rested against darkened as the bolts neared the floor. She wondered if the lower bolts were truly a dark blue or if they had fallen victim to the foot traffic bringing in the ever-increasing soot pervading the city.

Laying gentle hands on her hips from behind, Terren whispered in her ear, "How did you manage to convince me to stay so you could shop?"

"It is because I am exceedingly adorable and difficult to contradict," Kiira replied, without a beat of hesitation.

"As if I need reminding." He chuckled.

"Oh hush. Go down the way and look at the blacksmith's offerings. I'll be here for a while yet and I noticed the attention you gave the shop as we passed."

"I'm not leaving you alone," his flat statement ceasing his previously teasing lilt.

Kiira turned. Terren's eyes were serious. The intensity of his gaze made her question if there was more to his emphatic statement. Softly, she said, "Really T ... Jayan, We can't always be attached at the hip, even on our Lundemai."

He narrowed his eyes.

"I'll be fine," Kiira said, placing a palm on his chest. "Besides, you will only be a few shops away, nothing is going to happen."

Terren studied her for a moment. "Why do you want to purchase material? For that matter how do you plan to carry such an item?"

"Ah, well here is a lesson for you then, Husband." A smile teased the corners of her mouth. "If I decide to purchase something, have no worries for I'm quite *gifted* with packing."

Terren raised his brow. "That still doesn't answer my first question."

"Oh, that's simple. I only packed a basic traveling dress and I'm considering a purchase so I can have something nice to wear for you," Kiira said, and then continued her perusal.

Not realizing the impact of her statement, she quickly found herself in Terren's arms. His intense gaze searched hers. Kiira glanced around, but the other patrons were hidden behind hundreds of fabrics and people on the street were too preoccupied to look into a pitted grey window.

Blinking, she whispered, "Ter—" His kiss was soft, gentle, and it took the space of a heartbeat for Kiira's breath to hitch. He pulled back. She knew the shock that jolted her breathing was mimicked on her face. Terren smirked and put space between them.

"Alright, I will be at the blacksmith if you need me or when you are finished, but please do not go anywhere without me, and be wary." He placed a light kiss on both of her hands before exiting.

Kiira watched him as he passed the front of the shop.

What in the world was that for? The way he acted this morning, I didn't think I was going to get him to leave my side ... and what was that kiss for?!

Shaking her head, Kiira returned to her browsing, but couldn't focus on the bolts of cloth in front of her. Even a bright silk verging more on the side of pink than orange with fine golden threads hardly caught her attention and seemed as mundane as the other selections.

She was still puzzling over his actions when a familiar sensation crept up her spine. A sick feeling dropped the color from her face as she glanced out the window to see people panicking.

"It can't be," she gasped, but knew her instincts were true. Kiira dashed out the door and stopped short when she spotted the one person she had never desired to see again. Zerrec stood in total concentration as he organized the chaos in the wide street. She had to stop him.

Shoving her way through the increasingly panicked movements of shoppers, Kiira stormed up to Zerrec and pulled on his arm in an attempt to break his concentration. "Zerrec, stop this. Stop it right now! What are you doing here?"

He turned his eyes to her and smiled gently. "Why I should think it would be obvious, child; I'm here to rescue you. I have been waiting months for this opportunity."

"What? I don't need rescuing! You have no right to be inside these people's minds, Zerrec! Let them be!" She said, her voice rising in urgency. Zerrec reached out to touch her, and she flinched out of his reach. A flash of anger glazed his eyes so quickly that she almost doubted she had seen it.

"In time you will understand what I am doing for you," Zerrec said.

"I already know what you have done for me," Kiira spat. "Now leave these people alone!" Glaring at him, she summoned her magic, using a casting from Liem's school. This much power would drain her, but it would stop Zerrec. Before she could snap her fingers, rough hands pulled her off balance and shackled her wrist. The magic she was about to cast abruptly ended. She looked up into the eyes of a weathered bear of a man with a blank expression, staring at her with utter boredom. Furious, she tried to complete her casting, and blinding, intense pain shot up her arms, making her gasp and her eyes water.

Dizzy, she sank to the ground only to be hauled back up by the large tattooed man. With difficulty, she looked up at Zerrec and saw what appeared to be sympathy.

"Now, child, there is no need to be so brash. I'm not going to hurt you or any of these people. I'm trying to protect you," Zerrec said.

Unable to use magic, Kiira struggled bodily. Her attempts, however, were laughable compared to the hulking man's strength.

"Let her go," came a familiar voice from behind her.

Terren.

Kiira was spun around as Zerrec stalked past her and up to the prince with a polished silver knife in hand. Two horrible, grungy looking men ambled up behind Terren and grabbed his arms, one of them holding a knife just below his ribs.

Zerrec laughed, sliding his own knife up to Terren's throat. "I was going to kill you with my magic, but you're not worth the waste of energy."

A line of blood seeped from beneath the blade to trickle down his neck.

Kiira's heart locked. "Zerrec, stop!" He looked at her. "I'll do anything you want, just let him go."

"No, Kiira," Terren gritted out before one of the two men holding him shoved the knife into his skin. He winced with the pain.

She turned pleading eyes to her old mentor. "Please, Zerrec. I'll go with you, just don't kill him."

Zerrec narrowed his eyes at her. "If I do not kill him, he'll only come after you. I cannot have that." He turned back to his target.

"Zerrec, please"—she swallowed hard—"for the sake of what we once had." The words were ash in her mouth. It was a vague statement, but she trusted it was suggestive enough to spark the response she wanted from Zerrec. It was cruel, playing to the man's feelings for her, but Kiira would do anything to protect those she loved.

Her old mentor studied her, and with difficulty, Kiira held his eyes. "Please, Zerrec."

"Fine." Looking at the bear man holding her, he said, "Take her."

Kiira struggled. "No! Promise me, Zerrec. Promise me you will not kill him."

Zerrec sighed with impatience. "Trinesteo. I will not kill him this time, but if he comes after you, I will not keep such a promise."

Kiira nodded. She looked at Terren. "I love you." Tears sparkled in her eyes as she was pulled away.

"You two get rid of this filth," Zerrec said.

Kiira heard a grunt and boots being dragged. She choked on a sob.

Ny, Windrah, Apelgo, please hear me. Protect him. Bring him back to me.

As she was pulled from the market, the last face her eyes landed upon was that of the beggar's that she had given the loaf of bread to. Complete despair entered her heart. She was alone.

"You worry for no reason, my love. I have the perfect place for us, prepared just so that we can be together," Zerrec said.

Angered, Kiira growled, except the unshed tears in her throat made it sound like mangled coughing. "What do you want, Zerrec? Ten years is not enough time to let go of rejection?"

"Centuries would not be enough time if you lost the one you loved. Something I know you are all too familiar with," Zerrec spat.

He has no right to bring my mother into this.

Glaring at him, Kiira said, "You were a fool to believe I ever looked at you as anything more than a mentor and a friend. You mistook my kindness for more than what it was." She locked eyes with the man she once respected; a silent battle passed between them, each willing the other to look away first. She was physically and magically helpless, but she would not let him intimidate her.

Zerrec remained at ease. "You will change your mind once you see what I have done for you." Turning to his henchman, he said, "Ricker, time to go."

Pulled in a direction she didn't want to go, Kiira struggled against her captor. Strong arms picked her up and sacked her roughly across broad shoulders, pushing every ounce of air from her lungs. By the time she could draw any respectable amount of air, they were far from the chaos outside the city walls. Zerrec had transported them. Frustrated, she beat on the back of her captor and shouted angry words, but she might as well have been pounding a stone wall for all the good it did her. Tears threatened to spill, but she forced herself to be strong, despite the hopelessness she felt.

"Zerrec," Kiira begged weakly, "what are you going to do with me?"

"What I had always planned to do my dear, marry you. If the whelp of a prince is smart, he won't come after you, leaving us to live in peace," he said, then increased his pace.

His emphatic statement worried her, and she fell into silent despair as hope became shrouded with pitted blackness. At this point, she could only try to survive. Her former mentor was powerful, as an Elder Mage, and if he wanted her or Terren dead, all he needed was to snap his fingers.

A single tear managed to drip and stain the dirt.

Goddess, please help us.

DESPERATE SEARCH

Gingerly, Terren pushed himself up, tunnel vision moving in and out of focus and an annoying tension at the back of his mind keeping him from gaining his bearings.

'Terren!'

The voice urgently speaking his name was fearful and distant, as if being shouted to him across the Glazefire Canyon.

'Yepenzi!'

That name caught his attention and suddenly did not feel so remote. 'Kamaria?' He asked, unsure if it was real or a very plausible dream.

'Oh, thank the night! Yepenzi, are you alright?'

He folded his brow as he took stock of the situation. There was a slight pinch in his neck and Terren reached up to pull out a dart. He blinked several times as his mind cleared. He looked at the dart.

Pirates? Why was I attacked by pirates? In Letra Mera?

Terren studied his surroundings. There were two unfortunate looking dead men at his feet. Definitely pirates. Pools of their blood were already black, and in some spots, dried completely, staining the compacted earth.

How long was I unconscious?

From the placement and depth of the wounds, he knew he made those cuts, but he certainly didn't remember it. Looking around, Terren saw he sat in a long, shadowed alley, well away from any prying eyes and sounds of a disturbance. At the very end, in the deepest shadows, he could see Kamaria looking at him with concern. Her expressions matching the pulsating emotions dominating his mind. Pushing to his feet, he staggered toward her and walked through the opened passageway.

Knowing he was safe by his Bear, Terren fell raggedly against Kamaria's stout leg. She shifted, laying, and settled in such a way he could rest comfortably against her. Her massive head blocked him completely from view. It wasn't necessary, but he felt her contentment at being able to protect him within the folds of her body. They were silent as Terren waited for complete recovery from the effects of the dart.

'*Yepenzi?*' Kamaria asked.

'*I'm fine, my friend. I've had worse than this, but I'm having difficulty remembering what happened,*' he said.

'*Tell me what you do remember. One minute I felt your presence, and then nothing. I only found you as the drug began to wane,*' she said.

'*All I can remember is being at the blacksmith when complete chaos erupted. I imme-diately searched for Kiira—*' Jolted, he sat up. "Kiira!" Terren scrambled out of the protective embrace of his Bear. "Gods above! Kamaria, why didn't you say something?"

'*I did not think about it,*' she replied.

Terren gave her a stern look.

'*Alright, I did think of her briefly, but my chief concern was finding you.*'

"Kamaria…"

'*It will always be you,*' she said, resolute.

He sighed, disappointed. "I cannot fault you."

His Bear flattened her ears, attuned to his current feelings. '*I'm sorry for not saying anything sooner. I know how important she is to you and this time I'll do whatever I can to help you locate and rescue her.*'

Terren calmed and rested his forehead on her ice cold snout, allowing her warm, steady breaths to ruffle his hair. He permitted his love for Kamaria to relax him. She hummed in pleasure as she felt the emotion course through him. "I'm sorry for that. I'm just worried."

'*I know, but we will find her, I promise,*' Kamaria said.

"I pray you are right."

'*Have hope, Yepenzi, we will.*'

Terren nodded and rested for a few more minutes against her snout, willing her strength and comfort to bolster him.

Terren left the Dueling Bells burdened with belongings and leading the horses. He made his way toward the market, where the chaos erupted. It was his first stop after discussing a plan of action for finding his wife with Kamaria. Terren wanted to first see if Zerrec left any clues. Once his head cleared of the drug, he remembered every detail of the encounter. Kiira sacrificed herself to protect him. Part of him was angry. She had decided for him what should happen, but he also knew she had done her best with the situation handed to her, just like she always did.

Now it was his turn to return the favor.

Ny, help me find her.

Currently, Kamaria was checking the perimeter of the city from the shadows, and he would see what there was to learn within the walls. He needed to hurry. Patrons were being chased away by the setting sun and shops would soon close in response.

Stepping into the open marketplace, frustration tensed his fists when he saw how packed it was, even with the late hour and after their minds had been invaded, acting as if nothing occurred. Pushing through the crowd, Terren found the street of the fabric shop. He didn't really expect to find Kiira there, but wouldn't leave anything to chance. After speaking with the woman manning the shop and getting nothing, he moved on to the bakery. Discovering the doors locked and bolted tight, Terren set to banging until the baker opened the door with an angry jingle.

"What? I'm closed."

"Have you seen a petite woman with long honey blond hair, green eyes?"

"Ya, know, I'm pretty sure I saw the girl you're talkin' about. She has those pretty curls like my little Leina. You don't see that color hair very of'en. Why's a fellow like you askin'," he said with a hint of animosity.

Hiding his annoyance, Terren said, "Do you not remember us from earlier?"

"Can't say I do. Get a lot of customer comin' through my door," the baker replied, crossing his arms.

Terren wanted to rub his temples to clear the mounting headache. The man was purposely being difficult. Holding up his right hand so the man could see his ring, he said, "The woman is my wife, sir, and any information you have would be greatly appreciated." The words were pleasant, though forced through gritted teeth. Normally, he would attempt to be more genial, but his concern for Kiira held an iron sway over his emotions, and keeping his voice marginally even was all he could manage.

"Ah, well, tha's a shame. Le's see … she purchased two loaves of honey bread from me this mornin' an' I sees her give one to the beggar Old Man Dain. Thas' the last I saw of the lady."

"Maybe the beggar, Dain, saw something?"

"There's a chance, but I doubt it. Nice ol' thing, but he's crazy as me mother-in-law."

Terren ignored the baker's quip. He didn't have time for small talk. "Where can I find this beggar, Old Man Dain?"

"This time 'a night…" The baker fingered his beard. "I'd say he's probably near the cen'ral foun'ain beggin' for a coin or two. The crazy 'ol loon, he don' ever make much sense when you talk to 'em."

"Thank you, I appreciate your assistance," Terren quickly said, abruptly turning on his heel to make for the central fountain.

To his vexation, the fountain square was even more packed than the streets. Sighing, he took care to deliberately scan every beggar on the premises. Several homeless men and women filled the space, asking for money. Most people ignored them, except for a few compassionate shoppers with extra coin. Terren was about to give up looking when, in an alley just ahead of his position, he saw a man sitting in the shadow of a building. It was the beggar from this morning.

Finally, some fortune.

Eagerly, he pushed through the throng of shoppers and kneeled in front of the old man. Dain, muttering to himself, had eyes dancing to every inch of his surroundings except the space Terren occupied. His hands were out and cupped to receive anything from a passerby who cared enough to notice. His fractured words were incoherent, but Terren thought he heard the beggar mumble something about magic. It was so muffled in his frizzy beard, he couldn't be sure.

Laying a silver coin in palms tentatively, he asked, "Are you Dain?"

Pale blue milky eyes met his and then glanced back to the coin in his hands and then at him, as if the moment seemed unreal. The telling signs of fear and uncertainty crept into the old man's expression.

"I am not going to hurt you," Terren added. "I was hoping you could help me. I'm looking for my wife. Do you remember the lady from this morning with the bread?"

The old man rapidly nodded his head. "Pretty lady nice to me."

Terren smiled. "She is a kind person. Can you describe to me what she looked like?" He asked, to be certain. Following rabbit trails wasn't something he had time or energy for.

"Pretty lady gave honey bread. Tasted like her hair."

"Did this pretty lady have green eyes?"

"Pretty lady gave honey bread. Tasted like her hair," Dain mumbled again.

The baker had been correct about the old man's ramblings, but Terren was fairly certain the beggar was talking about Kiira. This was the man they'd seen this morning, but he needed to pull more information from Dain. This was going to be a long conversation and extreme forbearance was key. As much as he wanted the information now, the task before him needed to be handled with care. Even if he didn't get useful information, at least he would know he covered every possibility of finding information within the city walls.

Looking at the pathetic state of Dain, he could see why Kiira accorded the old man compassion. Terren hadn't been unaware of the beggar this morning, but his sour mood put him in a selfish frame of mind. This man needed to be shown the same kindness Kirra had given, not just because he responded favorably, but because the old man deserved his respect.

Clearing his throat, Terren said, "Dain, are you hungry? I will buy you some food if you talk to me about the pretty lady with the honey hair. I would like to know more."

The old man's eyes grew wide and then he scowled and said, "No, no, no, no, no, no. You trick Dain. Make fool, not believe what he saw."

"Dain, this is no trick. I will believe anything you tell me. I want to find the pretty lady."

The old beggar scowled and waved his arms wildly. "No! No, no, no, no, no. You hurt pretty lady like other men. Leave pretty lady alone!" He shouted.

Terren shuffled back a few inches and allowed the man to calm and begin muttering to himself again and then he said, "Dain, pretty lady is very special to me, she is my Ishaiio, I would never hurt her. I want to help and I need to know if you saw anything. Please, for some food and drink I am asking for your assistance."

The old man stared at him and held his gaze for several intense seconds. Terren did not falter in the staring contest, but only tried to convey his honesty. Finally the beggar said, "Dain help Kiivulii. He want hot food."

Terren was startled at the old man's name for him, but ignored it for the moment. He agreed to help. "Alright Dain, lead me to wherever you wish to eat and I will buy the meal of your choice."

Standing, he pulled the beggar to his feet. At an agonizingly slow shuffle, he followed Dain. Terren prayed for the gods to give him patience as he dealt with the old man. His increasing anxiety to find Kiira had the potential to make his words testy.

DAIN'S LONG GRAY BEARD, matted with years of dirt, skimmed the surface of the food bowl. The same hair from his head framed his weathered ebony skin. Leaning heavily opposite the table, Terren studied the old man. He imagined the beard to be snowy white if properly taken care of. Drawn and creased milk-blue eyes gave the beggar a tired look. He was definitely Shade Born, but why did Dain live here in the Sun Realm? All Shade Born found the harshness of the Sun Realm too much to handle, their eyes being more sensitive to the light. Even the traveling merchants wore special cloths over their eyes. Terren remembered thinking it was odd that his mother always covered her eyes until he later learned the reason. Only he could travel between the two realms with no aid.

Thoughts tumbled through Terren's mind as he watched Dain eat his chosen meal of a hearty beef stew with a smoky and spicy seasoned broth. It was no surprise the beggar chose the Glazen Tavern for food. It was the most popular in the city. He'd gotten several stares when ushering Dain inside and had to promise to pay the barkeep triple just to be given a place to sit. Terren understood the owner's reservations, and he respected them, but he made a promise to Dain. Plus, gaining information about Kiira was more important than the establishment's pride.

He finished his own meal some time ago and now played a waiting game for the old man to be ready to talk. Dain was a slow eater, and the pace wore on Terren's usually lengthy patience. They had been sitting for nearly an hour. Letting out a big sigh, Terren leaned against the wall of their shadowed corner table and rubbed his temples. He let his mind go blank momentarily, not really sure of what to think.

Out of nowhere, it occurred to him why Dain called him Kiivulii. Terren's tattoos were not visible when dressed, so there was nothing obvious to give away his status as a Stieti Tetsaa. The only other plausible explanation was the old beggar once attempted to complete the Ermyjek, and the Beast chose to leave during the process.

Terren remembered his instructors speaking of it. If a beast left in the middle of the forging, the person was left drastically different. One of the changes was having the ability to see things as they really are. It made perfect sense, then, why the old man seemed crazy to others. The poor beggar was not anchored to a Beast or the Shade Realm, which had serious repercussions on his mind. It would explain why it sounded like he may have been muttering about magic. Curious, Terren asked, "Dain, did you attempt the Ermyjek?"

Sadness filled the old man's eyes before they became unfocused and he stared at nothing. Then, Dain looked at him with complete clarity and said, "Pretty lady in trouble."—he slurped some broth—"Nice lady hurt."

Caught off guard, it took Terren a moment to formulate a reply. "Dain, please tell me what you saw. I am desperate to find the pretty lady."

"Pretty lady put in chains, cried in pain," Dain said, slurping again.

A grimace pinched Terren's face. He bet the shackles had a casting to prevent her from retaliating. Kiira mentioned the existence of such magic often used in her father's dungeon. She, of course, still tried to fight back in some way and suffered for it.

"Nice lady cry, Kiivulii hurt, pretty lady carried away." The beggar mumbled.

Terren stiffened. Dain witnessed the whole thing, and it only served to remind Terren of the inadequacies of his protection. The sooner he located and rescued his wife, the better, but it took a great amount of control to stuff down his impatience. He promised Dain a meal and he would see it through.

His biggest issue at the moment was where Zerrec had taken Kiira. Based on where he found Dain, he doubted the beggar followed, but he asked anyway. "Dain, can you tell me which direction the pretty lady and her captors went?"

The old beggar chewed on his food and rocked back and forth in his seat, humming. After a few minutes of no response, Terren asked again. This time Dain began to sway and rock even more violently. His face was distraught. Terren soothed the man before pondering what would have caused his reaction. "Dain, did the pretty lady go near the bridge?" He tentatively asked.

He started rocking again and mumbling, a low-pitched moan escaped his throat before he answered, "No, no, no, no, no, no. Dain afraid of edges. Central is safe. Sun not like Dain."

"Pretty lady was not taken toward the bridge?"

"No, no, no, no, no, no," Dain said, his voice steadily increasing.

Terren placed a gentle hand over the beggar's clenched fist. "Alright, Dain, it's alright. Thank you for your help." The old man stilled his movements and after a few moments, turned to look at him. Terren tried to convey every ounce of sincerity, compassion, and thankfulness he could for the beggar's help.

Closing Dain's hand around several coins, enough for the old man to not beg for some time, Terren wished he could do more, especially since this man was related to him in some way. But the only help the poor beggar would find would be in the Shade Realm. Switching to Isokanii, he gently said, "Dain, thank you again for your help. I understand going home may be difficult, but if you go back, there are places to assist you. You would not have to live on the street and beg for anything. Think about it alright?" Terren hoped his words would actually get through to him, since it was Dain's native tongue.

Dain looked away for a moment and then stared at him with a heavy gaze and simply nodded.

Leaving the beggar to finish his meal, Terren laid several gold coins on the bar, paying as promised for the 'inconvenience' to the owner, and left.

A MAGICIAN IN LOVE

Kiira struggled against the meaty hands of her captor, the shackles a discordant echo in the natural stone pathway. Her skin was being rubbed raw as she writhed, but it mattered little in the grand scheme of things. Her movements only made the ox-man's hands tighten all the more on her arms and he shoved her further into a perfectly round stone room. She would have dark, finger-shaped bruises on her arms for days. Catching her balance, Kiira twisted and sprinted for the door, but there was no reward for the effort, Zerrec had already erected a barrier. The chain of the manacles dropped to the floor with an ear-splitting clank. She pounded on the crimson, glittering shield, the color brightening where her fists connected, but otherwise remained resolute. Kiira tried to send magic into the barrier to destroy it, but with the metal cuffs still encircling her wrists, she only managed to send a streak of pain straight to her head.

After watching the two men walk away, she turned her back to her freedom, and sank, frustrated, exhausted, angry, and hopeless to the unyielding surface beneath her. Tears stung and reddened her eyes as she cried into her knees.

If only I had listened to Terren … to Liem … to Father …

Kiira eventually reigned in her emotions. She swiped the hot tears from her face, taking a few shuddering breaths. Standing, she took querying steps about the rather spacious cavern, taking stock of her surroundings. Placing her fingertips on the deep purple, nearly black stone, Kiira walked the perimeter of the domed space. They were in the Forest Wilds. She could tell by the way her magic hummed in contentment at being surrounded by plants. A lot of good it did her. She couldn't cast anything to make a difference.

She stepped around orbs of magically sustained lights spaced every few feet around the perimeter, and to her dismay, but not her surprise, she found no other exit. Several feet above her hung a chandelier with dripping candles, a busy but beautiful piece lavish in dramatic arcs from the ceiling.

Well, he certainly hasn't lost his taste for finery.

It was oddly comforting to know a part of Zerrec hadn't changed.

The essentials of a bedroom and dining area occupied tiny portions of the rather large cavern. The design of the furniture gave mention to the sea. It was beautiful. Elegant curves and subtle hints of blue could be seen in the otherwise white linens. Coppery plates, bowls, and cutlery preset on the table changed color as she shifted from one foot to the other. Zerrec was trying to impress her. She grimaced.

A squelching sound, like boots stuck fast in thick mud, caught her attention. Kiira spun to see Zerrec standing behind her, holding a tray of food. He smiled, but it wasn't warm and caring like Terren's. Zerrec's rich, sapphire eyes stood out against long, stark blonde hair. The Elder Mage was a respectable-looking man, and many of the court women had sought him as a husband.

"How do you find the accommodations?" He asked.

Gesturing to the space beside her, Kiira said, "This is impressive, thank you, but why do all of this for me?" She wanted to be rid of Zerrec's attention, but she wouldn't be ungrateful for the gesture. A bed was preferable to an unyielding floor.

"Because you are my love."

Kiira cringed.

"Is there anything else I can do for you?"

"You can let me go. Find someone else to love."

Zerrec returned her gaze with a single brow arced, silently asking if she really wanted to continue with such an ignorant thought. It was the same look he would give when she was his student years ago.

Kiira relented. "No, there is nothing more I need or want at the moment."

Zerrec bowed and left the room.

Three days passed as the first. Zerrec brought Kiira her meals and asked if she needed anything. Her request was always freedom, but Zerrec merely smiled and shook his head each time. So, Kiira tried a different tactic, and for another three days she asked for inconsequential things that might help her escape, but he still gave her the same silent expression. He would not be fooled. Giving up on the idea of escaping by herself, she settled for books and writing essentials. If she was going to spend so much time alone, writing her thoughts would at least keep her from going insane. Her captivity wasn't awful, but this was not living, and Kiira refused to lose hope that Terren would eventually find her.

On the seventh day of her confinement, Zerrec stepped through the barrier with the usual meal, but there was something different about him. She was lounging on the bed, reading and, instead of their usual routine, he left the tray on the table and came and sat on the edge. Kiira closed the book and pulled her legs in, crossing them as she sat up.

"How are you holding up, my love?" Zerrec asked.

Kiira stiffened at the endearment. She would never get used to it. "I am alright. I would be better if I was not stuck in a one room cave," she said. "Could I not have some glimpse of outside?"

"I will have a better place for us to live soon. When I can trust you will not run, you will have more freedom. I am only trying to help you."

Kiira fisted her hands to her forehead. "Zerrec, this is foolishness. You and I will never be."

He shook his head. "One day you will see what I have saved you from and you will thank me. We will be married and happy."

She looked down at her knees. The thought of being with Zerrec made her stomach roll. "I am already married, Zerrec. The gods will not ordain a union between us. Ten years. You would have found happiness with another."

"The years between then and now have not lessened my desire. It is why I have rescued you from a life you did not want. We will be happy." His sure tone frightened her more than the surges of anger she knew existed within him.

"How did you know I was unhappy before, Zerrec?"

"I have watched you since learning of the arrangement," he said.

She couldn't suppress the shiver inching down her spine. "I am no longer unhappy, you can release me and have peace knowing I am well."

"There is no need to resign yourself any longer, my love. We are together now," Zerrec said, reaching out to stroke her cheek. Kiira bit her tongue to focus on something other than the crawling sensation tingling her cheek from where he touched.

"It is not resignation. My feelings for you have not changed. I did not need to be rescued, Zerrec. I'm happy with Terren. I love him."

"That is a lie. You loved me first."

Kiira pulled away from his touch. Anger burned in his eyes. She needed to keep him talking, distract him. "You were always my mentor and friend. What made you believe I had feelings for you?"

He paused for a moment, studying her, puzzled. "It was the quilt you made for me," he said. "It was your token of unspoken declaration."

Kiira took in a breath, unable to utter a word.

That ratty haphazard quilt? An unspoken declaration? That way of courting died with the Mage War.

It finally all made sense. At the time of her mother's death, Kiira hadn't known how old Zerrec truly was. Hearing his confession now, she actually felt a measure of pity for him. "Zerrec, that quilt was nothing more than a gift to a friend. I will say it again, I love Terren," she said. "You need to release me."

"Why?" he asked, reaching out again. This time cupping her cheek. She wanted to pull away, but also didn't want to ignite his anger. "I can make you happy."

Kiira did her best to express a gentle rejection, and with a sorrowful shake of her head, pulled his hand away. "No, you cannot."

His expression soured. "How can you be so sure of that?"

"I have always been, and always will be a mere child in your eyes, Zerrec. You were my friend and my mentor, but nothing more, the age difference is far too great. Do you honestly believe your affections would be enough for me to tolerate being looked down upon?"

"It is not uncommon for there to be a gap in age, and I do not look down upon you," he said, offended. "You were one the strongest magicians I ever had the pleasure of teaching and I respect you as such. I love you."

"That is not what I meant, or did you forget I know your true age?"

"Age is but a number. We would have forever," he said.

Kiira closed her eyes and sighed. "I do not want forever, Zerrec."

"Why not?"

"I never want to forever outlive all of the people I love."

"You would have me to love you."

The topic was a losing battle. One they had debated many times before Zerrec had been banished. He did not understand her arguments against living forever then and clearly would not now. Why stay frozen in a world that should be constantly changing? It was the next generation's responsibility to shift and move society from one way of thinking to the next. Kiira was certain countless discoveries, like long burning candles, better saddles, and hideaway tables, would have been missed if not for the imaginations of those younger than her. Changing tactics, she asked, "Do you value me for my gift as a magician or as a person, Zerrec?"

"What is the difference? Who you are is a magician."

"Therein lies the problem. If I had not been gifted with magic, if I was never a princess, you would have never been inclined to know me. That is what makes my relationship with Terren special. He values me for who I am, not for my birthright or what I am capable of doing."

Anger dropped his face and pulled at the corners of his mouth. "So, that is your decision? There is nothing I can do to have you love me?"

Kiira attempted to settle her features into a kind, yet determined, mask. She needed him to understand, to truly hear her. "Nothing, Zerrec. I never meant to toy with your emotions and for you to believe more."

He slapped so hard, Kiira felt her eyes water and could feel a cut on her cheek caused by the ring on his finger. She refused to cry in front of him, despite the pain. Clenching her teeth, her previous calm turned into defiance.

Zerrec was shaking, attempting to control his rage. "If what you say is true, then you would never have looked at me the way you did when handing me the quilt. I refuse to believe your lies. You love me and soon you will be my wife," he said and strode through the door.

CHAPTER 52
REFRACTION

"I was willing to overlook the whelp of a prince, but as long as he is alive, Kiira will never be mine! I should have removed him from the picture when I had the opportunity. Once he's gone, she will be released from her bond and ultimately see I am the better man," Zerrec said, storming into the cavern used for cooking and dining, a proverbial and literal storm cloud following in his wake. A heavy breeze whipped through the enclosed space, scraping tables and chairs across the stone floor. Zerrec fisted his hand to disperse the heavy winds. The longer he'd lived, the more often he noticed his magic sometimes flowing without his control, usually matching the pace of his emotions. He paced, letting fury fuel his limbs. Zerrec felt Ricker's eyes following his every step. "What do you want?" He snarled, not caring to stop and give his full attention to the mercenary.

"You want me to track him down and kill 'im?"

"No. If their love is as strong as she says"—he sneered—"the prince will come after her, and I will not have to break my promise of not killing him."

"Seems a bit of a loophole," Ricker said.

"She should have thought of that when she extracted the promise from me."

Ricker grunted.

"Is there something else?" Zerrec bit out. He wished to be alone with his thoughts.

"Gorren and Hammle have not returned," Ricker said.

"Who?"

Ricker frowned. "The other two men you hired. My comrades."

"Oh, yes, the idiots. What about them?" Zerrec asked, still moving about the room and only half listening.

"They're dead, Sir," Ricker said with a hint of animosity.

He should have immediately punished the pirate for speaking to him in such a manner, but at the moment Zerrec was all too glad to hear that the needless task to kill them himself was not something added to his list. "How do you know?"

"When they did not return at the scheduled time, I made some inquiries."

"And?" Zerrec prompted, impressed the pirate had the foresight to procure the information himself, but it would be preferable to not have to pull the words from the mercenary like a horse pulling a plow through rocky soil.

"*And* they were found dead in an alley not far from where we obtained the princess. Only the two bodies of my comrades were found, but disturbances to the ground indicated three people."

Zerrec stopped and whirled to look at the corsair. "You are certain?"

Ricker gave one serious nod.

"Kreshkt!" Zerrec pushed past the hired man, making a bee-line to the room with his seeing crystal. Entering, he casted the magic to see his quarry, but nothing appeared.

I should be able to see him.

Zerrec tried again—nothing. A black void filled the crystal, which meant only one thing. The prince was using some kind of amulet to prevent himself from being found by magic. The boy was smart. "Kreshkt!" Zerrec pounded his fist against the wall.

He would have to continue to move their location to keep the whelp from finding them. However, with only one man to help, it would take time to discover and prep a new location. While he could contain Kiira's magic fairly well with the manacles, it was nothing compared to the solid barrier of stone to which he anchored his current castings. The prince was a severe miscalculation on his part, and Zerrec needed to dispose of the problem before finding suitable seclusion.

A slow smile crept across his lips. The prince was sure to be looking for Kiira. Zerrec had hidden their tracks well, but maybe he could let their location be found and use it to his advantage. He loved elements of surprise.

Zerrec strode into the Kiira's room, keeping a pleasant smile on his face.

She eyed him. He didn't blame her. The strike to her cheek still had an angry red line. She flinched when he sat down beside her and cupped her cheek. A faint crimson glow came from his wrist as he sent healing magic into her, making the skin soft and smooth once more. She pulled away with an angry jerk, flaring his ire. He needed her compliant, so settling his features, he said, "I apologize for hurting you."

"I do not want your apology."

"I admit my anger took the best of me, but you will see I am enough for you."

Kiira shrank away from him with a wary gaze.

"I have concluded that your prince is a problem."

Tears formed in her eyes and fear radiated from her. "What are you going to do?" It came out in a forced whisper.

"What I should have done in the market. I indulged you and and let him live, but he's tested me and my restraint is depleted. The only way solve this problem is to kill him," he said, with the patience of a teacher to an obstinate student.

Her eyes begged him, and he enjoyed having her at his mercy. "Monster. You promised."

"Ah ah ah, but there were conditions and they have been broken. Actions have consequences, my dear."

"Please, I'll do whatever you want"—she choked, swallowed a painful gulp of air—"I'll be with you forever, just don't hurt him."

"No!"

Kiira recoiled.

Calming again, he replied, "You have already proven to me your words are lies. If I do not kill him, he will never stop searching for you and you will never stop pining for him. Terren will be removed from the picture and then with some persuasion you will see what we can be with true clarity."

Zerrec ignored the pleas passing Kiira's lips as he left her, eager to set his new plan into motion.

CHAPTER 53
FAMILY

"Search the king's rooms, mine, and Kiira's. Search thoroughly, someone I don't know was using magic in this area," Liem barked.

Terren couldn't see the prince, hidden as he was, but the irritation was palatable. The sour attitude would not make the conversation he needed to have with Liem easy. A banquet was in progress, and the bit of magic Terren used to catch the prince's attention, stored within the night crystal pendant around his neck, proved effective in pulling him away from the frivolity. Terren considered being forthright about Kiira's disappearance and simply showing up in Lorea alone. No doubt Herretus would provide the means to find her, but in this instance a less was more and Kiira was his responsibility. He just wasn't naïve enough to face Zerrec alone. Liem knew the magician most of his life, which would give Terren an advantage over the Elder Mage, albeit a small one.

Terren edged around the stone column and saw the two other knights grimly nodding to their prince before striding to their assigned task. Terren recognized them as Folen and Merkus.

They must be wearing anti-casting armor if they are confident to take rooms alone. I am continually impressed by how well prepared Lorea is for a variety of attacks.

Turning his attention back to the prince, Terren watched as Liem headed down a perpendicular hallway to check the royal guest suites. He followed with careful steps, waiting for the perfect opportunity to reveal his presence to Liem. The other two knights were not part of his plan, and the conversation with the prince needed to happen without prying ears. Terren waited as restless protracted minutes passed. Normally, he could wait as long as necessary, but Kiira missing motivated his agitation. The heavy tread of the two knights came back to the split in the hallway.

"Anything?" Liem asked.

"Nothing, Liem," Merkus said while shaking his head.

"I thought I saw a glimpse of something in your chambers, but when I looked closer nothing was there, sorry, Liem," Folen added.

"That's alright," the prince said, then sighed in frustration. "Go back and enjoy the feast, I will be down in just a few minutes."

"Liem, I prefer not to leave you here alone, especially if there's someone here as you suspect," Folen said, and Merkus, his face grim, nodded in agreement.

"I do not feel the magic anymore, whoever it was must be gone," Liem said.

"You know that's not a logical conclusion," Folen said.

"I know that," Liem snapped. He scrubbed a hand over his mouth and jaw, letting it snag in his closely cropped hair.

"I've seen how tired you've been these last three days, Liem. Clearly you are not thinking as you should," Folen replied. Terren smirked at the knight's confidence. Only a best friend would be so bold to talk to a superior in such a manner.

"Only one of us needs to report to the king," Merkus added.

"There's no sign of anyone being here," Liem reminded.

"All the more reason for us to stay nearby," Merkus said.

"Really, my friends, I will be fine, I simply want a minute to myself before rejoining the banquet. If there is someone here, you know I am more than capable of handling them. Besides, the king saw us leave hastily, he'll be concerned. Go back and give a brief report. If I'm not there in twenty minutes, then come back for me."

Folen was about to say something else, but Liem's look must have been threatening enough to drain the words from his lips. Merkus frowned, but nodded, obeying the order. Folen, after a brief battle of wills, obeyed also, leaving Liem alone in the hallway. Terren still wanted more privacy, but if Liem didn't go into a room in the next few minutes, he would approach him in the hallway.

Hard lines carved unmistakable grooves around Liem's dark-rimmed eyes and his shoulders slumped. Terren could empathize with the prince.

Since Kiira's capture nearly three days ago, he slept very little. Liem and Kiira were too connected for the prince to not feel something.

The footsteps of Folen and Merkus were lost to the castle noises, and Terren was about to do something to get Liem's attention when the prince pushed off the wall and dragged his feet toward his room.

Perfect.

Terren whispered into the room before Liem shut the door and melted into a deep shadow. The prince leaned heavily against the stout wooden table in his sitting room, as if hoping the porous material would somehow absorb his burdens. The room rivaled that of a moonless night. It was now or never, and Terren needed Liem's help to ensure a favorable rescue of Kiira. He cupped the ebony crystal in his palms, covering his mouth, and whispered the trigger word to release the casting stored in the pendant.

Liem whirled and stared directly into his corner. "I know you're there. In the name of the king, show yourself!"

Terren took purposeful steps forward into the light of the only bare window, the silvered moon casting scant color into the otherwise dark space. Lights blazed as Liem used magic to flood the room with light. Terren momentarily squinted and there was the unmistakable sound of sword leaving sheath. He instinctively drew his blade in response.

"What are you doing here?" Liem asked, not bothering to disguise his distaste.

"I'm here for your help," Terren replied in a smooth and even tone. He was determined to show no emotion. Begging would only convince the prince he was weak and incapable. Liem would hate him even more.

"I am not helping you with anything," Liem said. "You were the one I felt using magic?"

"I think you will, once you know why I am here, and yes I was, to purposely gain your attention."

"Did Kiira tell you?" Liem asked, his look suggesting he felt betrayed.

"No, you just did, but it was something I knew about magicians already," Terren said.

Liem narrowed his eyes. He sheathed his sword and casually leaned a hip against a table. Terren would not be fooled by the relaxed stance. Liem was the training commander for a reason. In a gesture of good faith, Terren slid his scimitar into its protective cover. A silent battle of wills ensued for a few moments as they stared at one another.

Finally, Liem asked, "So why are you here?"

"As I said, I need your help," Terren said.

"I got that the first time, thanks," Liem said, rolling his eyes.

Terren tightened his lips briefly before smoothing his features again. He took a long cleansing breath, taking a moment to keep his impatience in check. When they locked eyes again, Liem looked at him for a fraction of a second before suddenly pushing away from the table in alarm. "Wait, you're alone. What happened to my sister?"

"She was taken by Zerrec," Terren said.

Immediate rage permeated Liem's entire being. "Kreshkt!" He pushed his hands through short hair, just beginning to curl and paced—a captive Wolfcat. It was only with great restraint he seemed able to speak. "Gods, Terren! I told you to be careful! Did my words mean nothing to you!" Liem's voice rose with each sentence.

"Of course," Terren said, his tone short and biting.

"Hmmph."

"Look Liem, be as angry with me as you wish, we can argue, and you can attempt to kill me later, but I do not want to fight Zerrec alone. I need your help. If I believed I could have rescued Kiira without either of us getting seriously hurt, I wouldn't have wasted precious time coming here to fetch you." Liem stopped. There was a murderous glint in the prince's eyes, but Terren remained composed. He needed to be the reasonable one at the moment. Liem went back to pacing. "Liem, are you going to help me or do I need to seek assistance elsewhere?"

The prince was intimidating, his bulky form crowding the space between them. Through a clenched jaw, he hissed, "You are a fool if you think I would abandon my sister."

"What is your answer?" Terren asked, narrowing his eyes. He dropped his hand to his side, resting it easily on the hilt of his sword. Liem noticed.

"Of course I am going to help you get my sister back, I'm simply determining what I may need. Zerrec is not to be trifled with," Liem said.

"That is all I needed to hear," Terren replied.

"What is that suppose—"

Terren touched a palmed crystal to Liem's neck, and the prince slumped forward in his arms. Grunting, Terren lowered the prince to the floor. The prince needed the bulk for his magic school, but still.

Wow, it's a wonder how he carries all that mass around.

'Kamaria,' he called as he moved to snuff out the candles in the room. The massive head and one paw emerged from the shadows. Through the doorway into the Shade Realm she opened, he could see stood on hind legs and leaned heavily against a sturdy tree to support her weight. She lowered her head to smell Liem. *'It's a good thing he's out cold,'* Terren said.

'They smell similar,' she said, *'but I like Kiira's scent better. She smells of the forest and he smells of dirt.'*

Terren wanted to say something sarcastic, but instructed Kamaria to lower herself as much as possible, and then hoisted the prince across her foreleg and onto her broad neck. After collecting a few items from the room he thought Liem might need, Terren climbed onto her back. *'Okay, let's go.'*

A DAY LATER, Terren slid off his Bear's back and lengthened tight muscles by moving first left, then right, wishing he thought to move more often while traveling. He lowered Liem to the ground and laid him in what looked to be a comfortable position before touching the prince's exposed neck with the ebony counter-crystal. It would be several hours before the knockout crystal Terren used on him wore off; especially after being under its influence for so long.

Removing all the items he packed from Kamaria's back, Terren decided a long run would be good for his overall sanity. Looking to his Bear, he asked, "I am going to get some exercise, would you be willing to watch the camp?" Terren knew better than to demand her vigilance.

'Yes, but do not be gone for long, I wish to nourish,' she said.

He nodded and, with a glance at the sun's position, low on the western horizon, ran north. The long, steady strides and heavy beat of his heart were the perfect release of pent energy. It didn't take long for Terren to feel a semblance of normalcy again. His worry for Kiira knotted twists of stress in his muscles, taking away his ability to relax. Worry still burned every inch of him, and that wouldn't go until she was safely in his arms again, but Kiira was still alive. He couldn't remove the wedding ring from his finger, giving him some comfort, and now, with Liem's help, his confidence at mounting a rescue was more than a dim hope.

An hour later, he returned to the camp with a renewed sense of purpose and two large hares to stifle the hunger settled in the depths of his stomach. Kamaria left as soon as she sensed his sight was upon the camp and, based on the current mood rolling between their connection, she wouldn't return for several hours, maybe more. She grumbled something about being a pack-horse as she disappeared through the doorway back into the Shade

Realm. Terren smiled and shook his head. His Bear was unbearably grumpy when she needed to eat.

Two hours saw the assembly of a well-fed campfire, a simmering stew, and, most importantly, a full stomach. Stretched out next to the cheerful fire, Terren's eyes roamed lazily across the dotted night sky. Still waiting for Liem to wake, he occupied his time by thinking through the Steasi Storja, and managed a few before it reminded him too much of Kiira. Instead, he admired the depths of the night sky, considering how small he was compared to the vast, sparkling blanket of night.

Every so often, he would whisper simple prayers of safety for Kiira. He tried not to dwell too much on what happened. If he did, his heart would ache. Desperate feelings wouldn't bring her back. Terren heard a groan and twisted up to see Liem stirring. Fully sitting, he grabbed a water skin for the prince, since he knew from experience the side effects of the crystal.

It took several minutes for Liem to become coherent. When he was, Terren said, "Your head is going to hurt for a while. I have water here if you can manage to sit up."

Painstakingly slow, the prince pushed himself onto his seat. He was unquestionably stiff and sore from the way he gingerly stretched his massive frame. Liem took a deep breath, looking at his surroundings.

He's definitely a strategist. Just awake and already he's assessing surroundings. Kiira might be right. We likely have much in common if he would get over his petty hatred of me.

Terren reached out to put the water skin into Liem's line of sight. The prince's eyes traveled up his arm to stare into his eyes, and then he snorted.

"I am not sure what you find so amusing," Terren said.

"I find it amusing that I see you here, of all people. This must be a dream because it includes you. I'm probably imagining you since I saw you in my room."

Terren raised his eyebrows, waiting for the prince to comprehend.

"Wait!" Liem twisted suddenly to get a good look at his surroundings, which turned out to be a bad decision as he immediately clutched his head. "Where am I, and how I did I get here?" He growled, the pain making him sound more like a snarling animal than a human, and Terren hid his amusement at the thought.

"We are camped just within the borders of the Forest Wilds, near Kiiroth, and I brought you here via knocking you out," Terren said.

Liem stopped, seeming to control the urge to vomit long enough to glare at Terren.

"You agreed to help me find Kiira," he added.

Something must have snapped, then, because Liem's eyes grew wide and his jaw twitched as if he wanted to say something but didn't know how to put words together in the correct order. The prince clenched his jaw, and a vein popped above his right eye. Terren waited for the inevitable storm and wondered if the prince's anger was making the headache worse.

"If my head did not feel as if a horse was repeatedly kicking against my skull, I would butcher you where you stood," Liem said.

"You could try," Terren mused, "although, Kiira wouldn't be very happy if you did manage to kill me."

Liem grunted and turned his attention to the steady flames of the campfire. He slowly sipped water, and the tension in his face seemed to lessen. Terren dug in his bag and found the painkillers he purchased from the temple. The special mixture was made of birch leaf and white willow bark, and flavored with dried cherries to make the plant concoction more palatable. As Terren handed them over, Liem gave him a suspicious look, but took the small button sized tablets and swallowed them with a mouthful of water. They sat in silence for a long time before either spoke.

"I really wish you would stop staring at me as if I have two heads. It's rather annoying," Terren said.

"I apologize, I had not realized," Liem said.

Terren doubted his words, but remarking on them was not worth the potential argument. "How is your head?"

"Better, I might actually feel up to murdering you later for losing my sister."

Terren sighed. "We were attacked, I was held captive with a knife to my throat, she sacrificed herself to save me. They drugged me, and when I awoke, Kiira was gone. Once I realized what had happened, I immediately started to look for her."

"Sure. She probably could not stand the sight of you and orchestrated the chance to get away," Liem retorted.

Terren closed his eyes and clenched his jaw for several seconds. He would like nothing better than to make a scathing remark, and he knew it was expected. But Kiira wouldn't want him to stoop to her brother's level. She mentioned on multiple occasions that Liem could hold a grudge. Responding to his jab was not worth his effort. Taking a deep breath, Terren leveled his gaze at Liem and said, "If you're going to continue with your sardonic and snide remarks, then let me give you money to purchase a horse and you can go home. I will find Kiira and rescue her myself."

Liem studied him with care then. Terren made sure to keep his face expressionless. He wanted an honest answer from the prince with nothing influencing his opinions.

After several minutes, Liem said, "You love her."

Terren gazed heavily at Liem. There didn't seem to be any malice in his statement, just a realization of the facts. He nodded and turned his attention to the fire, adding several logs to the diminished flames.

"I am sorry," Liem said.

Terren huffed. "Do not pretend you actually care, Liem. I know your opinion of me."

"True, but I can still be sympathetic. You love my sister and will do anything to save her. I may not like you, but I can respect your intentions."

Terren looked at him, genuinely surprised, before replying, "Thank you."

"Does she love you too?" Liem asked.

Terren nodded. "Very much." Clearing his throat, he poked at the orange and white embers.

Liem took a deep breath and asked, "May I have some stew?"

Terren lifted his chin, indicating the bowl and spoon near the fire. He settled into a comfortable position and waited until Liem was ready to talk again.

After a second helping, Liem said, "Tell me everything that happened."

In painstaking detail, Terren retold all he could remember. Everything from the sudden panic of the crowd at some unseen danger and how he immediately went to be at Kiira's side, to finally waking beside the two dead pirates. He didn't mention Kamaria, for obvious reasons, but ended the retelling with his conversation with the beggar.

"I hate that man," Liem growled. "He killed my mother and now he has the audacity to take my sister! He'll suffer a thousand times over for this."

"Liem, I'm not seeking to kill him, I just want Kiira back," Terren said.

"Are you not angry? How can you not want to kill him?"

"Of course I'm angry, he took my wife," Terren barked, and he had to pause for a moment to control the sudden rise of pain in his chest. "It's not my place to act as judge simply because of my anger. If it comes down to it, I will kill him in self-defense, but it is not my aim."

Liem scowled first at him and then at the fire, but said nothing. "Zerrec's going to try and kill you. He won't let go of Kiira for anything, and if he can't have her, he'll dispose of her, too. Zerrec. Does. Not. Share."

"I know, Liem, which is exactly why I came to you for help," Terren said.

"I am not arrogant enough to think—even with my abilities—I could defeat an Elder Magician easily."

Liem raised a brow. Several questions lingered behind his eyes, but thankfully, he kept them silent for the moment. "So, where do we start? Are we close to his location?"

"Our current position is my best guess. I found a set of hoof prints outside of Forchid leading in this direction. The trail disappeared at the edge of the forest, as if he was trying to hide his direction. It was definitely an error on his part," Terren said. That was only partially true. Kamaria had been a tremendous help, locating Kiira's scent. It was the only reason he'd gotten as far as he did.

"Maybe," Liem replied, shaking his head. "I think Zerrec is too smart for that."

"Okay. My tracking skills are excellent, but it's been five days since she was taken, so who knows how much has disturbed the area. Can you use your magic?"

Liem thought for a moment and then reluctantly nodded. "I'll have to be extremely careful. Since I was Zerrec's student, he knows the feel of my magic. Surprise is our best element, I don't want to give us away."

Terren acknowledged the limitation.

"Speaking of magic, I know you are not a magician, so what exactly did you do to get me here?" Liem asked, his voice as dry as the earth beneath him.

"I used magic to knock you out," Terren said, without missing a beat.

"What?" Liem asked, his alarm inching his voice up a few decibels.

"A gentleman never reveals all of his secrets, you of all people should know this," Terren replied and gave an indifferent shrug.

Liem flexed his jaw and a small part of Terren was having fun provoking the prince. The camp settled into quiet, allowing the crackle of wood to take up conversation. From the corner of his eye, Terren could see Liem holding back laughter.

"What, may I ask, do you find so amusing?"

Liem said, "As a gentleman, I cannot reveal all of my secrets."

Terren smiled. "Touché."

CHAPTER 54
A DIRECTIONAL POINT

Surprisingly, a modest chuckle escaped Terren's throat at the conclusion of Liem's story. If his mind wasn't so preoccupied with the reason the two of them were together, it was the kind of tale that might have actually made him laugh. The picture Liem painted of Kiira was a side she rarely showed, even around him, and it was amusing. The particular incident the prince described had earned the twins a full month's punishment of 'hard' labor. Picturing his wife scrubbing floors and washing laundry because she caused an egregious courtly humiliation and her uncle's broken limb was rather hilarious.

Terren absently poked a long stick at the coals, watching the sparks float away to non-existence. He and Liem had searched the Forest Wilds all day with no luck. They were miles into the thick trees, not the safest place to camp, but wasting time traveling to the fringes of the forest every day made little sense. It was only by Liem's insistence they rest, yet Terren's whole body itched to continue searching. At least having the prince around kept him from pushing himself to exhaustion. That, and the fact that Liem could not see well in the dark, and any use of magic to light his surroundings, was risky, forcing them to camp each evening. Terren agreed it was smart to be sparse with the magic, but it didn't mean the handicap wasn't a frustration or that it didn't bother him. Terren could see it chafed Liem as well, that his hands were figuratively tied, forcing him to limit the extent of his abilities.

Kamaria's search also bore no fruit. Terren had his Bear roaming the forest non-stop, attempting to pick up on Kiira's scent. Luckily, as a Shade Beast, she could go for days without rest when expending little energy, and she'd been searching consistently for the past several days. Unfortunately, it was the end of day three of their search, Kiira had been missing for eight days and the longer it took Kamaria to find her scent or signs of her passage, the more Terren's frustration wormed through their connection, making them irritable with one another. Even now he could sense her morose thoughts as she trundled through the thick trees, snuffling the air and ground, attempting to pick up a trail.

So far, Terren kept the revelation of his Bear's help to himself. He and Liem were separated throughout the day when searching, which was fortunate. While investigating, Terren intertwined with Kamaria. A strong smell or a flash of movement shifted his focus from his surroundings to her current position, causing him to stumble. Feeling as if he was in two places at once always disoriented him. It was a common sensation for new Shadow Walkers that would be less hindering the longer they were bonded. He readily anticipated that day. He was certain he looked the fool and was thankful Liem was not nearby to witness his clumsiness.

Kamaria's help and existence would eventually be known; the proximity to the prince was too close for it not to be, especially since Terren needed to meld with his Bear to have a marginal chance at confronting an Elder Mage. If Kiira's reaction to seeing Kamaria was anything to judge by, he didn't want to discover Liem's response. Delaying the meeting for now still seemed in the best interest for both of them.

Terren turned his mind to other musings as he sent another shower of sparks into the canopy with his stick, the embers sending fresh waves of heat out as he rolled them over. He was pleasantly surprised and grateful for how well he and the prince gelled in their short time together. Liem made no disparaging comments since the first exchange. In fact, he felt Liem was putting too much effort into friendliness—it was mildly annoying—yet it was infinitely better than the brazen hatred flaring from him only days before.

Terren was drawn out of his thoughts when he saw a hand in the corner of his vision. He shifted from his lounged position, feeling his legs going numb. "I apologize, Liem, what did you say?"

"I asked how you were holding up, you look utterly miserable," Liem said.

"I am miserable. It has been a week since Kiira went missing and the gods only know what she's endured. I have been praying fervently but it has not eased any of my fear."

Liem pulled in his lips and worked his jaw. "Completely trusting the gods is difficult, but we must try and do it, for, as you said, they alone have the answers. Though, if I may be honest, it doesn't sound as if you are at that point."

Terren was surprised to hear such an honest, vulnerable thought from his brother-in-law. He pondered for a few moments as his eyes focused beyond the flame of the fire, then huffed an amused breath. "I wasn't sure I would ever say this out loud, but you're correct. I have not completely trusted the gods, may they forgive me. I fear it is still in my nature to fight against them."

"I think it's that way for us all," Liem said.

"You seem to trust them implicitly," Terren replied.

Liem snorted. "Then you do not know me very well."

"You have never given me the opportunity." Terren said cautiously, not wanting to spoil the rapport he and Liem were sharing. It was a dangerous subject to breech and possibly not the best time for it, but Terren knew a rare moment when it passed his way and this definitely was a singular opportunity. He needed to begin mending the relationship between them or spend the rest of his life battling Liem with words. Mostly, Terren wanted to do it for Kiira.

Liem narrowed his eyes at him, probably hoping to decipher some ulterior meaning in the phrase, which did not exist. "Terren, you hurt my sister and then spent the remainder of the time before the wedding hardly saying a word to her, and whatever you said to make her run off into the Forest did not earn you any favorable marks. How did you expect me to react?"

"Liem … what I did was wrong. I admit it without reservation. But you have based your opinion of me on what Kiira said before we were married and her opinion of me then was less than favorable—"

"You did not want to marry her, either," Liem interjected, tipping the opened water skin accusingly in his direction.

"Not in the beginning."

"So, what changed?"

Terren thought back to what had really opened his eyes to what made Kiira special. "The catalyst was what she engraved on my ring. It was courageous, even though she was afraid. Then, after experiencing firsthand her kindness, loyalty, humor, and fierce spirit, one day, I found being around her was like breathing, and she felt the same about me. I'm grateful for the Lundemai, relationships are not an area where I am particularly gifted."

"Clearly," Liem said.

Terren held his tongue; he would not dignify Liem's childishness with a response.

Liem added quietly, "I'm making an effort to befriend you for my sister's sake. I'm glad you two are happy, that's all I would ever want for her. It is not easy, though, you're not an open book and that bothers me to no end."

Terren looked at him. "So, you dislike me because I'm a mystery?"

Liem nodded.

He wrinkled his brow. "That does not make any sense."

Liem refrained from rolling his eyes, but the exasperated tone was still apparent. "Really, Terr—"

"No, I mean it, Liem. It's not possible to know everything about everyone, even those closest to you. If you live by that rule, you will never find satisfaction in your relationships," Terren said.

"So, I should be like you, suspicious of everyone?"

"I'm not suspicious of everyone," Terren said.

Liem snorted.

"I'm cautious until I get to know a person. Those are very different."

Hesitantly, Liem said, "I'll concede to that."

They settled into a comfortable silence. Terren mulled over what Liem said about not trusting him, and the idea renewed his earlier worries. Liem would soon find out about Kamaria, and he still hadn't worked out what to say. With Kiira, it was easier. There was a foundation of trust that didn't exist between him and Liem.

Terren needed to change the direction of his thoughts. "Tell me more about Zerrec; his personality, his abilities, his magic strength. We still need a plan of how we are going to approach confronting him."

Liem leaned his chin onto his hands thoughtfully and Terren used the opportunity to quickly check-in with Kamaria. He connected to the small pressure at the base of his skull and was inundated with the sights and, more specifically, the smells registering in her mind as she searched. Weariness colored her emotions, and even though Terren knew she would search until she had little energy to offer, he encouraged her to stop. Kamaria's physical and mental health was as important as his own. Once he was satisfied she would bed down for the night, Terren severed the connection with her and brought himself back to his current surroundings just as Liem cleared his throat to speak.

The time passed quickly. Liem went into great detail, recounting all he knew of Zerrec. An interesting mixture of respect and bitterness poured from his tongue. The magician was brilliant and an excellent strategist. He always seemed to approach situations from an angle no one else considered. It was partly because of Zerrec that Liem learned to enjoy military strategy. Unfortunately, with the magician's brilliance, came a host of darker aspects. Zerrec never left things incomplete, not even the smallest tasks. He was meticulous and neat, but he was also rash and prone to violent outburst. He would do anything to get the results he desired.

As students, Liem and Kiira were subjected to surprise magical attacks. He would never physically harm them, but it kept the twins on high-alert for several years. The experiences taught Liem valuable lessons, but to this day, still annoyed him. The prince recounted the story of a casting that left him hanging upside down with his shoes stuck to the ceiling. Terren chuckled at that; the idea of the prince's hulking figure stuck to the ceiling was infinitely comical. Liem frowned at him, and Terren cleared his throat.

"If that is the case, then it surprises me Kiira was so easily captured in the market. How could she not expect him to have some kind of devious plan?"

"I love my sister's heart, but Kiira doesn't always think before she acts, or if she does, she ignores the potential consequences of her actions. I'm willing to bet she felt the use of Zerrec's magic and, concerned only for the people in the market, she attempted to stop him," Liem said.

Terren nodded. "I've seen evidence of that on more than one occasion." He studied the dark canopy for a moment. "It also surprises me Zerrec did not act sooner. As an Elder, why wait? Why now?"

"Terren," Liem said in a low, almost reverent voice, "Zerrec is smart and calculating, whatever the reason—even the smallest—it's purposeful. Has Kiira told you the story of how our mother died?"

"Your father did," Terren said.

"Really?"

"Yes, after Kiira and I argued."

"Hmm." Liem was silent for a moment. "You need to know something else my father never fully understood."

Terren sat straighter in response.

"Zerrec didn't just want to marry my sister. It was more than that. He was … obsessed with her. He did a decent job of concealing his feelings, but it was really obvious to me and my mother, and it was unnerving," Liem said.

Terren processed the words carefully. Herretus mentioned he was aware of the obsession, but Liem's words implied something dangerous. He said, "That explains why he reacted the way he did when he was not granted the marriage request."

Liem shrugged. "I suppose, but it seems rather extreme to me."

"Well, you're not mentally unhinged. Grayten did the same thing when he found my mother with another man." Terren scowled as memories of the outraged king stormed through his thoughts.

"Terren?" Liem asked, drawing out his name in his concern.

"What?"

"You've been staring angrily at nothing for quite some time."

Terren waved away the statement nonchalantly and Liem sat back in a huff, clearly frustrated, but he didn't push the issue. Terren did not need to discuss his morbid past, it wasn't relevant to their current objective.

"Tell me more about Zerrec, what school of magic is he in?"

"Zerrec is a magician of the crimson school, a Blood Mage."

"Healing," Terren mumbled to himself.

"Correct. He's been alive for as long as he has because of it. And here's the worst part, he's also had centuries to gain a firm grasp on the other schools as well."

"But it still affects him the same way, yes? He's not immune to the drain caused by castings outside his school?" If he could be drained, he could be defeated.

"Yes, thank the gods. Like me, he needs muscle mass to be at his magical best."

"Then how come he does not carry the same bulk as you?"

Liem scratched his chin. "I do remember him being on the slimmer side, but still muscular." He snorted. "It made him popular with the court women. He must know something as an Elder that I do not."

Terren nodded thoughtfully.

As Liem continued, the account turned lengthy and even more detailed, but by the end, there was only one conclusion. He and Liem were in for a proper fight. It made Terren wish for more help. Even with Kamaria's immunity to magic, this would not end the way he desired.

I will count us fortunate to walk away from this alive.

The magician had been around at least since the Mage War, and he was cunning and ruthless. Terren frowned, feeling unbalanced by understanding Zerrec's personality. It was hitting too close to home, and it had been a long time since the feeling had surfaced, not since his time aboard *The Surveysor.*

He could feel the tension in his shoulders building again, giving him an awful headache. Without a word, Terren stood and strode into the night, letting his steps quicken into a run, leaving Liem's surprised shouts to dwindle as they were absorbed by distance.

No sooner had Terren found a seat near the warmth of the fire than a harsh accusation came from his companion.

"Where have you been?" Liem's tone was short and flat as he stared hatefully at the large lizard glistening in the light. "I hate lizard."

Terren raised his brows at the sudden hostility, but said nothing. Instead, he stretched out on his bedroll, enjoying the warmth of the fire. Liem continued to glower at the lizard and shuffle his massive shoulders in the forced silence. The sour mood was not unexpected. Today had been another unsuccessful venture, and Terren would have liked to join the prince, but having both of them morose was only asking for a headache.

After dinner, the overall air of the camp improved significantly, despite a meal that left them both wanting more. Terren considered talking with Liem, but didn't particularly care to rehash a disappointing day, so he watched his surroundings. The distant flicker of a few stars peeked through the boughs of the thick trees, but otherwise a moonless night kept them pressed in on all sides by darkness, their campfire a beacon in an ocean of black. Reflective eyes blinked in and out of view, pausing long enough to study the odd light before going about their nightly activities. The hoots of owls echoed through the trees as they staked their claims. It was the perfect night for a Shadow Walker as it was the closest the Sun Realm came to matching the Shade Realm. Terren could even feel Kamaria's pleasure at the deep shadows as she continued her nightly search.

Terren glanced at the prince to find him scowling again.

Liem is as frantic as the stormy seas. I wonder if there is anything he does not concern himself with.

Curiosity got the better of him, so he asked, "What are you thinking about?"

Liem's frown did not change. "I'm considering how to best manipulate a casting to make me invisible without discovery. It's possible to shield the use of magic, but from Zerrec … it's more difficult."

Terren could hear the pained uncertainty in Liem's voice.

"I may have something that can help," he said, rolling up to dig through his belongings.

It occurred to Terren this was the first time he could help the prince with something. Liem watched him with great interest as he dug through his pack, pulling out several rolled leather bundles. Each one he stacked in a neat pile until he came to the pouch he was looking for and tipped out a small black crystal the size of a coin, sculpted into the shape of a swan. Picking up the thin leather cord from which it hung, Terren presented the object to Liem. "I would have this back. It wasn't easy to come by," he said as the trinket fell with a soft thud into the prince's outstretched palm.

Liem studied the piece briefly before saying, "No, I suppose it would not have been."

"The action words are Kreden and Juston," Terren said.

"It's heavier than I would have thought." Slipping the item around his neck, Liem said the first word, and his body immediately vanished. He said the second word and was once again looking at his knees. "Cray-den and Joos-Ton? What kind of ridiculous words are those?" He asked, not bothering to hide the incredulity in his voice.

"How should I know? The item was not specifically made for me and to answer your impending question, no, I'm not going to tell you how I came by such a trinket."

"I would not expect you to tell me," Liem said with a sneer. "Put this on and activate it, I want to test this against various castings."

Terren narrowed his eyes. He didn't appreciate the disbelief. Well, that and the disdain Liem was not disguising. Quietly, with just a hint of annoyance to color his words, he said, "It will hold against whatever castings are used."

Liem rolled his eyes. "I trust you, Terren, but it will still make me feel better. This is my sister's life we're staking on a trinket."

Terren wouldn't argue. He would likely do the same if the tables were reversed. Without a response, he whispered the activation word and blinked from sight. After settling into a comfortable position, he used the time to check-in with Kamaria.

'How are you, Yepenzi?' He asked.

'Miserable. I have been sniffing out a trail for days with nothing,' she replied.

'We'll find her, and you know I appreciate your help.'

'She has such a unique scent. Kiira is like light in darkness to my senses and NOTHING!'

Terren frowned. The mental strength behind the last word pounded at the base of his skull. He had never felt his Bear this frustrated before. *'Kamaria, my friend, we will find her. I am anxious to find my wife, but being emotional will not find her any faster.'*

'I know, but I'm tired, and frustrated, and hungry,' Kamaria said.

'Then rest, taking an hour to hunt or forage will not be a set back and your health is important. I'm going to need you when I face Zerrec,' Terren reminded her.

She grunted, but did not stop her searching. *'I do not like that your rescue plan hinges on me, I'm not an infallible resource.'*

'Of course you're not. You know me better than that. I always have a back-up plan.'

'And that would be?'

'Liem.'

Kamaria snorted. Her feelings for the prince were as favorable as the fish she preyed upon.

Terren mentally sighed. *'Yepenzi, he is a gifted magician and related to me. Be nice.'*

'Why? You don't like him,' she said.

'He's starting to grow on me,' Terren replied.

Kamaria physically growled.

'Gods above, Kamaria, you knew sharing me was going to happen eventually, it just happened sooner than you would have liked. You are acting like a cub.'

'Do NOT compare me to those minuscule monsters!'

Terren smirked. Her feelings at being demoted and compared to the irrational Shade Beastlings were entertaining. Her reaction was justifiable. The small, curious creatures would occasionally wander into the Sun Realm during the night, unaware a portal opened, and their resulting mischief often scared people. Not that he could blame Sun Born; Shade Beastlings were as large as an adult Wolfcat. Unfortunately, their wanderings happened more often than it should. He and Kamaria, after bonding, had been asked to track some down on more than one occasion. Though the Beastlings were smart enough to comprehend that being in the Sun Realm as day broke was incredibly dangerous, most would still fight bitterly at being dragged back.

While his Bear stewed, Terren brought his mental awareness away long enough to find Liem still testing different castings. Conversing with Terren seemed to help Kamaria with the dreary task of scenting out Kiira. They continued to talk about inconsequential topics and every so often scents would invade his nose so strongly he had to fight back a sneeze. Inconsistent, random sneezes would have been awkward to explain to Liem.

Terren was about to pull away from Kamaria when she caught Kiira's unmistakable scent, clove and jasmine, and magic. He shifted his boots, scraping them against the loamy surface, his back ramrod straight. He vaguely heard Liem, but ignored the inquiry as Kamaria hurried along the path, the scent getting stronger with every stride.

"Terren," Liem said.

"Hush," he replied.

Liem glared, but Terren didn't care in light of the discovery. Minutes passed as Kamaria followed the trail. Finally, far in the distance, she could just make out the formation of a cave system. She moved to take a step closer. *'Kamaria, no! Don't go any closer.'*

'Why not?'

'You're sure that's her?'

'Positive. It can't be anything else. It's not like Zerrec could fool me,' she said.

'Okay, show me where you are.'

Kamaria looked around, giving Terren a clear view of her surroundings, and then turned to face the direction of their camp.

'Thank you, Yepenzi. Eat, rest, I will tell you how Liem and I decide to move forward.'

Kamaria grunted just as Liem's exclamation cut into his conversation.

"For the gods' sake, Terren, tell me what's going on!" Liem snapped.

Terren's form rippled as he whispered the release word on the necklace. He turned to him and the prince instantly knew.

"Where?" Liem asked, the single-word question weighted and heavy.

Terren was torn with indecision. He wanted to race toward Kiira without a second thought, but he, Liem, and Kamaria needed to be well rested to face a man like Zerrec. They needed to be rational.

I need to be rational.

Unfortunately, the slight twitch in his fingers betrayed the calm forced into his features.

Liem saw completely through it and was, thankfully, the more level-headed one at the moment. "Terren, how far away is she? How long will it take us to get there?"

He paused long enough to picture again what Kamaria had just shown him. "Not far actually. We could make it to the cave within two hours."

"They're in a cave? I have never seen a cave within the Forest Wilds. Then again, I've never had to venture this far in, either." Liem paused for a long moment, then asked, "how is it you know all this?"

Terren leveled his gaze and said, "You will find out soon enough."

Liem narrowed his eyes and pushed out his lower jaw, gritting his teeth.

"Tell me how you know this, Terren! You could have potentially alerted Zerrec to our presence."

Terren scoffed. "If anything has alerted him to our location, it was your insistence on testing the necklace."

"Do not try to shift the attention here, Terren." Liem spoke low, his tone holding a warning.

Terren took a deep breath and let it slowly go. "You're right. I apologize."

"So, how do you know of Kiira's location?"

"It's a long story and will be explained tomorrow."

Liem gave him an incredulous look.

"Just trust me," Terren said.

"This,"—Liem gestured between them—"is exactly why I have a difficult time liking you. All of your ridiculous secrecy, especially when my sister's life hangs in the balance!"

"Do not lecture me, Liem. This is not about secrecy. I said you would find out soon enough and that is the truth. You need to trust me. I know where Kiira is and how I came to know the information should not be the point on which you fixate."

Liem let out a frustrated growl. "Fine, if she is as close as you say, then we sleep. I will make sure we wake two hours before dawn. May I point out, despite all of our discussions, we still do not have a solid plan."

"What do you suggest? You know Zerrec better than I and he may be expecting me. I let you borrow the necklace thinking you could act as an element of surprise," Terren said as he prepared his bedroll.

"Except, he has probably been tracking your movements, so he knows I'm with you."

"Not possible," Terren said, shaking his head. "Since Kiira's capture, as a precaution, I have made sure he could not scry me."

"Let me guess, some trinket or other?" Liem asked.

"Yes," Terren replied and lifted his left hand to move his thumb. "This ring allows me invisibility, magically speaking."

"Why am I not surprised," Liem said, dramatizing each word.

Terren wanted to retort, but the air was still sour between them. Instead, he turned his back on the prince and said, "I know you mentioned an idea of how you wanted to approach this, so what is your plan?" He purposefully kept his tone flat, lifeless, and to the point.

Liem, in the same business-like manner, said, "Since you are so certain he has not tracked you, then I suggest you sneak in. You have this weird ability to seemingly pop out of nowhere. Once you're in, find my sister and

I'll work to clear the area. You can come back here and we'll raid the cave together. Whatever Zerrec has planned, it will be magical, so unless you have some fancy crystal stowed in your pack, We'll work together to kill Zerrec and then free my sister."

Terren thought for a moment and said, "We don't know the extent of his plans. Kiira will be my responsibility and you work on the surrounding area to secure everything else before coming to my aid."

"Why do you get to be the only one to rescue Kiira?"

Terren turned from digging through his pack and gave Liem an enigmatic stare.

Liem threw up his hands. "Alright, no need to get all huffy about it."

Terren handed the prince the item he procured, a leather tube with several Night Crystals. This bundle held crystals to absorb, dissipate, or shield from magic attacks. "Those should be helpful to you."

Liem unrolled the bundle and looked at the ebony crystals. Sitting up in shock, he said, "Kreshkt, Terren! Do you go around expecting magicians to attack you?"

"No, but I never travel anywhere without protection, and I took your words of caution seriously. You wouldn't have said something to me in Lorea if it hadn't been important, especially with statements as cryptic as yours," Terren said.

Liem stared at him, dumbfounded.

"What?"

The prince shook his head. "Nothing. Thank you for these."

Terren nodded. Laying on his bedroll, he watched the swaying of the boughs for another moment before closing his eyes.

Gods, give me strength to rescue Kiira.

CHAPTER 55
BOND PARTNER

Terren stalked between the tall, widely spaced oaks, using each tree to hide as they neared the place of Kiira's captivity. They were close. He could feel his connection with Kamaria growing stronger. Liem ran just behind him with matching stealth, surprising since the prince could barely see in the nearly lightless forest.

Sorted images filtered through his mind as he followed the path Kamaria showed him. The images with the combination of smells and sounds seared his memory with surprising clarity, which disturbed him; only blood could tinge the air with such potency. With each step closer, his heart beat in earnest for the tasks ahead.

He would soon reveal his Bear to Liem and the prince's reaction was at the forefront of Terren's mind. How he was going to explain their connection in a limited amount of time, he did not know; hopefully inspiration would strike at the perfect moment. The last thing he needed was to create an enemy and lose an ally at the same time.

Terren mis-stepped and a resounding crack bounced from tree to tree. He cringed and whispered a curse as he froze until he was sure the sound had alerted no one to their presence. He could feel Liem's annoyed glare burning a hole in his back. He took a deep breath, choosing not to acknowledge the prince.

That is what I get for being so distracted.

Terren completely opened his mind to Kamaria, and her nearness surprised him. He and Liem traveled more swiftly than he thought. She retreated some from her watchful position upon the cave entrance and he soon spotted her massive form blending seamlessly with the surrounding black shadows. She'd chosen her hiding spot well. Even when Terren stopped just in front of her snout, she remained perfectly still, aware of Liem's presence and knowing not to reveal herself until necessary.

'*Could you have been more obvious in your approach?*' She asked drily.

'*Not one of my finer moments to be sure,*' he said.

'*Master Topeko would be disgusted with you.*'

Terren smirked. '*Yes, he would. I expected to meet you closer to the cave.*'

'*This position was more advantageous for when I am to join with you and it was safer for me as it has more shadows. I was not sure how long it would take you to arrive. You have such short strides.*'

'*I am not an enormous Beast you miscreant.*'

Kamaria flashed amusement and his heart lifted momentarily, then sank back into a despondent gloom that had bogged him down since waking.

'*Sadness does not become you, you know.*'

'*I do not wish to put you through this ordeal,*' Terren said. '*Zerrec is very powerful, but I know of no other way to defeat him than with the help of your immunity. I am helpless without you and that bothers me.*'

'*Terren, you are strong, but together we are stronger. It is why I chose you. Worry not about me, magic cannot kill me when I exist as my essence, you know this,*' Kamaria said.

'*Yes, but it can still hurt and that is what concerns me; whatever Zerrec has planned is certainly intended to kill me,*' he said, grimacing. '*My only advantage is he is not aware of your existence or my connection with you. I care very much for you and I do not wish to see you in pain.*'

Kamaria let a rumble vibrate through her chest. '*Your concern comforts me. It is only to be expected as my bond partner. I know how much you love Kiira, your smell is strong when she is near. However, you should know I do this not just for you, but for my brethren as well. Zerrec has killed too many of my kind. We all know his scent and it is foul.*'

The force of Kamaria's disposition hit him solidly in his mind, and he felt every ounce of sadness and anger she felt toward the magician. Terren even felt the force of restraint keeping her from storming the cave last night alone.

"Terren, did you hear that noise?" Liem whispered, then a little louder and with greater confusion, "Why are you petting a boulder?"

Terren snatched his hand away from Kamaria's snout and cleared his throat. "I am not petting a boulder. I"—he let out a defeated sigh—"Liem how much do you know about Shade Beast?"

"Do you mean Shade Demons, like the Oranta Kiira and I killed?"

"No." Terren had to send calming thoughts to Kamaria to keep her from outright growling. Reeducating people on the truth of Shade Beasts was becoming a burden. One he was willing to bear, but a burden nonetheless. "Shade Demons are an abomination of the beautiful creature that is a Shade Beast."

"What does this have to do with anything?" Liem asked, confusion marring his features and his voice.

"I don't have time to explain this in detail as I did with Kiira. Liem, I need you to be very understanding. I promise I will answer all of your questions *after* Kiira has been rescued, just know that what I am about to tell and show you is necessary, and not harmful to either you or Kiira," Terren said. He hoped they built enough of a friendship, and saving Kiira was important enough that Liem would quickly move past the introduction without threatening violence.

"Alright," Liem said, but it came out sounding more like a hesitant question.

Terren nodded. That was the best he would get for now. Taking an encouraging breath, he said, "I am a Shadow Walker, which means I'm bonded with a Shade Beast."

Liem's eyes narrowed. "Shadow Walkers are as real as the sea serpents sailors carry on about."

Terren pointed at him. "Sea serpents are real, I've seen them, and I assure you the tales of Shadow Walkers are more than myth, as you're about to find out. For the moment I need two things from you. One, I need you to trust me. If we have any fighting chance against Zerrec it is going to be with her help." Terren pointed to Kamaria's head, which remained unmoving. "Two, I need to know you will not abandon me. Neither of us can do this alone."

Liem gave him an incredulous look. Pointing to the same space, he said, "Terren, that is a boulder."

Terren just shook his head, unwilling to offer more until the prince gave his word.

Liem must have seen the truth, for he scowled at the ground longer than Terren would have liked. Finally, he cautiously said, "I will reserve my judgments and questions until after my sister is safe. I trust you have put her first in this situation and are using the resources available to you with the best of your knowledge. I will not leave your side."

It was more than he had expected. Liem's assurance gave him hope that the slowly building camaraderie between them would not be demolished, as he had previously assumed.

"I will warn you, then, what you are about to witness is rather … violent," Terren said.

"What are you doing?"

"Kamaria will be joining with me. It is a painful process. No matter what you see or hear, do not interfere."

At the sound of her name spoken out loud, his Bear lifted her head, focused large ebony eyes at Liem. Terren watched the prince carefully, monitoring his reaction as Kamaria raised to her full height, which towered another fifteen meters above his own almost six-foot stature, and she was still on four paws.

Other than his eyes growing wide, seemingly in disbelief, Liem held fast. "I will certainly have a lot of questions for you later," he breathed.

Terren barked a humorless laugh. Stepping in front of Kamaria, he took several deep breaths, clearing his mind of everything except for her presence. If he was distracted, even in the slightest, this painful process would be even more taxing. It was difficult to concentrate when someone stood just a few feet behind him, watching, no doubt with inordinate amounts of curiosity. Terren focused solely on Kamaria's glistening black nose until complete calm took over his mind and, little by little, he let his consciousness meld with hers. When his thoughts were no longer his own and he was no longer aware of his own body, when felt as if he was Kamaria, Terren waited; his Bear knew the precise moment to begin the joining.

As the process began, a deep-seated pain blossomed in the center of his chest. This was nothing compared to the first time they bonded, and the pain would be distracting if he'd not trained himself to ignore the fire burning him from inside. As Kamaria pushed her essence through his body, the sting coursing through him grew tenfold. She invaded every part, making him completely aware of every kindled cell. He hissed, straining to keep from making a sound; despite his best efforts, he let out a raw scream that sounded more like a vicious roar. Still, he kept focused.

With great effort, Terren minimized the thrashing of his limbs; he did not want to accidentally harm Liem. The changes to his body were incredible. His bones turned dense and heavy, muscles became empowered, teeth sharpened and shrank, and nails turned to four-inch claws before disappearing; his entire form changing and restoring in a matter of minutes. When the process was complete, Terren could shift seamlessly between a normal sized humped bear and man, and now he could quickly channel the capabilities of a Shade Beast. The worthwhile pain eased, but weakened his knees. He lowered one knee to the ground while clean air filtered into his lungs. Terren looked at his hands, forcing his attention to something other than the residual discomfort.

"Terren?" Liem asked.

He turned. Liem looked startled.

"Your eyes. That was,"—Liem tapped his chin as he studied the tree canopy—"interesting, no, fascinating, no … the number of my questions just multiplied."

Terren gave him a wry smile. Liem's words betrayed the nervousness he could smell with his newly sensitive nose. "I did warn you."

Liem eyed him. "Wasn't much of a warning, considering what just happened. By the way, a big ugly brute of a man wandered pretty close just as you knelt to the ground."

"I know, I could smell him," Terren said, shifting uncomfortably. Liem cracked a smile but blessedly said nothing. Terren was sure a thousand quips were going through the prince's mind amongst the thousands of questions. "Did he see you?"

"No, I heard him even over the noise you were making. A skilled woodsman he was not. I activated the necklace, but he was more focused on you. My assumption would be he was instructed to be specifically looking for you."

Terren nodded, then asked seriously, "Are you ready?"

"One question first."

Terren raised his eyebrows.

"Does this mean you can smell me, too?"

Terren gave him a blank stare. He refused to answer the question, since Liem obviously already knew the answer. A shiver went down the prince's spine and his scent changed.

"That is just unnerving," Liem muttered.

Before Terren could respond to the comment, steel entered Liem's eye, and he nodded to Terren.

"Now I'm ready." He whispered the necessary word and his body vanished. With his Bear's immunity to magic, Liem's form was visible to him but hazy, and the prince's smell was definitely still there. Turning, Terren made his way toward the cave holding Kiira, her scent invading his nose and guiding his steps.

Soon she would be free, and Terren could hold her in his arms again.

CHAPTER 56
COUP DE GRACE

Zerrec couldn't help the small upturn of his lips as he took in Kiira's exhausted body. In the days since discovering Terren still lived, his relationship with Kiira festered beyond his tolerance. Zerrec realized she needed to break before she could be molded into the partner he wanted. It was a last resort, but had always proved to be an effective tool at his disposal. Except, his attempts to gain knowledge of Terren's weaknesses proved fruitless. Zerrec's niceties and the pain he caused did nothing to loosen Kiira's tongue. Her unrelenting willfulness left him little choice.

Serves her right for rejecting me. He narrowed his eyes a fraction. *She will learn to love me ... no matter what it takes.*

"It is time to set my plan into motion," he said, walking toward her hunched form against the far wall and crouching to her eye level. "The satisfaction that Terren will soon be dead and you will be forever mine is quite exhilarating." His tone was light, almost teasing.

"No, Zerrec, please do not hide your enthusiasm simply to be considerate of my feelings," Kiira said, as she lifted her head from her knees, every word dripping with sarcasm.

He clenched his jaw briefly before relaxing and rolling his shoulders. "Lucky for you I am in such a glorious mood, otherwise I would punish for such an insolent comment."

Kiira's eyes betrayed nothing. In fact, it was the most enigmatic expression he had ever seen from her. "It doesn't matter what you do or say, I will never love you and I have lost all respect for you. You are the monster my mother saw. You have stayed your hand for false hope. I will be dead by Terren's side before I live a day with *you*."

The eerie collectedness to her voice twinged something inside him. Zerrec drew out the silence with pinched lips as he studied her expressionless features, searching for the authenticity of her seemingly benign words. Her rich green eyes, so like Loralyn's, were one reason he loved her in the first place. Except, nothing sparked within their depths. Flat. Zerrec foresaw the truth of her words. No matter which way he twisted or pulled, Kiira would always fight him, and in a moment of carelessness on his part, she would take revenge for the loved ones lost by his hand.

His dreams of rebuilding his first life with his re-birthed Loralyn crumbled. The balm that Kiira's presence had been was suddenly a hot brand digging into his centuries-deep wound.

Am I fated to never find happiness or peace again?

His calm façade cracked ever so slightly as his anger boiled from the verity of her claim, and if he could not have her for his own, he would remove the festering desire from his life. She would no longer torment him. He would start anew with another. Taking a deep, releasing breath, he said, "You have asked for your fate and you shall have it."

Kiira shrugged. "Terren is not a fool, Zerrec, you may have lured him here, but he will be expecting something."

His back stiffened, and he focused on a divot in the cavern wall. "Oh yes, the ever knowledgeable peripatetic prince, as the rumors say. How could I forget?" Zerrec turned to eye Kiira. His lip briefly curled in disgust before facing her fully with a plastered on amiable smile. "Here's the genius part of my plan, would you like to hear it? It's really quite clever."

Kiira raised a single brow. "I suppose you are going to tell me, regardless."

It was his turn to shrug. "I was not going to, and your impertinence is not inspiring me to be divulging," Zerrec said.

"Tell me, Zerrec, I see no reason why I should be kept in the dark, you have been straightforward with me up to this point and you are only going to kill me after."

"True, honesty is always the best course of action," he mused.

"As if you would know the meaning of it," she scoffed.

A languid smirk crossed his lips. "I think it would be quite fitting, since he loves you so much more than I ever could, that he dies by the kiss of death, don't you?"

Zerrec couldn't help laughing at her horrified expression.

She would remember this casting from their lessons as something only a high-ranking Blood Mage could do. Another school of magic to attempt such would drain them to the point of death. The curse was simple, but it put the receiver in unbearable amounts of pain before dimming their spirit into nothing. He considered gloating more. Watching her turn ashen was such an enticing game, but the promise of his curse had been just enough.

It was perfect, actually. Any more would overdo it, and it's always best to keep them guessing.

Zerrec walked closer, and Kiira attempted to scramble away from him. The solid wall of the cave stopped her progress. He grasped her chin. She squeezed her eyes in pain, trying and failing to wrench free of his grip. The symbol on his wrist glowed a bright, cruel crimson as he said, "Death's kiss be upon your lips, and may you know the pain of loss as I have." The words were a formality, as he needed nothing to direct the casting, but they felt good to say. Zerrec pushed his lips against Kiira's. It was swift. She didn't even have time to struggle or retaliate. The kiss was more for his benefit, to see her skin crawl. Watching the gooseflesh inch across her skin and seeing the ill expression creasing her features pleased him.

Kiira wiped uselessly at her lips.

Stepping away, Zerrec waved his hand and a pair of shackles on her wrists and ankles clanked into place, securing Kiira so he could remove the magic barrier. Her lip trembled before she lost control and sobbed into her hands, the chains jangling.

He moved with a new purpose as he made preparations for Terren's arrival. Zerrec turned back at the door, studying Kiira one last time. It truly was a shame to kill such a talented and beautiful magician.

Maybe in another century he would again find love.

CHAPTER 57
EIDOLON

Pain ripped through Kiira's throat as she uttered agonizing cries, the searing heat shooting up her spine and slamming into the base of her skull like a blacksmith striking with a hammer. Tears poured from her bleary eyes and she found not even a whimper could escape. Despite her best efforts to not show weakness at Zerrec's sudden change of heart toward her, soft sobs raked her body as she sought the comfort of the cold, unyielding stone beneath her cheek. She panted deep, gulping breaths as her heart beat a frantic rhythm from the desire to be safe. A bead of salty water dripped down her temples, stinging her eyes, and, despite the cool temperature of the cavern, Kiira felt feverish.

"Tell me," Zerrec growled, his voice pitched low.

"Even if I did want to tell you, I cannot," she replied in a hoarse whisper. She tried to push up, but collapsed when her muscles shook involuntarily. "I erased the information from my memory."

"Liar, I taught you better than that. It's locked in your memories, give me the key to Terren's disadvantage and I will make his death painless."

"No."

Another wave of searing heat punched her in the stomach, and Kiira searched desperately for air. Her vision blurred as she teetered on the edge of unconsciousness, unable to think of anything but the pain. At least this was slightly better than feeling as if she was drowning or having her skin sliced open in a thousand places. This felt more like heavy hits, and hits she could bear, though she could feel herself standing on the precipice of a cliff. Soon, she might consider jumping just to find a measure of peace.

Since learning Terren killed the hired men and was likely coming for her, Zerrec had turned violent, mentally and physically, relentlessly brutal with his magic. Within the span of two seemingly endless days, she suffered through physical pain and visions of those she loved dying horrible deaths again and again. Zerrec had even gone so far as to recreate her mother's death for her, turning the scenes over and over in her mind to see her mother's warm and loving smile twisted into utter terror and pain. Each planted vision felt so real they haunted her in her sleep, making for fitful nights. Cognizant the visions were illusions, yet it never stopped her pounding heart as she jolted from unsettled sleep, screaming as much as an already raw throat would allow.

Only by sheer force of will and strength from the gods, she kept her mouth tightly clamped.

The only reason Kiira had any opportunity to recover was because he did not wish to kill her—yet. She prayed desperately for Terren to find her soon, not truly knowing how much longer she could grasp at strength and sanity. Terren would never abandon her, but Zerrec's torture had been so consuming, she nearly preferred death over rescue.

Zerrec stooped next to her prone form, a looming shadow in the dim space. Strong hands gripped her jaw, forcing her to look at him. Kiira winced from the pain before finding the courage to look into her old mentor's incensed eyes. He stared at her for several minutes, studying her bedraggled appearance. She could only imagine how she looked, black and blue, clothes disheveled, weak and pathetic, a helpless child. Zerrec released her head with a disgusted growl.

"You are strong Kiira, I commend you. Between the visions and our daily sessions together, you have managed quite well at evading my desire for information. I have tortured stronger men with better results."

Kiira tried to laugh at his ridiculous compliment, but it came out sounding more like a dying animal and left her coughing and gasping for more air.

"Ricker," Zerrec shouted!

The familiar heavy footsteps of the ox-man reverberated across the stone. Since her capture, Kiira had learned to fear those steps. He was as unyielding as stone and spoke only when absolutely necessary, otherwise communicating through nods and grunts.

"Get her some food and drink," Zerrec commanded and strode away.

Relief flooded Kiira and she let her body completely melt upon the hard surface. Welcoming blackness creeped into the edge of her vision.

It would be so nice to just ... let ... go.

Tempting, and she seriously considered it, smiling blissfully at the thought as she closed her eyes. Kiira did not fear death, and her worn and weary mind easily slipped away into a delicious nothingness.

SHE STOOD IN UNWAVERING DARKNESS. It was not the type of darkness where light just did not exist, this was absolutely nothing. Yet, strangely, the world around her still felt tangible, immaterial, save for the solid ground on which she stood.

Void is not the right term either, but how else do I describe this ... negative space? I thought I would be standing in Apelgo's Hall.

Kiira then remembered that this was how most of the visions over the last two days had begun. With a sigh of resignation, knowing she wasn't dead, she waited for the worst.

After several increasingly confusing moments of nothing, she wondered if Zerrec had felt sorry for her predicament. She snorted.

That's when she noticed a pinprick of light appearing in the distance. Cringing, Kiira prepared once more for the haunting images. The point of illumination glittered and sparkled as it grew in circumference. Feelings of joy, comfort, and warmth replaced the usual fear and dread. The brilliance of the light soon became unbearable, and she had to cover her eyes to block it out.

A rush of wind pushed her back a step, tugging at her hair before calming to a gentle breeze tickling her cheeks. Slowly, Kiira lowered her hands, letting her eyes adjust to the gleaming surroundings. She gasped as her eyes drank in the lush meadow. She was standing amid The Springs. Washed with bright winter sun, the space felt warm and breathtaking. Every color, sound, and scent intensified. Joy filled Kiira's heart at being in the sacred space. Just standing in the glen gave her the courage she craved.

Kiira turned, letting her eyes hungrily devour every detail, knowing this was only temporary. It would be the image she clung to during Zerrec's administrations. Halfway through her reverent spin, Windrah appeared.

The goddess stood in the soft springy grass near the edge of a large ground pool, her hands demurely clasped in front of her, a serene smile. At the sight of her, Kiira lost all sense of decorum. Running to the deity, she threw her arms around the goddess, collapsing into agonizing sobs. Protective, loving arms encircled her and supported her as she cried. A soft, gentle hand ran over her curls, a mother soothing her child.

When her cries lessened to gasping hiccups, Windrah said, "My daughter, I sense your heart, never ever fear coming to me and wrapping your arms around me. I shall always welcome you."

"Goddess, please take me away. I cannot endure this anymore," Kiira cried, desperation cracking her voice.

"My child, it is not yet your time to join the gods and dine with Apelgo. You and your gifts are still needed in the world. Your time to be with us is still many years to come."

"I have needed you. How could you let me be tortured? Could you not at least help me in some way? If I am still alive, I am struggling to cling to what little life I have left." Kiira babbled shamelessly, voicing every doubt and question that had plagued her over the last few days.

"Daughter, I know it may not seem like it, but the gods have been giving you the strength you need to resist Zerrec. Our hearts break at the pain you are feeling."

"How? I have never felt so alone."

"You are never alone, but certainly painful circumstances can make it seem as such. Resisting Zerrec's attacks is not easy, for his power is real and unrelenting, but you must always remember you have the strength of the gods fighting for you; a power greater than his."

Kiira dissolved, her thoughts and emotions frayed. The goddess pulled her to the ground and continued to cradle her until the shuddering ceased and the tears dried. For the first time since Zerrec had lost his mind, Kiira felt absolute relief.

"Windrah, why come to me now?"

"You did not let me come sooner. I so dearly wanted to come to you and comfort you, but you felt as if you had to endure this challenge alone. Until you let me in, I helped you with this trial in whatever way I could."

Kiira winced. Being self-reliant was her biggest weakness. Terren had told her as much, and the goddess would never lie to her. "Forgive me, Windrah. Thank you for coming now, I needed this."

"Of course, my child," the goddess said. Pulling Kiira to see her properly, she said, "I came to tell you to keep your courage, for Terren has discovered your location and is coming with the aid of Liem."

"No!" Kiira back peddled from the goddess. Visions of his death slammed full force into the front of her mind. "They will be killed, better to let me die than them!"

"And how would your husband feel if he heard you speak those words? Your brother? Do you think so little of yourself? Fear not. Surely, I tell you, have faith in the abilities the gods have given to you and to them. Their lives, and yours, are under our protection, you cannot save them."

Kiira gripped the long, soft grass at her side, clamping down on the fear galloping in her heart. The thought of Terren and Liem dying trying to save her frightened her to speechlessness. She squeezed her eyes shut, wishing all of it was an awful dream. Kiira hated not having control, but she needed to trust the gods. The words were almost difficult to utter, but they were a promise and a soothing reminder to her soul.

"I trust you will protect us."

The vision faded to the black void once more and Kiira's salt-caked eyes focused on a tin cup so close it blocked her direct line of sight. Pushing herself up, she winced as her aching body protested the movement. Bruised and partially fractured ribs made it difficult to breathe as she took in shallow amounts of air. Gingerly, she picked up the metal cup and, with shaking hands, drank the cool liquid. It stung her raw throat, but was soothing as the waters from the Springs. Icy coolness flowed through her veins and healed the physical pain.

Kiira alternated between taking small sips of water and eating the sad, stale loaf. She realized this was the most mentally alert she had felt in the last few days. Fear no longer gripped her, but it was still there, coloring all of her ragged emotions. If she wasn't careful, it would be easy to slip into dark thoughts once more. Despite all of it, a river of peace winded through her, the goddess giving her hope.

KIIRA SQUINTED at the vaulted cave and pursed her lips, willing the roof to come into focus. But it was useless. It was pitch dark save for a single flameless orb near her shackled feet. After their last encounter, Zerrec took all of her comforts just to be spiteful. Staring at the ceiling was more about giving her mind something to do, so she didn't focus on other, more dreary things. Kiira wanted to believe her tears and emotions were long dried and gone, but any thought of Terren and his impending death twisted her insides to make her sick. Her only comfort, when thoughts threatened to overwhelm her, were the words of the goddess.

The gods have a plan for me. I have a hope and a future.

Still, the promise did not always combat the shades of gray pressing at the edges of her mind. Zerrec's casting had been perfectly clear and sometimes her hope for a favorable outcome would diminish at the thought, sending her into a spiraling depression.

If Liem could see me now. She mused about what he might tell her. *He'd probably tell me I need to think like a soldier, think of the task at hand and not have such a bleeding heart. Then again, he might just be sympathetic to my plight and give me a hug.*

The idea of her brother holding her in such a familiar and safe gesture sent a fountain of tears to her eyes she refused to let fall. Kiira prayed fervently for both Terren and Liem's protection at their impending duel with Zerrec.

Painful spasms pushed through her chest, making it difficult to breathe. How could they survive? Zerrec was so powerful and cunning. Fear warred with hope, creating a headache that pulsed behind her eyes. Kiira would welcome any death Zerrec had planned if she lost both her brother and husband.

The dark fizzled away as she heard the most beautiful sound in the world. It was a sound of her hope, joy, and fear all at once.

Kiira sat up to better look for the sweet voice caressing her name. The chains binding her shifted with a dull clink. Still, she listened and glanced eagerly around the cavern as her name came again. She checked to make sure she was not dreaming, and this was not some cruel vision created by Zerrec. Sure enough, when she attempted a small casting, pain raced up her arms. This was no dream.

"Kiira," the soft male voice repeated.

She fervently whispered, "Terren?"

Terren coalesced from the shadows, insubstantial at first, then completely solid. His eyes drank in her form, showing relief, shock, anger, but mostly love. Kiira held his gaze with equal ardor, absorbing all the emotions flashing in his eyes like it was the sweetest wine.

Terren's arrival had been expected, but still his presence seemed too good to be true. She couldn't help the overflow of passion bubbling in her chest as it escaped through tears of joy and grateful sobs. After days of uncertainty, he was finally here. Kiira buried her face behind hands and within seconds Terren's very real arms wrapped around her. He pulled her into his lap to hold her close and she relished the feel of him, so very real, next to her. Terren was strong and quiet as he held tightly, stroking her hair.

"Kiira, my love, I know you are weary, but I need to get you out of here," he said, pulling her back enough to look at her.

"Terren, you cannot. You must leave! Freeing me will only kill you," she said, shaking her head, though her heart disagreed.

Hardness glazed his eyes. "I am not leaving here without you."

"Terren," she pleaded.

"No."

The word was weighted, the scale not tipping in her favor. At this point, Kiira was so tired from the ordeal she wasn't sure she had it in her to argue. Looking at the manacles on her wrist in defeat, she whispered, "The only way to break the chains is to kiss me, but the action will kill you. I beg you, please leave, the thought of your death breaks my heart. The casting Zerrec placed on me is…"

Lifting her chin, Terren forced her to look him in the eyes. "The thought of leaving you here to suffer and perish at that magician's hands breaks mine. Let me try something else before the kiss, however, I will do whatever it takes to ensure your safety."

The sweet warmth radiating from his eyes promptly leeched away as a slow clap echoed in the cavern, and Zerrec stepped through the entrance.

"Wonderful! Just wonderful! This, this right here makes my plan perfect!" Zerrec said.

Kiira shrank closer to Terren, and his grip around her tightened. She could feel the tension in his body and, although his grip on her arm became uncomfortably tight, it hardly mattered.

"I assure you, whatever trick you have planned will not work, prince, but please, don't let me interrupt your lover's reunion. Continue," Zerrec said, a nefarious grin punctuating the expression with a sweeping gesture of his arm.

Kiira glared at him, her patience running thin with his gloating. Terren gently turned her head and rubbed his thumb along her cut cheekbone. She winced at the touch and his clenched jaw said more than words.

Crushing her close, his lips were soft against her ear as he whispered, "Do you trust me?"

A tear rolled down her cheek. The voice in her mind screamed no, but she did. She trusted him with everything. Kiira nodded, though it was emotionally painful to make even such a simple gesture.

When Terren looked at her again, she saw they were not the beautiful ice-blue she loved, but complete obsidian black with a light ring of grey. Her eyes widened, but she quickly looked away, hiding her shock.

She knew those eyes.

Memories from the night around the campfire when Terren revealed Kamaria to her flooded her mind, and she was forming a realization, when suddenly, Terren's lips were on hers.

His kiss was passionate and desperate, every ounce of his love for her pouring through his lips. Tears salted her lips, both her love for him and the terror of what would happen next.

He was sacrificing himself for her, and he would live. She believed he would.

Kiira could feel Zerrec's casting working its evil purpose. Terren's hands stiffened, clamping the back of her neck just as the manacles fell from her wrist. A loud echo clanged around the cavern as they dropped to the floor. He pulled away from her and smiled briefly before his face went blank. He fell into her arms and Kiira gently laid him on the floor.

She cried with no tears, fisting his shirt in her hands, beating his chest, willing him to live. Why did he have to be so damned noble!?

He's going to be alright. The goddess said it would all be fine. Goddess, please, please, please. I beg you.

Kiira was vaguely aware Zerrec had drawn closer. When he spoke, she clenched her jaw to the point of aching.

"I told you, my dear, I always win. Your puny faith in the gods could not stop me," Zerrec raved. "I promise to make your death less painful. I'll even notify your father and brother of your tragic demise."

Kiira shivered in anger, words failing. She turned and glared at the man she once respected and admired.

Zerrec spoke with a hint of remorse. "Such a waste, really. With me by your side, you could have been a great magician."

"I became a great magician despite you," Kiira spat back at him.

A beautifully crafted dagger flashed into his hands, and Kiira recognized it as one of hers.

This is how I die.

Zerrec raised his arm, and she could hear the roar of a heavy, beating heart in her ears.

A still, small voice whispered through her thoughts, reminding her she was no longer bound by chains. Focusing on this idea, her heart slowed and renewed clarity sent a jolt of remembrance through her muscles.

If I die, it will not be without a fight!

Kiira shifted to protect Terren's body and hide her intentions of evasion.

Thank the gods Zerrec didn't seem to notice, so focused he was on her death.

She concentrated on the knife in the magician's hand, but also watched for subtle changes in Zerrec's features in her periphery. His face would tell her more than the beginning movement to strike. Years of training tensed her muscles, preparing her to dodge and block the attack. Her goal was to move him away from Terren's body.

Before she could take action, a throwing blade whistled past her ear and she stumbled away in fright. Gasping at the thin, steel blade penetrating Zerrec's hand, Kiira glanced between it and the man who threw it. Terren. Alive! Already he was standing with his scimitar unsheathed, placing himself in her defense.

"Kiira, gaan!" Terren commanded.

She stood an addle-brained fool, knowing it was not impossible, but still not believing what her eyes were telling her. He was *alive!*

"Kiira! Go!" Terren commanded again.

A howl left Zerrec's lips as the shock registered. The sound jolted Kiira's body into responding, and she sprinted for the door.

He's alive! Thank the gods, he's alive! She stopped, frozen in the hallway. Oh, gods above, he could still be killed. He's completely alone. Where is Liem!?

Kiira spun, intending to go back and assist her husband even if it made him angry, except she came in contact with a sword hilt, smashing into her forehead, and her world went black.

CHAPTER 58
DEATH UNTO DEATH

Searing heat ran through Terren's lips and into his veins as he kissed Kiira, the poisonous casting completing its evil purpose. A whisper of a touch would have been more than sufficient, but Terren pressed deeply into the kiss. If this was the only way to free his wife, then he would show her how much he loved her and enjoy the moment before paying the price for her freedom. Kiira's salty tears wetted his cheeks and lips as death seeped into every corner of his being. Terren held onto his own body as long as possible. He was playing with fire, waiting this long before giving control to Kamaria, but it was such a relief to be near and see Kiira again he would let himself burn before relinquishing to his Bear.

Terren allowed one last weak kiss before death stiffened his fingers and a last surge of pain coursed through his body. He managed a smile, and then, giving his Bear control, faded into darkness.

Time was a whisper, a concept, as he floated somewhere between life and death. It was a similar sensation to when he first bonded with Kamaria, only less painful. Terren could feel the heavy weight of death in his body. A black disease racing through his veins, consuming him with glee, eagerly wanting to carve away his soul, to snuff him out.

Darkness like he'd never known toyed at the edge of his mind, growing by the second. Terren thought he understood darkness, having lived the life as a half-child of the Shade Realm, yet this darkness doused everything; it was an unbreachable wall before him. Not to be heard or seen, this darkness ended all that was good. His very soul hungered for light. A flicker of any kind would be welcome. The utter sense of loss consuming him inside the curse would have driven him mad if not for his connection to Kamaria. Only her rapid absorption, dispelling the evil intent of the casting, kept it at bay.

His Bear pushed and strained at the recesses of his mind, nudging him to completely let go, to let her protect him. Could he? If the casting was doing this to him, how much would his Bear suffer? He could give his life in exchange and be at peace.

'Yepenzi.' Her voice, soft and soothing, echoed in his mind. *'You are not allowed to give in, do you hear me? What about Kiira? Your sister? Your people? This will not destroy me, but if you give in, I chose poorly. If you give in, you are not the person I know you to be. Let me save you!'*

Something sparked inside him. What was he doing? This was not his end. Kamaria was right, this would not extinguish her and he had much to live for; to give in would be selfish. They were partners, and he trusted her. Terren relinquished control, knowing it would soon bring him back to the light. The effect was immediate. Death receded, the edges of darkness pushing away, but at a great cost to his Bear. She roared and whined as the pain from absorbing the curse engulfed her essence, turning her very being into an inferno.

Still, she pushed through.

Her agony wrenched at his heart, and he felt every lasting moment of it. She would not be consumed by the casting, but it left her essence frayed. Terren almost wished death would come for her, if only to give her some measure of peace. He desperately wanted to ease her suffering, but in his current state, he was helpless. Instead, he poured every thought and feeling of love he had for his friend, knowing it would not lessen the pain, but hoping it would soothe her mind.

It was impossible to know how long it was taking to absorb the curse. He just hoped it would not be too late to actually save Kiira. With Zerrec standing over them, the kiss had been the fastest option to release her. Except, if the magician had planned his attack well, freeing Kiira put all of them in a vulnerable position. It forced him into a place he didn't like.

As the effects of the casting burned off and pain was no longer a dominating force within his spirit, anger took its place. Rage raced through his veins, bringing life to his dead fingers.

He twitched them.

Kamaria's presence faded to the back of his mind as he once again became aware. Her weakness taxed his conscience. She would need a considerable amount of time to recover. For the moment, he lost the ability to shift his form while fighting against Zerrec. A small price to pay for his life. Terren's skill with a blade and magical trinkets would be enough protection.

He fully opened and closed his hand, and in seconds, his entire being was alive once again. Terren blinked as his ears processed everything around him. He looked to see Zerrec poised to strike Kiira. It did not go unnoticed, even now, in such awful circumstances, she didn't beg for mercy, and this made him incredibly proud of her.

Just as the magician moved to plunge the knife in a smooth, practiced motion, Terren rolled up while throwing a long, thin blade. It pierced Zerrec's hand, forcing him to drop his weapon. He yelled at Kiira to run before the scream escaping the magician's lips jolted her into action. Terren stood ready with his Solpur Blade, the gleaming curved obsidian shone with a dull hunger in the meager light flickering in the cavernous space. Blood spattered his clothes as Zerrec flung his bleeding hand out and away, surprise, confusion, and anger registering on the magician's face as he directed his hateful gaze to him.

Terren's tone and words did not match his tame expression as he said, "Touch her again and you will regret ever crossing paths with me."

"Impossible!" Zerrec raged. "Impossible! How are you alive?"

Terren ignored the question and moved into a more advantageous position for fighting. He would wait for the raving magician to make the first strike. His eyes studied Zerrec, learning his opponent; looking for weaknesses or any favored parts of the body.

Zerrec continued to howl and scream for several moments before sense finally took over. The calm and quiet came suddenly, and in an instant the magician healed his hand and conjured a wicked blade crackling with a magic meant to devour.

Terren adjusted his grip, glad his own blade would disperse any spells attached to Zerrec's weapon.

Zerrec moved abruptly and with amazing speed, but Terren blocked the first strike easily, retaliating with several quick strikes of his own, forcing Zerrec to take a few steps back. He expected some level of skill based on Liem's description, but the speed with which the magician struck exceeded his original estimation. In the first few moves, Terren learned his enemy. His blade skill while maintaining a powerful casting was impressive. Although, for a century's old magician, this was likely nothing more than child's play.

Zerrec pounced and the magical energy of his weapon fizzed as fingers of light danced up and down the blade with each connection of their swords. Terren's scimitar absorbed every ounce of magic Zerrec poured into his weapon, each strike consuming the destructive energy with a fiendish hunger. The night crystals decorating the guard glowed with the same dull glow of his blade as the empty vessels stored the magic.

Their dance of blocks and strikes continued, and every passing minute increased the visible frustration on Zerrec's face. Several quick strikes locked their swords and brought them face-to-face.

"How did you survive, boy? That spell was more than enough to kill you and destroy your soul," Zerrec growled, pushing a little against Terren and trying to gain an advantage.

"You actually believe I will tell you?" Terren asked, planting his feet to keep the magician from taking any ground. Zerrec played a game—this time with words—and he would not give the magician the satisfaction of showing emotion.

Zerrec narrowed his eyes and pitched his voice to a menacing growl. "I spent months learning about you. The places you traveled and the people with which you had interacted. The casting should have worked! You were dead!"

"I was dead," Terren replied, as Zerrec unlocked their blades and stepped back.

Magic flared across Zerrec's sword as he gave an enraged howl. The bright glow of his magic danced across the blade in an eerie, wispy white and navy blue flame. The new casting bathed a disheartening glow across the walls of the cavern.

The space between them increased in temperature, causing sweat to slick Terren's brow. He continued to maintain an inscrutable expression, though fight progression pleased him. An angry opponent was a lazy opponent. It didn't matter if Zerrec had centuries of practice. He would eventually make a mistake.

The magician leapt, Terren blocking just barely. The two of them exchanged another set of lightning fast parries and blocks; his Solpur Blade eating every ounce of magic grazing the surface, and the night crystals in his guard lapping up every joule. The stored energy converted and fed sustaining life into Terren's limbs, allowing him to maintain this fight for hours beyond his opponent with the help the crystals gave.

Zerrec renewed his onslaught, hacking forward wildly in an attempt to push Terren back. When Terren held his ground, a brief flicker of recognition scrolled across the magician's eyes before he pushed away, extracting himself.

"Your blade is enchanted to block magic," Zerrec hissed, as the white and blue flames extinguished, plunging the cavern into darkness.

Terren shrugged. For someone who was supposedly very smart, it had taken the old man a long time to realize.

"In my seven-hundred years I have never come across such a blade," Zerrec said.

Terren shrugged again. He was not about to tell Zerrec that a Solpur Blade was given only to Shadow Walkers and the forging of such weapons had been around since before the Mage War.

Zerrec sneered. "I will kill you, boy."

Terren huffed. Not because of what the magician said, but because he could smell when Liem reentered the room. It was a moist scent, telling him the prince had probably been running. Terren could see the prince's bulky form ghost up behind Zerrec.

Terren adjusted his stance to keep Zerrec's attention on him and readied for another series of exchanges. Before either could make a move, a crimson blade erupted through Zerrec's chest. Genuine shock crossed the magician's face.

"Not unless I kill you first," Liem hissed. Shoving the blade deeper, he said, "That is for what you have done to my sister"—he twisted the sword, causing Zerrec to gasp in agony—"and that is for my mother."

The sickening sound of the steel scraping against bone and slicing flesh resounded through the cavern, followed by the dying man's blood-filled gurgles. Liem shoved Zerrec to his knees as he removed his sword. There was a loud crack of bone against stone as the magician fell against the hard surface.

"Heal from that, Zerrec," Liem said, panting with rage.

Terren didn't relax as the light of life dimmed in the man's eyes. He watched, detached, as Kiira's captor took his last breaths. The magician fell to his side, blood pooling, staining everything around him. His lips moved, seeming to form words, but no sound came. A few spasms danced through his limbs before he stilled and his eyes stared at nothing. Zerrec was gone.

Terren stood over the man for a long time, not entirely certain why he stayed. He knew the magician was dead, but with everything that happened, it took his mind a long time to process the reality. Liem remained on the other side of the body, looking as well. Something about Zerrec's lips moving bothered Terren, but he was the only one to see the action and wasn't sure if it meant anything or if they were muttered wishes.

Several minutes passed. Without removing his eyes from Zerrec's body, Terren asked, "Where is Kiira?"

"I have her hidden and protected outside, not far from the entrance," Liem said.

Terren nodded. Tearing his eyes from the corpse, he stepped around the body and left, wanting nothing more to do with the despicable place. He stopped just before exiting the cavern when he noticed Liem was not following. He still stared at the body.

"Part of me is sad this happened. There are so few magicians in the world, especially an Elder Mage. As much as I hated him..." Liem drifted off, leaving the phrase hanging in the air.

Terren did not finish the statement. He didn't need to; he understood. Sadness sometimes accompanied necessity. With a sigh, Liem turned his back on his former mentor, grim.

Neither of them spoke as they traversed the network of tunnels, each lost in their thoughts. Stepping into the soft loam of the forest, Terren noticed the oddity of silence. The area seemed to know death had just occurred. The crunch of dry leaves and sticks softened the eerie lack of noise.

Liem led Terren to a small natural overhang in a stack of rocks, with a lively brook flowing nearby. The prince moved the loose bushes to reveal Kiira, her breaths heavy with sleep. Terren gripped the hilt of his sword, making the leather creak as he surveyed the damage done to his wife's body. Her injuries were extensive and probably more than he could see. Terren strained to keep his limbs under control. Kamaria's essence still lingered inside of him, making his emotions more volatile. Terren took several deep, loud, and forced breaths to calm his mind.

"I need to see the extent of the damage and do what I can to heal her, but I would rather be at our camp," Liem said.

"Go, I will join you later."

Liem studied him for a moment. "Are you alright?"

Terren longed to follow him, to be close to Kiira, but at the moment, Kamaria was his priority. "I will be fine, I just need a minute to reverse the joining with Kamaria. She needs time to recover from this ordeal and cannot be joined with me to do so."

Liem nodded and scooped Kiira up, securing her in his arms. Terren watched as the distance increased between him and his wife, wishing he was the one carrying her from this place. Still, the sight of them going sent waves of relief through his core, helping him to let go of the lingering knot in his shoulders. Terren quickly slipped into the mental state he needed to begin the division process.

He could, for the first time in a week, almost completely relax.

CHAPTER 59
HEALING

Liem looked as Terren entered the light of the strong campfire, blinking in surprise. He couldn't blame the prince. He'd been gone for most of the day and the hour was late.

Liem's hands were on Kiira's temple and his eyes were heavy, as if just coming out of deep concentration. Terren acknowledged Liem before scooping a generous portion of the rabbit stew bubbling over the fire into a wooden bowl. With the first bite, he was pleased to find the prince to be a decent cook, and the warm food soothed his hunger and his weariness. The last thing he wanted after a day like today was bad food.

After a few minutes, Liem sat back with a weary exhale. He moved away from Kiira before also serving himself a generous portion of stew. After finishing his bowl, Terren took up Liem's place and gently cradled Kiira's head in his crossed ankles, tracing the outlines of her features. It was one thing she enjoyed while he recounted the Steasi Storja. Even if she couldn't react to his touch, the familiarity of the action comforted him.

She's not out of harm's way yet, but at least she is where I can protect her.

As he stroked her face, Terren found it amazing how two very different people came from the same parentage. It had become even more obvious to him after spending one-on-one time with Liem. Other than their similar hair color, the brother and sister didn't really share any physical characteristics. Her slight and lean frame was a complete contrast to the prince's vigilantly maintained bulk. "If I didn't know you two were related, I would never guess it," Terren said.

Liem huffed. "She looks a lot like my mother. What made you say that?"

"I saw a picture of the queen in the gallery, your mother was lovely. I suppose what I mean is, after getting to know you this week, the two of you could not be more opposite," Terren said.

Liem let a single amused bark escape his lips. "We're opposites in most things, but we complement each other well. Kiira is not as erratic as I can be, and I keep her from being overly serious," Liem said the last part of his sentence with a mild tease. His gaze, though, when he looked at his sister's fragile form, could only be described as unselfish love. Looking back up to meet Terren's eyes, he asked, "What took you so long?"

"I spent some time with Kamaria after we were no longer united. I had a few things I wished to discuss with her and I needed to give her my attentions as well; she did a lot for me today. Then I ventured back into the cave because I remembered Kiira was wearing her cloak and had a few daggers on her"—Terren gestured to the items—"when she was taken. I would have come back sooner, except I knew she was in good hands."

Liem smiled. "She would have insisted on looking for her weapons," he said, looking at the small pile of items, "had you not gotten them."

Terren nodded. "The cloak was a gift from a dear friend. Kiira would be upset to have lost it." They were quiet for a few moments. Both he and Liem staring into the campfire, but he suspected the prince was looking beyond it, the same as him. "How is she doing?" Terren asked.

"Kiira is in poor condition. She was not fed well for a few days and the strain on her body was beginning to show. There are multiple internal and external contusions. Kiira's ribs are the worst, she's lucky something wasn't punctured. And, of course, the cuts and scrapes you can see." Liem scowled. "What's worse is the evidence of Zerrec's mind games."

Terren looked down at Kiira.

You are so strong for surviving, my love, for having the will to live. Thank you, Ny. Thank you for protecting her.

"There are lingering traces of his castings in her system. I'll need more time to dissect and pick apart the threads of his magic," Liem added.

"Do you have an idea of what he did?"

"Some," Liem said reluctantly. "She's strong ... stronger than me."

Terren looked up. "You are both strong. I have no doubt of that."

"You don't understand." Liem shook his head. "Zerrec, he made her see things. I've only glimpsed parts of what she was subjected to and it turns my stomach."

"Like what?"

"Do you really want me to tell you?"

Terren worked his jaw for a moment. "No. I'll let Kiira tell me if she wishes. Besides, I'm completely spent from today. I don't need to think on such black thoughts while my nerves are already frayed."

"I understand how you feel. I barely fought, but even these castings are more of a drain than I am used to," Liem admitted.

Terren looked to see dark circles under the prince's eyes, and he seemed thinner than before. Terren gave Liem an unhappy but grateful smile. "Let's get some rest. We'll both be able to face tomorrow after some sleep."

"Terren, I'd prefer not to stay in the Forest Wilds any longer than we have to."

"I agree. We can head back toward Kiiroth where I stabled the horses. That should be a safe enough place until we can come up with a more cohesive plan. I met an apothercarist from there once," Terren said.

Liem nodded once. "That will be perfect; we can remain anonymous, but give her the care she needs. How long will it take to travel?"

"At the pace we will need to take, I would estimate a full day maybe a day and half," Terren said.

"Excellent. Leave at first light?"

Terren nodded his agreement, then gingerly moved Kiira from his lap. Standing, he stretched and said, "I need a decent sleep after today"—a wry smile crossed his face—"I did die and come back to life after all."

Confused, Liem asked, "You died?"

"Yes, in order for my Bear to protect me, I had to first absorb Zerrec's casting. So the magic was both effective and painful," Terren said. Liem stared at the water pouch in his hands absently. "If you have a question, speak your mind."

Liem frowned. "You were out briefly, not more than a minute if I had to guess. Even Zerrec thought you were dead."

"That's not technically a question, but I assume you want me to tell you about my abilities as a Shadow Walker," Terren teased.

Liem flexed his jaw.

"We have at least a full day's journey, giving us plenty of time to converse. I'll answer your questions as best I can then," Terren said.

After Liem agreed, Terren put his bedroll next to Kiira and wrapped her in a protective arm. He listened to the prince rustle for a few minutes before only the gentle crackle of a fire stood between them, lulling them to sleep.

CHAPTER 60
FORCED SLUMBER

Magic fueled her sleep. Looking 'up,' she could see a shimmering amber barrier. Reaching forward, a gelatinous substance coated her hand and would not allow more than a few inches give. Liem's magic tickled her fingertips with familiarity. She tried a few more times before deciding it was a waste.

Instead of standing on a 'solid surface,' she hovered. Though floating might be a better description.

It wasn't the same sensation as floating in water and neither did it feel like floating on air, since her movements were slow and restrained. It took a combination of 'swimming' and 'walking' to move around—not that she had anywhere to go. Altogether, it felt like an awkward dance no one had taught her the movements for. Kiira remembered this sensation from only one other time in her life. It had been years ago when she had fallen from a horse and the royal healers had put her in this state to ensure her concussion was not life threatening.

Resigned to floating, Kiira pondered her situation. The last thing she remembered was being pummeled in the head by the ox-man. She huffed and crossed her arms across her chest. Some information would be nice. Terren and Liem must be alive, but were they okay? Were the three of them still in the Forest Wilds? Was Zerrec dead? How long would she remain like this? These and other pertinent questions paraded through her mind, making her increasingly agitated in her unenlightened state. What Kiira wouldn't give to have the goddess show up right now.

CHAPTER 61

DRIFTING

A cloudy mist leaked from the blue, lifeless lips to float in a loose, ever-shifting ball above the corpse's head. The essence condensed, and a small sphere of light glowed with an ethereal haze.

Zerrec extracted his soul from this body to occupy another. This form was only to be used in the most dire of circumstances—and this moment absolutely qualified—as it was better to be in physical contact with someone to make the transfer. Immediately, the long blonde hair turned stark white and deep lines etched around the eyes and mouth. The skin spotted, sagged, and thinned as the mark of the magician dissolved from the wrist. It had been only through his magic and constantly healing that the body remained so well preserved. In a matter of days, this body would be dust.

This body served him well for nearly a century. It was a pleasant face, one he'd known intimately. The trusting facial features helped Zerrec to earn a place amongst the royals. It was a shame it had been taken.

Zerrec thought back to all that this body had provided for him over the years. He had done and experienced so much. Time ravaged his memory, and he didn't even remember this body's birth name, forgotten long ago with other unimportant things. He remembered this body being a farmer. Lean, agile, and strong. Of course, he hated Liem for taking away his shell and being forced into something new, but revenge could come later. Now it was time to start again.

Drying blood soaked the chest, and dull, lifeless eyes stared into nothing. His essence flared a bright red before settling into a stormy black. Before him was laughing evidence that his plan failed. He trivialized the whelp's abilities, especially his unexplainable immunity to a death curse. It should not have been possible! Zerrec's essence changed from stormy to crackling, a miniature violet storm.

It had killed him. There was no pulse. I sensed it. The prince should not have lived!

He briefly considered the gods sparing the whelp's life, but quickly dismissed the idea. The gods were unsympathetic to anyone. His essence took on a hint of yellow as discontentment colored his thoughts. No, there had to have been something else aiding in Terren's defense; a trinket or maybe another's casting, except the strength of his magic, born of centuries of practice, should have negated anything.

Liem could have done something.

Zerrec's essence bobbed as he disregarded that thought as well. Again, it didn't fit. Liem was nowhere near as powerful as him. A flaring and pulsing blood red light lit the cavern. No one bested him, ever!

I will have my revenge. The only thing to do is find out more about Terren.

Zerrec scanned through the options of how he could best weave his way into the whelp's life. This time he needed to be mindful and subtle, taking his actions with care so his hand pulling the strings would not be recognized until it was too late. Zerrec's essence turned limpid as a thought occurred to him. Was it too brash? Was he setting himself up for vulnerability or success? As his idea seemed more and more workable, a deep blue-violet swirled lazily through the translucent cloud, darkening in opacity as his plan solidified.

Zerrec whisked out of the cave he called home for the last several months into the open air. He paused to hover over Ricker. The man was dead, but only just. He could save himself energy by occupying using the corsair's body as a host before taking over his new intended target.

No. I do not wish to waste months setting up the perfect opportunity for an ideal transfer. This will have to do.

Zerrec's soul floated above the trees, and the setting sun gave him the heading for his new home. His priority was to find a new host, and he knew exactly where he would find one.

He sped toward the western edge of the forest, the trees a solid blur as one trunk bled into the next. Zerrec needed a host with past knowledge of Terren. He needed an advantage for him to lay the groundwork for the perfect trap to solicit his revenge. It was be risky plan, taking over a host with an established influence in Terren and Kiira's life, but sometimes high risk meant high reward, and in this instance, the knowledge gained would be more than worth it.

A flash of white pulsed once as he sped through the night.

Zerrec knew precisely where he was going.

REVIEW

I know this is the last thing you want to do after reading a good book. Personally, I would already be on the hunt for my next adventure, but reviews for Indie Authors are important. It is the lifeblood to our success. It doesn't have to take long. One sentence with an honest star rating will do. Can you give me less than five minutes of your time? It's so easy. All you need to do is scan the QR code (psst, for digital you can click on it), and it will take you directly to the review page. If I could say thank in person I would. Instead, I'll leave it here. "Thank you, thank you, THANK YOU for bolstering your bookshelf!"

REFERENCE & PRONUNCIATION

Albea — AL-Bey-uh: The city at the Eastern base of the Klaroni Cordillera. This is the first city that Kiira and Terren are in after leaving the Temple of Ny.

Apelgo — Ah-pell-Go: Considered the third god of the trinity and the messenger of the gods. A chain of islands is named after the god and is credited with having a feasting hall for those that have died.

Aradyll — Are-uh-dill: The capital of Klynotia.

The Aria Bells: The lower mountains running north to south dividing the kingdoms of Lorea and Klynotia.

Ariella — Are-EE-ella: The lady Liem is courting that Kiira references just after she is married to get a rile out of her brother.

Asimesta — Ah-sEYE-Mess-Ta: The tools and weapons makers for the Isokanii people. They produce everything from farming tools to the weapons of the Royal Guard and Shadow Walkers.

Barikkaa — Bare-eye-Kay: The judges of the Isokanii people. They are the law regulators and settle disputes between individual tribe members and the tribes. Often used in business dealings to make sure that all parties present are honest and abiding by the law.

The Burnished Plains: Kiira and Terren cross a portion of these plains when making the journey to Fellos and again toward Letra Mera or Forchid.

Byloraan — By-Lore-An: Also known as the Ristern Mera. The city is in the Shade Realm and is enormous. Considered one of the sister cities.

Ceress — Sare-Ess: An established identity of Terren's from the time he was traveling to keep people from learning of his true identity and creating a trail for his father to follow.

The Charlarae River — S-Har-lu-Ray: The river running from the splitting point of the Rustean River, eventually flowing to the sea.

Chausekkii — Chow-sek-Kee: The royal family of the Isokanii people. They are also the only family within the tribes that can become Shadow Walkers.

Coran — Cor-AN: An experienced archer under Kiira's command, who she will miss after her marriage.

Corsair Cay: The rough skerry where pirates live and Zerrec finds his mercenaries.

Curavailed — Cure-ah-Veiled: The term for the excommunication from the Nyuten Priesthood.

Dain — Day-N: The old beggar Terren speaks with to gain clues about Kiira's disappearance. He is a Pheneojek, so most people see him as addled, even though he is very intelligent.

Danel — Dan-EL: The Cook Master for Lorea.

Daswadii — Das-wad-ee: The leading tribe over the Isokanii people. The tribe is a part of the royal line, but they can not become Shadow Walkers.

Drenton's Ascent — Drenn-Tun: Named after the first priest to discover Klaron Point. It is the steep incline that you must ascend in order to gain access to the point and exit the caverns.

The Dueling Bells Inn: The inn in the Forchid, also known as Letra Mera. It is a well-kept popular inn in the heart of the maze-like city. Terren knows the owner, but under a false name.

The Ebony Spires: The strange tall rock columns of the northwest coast of the Sun Realm.

Ermyjek — Err-meh-Jzsh-ek: The ceremony that takes place for a Shadow Seeker to become a Shadow Walker. It is a painful process and extremely taxing on the body, especially the mind. The process can go wrong and have some serious side effects.

Eshalahee — Esh-ah-La-he: The merchant tribe of the Isokanii people. They deal in every manner of trade, buying, and selling. This is both in the Shade Realm between the tribes and the Sun Realm.

Fellos — Fell-Ohs: The town at the Western base of the Klaroni Cordillera. This is where Terren and Kiira stop and rest after the wind storm before ascending the path up the mountain to the temple.

The Fire Falls: The location on the beach Kiira takes Terren on their first required outing. These falls are very colorful when the light hits the water a certain way.

Folen — Foal-En: Prince Liem's best friend. He is a laid back and easy-going guy and a terrible flirt with all the women, especially Kiira because he has known her for so long.

Forchid — Fore-Ked: Also known as Letra Mera of the sister cities. It is a massive maze-like city on the Western side of the Kilunys Bridge. Though it is so close to the Shade Realm, Shade Born are rarely seen walking the streets. If any Shade Dwellers are seen, they are usually merchants or traders. The city is described as always being covered in a layer of soot because of the proximity to the canyon.

Gahijett — G-ah-ee-Jet: One of the two tribes that trains warriors and guards for Isokanii people. The people from these tribes serve in every capacity of protection, from guarding the royal family to helping the merchants guard their goods.

Gettii — GeT-Tee: The traveling merchant both Kiira and Terren have met.

Gimetii — Gi-Meh-Tee: The god of the Isokanii responsible for creating the massive trees of the forest for the Shade Beast to roam.

Glazefire Canyon: A deep and wide canyon separating the Shade Realm and Sun Realm; it was created during the

Mage War and it is the rift that exists between the two realms. It is the unbalance of the Shade Realm and the Sun Realm being forced to exist side by side, producing spectacular and dangerous flames within the canyon.

Glazen Tavern: The tavern that the old beggar Dain takes Terren to for the offered meal. It is considered one of the best taverns in Forchid because of its excellent ales and delicious food.

Grayten — Grey-Ten: The king of Klynotia and Terren's father. He is a hard man and rules his people with intimidation and fear. He is especially brutal towards his children, expecting perfect results when it is sometimes not possible, and harbors an extreme dislike for magic and magicians.

Gresher — Gresh-Er: The Master Priest of the gods for Lorea and the officiate for the royal wedding.

Harmend — HAR-mend: a guard assigned to Terren.

Hayla — Hay-Luh: A newer archers that Kiira plucks a drink from her hand during The Yielding Festival.

Herretus — Hair-eT-Us: The king of Lorea and the father to Kiira and Liem. He is a kind man the people love and respect. He cares for others, but also expects to be obeyed when he has given the final say in a situation.

Iamloruu — Eye-am-lore-U: The tribe dedicated to the making and coloring of cloth. They also create and design all the clothing that is sold by the merchants.

Isokanii — Eye-so-Kahn-EE: The name of the people that dwell in the Shade Realm. The people group is built upon twelve tribes that all have a specific function that helps protect and advance the culture. Everyone of pure Isokanii blood is very dark-skinned and they all have the same eye coloring that is unique to their people. The eye color allows them to see vividly in the Shade Realm.

Ishaiio — Eye-SH-ee-oh: The name given to a beloved among the Isokanii. It roughly translates to "the missing half of my heart".

Jaburshelee — Jaw-bor-Shell-ee: One of the two tribes that trains warriors and guards for Isokanii people. The people from these tribes serve in every capacity of protection, from guarding the royal family to helping the merchants guard their goods.

Jayan — J-eye-Ann: An established identity of Terren's from the time he was traveling to keep people from learning of his true identity and creating a trail for his father to follow.

Jearut Oasis — Jay-rooT: The capital of the Isokanii people.

Jemma — Gym-uh: Kiira's lady's maid and one of her dearest friends. She is quiet and does not say much, but fusses over Kiira and is almost constantly worried about her whereabouts and the way she looks.

Jiirus — JEEr-us: The Horse Master for Lorea.

Johsh — Joe-sh: The priest greets Terren and Kiira when they first arrive at the temple. He is the second attendant to the Master Librarian. He is a stickler for protocol and is very proud of his position within the temple.

Jurica — Jzhur-EES-Uh: The queen of Lorea who died while trying to calm Zerrec. Kiira cherished her mother. It was a hard loss for their family, but her death affected the princess the most.

Juston — Joos-Tun: The deactivating word used on the invisibility necklace Terren gives to Liem to borrow.

Kamaria — Kah-Marr-ee-ah: The Shade Beast that Terren is bonded to via the Ermyjek. As Shade Beast, she is massive and Kamaria, raised to her full height, towers another fifteen meters above Terren's own almost six-foot stature while still on four paws. She is a Beast, both material and immaterial, and grants Terren a range of abilities.

Kessa — Kess-Uh: The name that Terren picks for Kiira while staying in Fellos. It is one of her cover identities to keep anyone from knowing that she is the princess of Lorea, since many of the people they meet in their travels do not know of Terren's true identity.

Kiira — Keer-uh: The princess of the Lorea and is the twin to Liem. She marries Terren through an arranged marriage, but has a secret love for Leo an Earl and her second in command of the archers. She loves her family and the people of the kingdom, but she is also incredibly stubborn, which often gets her into trouble. Kiira is often compared in likeness to her mother.

Kiiroth — Keer-Oth: The large town on the northern edge of the Forest Wilds near the Glazefire Canyon. It is where Terren and Liem travel to while waiting for Kiira's injuries to heal.

Kilunys Bridge — K-eye-loon-iss: The massive bridge that expands the Glazefire Canyon connecting the Shade Realm and the Sun Realm. It takes an hour to cross the bridge.

Kiivulii - KEE-vul-EE: The actual name of those among the Isokanii that bond with Beast and can travel the realms. It is a lost name from before the realms were broken, but a few still remember the term. Most, however, refer to them as Stieti Tetsaa (Shadow Walker).

Klaron Point — Klair-On: A flat landing on a tall peak in the Klaroni Cordillera. It can only be accessed via the temple and was discovered by the priest Drenton.

Klaroni Cordillera — Klair-Oh-N-eye: The mountain range that stretches across most of the northern edge of the Sun Realm. The peaks are tall, soaring to heights above an estimated 10,000 kilometers. This is also where the Nyan Temple is located and the Nyuten Priest dwell.

Klynotia — Kleh-Noht-sha: The neighboring kingdom to Lorea. It is known for its gem exports, as much of the kingdom is bordered by mountains. It has some beaches, but a vast majority of the kingdom is rocky and barely fertile soil. A lot of goods are imported into the kingdom and it is afforded because of the gem exports.

The Knobby Seas Pub: The pub where Zerrec waits to find mercenaries to hire. It is a disgusting place and sadly the best pub on Corsair Island.

Kreden — Kray-Den: The activating word used on the invisibility necklace Terren gives to Liem to borrow.

Kreshkt — Kresh-Kt: An expletive that various characters used to convey great anger. It is a word not used often, so when it is spoken, one understands the upset of the speaker.

Lady Liane — Lee-Ain: The wife of Marko, sister-in-law to Herretus, and aunt to Kiira and Liem.

Lenden — Len-Den: A guard assigned to Terren.

Leo Moredell: The second in command of the archers after Kiira. He is an Earl of Wirlen and the princess' secret love. The two courted each other without the king's knowledge for several months.

Letra Mera — Let-Ruh Mare-Uh: Also known as Forchid and one of the sister cities. It is a massive maze-like city on the Western side of the Kilunys Bridge. The city is described as always being covered in a layer of soot because of the proximity to the canyon.

Liioh — lee-Oh: The twin god to Gimetii and the creator of the Shade Beast, according to the Isokanii.

Liem — Lee-em: The prince of Lorea and Kiira's twin brother. He is bulky and stands at five foot eight. His size is because of his school of magic. If he ever depletes his core magic, fuel is then pulled from his muscles. He loves his family fiercely and will do anything necessary to protect them, even if it means bending the rules. He looks more like his father in build and demeanor.

The Lieta Springs — Ly-eh-Ta: The Lieta Springs, or more commonly known as The Springs of Windrah. This is the clearing that Kiira stumbles into after running into the Forest Wilds and meets the goddess.

Loracia — Lore-ay-see-uh: The capital of Lorea

Loralyn — Lore-uh-lin: Zerrec's first wife. The mage considers Kiira the reincarnation of her and, therefore, destined to be his.

Lorea — Lore-ay-uh: The neighboring kingdom to Klynotia. It is a prosperous and fertile kingdom that exports many goods. Produce, woodwork, clothing, and glass are just a few examples. Most of the land is covered by the Forest Wilds and it is known to have beautiful black sand beaches. The people of the kingdom are generally happy and loyal to the crown.

Lorestan — Lore-Ess-Tan: The surname of the royal family of Lorea.

Lorestan Lake: An immense lake located almost in the center of the Lorean kingdom. It is home to a variety of fish and almost always has calm waters because of the surrounding forest and mountains that block much of the wind. The water is relatively clear and one can see rather deep into the lake.

Lunedemai — Loon-Deh-My: The yearlong trip that newly married couples take. It was a tradition started before the Mage War and it is meant to act as a way for the newly married to get to know one another. There are no restrictions on the Lundemai on what a couple can do during the year, but it is frowned upon to have contact with anything familiar.

Lucen — Loose-en: Terren's personal servant. He is a loyal to the prince even though he was abused by the king after the prince fled Klynotia.

Mafelbno — Ma-Fell-B-no: The title of emperor within the Isokanii people.

The Magician's Cloister: The smallest island of The Tears of Apelgo, a refuge and sanctuary for magicians.

The Mage War: The devastating war that brought the Shade Realm into alignment with the Sun Realm and created the Glazefire Canyon. The war started because of a young mage that believed that those with more powerful magic should be in leadership and many disagreed. It was a civil war that pitted children against parents and friend against friends. The conflict lasted a century until a last act by hundreds of Elder Mages misaligned the two realms that sent a shockwave killing almost everyone.

Maireen — My-Ree-N: The wife of Tanan and the cook for the Starbryt Inn and Tavern in the town of Fellos near the base of the Klaroni Cordillera.

Mag jou tafii ke ya nagligte gaan — (Mag) (jzhou) (tah-fee) (kay) (ya) (nah-glee-G-tay) (gay-an): Translated means "May your journeys go by the lights of night." Kiira says this to Dain the beggar as she leaves after giving him a loaf of honey bread.

Mandalltii — M-ahn-doll-tee: The tribe responsible for mining the Night Crystals. They are also the smallest of all the tribes.

Marko — Marr-Ko: The younger brother to Herretus and uncle to Kiira and Liem.

The Meladaai River — Mel-uh-day: The river running from Loel Lake to Lorestan Lake.

Merkus — Merr-Kuss: One of Liem's closest friends next to Folen. He helps with searching the royal quarters because Liem feels magic being used.

Mythieres — Mith-Ear-es: The surname for the royal family of Klynotia.

Ngozee — Nuh-go-Zee: The tribe specializes in the jewelry that all the Isokanii people wear. It is even highly prized and traded within the Sun Realm.

Night Crystal Quarries: Rocky cliffs where the Mandalltii Tribe harvest the Night Crystals used in jewelry and sold to magicians.

Ny — N-eye: The head god of the trinity. He is the god of both light and dark and the creator of the realms.

Nyuten Priesthood — N-eye-you-ten: The priests that have dedicated their lives to serving and worshiping the god Ny. They live in seclusion, high in the Klaroni Cordillera, and are known for their fighting skills with a bo staff. Their ways are only taught to those who are a part of the order, but all are welcome to the temple as long as they are pure of heart. Both men and women are welcome to join the priesthood.

Oranta — Ore-anT-uh: A sleek wolf-like animal that attacked a caravan outside of the citadel in Lorea. The beast is as large as a manor house and black as midnight.

Pheneojek — P-heno-Jzsh-ek: A Shadow Seeker that failed the Ermyjek or the bonding process with a Shade Beast. They are often considered insane because of the mindless babble. These Shade Born are not anchored to the Shade Realm or to a Shade Beast, so it has serious repercussions on the mind.

Ramilkretna — Ram-ill-Kreet-Na: The spiritual guides for the Isokanii people. The specific beliefs of the people are unknown in this novel.

Reberak Peninsula — Reb-AIR-aK: The most common place for fishermen to go in the Kingdom of Lorea.

Ristern Mera — Res-Tern Mare-uh: Also known as Byloraan and one of the sister cities. A massive maze-like city on the Eastern side of the Kilunys Bridge in the Shade Realm. The description of this city is unknown.

Rustean River — Rus-TeeN: The river is fed from Loel Lake and surrounds the capital of Klynotia before going to the sea.

Sael — Say-El: The hunter that brings Zerrec food and news from Lorea.

Sairah — Say-Ruh: The princess of Klynotia and Terren's younger sister. She is seven years younger, so she was only ten when the prince disappeared. She is considered pretty, but has a difficult life, so most of the time she pushes people away. Her relationship with Terren is strained, but is on the mend.

Sartenn — Sar-Ten: The Horse Master in the Nyan Temple that Terren makes a deal with for practicing. This is also the same man that gave him Tempest.

The Seas of Reana — Ray-ana: The seas bordering the western edge of the Sun Realm. They are a darker blue and can seem like a deep purple in the right light.

Senuresko — Sin-Yur-es-Ko: The tribe responsible for building and assisting with any transportation needs for the Isokanii people.

The Shadow Desert: The dark, massive sand dunes that make up where the main gathering of Isokanii live.

Shadow Walkers: The ultimate protectors of the culture, people, and the Shade Realm; since The Mage War, their job is even more important.

Skehtra — Sk-Eh-T-Rah: Kiira's Wolfcat cub she rescued from a sprung rabbit trap. The cub refused to leave her side even with encouragement and was kept as a pet.

The Slate Cliffs: Dark cliffs rising from the sandy beach and are the conduit for the Fire Falls.

Staesi Storja — Stay-See Store-Jha: The star stories that the Veripoi tell. They are a history of their culture and existence, giving the listener life lessons.

Starbryt Inn — Star-Brite: An inn in Fellos where Terren and Kiira stay after dealing with the Windstorm.

Starfire: A uniquely colored gelding that Kiira absolutely adores. He has a playful and stubborn personality and does not warm up to others quickly.

Stietii Tetsa — Sty-ET-ee TET-sah: Shadow Walker in Isokanii.

Storm Gulf: The end of the Whispering River coming out of the canyon so forcefully it makes a loud thunderclap sound.

Surveysor — Sir-vey-Sore: The name of the pirate ship Terren sailed with for a time during his travels.

Taam — Tay-Am: The other hunter that will sometimes bring meat to Zerrec.

Tanan — Tan-ann: The owner of the Starbryt Inn in Fellos. He is a portly man that is always in a jolly mood and thinks of Terren as a son.

The Tears of Apelgo: A chain of three islands south of the Shade Realm. These islands were not pulled into the Sun Realm at the conclusion of the Mage War, however, they were formed after and are part of the Sun Realm.

Tereyssa — Tare-Ess-Uh: The older priestess Kiira becomes very close to in the months she is there. The old woman is wise, a little mysterious, and has a witty sense of humor.

Terren — Tare-En: The prince of Klynotia. He marries Kiira through an arranged marriage. He is a mysterious character, not a lot is known about him. It is known that he traveled and he obviously has some skill in fighting and being sneaky, but not much else is known to others. The truth of him emerges through Kiira's eyes, but he still has a lot to hide.

Trinesteo - Trin-Es-Tayo: A casting that is used to show you are telling the truth. It is a binding spell that will hurt the person with physical pain should they lie.

The Shade Realm: A shadow of the Sun Realm physically, but has unique animals and people.

The Sun Realm: A wild and beautiful land that has dangers, but many adventures for those willing to take the chance. It has extreme landscapes, with mountains and seas being very close to each other.

The Tayros River: The river running from Lorestan Lake to the Reberak Peninsula.

Tilkt Point — Till-Kt: The cliffs on the southern end of the Shade Realm riddled with caves; created by the high waves of the sea.

Torrel — Tore-ell: The owner of the Dueling Bells in Forchid.

The Velpani River — Vell-pah-Nee: The river that runs from the Klaroni Cordillera down the base of the Aria Bells and feeds Loel Lake and Lorestan Lake.

Veripoi — Ver-eh-Poy: Nomadic people group that live in both the northern tip of the Forest Wilds and the tall grasses of the plains.

The Whispering River: The river used to run between the two halves of the Sun Realm before the Mage War and fell into the canyon upon the splitting of the realms.

Windrah — When-druh: The goddess of the story and physical representation of the gods. She appears to Kiira multiple times in the book. This is due to the princess's strong devotion and worship of the goddess that she appears before her. Normally, messages from the gods are sent through Apelgo.

Wolfcat: A large cat vicious in its attacks and weighs up to 1,000 pounds. It has a silvery grey fluffy fur, lilac eyes, and lives in the Forest Wilds and prefers to hunt at night, but will also sometimes roam during the day.

Yven — Yeh-Ven: A guard assigned to Terren.

Zainabdee — Z-ain-uh-B-dee: The tribe responsible for farming and fishing among the Isokanii people.

Zerrec — Zehr-eK: An evil magician and incredibly powerful. He is an Elder Mage and used to be Kiira and Liem's teacher. He was also an advisor to King Herretus before turning on the royal family and killing the queen. Banished from the kingdom and disappeared for ten years, he has resurfaced after hearing news of Kiira's arranged marriage. He is also centuries old, having kept himself alive with his healing magic.

Acknowledgments

I have to admit that this part is tough for me. It's not that I don't want to show appreciation or thank those in my life, it's just that I struggle to find the right words to express my gratitude. I write entire stories and somehow cannot find the words to thank people. I'm indebted to them. My dream is coming true thanks to the people in my life, so I will give it my best shot.

I owe it to my Father for allowing me to see entire worlds when I close my eyes. I wouldn't be an author without being able to see things differently.

To my husband, who'd rather read police procedurals instead of fantasy, I won't consider it a betrayal. His hard work makes it possible for me to get lost in other worlds. I'll always be grateful for his sacrifice.

Addressing my editor and friend. Your challenge honed me into a writer and I am thankful for that. You have my fealty.

Finally, to the loyal readers who have been clamoring for another book since Heart published in 2018. I know it's not the next in the series. Really, it's a step backwards since this is a rewrite of the first, but I promise that the second book is coming soon.

ABOUT THE AUTHOR

T.J. Fisher is the author of *The Broken Realms Chronicle*. As a former mermaid, T.J. is a lover of all things fantastical and magical. After decades of watching humans write stories about her kind; she joined the fray and added her knowledge of magic to give characters a 'breath' of fresh air—so to speak. Lured to land by the love of a halfling and his endless supply of delicious culinary creations; T.J. now dines on the delicacies of enchiladas, breakfast tacos, milkshakes, and chocolate chip cookies. She may have lost her fins, but she still loves water in all forms.

Also by T.J. Fisher

Divided - A Broken Realms Novella

Shadow's Son

<u>**Coming Soon**</u>

Mage's Legacy - 2026

Sign up for news from the broken realms via **the fictioneer's inkwell**. A monthly report of all happenings in the kingdom. Become a fictionado today and stay in the know!